Fatal
Attractions

Fatal Attractions 2

Cataloging-in-Publication Data is on file with the Library of Congress.

Paperback ISBN: 978-0-9913338-2-0
E-book ISBN: 978-0-9913338-3-7

(Previously published in 2002 as
Fatal Impressions ISBN 0971681295)

Fatal Attractions 4

Chapter 1

Rocks hurtled down the steep mountainside, and bounced onto the gravel road bare inches in front of the Suburban's bumper.

Ambush!

Ariel swerved to avoid a big stone just as a mountain goat leaped in front of her vehicle. She stomped on the Suburban's brakes and wrenched the wheel. The front grill swooped past the startled animal, and hurtled toward a flimsy guardrail that protected them from the chasm. She heaved the steering wheel toward the sheer mountainside, but it fishtailed out of control. As she fought to regain command, she observed movement in her rearview mirror; a moment later, the goat vanished in the thick rooster-tail of dust spewed by the tires.

She didn't have time to worry over the animal's fate she needed to worry about herself and Tempest. Ariel threw all her strength and one-hundred-twenty-pounds into recovering control of her armor-plated vehicle and keeping it from plummeting into the gorge on the left side of the thin dirt road they were following through the Rocky Mountains.

The bumper hit the rusted guardrail. Metal shrieked. The impact threw her against the shoulder harnesses, numbing her from right shoulder to fingertips. With only her left hand, Ariel whipped the wheel toward the road.

Her muscles screamed.

So did Tempest and Mozart.

Ariel bit the insides of her cheeks so hard she tasted blood.

Then finally, miraculously, the suburban stopped.

Heart slamming against her ribs, Ariel stared through a haze of dust at the boulder-strew gorge, a hundred yards below.

"We're alive," she whispered in surprise. She tore her attention from the chasm and looked at her sister.

Tempest's eyes were pools of white. "Is that poor animal okay?"

Trust her fifteen-year-old sister to worry more about a wild creature than herself. Did the kid realize that if it hadn't been for the defensive driving course she'd taken, they'd be dead? Or had the five years they'd been on the run made Tempest take this sort of situation for granted? Ariel grimaced, this wasn't the first time those lessons had saved them.

And knowing Peter's persistence, it wouldn't be the last.

Hanging onto the one safe topic, Ariel glanced at the rearview mirror where she'd last seen the goat, but the only thing visible was billowing dust. She cleared her throat. "I think so." She closed her eyes then leaned her head against the seat, and controlled her breathing as she waited for her racing heart to still. When her blood pressure edged downward, she admitted, "After all the car chases and close escapes from your father, I never imagined a goat could give me such a scare."

"Uncle Mitch sure taught you good," Tempest said. Ariel grunted in agreement. Tempest's white knuckled grip relaxed and she turned to face Ariel. "I wish he'd taught me before we had to leave." Her tone brightened. "But you can teach me to drive like that."

"I'll probably have to." *Someday, but not today. Or tomorrow. Maybe not even next year.* But Tempest surely would need to learn, eventually, after all, her father had vowed to kill them and the one thing everyone could be certain about was that Peter always kept his word. Tempest flexed her fingers, restoring circulation. *Sitting in the passenger seat without any control had to be worse than fighting fate.* A glance in the rearview mirror showed the plume of dust concealing the isolated mountain pass they'd just come through. It billowed so high, that even the snow-topped peaks of the Rocky Mountains were hidden. She hoped it didn't mask something worse: Peter. Stomach tight, Ariel moved the suburban into the middle of the winding gravel road.

"We lost him three days ago," Tempest said, as if reading her mind.

Ariel nodded in agreement and hoped that for once they had actually gotten away and Tempest's perverse father wasn't just playing some sort of cat and mouse game. *Please let that black Bronco have lost our trail in Montana. Please let this be their last move and the last time she had to remember a new identity or not jump when she saw a stranger in the mirror. Please don't let Peter find them in Fairbanks.* She wished there was a way to tell if they'd finally outsmarted him or if he was merely keeping track of them from a distance. Either way, Peter's specter hung over them, like the death shroud he'd promised them. Ariel wondered if he had let them go instead of outright murder them because their efforts and fear entertained him.

Despite the long pause, the rear-view mirror only showed

dust. Still, Ariel didn't fully believe they'd managed to evade Peter's lackey.

Was there anywhere, short of the grave, where Peter couldn't find them?

She pushed aside her paranoia, shoved the suburban into drive, focused on the road and gently pushed on the accelerator. She wanted to floor it, but knew better than to give into panic.

Alaska. She shivered at the forbidding thought of ice and polar bears. Surely he'll never look for them in a land of perpetual winter.

Neither she nor her half-sister spoke for a long time. When the afternoon passed without any sign of a tail, Ariel's heart stopped pounding like a frenzied drummer. Then, she became concerned because she hadn't seen another vehicle in hours and the gas gauge was inching toward a quarter tank. Her foot eased back on the accelerator, the goon Peter had hired still didn't appear.

Tempest stared at the bleak mountain peaks long after her fright wore off. Gradually, her gaze dropped to the equally barren slopes on the far side of the wide gorge bordering the twisting road. "The trees are sure little here. Guess loggers got all the big ones, and these are all babies, huh?"

"The closer trees are to the Arctic circle, the smaller they are and they don't grow *in it* at all," Ariel hoped she didn't sound like a know it all. "They're not like the ones we're used to, either… No oaks or elms." Ariel forced herself to focus on the road to freedom and not think about Mecklenburg County's southern temperate forests or all the friends and family they'd left behind when they'd run for their lives and to protect the ones they loved. She couldn't prove it, but intuition told her Peter had tried to murder Mitch for helping them learn the skills they needed to protect themselves.

"No green pollen ponds in spring?" Tempest wrinkled her nose.

Ariel glanced at the trees across the gorge. "Pine pollen probably does that, too." Talking about trees was much better than thinking about what the swirling dust could hide, or what would surely happen when Peter found the only two people who'd had the audacity to testify against him. "In the Arctic Circle bushes are tiny, like bonsai."

"Ya mean they're in fancy pots?" Ariel glanced at Tempest in time to see the well-know mischievous grin beneath the chocolate brown eyes and short, spiked black hair. "Sherry-"

"Forget I'm your sister. Forget I'm a pediatrician. Forget Grandma, Kelsey, Jade and all our other cousins. Forget every name we've had before. Now, we're simply Ariel and Tempest Danner. Mother and daughter." The road shimmered through her unshed tears. "We can not afford to create suspicion. Not after we worked so hard to create these identities." She slowed down, even more and massaged the tight muscles at her nape. "I'm tired of creating new pasts and trying to remember who I am. From this point on, you must remember to call me Mom, Mama or whatever you want, as long as it's not Sis or Sherry."

Tempest wrinkled her nose. "I hate moving. I hate correspondence school. I hate not getting to go to the prom or have a boyfriend. Go on a real date. Maybe have a bunch of girlfriends over for a slumber party... I want to do all the stuff you got to do when you were my age."

"It wasn't that great."

"Yeah right," she scoffed. "I've seen the pictures. You had all kinds of fun."

"Sometimes. Not every day." Certainly not since her father had died or the day she'd seen her mother murdered. Definitely not the day when the judge freed Peter and had accused her of slander, then threatened to incarcerate her for libeling a man who'd given her and her mother a home, name and new future. Ariel swallowed. "Think about this: we get to play dress up and masquerade every day. Some people would think that's fun."

Tempest looked back over the seat to Mozart, who had his red head tucked under an emerald wing. "You're lucky there's no way to dye feathers." When the parrot didn't respond, silence descended. Tempest shifted in her seat, toyed with the CD player, wiggled some more, then finally said, "Sh-Ariel, can't I go to a real school?" Ariel shook her head. "Pull-ease?" Again, Ariel showed her disapproval. "Well why not?" *She had to ask?* "I mean, you are."

Her stomach clenched. "I'm working so we can eat." If she got any tenser, her fingernails would rip the leather cover off the steering wheel. Ariel glanced at Tempest. "A roof is nice, too. And you love clothes." She couldn't resist teasing, "Even though the ones you pick look like they were made for someone twice your size."

"I'm fashionable." Tempest turned toward her, a belligerent expression on her face. "And you shouldn't talk about baggy clothes, not when you're still wearing what you bought twenty pounds ago." Tempest glared at her. Ariel ignored the jibe; after all, the weight she had lost due to stress was the truth. When the silence stretched, Tempest said, "Home schools don't have proms."

"True." Years ago, she'd been forced to sit at home because their mother had made her respect her step-father's wishes. She could still remember her anger and the resentment toward the man who'd dared to usurp her father's place. Was she being as unreasonable and overly protective as Peter had been? Was her little sister's situation similar to what she'd resented? She shuddered at the thought. Should she set aside her fears and simply let them try to enjoy a normal life instead of view everything as a survival issue? "It's only a dance," she muttered. As she listened to herself, Ariel winced; their mother had said the exact same thing to Peter.

"Oh, you think so, do you? Trust me on this - the prom is not just any ole dance. Just like I'm not just any ole gal." Tempest patted her short black spiked hair. "I'm gorgeous and cool. Someone equally cool should ask me - at least they would if they knew me. But if I home school, no one will ask me 'cause you'll make sure we live like mushrooms and no one will know I exist." Her expression became thoughtful. "Maybe I should ask someone. Preferably someone totally gorgeous... You know, the drop dead kind."

Ariel shivered involuntarily, as she pictured Peter, who epitomized 'the drop dead kind', in far too many ways. Tall, dark, handsome men were worse than Ebola. Another shudder shook her. If it weren't for Peter's promise of death, she'd have a pediatric practice, not a phony master's degree in biology, a bulletproof Suburban, brown contacts and matching drab hair along with an alias she hoped would keep her alive.

"Even if I don't always remember our new names, Father'll find us," Tempest predicted. "He always does."

"Not this time." If she said it enough and prayed hard

enough it would be so. Ariel glanced at the rearview mirror. A prickle of panic coursed through her when she didn't immediately recognize the woman with the dark wavy hair and tense brown eyes.

"Like he'll ever give up." Tempest snorted as she crossed her thin arms over her stomach. "Even if we were dead, Father'd probably dig us up and kill us all over again, just to make positive certain he got his revenge." Tempest balled her fist and hit her open palm. "I hate him, I hate him, I hate him!"

"I know you do. And believe me I understand, but try to realize that while we can dislike things he does, we must love, not ha-"

"I don't want to hear it."

"Lo-"

"I don't want to hear about love! You know how horrible he is!"

"Yes, but all human life is-"

"Sacred," Tempest interrupted. "That's what you always say, but do you really mean it or are you just all screwed up from taking that hypo critic oath?"

"Hippocratic oath," Ariel corrected. "It's something I believe in because it focuses on good, not evil." Tempest screeched with irritation. From the back, Mozart, their parrot, shrieked and flapped his emerald wings. "Now you've upset Mozart. Better pop in a concerto to get him calmed down." Tempest was already pushing buttons on the player. Soon, the tones of Sonata in F Major came from the speakers. After several bars, the parrot calmed. Ariel wished Tempest were as easily mollified. "We should try to find something good we can focus on. After all, he is your father, and you're pretty terrific, so there has to be something good to say about him." When it came to Peter, Ariel knew she was asking the impossible.

"Like what? The way he tortures animals?" Sarcasm infused her tone. "Or, how about the way he treats people? Like when he makes us feel guilty when he's the one who's wrong?" Her mouth flattened. "Can you forget him pushing mom in front of that bus or did the judge convince you that we were just a couple vindictive brats, who imagined it?"

Ariel blinked hard to hold back the tears that always welled at the horrible memory and its demeaning aftermath. "No one is totally bad," she whispered. Tempest snorted in disagreement. "I know how easy it would be to hate him, but it only would hurt us. Please, try to find something positive to think about."

"Like what? All those dead animals he hung on the walls?"

"At least he never stuffed Mozart."

"Well, there is that," Tempest conceded, before she lapsed into silence. For several miles, the only sounds were from the gravel road and classical music. Ariel stared out the dusty windows at the scenery, which looked different from anywhere they'd ever been.

Hours later, exhausted from the trip, they followed the crudely sketched map to a quiet residential street and parked in front of the white clapboard townhouse, which would be their home for the foreseeable future.

"It looks weird," Tempest said. "Maybe barren is a better word." She frowned. "Do you think it'll take a long time to get used to such small trees?"

"I don't know." Unlike the big beautiful oaks surrounding the home they'd been raised in, these trunks barely looked big enough for a bunny to hide behind. For the zillionth time she wondered if Peter had wanted their mother for herself or for her family's prestige and money.

Ariel got out of their mud-splattered Suburban and stretched her aching back as she studied the simple white clapboard two-story building. Black shutters flanked the windows. A huge rose-colored peony covered in dinner-plate-sized blooms appeared to be making up for the lack of other foundation plantings. She looked up and down the block-long apartment building and counted a total of three spindly trees. At least it wouldn't be easy to be a peeping tom here.

Tempest opened the cigarette tray and grabbed the house key, then snatched Mozart's perch and headed for the door.

Ariel leaned over the back of her seat, petted Mozart's head, and then offered her finger to step up on. He stared at her for a brief moment before he backed away. She tickled him under the chin and offered her hand again, but he refused to come close enough for her to pick him up. "You stubborn old bird," she teased. "I know what you want." She opened a Tupperware canister of sunflower seeds and tempted Mozart toward her. He tilted his head, eyeing the seed as if to determine if she was trying to bribe him with substandard millet. He took a small step forward. Then another. Almost there. He took two more quick steps.

As he grabbed a seed, Ariel held the container with one hand and grabbed Mozart's red-feathered body with the other. When he bobbed his head to eat, she backed out of the suburban.

Suddenly, a dog began barking. Ariel twisted around in time to see a large black and white beast barrel around the end of the long building, and leap toward the chain-link fence that enclosed the townhouse next to theirs. The animal landed against the barrier with a resounding clamor. Mozart shrieked and flailed his wings. The seed container flew upward. Ariel lost her grip on Mozart and the container. He flapped back into the Suburban, while the Tupperware hit the ground. A second dog joined the first, but instead of beating the fence, the new one sat on the sparse grass and howled.

If they had to listen to this noise every day, she'd shoot the creatures. She snorted. As if she'd ever do anything that labeled her like Peter.

A third dog joined the pack. This one silently reared up and pawed at the fence-wire. Ariel swallowed. Though the chain-link fence appeared tall enough and strong enough, to keep beasts at bay, having anything with long claws and big sharp teeth this close reminded her of the toddler who'd been her first patient; a pit-bull had mauled the tike and ripped his throat to within a tendon of the jugular, it was a wonder the little guy had made it to the ER alive.

Tempest rushed back outside, nearly tripping over her own feet when she spotted the dogs. Instead of fleeing, she moved toward the howling pack. "Hello," she purred. "You're so pretty and handsome. I'm sure we'll be great friends."

Ariel rolled her eyes to heaven, as the howls doubled in strength.

Tempest glanced over her shoulder and grinned at her. "Aren't they gorgeous? This is almost as good as having a dog of my own."

Ariel grunted and motioned her to come away from the fence. After a moment's hesitation, Tempest trudged toward the suburban "I feel safe knowing they're there and that they bark at strangers."

"Valid point." One she'd have to consider later. "But, right now, you know you live here, but they still have to figure it out." Tempest grabbed the Tupperware, then crawled over the back seat and lunged at Mozart. The bird evaded her. Ariel slung her backpack over her shoulder then started crawling over the seat to help her.

Suddenly sunflower seeds exploded from Tempest's hand. Ariel felt several hit her head. "Ah!" She backed out of the door, while fluffing her dark, wavy hair. Suddenly, half in, half out of the suburban, something heavy thudded against her head and claws gripped her hair. Ariel fell backward.

Tempest laughed.

Mozart squawked as his wings beat her ears.

The dogs howled.

Claws grazed Ariel's scalp. She gasped in pain and flailed for balance.

In the distance a deep voice said, "Afternoon, you must be Ariel Danner."

Her shoulder jolted against the suburban's door. Mozart screeched and his wings beat harder. It felt like huge globs of hair were being pulled out. *I survived ER and morgue residency; I can endure this*. Ariel blindly grabbed for support. Her hands clutched something soft yet hard.

"Why'd you make her scream?" another male voice asked.

"Help me out, would you?" When the words vibrated beneath her hands, Ariel realized she was clutching a man's torso.

"I did not scream," Ariel snapped, as she held on tight. "Mozart did." As if acknowledging the fact, Mozart let loose with an ear-numbing shriek, as something ripped at her scalp.

"It's my fault," Tempest said. "I was trying to get him to come out of the car, but he didn't want to come because of those wolves howling and-"

"Huskies." The chest beneath her palms vibrated with the word. Her hands tingled. "They can't get through the fence." The deep voice sounded amused.

"Poor Mozart doesn't know that," Tempest said. "Getting his seed in Sh-Ariel's hair was a really stupid mistake, and I don't know how I did that." Embarrassment infused her tone.

"I've seen worse problems." The deep voice assured her.

Mozart suddenly stopped moving, then let loose with a string of Farsi curses that brought blood rushing to Ariel's face. He ended in "Insha Allah." *Surely Tempest and I are the only ones who understood the vile phrases he picked up from Peter.* Her hair was yanked so hard she stood on tiptoe. When some ripped free, she gasped in pain, then eyes watering, she bit her lower lip and held her breath so she wouldn't scream.

"Sorry if I'm hurting you. Without scissors, there doesn't seem to be any other way." The man had a soothing bedside manner that even Mozart's terror couldn't disturb. "I've almost got him free." His calm tone washed over her like a soothing caress. "The bird has a talon tangled in your ha-" Mozart's wings beat the air and another lock of her hair ripped free. Ariel cried out in pain, and her own nails sank into the man's muscular torso.

"Steady, gal." The wings stilled. He chuckled.

What a nice laugh the man had. Despite feeling as if she'd just been partially scalped, this was the safest she'd felt in five years.

"He's a boy." Tempest sounded offended. "And he's named Mozart, 'cause he loves classical music."

"One last strand and you'll be free." Was he speaking to Mozart or her?

Abruptly, the weight was gone and there was a rush of wings. "Thank you." Ariel released her hold on the stranger's waist, pushed her shoulder-length hair out of her face and straightened. She stood nose to chambray shirt. The top two open buttons gave her a glimpse of dark hair and a hard, all male torso. Her mouth went dry.

"Yes, thanks," Tempest chimed in. "Do your wolves-er-huskies, always bark this much at strangers?"

"I don't believe they've ever seen a parrot before. Particularly not one that was living out a fantasy of being a hat."

Ariel looked up. Laughter twinkled in the man's amazing blue eyes. Ariel stuffed her hands into her pockets and tried to smile. "Thank you, I don't know what we would have done if you hadn't happened by."

"I'm Stone O'Banyon and this is my partner, Link Gavallan. We live there." He gestured to the townhouse adjacent to the one they'd rented.

She looked past Stone's broad shoulder to see a blond with a duplicate body. Link winked at her. When her cheeks warmed with the warning of another blush, Ariel looked back at Stone. One small emerald feather fluttered in his dark unruly hair. The corner of her mouth twitched at the comical sight. Stone smiled back at her. Her stomach clinched.

"Aren't you afraid your bird will fly away?" Link glanced meaningfully from the three huge dogs that were howling as they tried to rip the fence down to get to Mozart, who was trying to retrieve a plump sunflower seed from under the Suburban's tire.

Tempest shook her head. "Mozart is more-n twenty years old an' that's plenty old enough to develop some common sense. A'course, you probably wouldn't think so after his-" Tempest crossed her eyes, flapped her arms, then yanked her own hair.

Stone's laugh sounded soul warming. Without thinking, Ariel reached up and plucked the feather from his hair. Horrified at her forwardness, she hastily tucked it into his shirt pocket. He winked at her. "Thank you, Ma'am. I'll cherish the souvenir of our meeting."

Face burning, Ariel took a step backward. Her bottom collided with the open door. Stone's smile widened. Of all the apartments in Fairbanks, she had to rent one next to a pair of tall, handsome charmers, the dark half of which apparently enjoyed seeing her mortify herself.

Ariel swallowed and spoke to the hair peeking from the chambray shirt's collar. "I really appreciate your assistance. However, we've got a lot to do." She cleared her throat. "If you'll excuse us, we really need to get things moved inside while we still have light."

Stone and Link laughed as if she was funnier than a circus. Ariel clamped her jaws together and reached inside the Suburban for a suitcase. As she stalked toward her new front door, a warm hand grasped her shoulder. She stopped and held her breath, waiting for the fingernails to dig into her flesh, but the pain never came. Instead, while gently holding her still with one hand, Stone ran his thumb against her neck. "Don't worry, everyone comes out with prize-winners like that."

What was he talking about? Tiny tremors shot up and down her spine. She ignored them, squared her shoulders and risked a glace upward. "Care to share the punch-line?"

Instead, Stone's long legs smoothly moved toward the open door to her townhouse. She tried to grab her luggage, but missed. Ignoring her alarm, he kept talking as if nothing was wrong with his behavior. "When I first came up from the Lower Forty-Eight, I made bloopers like that too."

Ariel hurried to keep up with his long-legged stride. "Tell me what I said."

He stopped and turned toward her, eyes twinkling with suppressed laughter. "In mid-summer, the sun never really sets." Link passed them, his arms full of boxes. Stone's smile widened and he added, "The flip side is that in mid-winter, it never really rises."

Tempest grabbed Mozart and efficiently tucked him under her arm, then snorted. "Like I'm really gonna believe that." With that comment ringing in the air, she hurried toward the townhouse.

"It's because we're so far north, isn't it?" Ariel asked. Tempest whirled around and came back. "The angle of the earth-"

"Bingo." Stone cocked a finger at her and pretended to fire it like a gun. A shiver raced up her spine.

"Sh-Mama, can't you ever just spit something straight out?" Mozart squawked, either in protest at the unceremonious way Tempest had him tucked under her arm, or in frustration at still being the dog's entertainment.

"It's like this." Stone put the suitcase down and fisted both his hands. "This is the sun and this is the earth. See where the rays hit?" Tempest's head bobbed up and down. Ariel had to fight not to nod, too. "Good. Now did you know that when the seasons change the earth tilts on its axis?"

"I studied earth science," Tempest said, as if the course had taught her everything worth knowing.

Stone slanted the hand, which represented the earth. "See how the top of my hand is toward the sun? So even though it's rotating, sunshine is always close." He abruptly angled his hand the opposite way. "But in the winter-"

"The sun is hitting your thumb all the time," Tempest concluded. She grinned up at him.

"Antarctica, actually, but you've got the concept." Stone looked from Tempest and grinned at Ariel. Her breath caught in her throat and all she could do was look at him.

Link came back by, another pile of boxes in his arms. "Any idea which room you want these in?"

"Just put them on the stoop. I'll-"

"I'll haul and carry the stuff for you." Link interrupted, than did exactly that.

"But-"

"You look beat," Stone said. "And you should probably have a doctor look at your head. There's blood trickling down your forehead." To underscore his point, he stroked her hairline with his forefinger, then held it up. The tip was bright red.

"Tempest, can you get my-"

"Bag." Tempest finished, as she thrust Mozart inside the open door.

"First aid kit," Ariel corrected.

Stone cupped her chin in his palm. His eyes didn't twinkle as he held her steady and tenderly eased her hair aside. Ariel stared at the tanned skin beneath his half-buttoned shirt and tried to breathe evenly. He pressed lightly. "It's not bleeding too bad, but maybe I should take you to the hospital. There's no telling how many germs could ha-"

Hospitals asked too many questions. Ariel jerked free from him. "I'll look at it."

Tempest thrust the fishing tackle box, which she kept her medical supplies in, at her. "Mama's a good doctor."

Stone straightened. "I thought you were a prof."

"I am." Ariel glanced meaningfully at Tempest, whose eyes widened, as she realized her mistake. Face crimson, she scooted toward the townhouse. Ariel tried to diffuse the comment by adding, "When you're a mother, it seems like kids automatically assume we have a Ph.D. in cuts and bruises." She hoped he'd accept her explanation and let Tempest's revealing comment pass.

Stone smiled at her. Her stomach did a flip-flop. Why did tall, dark, and sinfully handsome men still appeal to her? Perhaps it was his sincere blue eyes.

Link and Tempest came out of the house and ambled toward the Suburban; she was leaning toward the big blond man, hanging on his every word. "Believe it or not," Link said, "that's not all that unusual up here. A bunch of riggers came from the Lone Star when oil was discovered."

Tempest stopped as if struck; a frightened look on her face.

Ariel wrenched her attention from the mesmerizing effect Stone had on her and seized Tempest's upper arm. She towed her back toward the townhouse's maroon door, hoping neither of the men had noticed the kid's face. "The scratch probably looks worse than it is," she said loudly, to cover the latest blunder. And Tempest wondered why she needed to be home schooled! Come with me and help me clean the cut. I can't see the top of my head."

"But-"

"You can do it."

"But-"

"Shhh." Ariel yanked Tempest into the small foyer. Stone was a couple paces behind and coming fast. "Show me where the bathroom is." Tempest pointed down the short hall to the left door. Ariel pulled her into a refrigerator sized half-bath and closed the door. Leaning close, she murmured, "Get a grip and remember who you are supposed to be."

"But there's oil here." The whispered statement echoed in the tiny room. Outside, the dogs stopped barking. Ariel and Tempest stared into each other's eyes and the implication-filled silence stretched.

"Not right here. The only oil in Fairbanks is what goes through the pipeline or is sold in stores. The wells are hundreds of miles away on the North Shore. I studied all this. There is no way we'll accidentally run into him." Ariel brushed Tempest's wild hair away from her face then hugged her close. "I promise you, this time we'll be safe." She fervently hoped it was the truth.

Tempest's thin arms wrapped around her like a vise. "I was so scared."

"I know. I was, too." Ariel held her tight a moment longer, then straightened and looked for a counter to place the tackle box on, but there was only a pedestal sink. The white porcelain coupled with white walls brought forth an old memory of being shoved into an abandoned refrigerator by her stepbrother. Ariel sat down hard on the toilet seat. Her knapsack hit the back of her head. She shrugged out of it and placed it next to her.

While Ariel tried to forget the past, Tempest pawed through her hair. "There seems to be lots more blood than there should be for the dinky little pokes I've found."

"Head injuries always bleed more," Ariel assured her. "Blood flushes out germs."

"Well, you must be real well flushed." Tempest laughed at her own joke. "Get it? … You're sitting on the toilet."

Ariel rolled her eyes. Tempest prodded a particularly sore spot. Ariel clenched her jaws to stifle a scream. Through clenched teeth, she added, "If the punctures have stopped oozing, swab iodine on them."

"I'll try."

Someone rapped on the door. Tempest jerked and Ariel hugged her stomach. "You all right in there?" Why was Stone still out there?

"Just fine," Ariel said.

"Right." His tone didn't sound like he believed her. After several thundering heartbeats, he asked, "Do you prefer the boxes in the living room with your bird or would your rather have them in the dinning room?"

"Just leave them in the car."

"We've already got most of the stuff in."

"That's not nec-"

"Wrong. You got hurt because my dogs scared your bird. I'm trying to make it up to you."

"It wasn't as if you sicced them on Mozart or didn't have them penned up." Ariel sighed, desperate to get the man out of her life. "I'm sure you have better things to do."

Stone laughed. The sound warmed Ariel until she remembered the way Stone's eyes made his chambray shirt seem faded. The antiseptic smarted as it hit a gash. Ariel gulped.

"I'm sorry," Tempest said. "I didn't mean to hurt you." She backed up a step and smacked into the sink.

"I'm fine. Just fine." Tempest stared at her. Ariel sighed. "It has to be done. Finish."

Tempest splashed more iodine over the top of her head, then escaped from the half bath, the door slamming behind her. Ariel looked at her reflection. Blood and antiseptic oozed from her hairline bringing a memory of death she'd tried to forget. She sat back down on the toilet until she gained control over her emotions, then washed her face and carefully secured her hair into a ponytail that camouflaged the damage. When she finished, she shouldered her ever-present forest green backpack, which contained every essential when they needed to flee, and opened the door. Stone was leaning against the opposite wall, ankles crossed, as if prepared to wait for her indefinitely. What did he expect? Why was he being so considerate? He smiled at her. Dear Lord, the man had dimples.

"I like your hair up like that."

"Thank you." Ariel's throat tightened. "Is there some reason you're still here?"

"Sure is." Link's voice came from the front room. She glanced to her left. Link offered Mozart a slice of cantaloupe. This had to be some sort of trap. Ariel wouldn't put anything past Peter, not even having some of his good looking flunkies hold them hostage until it suited his schedule to come deal with them. But how had they known where she'd be far enough in advance to plan this ambush?

Or were they just playing it by ear?

A shiver coursed down her back.

"I put your sleeping bags in the bedrooms." With his free hand, Link gestured toward the stairway. "You don't have much furniture. If you're planning on renting, there really isn't anywhere good."

"Actually, Mama figured on garage sales. She says that with the Army and Air Force forts nearby, lots of people must come and go."

Link grinned. Thankfully, he didn't have dimples. "Good idea. Tomorrow is Saturday and it seems like I've seen advertisements in the want ads. I'll give you my paper. Better yet, I'll take you around to our storage barn. You can root through and see if you can use anything that we've salvaged. How'd that be?"

"Well, I don't know." Ariel glanced at Stone, who was scowling at his counterpart.

"Don't worry," Link assured her. "That is stuff other tenants left behind. We had to do something when we cleaned up the apartments."

"You're the janitor?" Tempest looked surprised.

Link's laugh was rich and warm. "You could say so. We own this block of townhouses."

They were her landlords? Ariel clamped her teeth together and vowed that even if they lived next door, she'd send them their check in the mail. She blinked. If they owned the apartments, then they probably didn't work for Peter. Ariel took a deep breath.

Outside, the huskies began barking. Stone pushed away

from the wall. "I'd better check on the Greeks." He moved toward the door. Thrilled to get him out of her house, Ariel dashed to the door and threw it wide. The barking was deafening.

"I thought you said they were huskies," Tempest called after him.

He paused in the doorway, so close that Ariel could feel heat radiate from him. "I did." She could feel his breath on her back. She swallowed and held onto the knob. "Hercules … Megara," Stone shouted, "quit scaring Mrs. Cabot's cat."

Link laughed and pushed Stone out the door. "Cats were made to be barked at." He turned and winked at Ariel in a conspiratorial fashion. "Gotta go. Tonight is my night to cook." He stepped around Stone and moved out of sight.

As soon as Stone followed him, she secured the deadbolt. Knees weak, with relief, she slumped against the door.

Chapter 2

The moment their front door clicked shut, Stone stomped toward the stairs, tension radiated from him. Link's expression became concerned. "Is Megara okay?"

"Far as I know." Stone wished Link would go fishing, or something; anything but stand there looking harmless and asking questions. Questions that had no answers; at least they didn't have answers Stone wanted to acknowledge.

Link's brow furrowed. "Is it the bird?"

Stone hadn't been able to think straight since Ariel tossed her hair back and looked up at him. He couldn't quite place his finger on what was unusual about her, but there was something. Nothing really seemed to match; yet everything about her was perfect. Marishka had affected him the same way and that relationship had been a disaster on all levels. "Just drop it, okay?"

Link shook his head. "I really don't get it. You haven't been-"

Since his marriage, his treacherous mind finished the thought. "I said drop it."

This time, Link put up his hands in surrender. "Okay. You don't have to shout."

Stone, who knew he'd only used a warning tone, made a sound halfway between a grunt and a snort, then stomped the rest of the way upstairs.

"Fine, I'll go clean the fish." Link sounded as surly as he felt. "When are you heading down to Valdez? After dinner or first thing in the morning?"

"I'm going right now," Stone snapped. "Dolly doesn't ask stupid questions."

"Good, go polish her brass and get whatever is bothering you out of your system."

Stone took the last steps two at a time. He tossed his clothes into his duffel bag and mentally debated if friendships begun in college should disintegrate after graduation, or form business partnerships. He and Link had gotten on well as roommates at Texas A & M, and it had seemed sensible to combine work with companionship by living together after his divorce from Marishka, but they seemed to have grown past the stage where the arrangement worked. Though their business wasn't suffering, living together was putting a crimp in their friendship.

Marishka. The woman had been a typhoon in the smooth sail of his life. After the divorce, he'd felt tattered and beaten; he'd obsessed about her and their marriage for months and still occasionally wondered what he could have done differently. However, since the wounds had begun to heal, he'd discovered that having a marriage fail didn't make him a failure. Until he'd locked eyes with Ariel, he'd thought he was finally on the path to mental health. Stone shuddered. He needed to get to Valdez as fast as possible and loose himself in Dolly.

~0~

Tempest gazed up at the joists supporting the floor overhead. "That hole is big enough to stick a rope through." She looked optimistic.

"And why do you care about that?" Ariel asked.

"I was kinda hoping we'd be here awhile." She looked Ariel in the eye. "And I miss working out."

Ariel studied the basement rafter's empty knothole. It looked too close to the bottom edge to support the weight of a body bag. "I miss working out, too, but I think we'd need a better support."

"Then we can get one?" Tempest said. Ariel nodded. "Fabulous! I'm gonna get as good as you. Maybe I'll glue Father's picture on it. That should be motivational, don't you think?"

Before she answered, the doorbell rang. Tempest dashed up the basement stairs and Ariel's breath caught. Two years ago, Peter's goons had gone door to door in their apartment building. Ariel stood still as a statue and prayed for deliverance, while Tempest took the stairs up to the main level, two at a time. The doorbell rang a second time. "Hello? Ariel?" Link called. "Tempest? Are you awake?"

Air surged into Ariel's lungs.

"Coming," Tempest called, as her footfalls pounded down the hallway overhead.

"Am I disturbing you? I can come back."

"Nope."

Would Tempest ever fully grasp the concept of safety? Unsteadily, Ariel walked toward the stairs. She paused hand on the rail. Please God, let Link be alone, don't let Peter or anyone who can identify us be with him. Taking a deep breath, she headed upstairs.

"Did you forget something?" Tempest asked, her tone curious. Surely the naïve kid wouldn't sound so casual if anyone was with Link.

"Nope," Link said, as Ariel stepped into the hallway. Link gave Tempest a boyish grin, punctuated by a wink. "Stone flew down to Valdez earlier than we'd originally planned and I'm hoping to talk you and your mom into helping me eat a trout I caught." Link's smile widened. "How about it? You like fresh seafood?"

"Love it!" Tempest's stomach growled loud enough for Ariel to hear it. "You fish a lot?" her sister asked.

He nodded. "I love to fish and I like to cook, but I hate eating alone." His soft Texas accent coupled with the boyish smile seemed innocent. He grinned, looking from Tempest to Ariel. "How about it? Will you come?"

Tempest looked up at her, eyes huge with hope. "Pull-ease?"

He seemed genuine and it could be a good opportunity to learn more about the area. Ariel shoved aside her doubts and grasped the sheer delight of a nice looking man offering to cook for her. "You just gave us the nicest offer we've had in days." Tempest whooped with delight as she twirled around, then she sprinted toward the stairs to the upper level.

"That means she's glad you agreed, right?" he whispered.

Ariel laughed. "It means she's beating me to the shower so she'll be ready on time." A whoop of delight came from above. "Does that answer your question?" He nodded. Ariel added, "I hope this unit has a good water heater, because she's been known to use tons getting ready for a special dinner." It had been a long time since either of them had been invited anywhere. Longer since they'd felt safe enough to accept. She hadn't done anything this spontaneous in years. Ariel smiled at him, feeling a bit giddy. "What can I contribute?"

"No need to contribute. Especially not when you're busy moving in." She opened her mouth to protest, but he added, "See you in an hour or so." Link looped down the steps, vaulted up the steps next door, then turned and waved.

Ariel closed the door. Heart light with anticipation, she grabbed her pocket book and keys. For the first time in years, an attractive, intelligent gentleman seemed interested in her, even after meeting Tempest. Of course, it was doubtful if anything would ever come of the situation. They never stayed anywhere long enough to establish real relationships. But at least she could imagine the possibility. An image of Stone intruded on her thoughts. Ariel shivered. Despite the somewhat tender way he'd assisted her with Mozart, Stone didn't seem like the type who had deep relationships. Worse, his dark coloring and wide shoulders were an unwanted reminder of Peter.

Despite what Link had said, Ariel drove to the store they'd passed on the way to the townhouse complex.

Later, standing at Link's front door, Ariel fought a nervous tremor as Tempest rang the doorbell. The door opened before Tempest's finger left the button. Had he been watching them through the peephole? Ariel fought against the need to flee. "Welcome." Link's tone was tinged with thinly veiled irritation, which flamed Ariel's paranoia. "Come on in. Make yourselves at home."

Tempest giggled and did just that. "Mama found a lemon-meringue pie," Tempest announced. Ariel prayed her overly trusting sister wasn't stepping into a trap. "Ooooooh, it smells wonderful. Seafood is my favorite. I love lemon pie with fish." She thrust the pie at Link. "You can really cook? I've never heard of men cooking."

Link tousled Tempest's black spiked hair as he winked at Ariel. Was he really this friendly, or was his behavior an act to calm them so Peter had time to set up something? Her fingers tightened around the neck of the bottle of wine she'd purchased as a friendship offering and thought that it would make a good weapon. But for now, it was best to play along with Link and act as if her paranoia wasn't warranted. It would be nice to have the possibility of romance. Ariel smiled as she thrust the bottle of wine at him.

Link wiped his free hand on his jeans before he took it. Despite the rugged work shirt, his fingers didn't look like he did manual labor. Neither had Stone's. Both of them had hands as smooth and innocent looking as Peter's. A shiver went down Ariel's spine. "Cabernet Sauvignon," he said." If you always come bearing gifts like this, I'm going to have you two over a lot." Link sniffed the air. "Gotta check the oven. Come on into the kitchen if you want, or sit in the living room, whichever makes you more comfortable."

Tempest trotted behind Link.

Ariel lagged behind. Trying to appear casually snoopy, she looked through the archway to her left. Their living room's deep forest green walls complimented the burgundies and dark blues of the leather furniture all of which combined to give the room a sense of masculine permanence, which was almost as reassuring as not finding an ambush. On the other hand, there wasn't a speck of clutter. Either Link and Stone had a great house cleaner and she'd left five minutes ago or they were vastly different from her stepbrother … or someone had gone to a lot of trouble to make it look like Link and Stone had lived here for a long time.

No ashtrays, which could leave behind butts and their accompanying DNA. Which was probably why Peter had been scrupulously tidy. She wrapped her hands over her roiling stomach, as she peered around the space, wondering what made it feel like one of Peter's sham settings, which she now understood had been designed more to give people an impression of him, than for comfort.

She sniffed the aroma of fresh bread. At least that seemed real and safe. Ariel hurried into the kitchen, where Link was peeking into the oven while Tempest stared out the window, her back to the room. How often had she told her sister not to leave herself in such a vulnerable position? Ariel looked around the room's black-lacquer cabinets, chrome appliances and crimson walls, cataloguing everything that could be used for a weapon - if necessary - and ignoring useless things like the chalk board hanging next to the old-fashioned black wall phone. "Can I help with anything?"

Link tilted his head toward the breakfast bar, where a big butcher-block chopping board half covered with lettuce, carrots, peppers and tomatoes sat under a black wrought iron rack of pots and knives. "How are you at making salad?"

"Not bad." Glad to have a viable reason to clutch a knife, even if the offer might have been made to give her a false sense of security, Ariel began slicing tomato wedges. Having the weapon in her hand eased the tension and sense of imposing doom. Cut by cut, her sense of security returned.

Tempest pressed her nose against the window, which overlooked the fenced in back yard. "Are the dogs friendly?"

"Sure - once they've been introduced to a person." Link

tossed his potholders on the counter. "What do you say, Ariel?" He gave her a questioning look. "Can she meet them?"

Tempest whirled away from the window, her hands clasped as if in prayer. Ariel looked from her pleading expression to the dogs. By comparison to her first glimpse, they appeared peaceful. Of course, anything short of a full-fledged riot would look serene. "Pull-ease?" Tempest begged

Against her better judgment, Ariel said, "If Link thinks it's safe."

"Oooooo, thank you!" Tempest threw her arms around Ariel's waist and whooped with excitement, then she spun away and leaped toward the door. She paused, uncertainty in her expression. "Mr. Gavallan —"

Link blinked in an exaggerated manner. "I'm Link. Mr. Gavallan is my father."

"Oh, okay." Tempest cast a worried glance at Ariel, then she directed the full force of her excitement on Link. "What are their names? What games do they like to play? How long have you had them?" Her questions came too fast for him to answer.

He laughed. "I'll introduce you." He opened the door and motioned Tempest to follow him. Two of the lounging dogs rose and bounded toward them; the other two, in chain link cages, merely raised their heads with interest.

Ariel, knife ready to throw, moved toward the door, but unlike their earlier behavior, the dogs' tails were wagging. In fact, the bigger one's tail was beating so hard it looked like the husky was vibrating with excitement. She stood in the open door, consciously adopting what would look like a casual pose, but prepared to do whatever the situation warranted.

Link picked up a small purple football and tossed it. The

bigger dog raced away, leaped high and caught it mid-air. When Link gestured toward Tempest, the big black and white furry husky gently dropped it into her hands. Tongue lolling out of its mouth, muscles rippling with energy, the dog seemed to be silently urging her to throw it for him.

Tempest's giggle sounded carefree as she threw it. The ball hit the ground a mere pace away. Link chuckled as the dog pounced on it. "Here, let me show you how to throw." As if it understood, the dog brought Link the ball. Link patiently showed Tempest where to put her fingers, then demonstrated the proper arm movement. Tempest's second throw sailed high and long. She squealed with glee, as the dog streaked under the purple projectile, jumped, and caught it.

Persuaded that Tempest was relatively safe, but not enough to close the door, Ariel returned to the cutting board and began slicing a cucumber. She told herself it was good for Tempest to have a decent male role model. The phone shrilled. She jumped.

"Ariel, could you get that?" Link called from the backyard.

"Sure," she said, grateful that her voice didn't betray her. She took a deep breath and picked up the receiver. "Hello?"

There was a long pause, but fortunately no deep breathing. Ariel swallowed and wondered if she should hang up. "Get me Stone," a woman's commanding voice said.

"He isn't here." Ariel cleared her throat. "Could I take a message?" She picked up a stick of chalk from the blackboard's tray and stood poised to write.

The silence lengthened. "Where is he?" The woman's voice snapped like a whip.

"Link said he'd gone someplace." She frowned in

concentration. "I can't remember the place's name. I think it started with V."

"So he's on his way here. Good."

"Is there a mes-"

"I'll try Dolly."

There was a reverberating bang. Ariel stared at the receiver. Who was Dolly? If she was some sort of girlfriend, why had Stone insinuated he and Link were partners? She thoughtfully replaced the receiver. Was she happy that Stone might have a lady friend or not? She envisioned his dark hair and the blue eyes that could render a woman senseless. Yes, she was definitely glad he had a girlfriend. She twirled the chalk back between her fingers before replacing it. That didn't mean she couldn't fantasize about having both men interested in her. She smiled. Fantasies were often safer than reality. With those dimples, Stone would make a dynamite gigolo. Perhaps he had two girlfriends, the one on the phone and Dolly. If so, obviously one knew about the other. He had seemed nice enough to fight for, so she could understand why two women would be willing to feud over him.

Ariel pinched the bridge of her nose at the tender spot between her eyes; something she did to relieve headaches. And the thought of romance certainly qualified as a headache. A relationship was the last thing she needed, particularly a liaison with someone who turned her mind to mush. She needed to be alert for danger. Having Stone and Link living next door was going to be distracting enough.

She glanced out the window, where laughter, shrieks of delight and barks punctuated the lively fetch-match. Stone probably collected women like dogs collected fleas.

What on earth was wrong with her? Had she lost her mind when she'd looked into his eyes? She wiped the chalk dust on her khaki cargo pants, grabbed the knife and attacked the cucumber. She was in no position to have a relationship with anyone. Whack. She didn't need to keep thinking about Stone. Whack. If the past was any clue, the Ariel and Tempest Danner identities wouldn't last a year. Whack. Whack. Whack.

She took a deep breath, closed her eyes and cleared the unwanted thoughts away.

The last time she'd felt anything similar to this, she'd been coping with her first alias, Maria, a Latina fast order cook with a marginal grasp of Spanish and worse culinary skills. Peter had found them within a month, but she'd learned a lot about survival in those twenty-four days. Ariel looked around the immaculate kitchen with its copper pots and well-honed knives. Why had this immaculate room brought back memories of that greasy spoon and her first alias? While they'd gotten better at building identities, Peter still seemed to be able to find them once they started feeling safe. She frowned. Practice usually did make perfect and so far she liked being Ariel Danner, but if experience offered any suggestion, she'd probably be someone else before Christmas.

So by then, any worries about Link, Stone, their dogs, or surviving an Alaskan winter would be irrelevant memories. Ariel started humming Silent Night, adjusted her grip on the knife, then chopped the rest of the vegetables - properly, instead of making mush. Working in a kitchen with the right equipment, was fun.

By the time Link returned, sweat dotted his flushed face, and he looked like he'd run a marathon. "You took the fish out of the oven. Thanks." He gave her a huge smile. "Some host I am, inviting you to dinner, then playing while you cooked it."

"I didn't mind." She bit her tongue before she blurted out her thoughts about the way his kitchen reminded her of the homey things she'd left behind.

"She sure loves the dogs," Link said.

Ariel nodded and silently thanked him for putting an innocent spin on her unsaid reflections. "Not just dogs. All animals." Outside, Tempest and the bigger dog were still having a rousing game of fetch. "She hasn't had this much fun since-" Ariel bit her tongue and shrugged.

"Neither have I." Link sliced the fish and began placing it on a platter. "So, who called?"

"A woman wanted to speak to Stone. Before I could get her name or take a message, she hung up."

"Abrupt to the point of rudeness?" Link's expression was somewhere between amusement and annoyance.

"You might say that." Ariel tossed the salad.

"Mavis." He sighed. "She's our office manager."

"You and Stone work together?"

"We own Linkstone."

"Then why didn't she want to speak to you?"

"At the moment, I'm on Mavis's roster, so she's avoiding me." He chuckled. "Pretty easy since she works out of our Valdez office."

"You let your employees mouth off like that?"

"Just Mavis." Link positioned lemon slices on top of the fish. "We began our company when we were first out of college – youth and arrogance were our main assets. Mavis knew people and understood how to build a business. So we owe her big time." He grinned. "Plus, it'd be hard to fire someone you halfway think of as your grandma." He chuckled.

"So you and Stone live and work together."

"Only in the broadest sense. He keeps a bedroom here, but mainly stays in Valdez."

"And Dolly is there?"

"Oh, so you've heard about the love of his life." Link chuckled and winked at her. "Mavis tell you?"

Ariel indicated agreement. Stone had a 'love of his life' and her name was Dolly. Disappointment mixed with relief made Ariel realize how exhausted she felt. Perhaps she shouldn't have accepted Link's invitation after five long tiring days on the road.

Link picked up the platter of fish and carried it into the dining room. Ariel followed with the salad. Then, while she called Tempest in to wash, Link carried in the rest of the feast.

Ariel gently massaged the tight muscles at her nape, then smoothed a loose hair back into the tight chignon, which she hoped made her appear matronly, or at least stodgy enough to teach college.

Tempest barreled into the kitchen. "Herc is so much fun. Did you see how high he can jump?"

"Wash your hands," Ariel said.

Tempest grabbed the soap. "Megara is cool, too. She's the chubby white one, who's locked up. Did Mr. Gavallan tell you that she 'n' Electra are gonna have puppies?" Water sloshed away the suds. "Do you think I could watch them being born? That'd be so cool."

Link laughed as he returned with the empty tray. "You'll have to ask Stone and your mother if it's okay." Ariel gave Link a sharp look. He grinned. "Even though I seem to end up feeding them most of the time, they're Stone's dogs."

"Why so many?" Tempest asked.

"He breeds and trains sled dogs for a hobby."

"How soon'll he be back so I can ask him?" Tempest asked.

"It's hard to say, but normally he's here a day or two each week and I spend about the same amount of time in Valdez."

"That's a weird way to be partners." Trust Tempest to blurt out what should only be thought.

"Not when we each run one of the offices." Link laughed at Tempest's befuddled expression. "Lets eat while the fish is still warm."

Ariel knew she should be pleased to know that Stone wouldn't be next door every day, and that he would be safely tucked away in Valdez with his beloved and that prima-donna secretary. But she wasn't.

"Sir," Tempest asked, "can I come over 'n' play with them again or do I have to ask Mr. Stone permission for that?"

"You can come whenever your mom says it's okay, but you have to promise to always latch the gate. Okay?" Tempest nodded.

They sat down at the table. Ariel looked at the table and some of her tension dissipated.

"Sir-"

"I'm not a sir or a mister, I'm just plain Link."

Tempest's expression became worried. "It's not respectful to speak to your elders as if they're your equals. At least it isn't unless they're family and that's not even-" She clamped her mouth shut and looked miserable.

Link's eyebrows merged with the blond curls flopping across

his forehead. "Maybe there's hope for the next generation after all." Tempest stared at Link as if his hair had turned purple. He smiled at Ariel. "You taught her well." She tried to curve her wooden lips into the semblance of a casual smile, but she knew where Tempest had been taught respect and doubted that Link's simple request could undo the beatings, which had typified Peter's definition of the way she should 'respect her elders'.

"Sir-"

"If it makes you uncomfortable, maybe you could call me Uncle Link." He looked at Ariel. "You look a little like my sister, Carmen, and I've always wanted a niece."

Eye's huge, Tempest chewed her lower lip and studied Link. Ariel imagined her sister was searching for the verbal trap that would lead to the irrational rage, which always ended in violence. Ariel cleared her throat. "I don't think it would do any harm, if you don't mind her calling you uncle, but don't think that'll translate into any special favors." She gave him a hard look. The surprise, which flooded his eyes told her more than she'd hoped to learn.

Tempest's expression remained suspicious, but she nodded in agreement. "Okay. You're my Uncle Link." Tempest seemed to savor the feel of it on her tongue before she took a bite of fish. "Mmmm. This tastes good." Surprise suffused her face. "Really good! You really made it?" She looked over the table. "All this?"

Linked laughed at her obvious doubt and nodded. "I learned to cook when Stone and I were roommates in college. It was either that or be poisoned by his cooking." By the time they'd finished the main course, Link had told them how he and Stone had been become best friends in college. As they ate pie, he regaled them with stories about moving to Alaska and starting their company.

Later, ensconced on the comfortable leather sofa, Ariel could barely keep her eyes open. She surreptitiously glanced at her watch. Eleven, which would only be seven p.m. Eastern Time. Ridiculous to be so tired.

Tempest giggled. "I think I like having an uncle who likes to fish and cook. You're a whole lot better'n my real uncles." She wrinkled her nose, then her eyes widened, as she realized how much she had revealed.

Let the kid get comfortable and she'd blurt out anything.

Ariel gave an exaggerated yawn. "Link, it's been a great evening, but we've been up since five this morning." She stood up. "When we get settled, we'll have you over for a meal."

"I'd like that," Link said.

After the door shut behind them, Tempest sniffed. "I'm hopeless, aren't I?" It sounded like she was ready to cry over what she'd almost said. "I can never remember to keep my mouth shut."

Ariel put her arm around Tempest's trembling shoulders. "It's all right. You did fine."

"But I talked about family."

"True, but you didn't name names." Her arm tightened. "It's not unusual to have uncles who can't cook or fish."

Tempest gave her a watery smile. "I wish we didn't have to live like this." She swallowed. "All the lies and pretending."

"I don't like it either, but it's better than the alternative." Ariel and Tempest both shivered. Even if everyone had to die sometime, she intended to postpone the inevitable as long as possible.

But if fate brought them a confrontation, she intended to do everything possible to protect herself and Tempest, too. So, as Tempest headed up the stairs to bed, Ariel headed down to the basement to practice Tai Chi. She studied the empty knothole for a few moments, thinking how much more satisfying it was to kick a boxing bag until dust mingled with perspiration, than the meditative fluidity of Tai Chi, than allowed herself to relax into the well-known movements.

Chapter 3

Ariel's heel savagely connected with their new boxing bag. *What had she been thinking when she'd invited Link to dinner?* Kick. *How dare Tempest set a date?* Kick. *Particularly for tonight.* Kick, kick, kick. She wiped perspiration out of her eyes with her forearm, then attacked the bag, again. At least she'd only asked her beloved 'Uncle Link' and not Stone. Kick, kick.

"Sherry!"

She whirled to face her sister. Grabbed her by the shoulders, and snapped, "Ariel." She gave her a tiny shake. "You've got to remember."

"How come we can't keep the same first names?" Tempest whispered.

"Do I really have to explain?" Tempest shook her head. "I didn't think so." She released her sister. "So what did you want?" It had to be something important for her to interrupt a workout.

"Is there enough food for one more person?"

"Probably. Why?"

"I was just over playing ball with Herc and Mr. Stone came home. "She rushed to add. "He looked exhausted. Almost like he hadn't slept since we last saw him."

"Interesting," Ariel said. Tempest looked startled by her harsh tone. "You didn't invite him, did you?"

Tempest nodded. "How come you're angry?" Fear flickered over her face. "Did I do something bad-wrong?"

Ariel sighed. "No." Tempest stared at her, waiting for an explanation. "Was there anything else, that you wanted to interrupt my workout with?" Tempest shook her head. "Good, then since you invited him, you can make more salad and peel a couple more potatoes and I'll make extra pasta."

"Fine." Tempest stomped toward the stairs.

Ariel turned back to the kick-bag. *The guy had looked exhausted, had he?* Kick, kick. *Perhaps he came to Fairbanks because he needed to get some rest from the 'love of his life'.* Kick, kick, kick. The mental image of him and a faceless woman named Dolly moving sensually beneath the covers brought on a frenzy of kicks.

Later, she sat across the card table from her sister, Link on her left and Stone on her right. How inadequate this meal looked compared to the one Link had served. How bare their townhouse's blah white walls seemed. If she knew they'd be able to stay, it'd be wonderful to make this unit into a cozy home as Link had. But that wouldn't happen, so she'd better get used to having beanbags for living room furniture and calling the cheap set of folding chairs and faux leather table a dinning room set. She stabbed some lettuce. Link put down his fork and leaned toward Tempest, his eyes bright with enthusiasm. Alarm skittered up Ariel's spine. Pretending to focus on her food, she listened to Link tell Tempest about an upcoming trip that he and Stone were planning to some God-awful sounding place that probably looked as sorry as the shoddy furniture and felt as uncomfortable as the blister on her heel, but his description of the place held her animal-loving sister spellbound. Convinced that the conversation was innocent, she returned her attention to her plate, but she was all too aware of Stone's silent presence to taste the food.

Suddenly, Tempest leapt up, her folding chair flipped backwards, Mozart shrieked from his perch in the corner and Tempest began bouncing on the balls of her feet. Mozart shrieked and beat his wings. Hands in prayer pose, her expression bursting with excitement, Tempest dropped to her knees next to Ariel's chair. *Oh, no! No. No. No. No. No. This could not be good.* "Can we, can we, can we? Oh, pull-ease say yes!"

"To what?"

"The trip. Can we go? Oh, pull-ease say yes!"

"Where?"

Link gestured northward. *Surely Link hadn't asked them to come with him*! Ariel shot a look at the man. Link smiled and raised a brow, as if daring her to accept. She wet her lips and turned her attention to her right.

Stone's eyes appeared hooded. "Just say yes and get the suspense over with."

"Camping?" she asked, in an effort to determine what her sister was begging for. He nodded and she hoped he had not noticed the squeak of alarm in her tone. "In the actual Arctic, with you and Link?" He nodded, again, but this time, the corners of his mouth tilted up. Her stomach did a tiny dance of excitement, then reality crashed in. Stone O'Banyon exuded the strongest aura of male sexuality she'd ever encountered. It was even stronger than Peter's had been, and that had been strong enough to blind her mother. She inched back from the table.

Tempest grabbed her left hand in both of her own, her eyes

beseeching. "Puuuullll-ease?"

Ariel's heart hammered against her ribs, she tore her gaze from Tempest to Link, who seemed to find her hesitant reaction amusing. A tiny sound from her right brought her attention back to the man, who seemed to define 'drop dead gorgeous'. How would she survive camping for a night or two with only thin canvas protecting her from Stone? No matter how hard she practiced self-protection, she didn't have any defense against the feelings she got around him. Her stomach knotted around the Pasta Alfredo she'd just eaten and her lips formed an N.

"Pull-ease, Sh-er-Mama. We might never get a chance to see real tundra ever again."

"It really is beautiful up there in a stark kind of way," Link added.

Stone tilted his head toward Tempest. "You owe it to your daughter."

Stone O'Banyon was the last person on earth she wanted to share a trip with. Particularly a camping trip to a remote area. Ariel straightened her back, squared her shoulders and looked directly into his face, then wet her lips to tell him so. He smiled. Her heart stopped for while his gaze stayed on her, and he seemed to see every shadowed corner of her soul.

"Pull-ease!" Tempest yanked hard enough on her hand to wrench her attention from Stone's mesmerizing gaze. She shivered, now knowing how snakes lulled their defenseless prey.

"Say yes," Stone said.

"Yes." Ariel clamped her jaws shut and crossed her arms over her stomach. What had he done to her mind? How had he gotten her to agree when it was the last thing she knew she should do? The man must be even more lethal than she'd suspected.

"Yes!" Tempest jumped up and did an impromptu jig. "We get to do something fun for a change! Oh, this'll be so great! Thank you, Uncle Link." She quit hopping and gave Link an impulsive hug.

The big blond mussed Tempest's hair, then he eased off his chair, stood up, and taking her sister's hand, spun her around in a classic dance move. "It's a date, then." Link winked at her over her sister's head. Ariel wanted to scream with frustration. "Plan to pack light," Link continued. "We don't have much extra room." He gave Tempest another spin, quickly followed by a brotherly hug ending with a chuckle under the chin, then he headed toward the front door.

Except for the dance moves and hug, Stone followed Link's example with Tempest, but then he turned in her direction. Her blood ran cold; his gaze appeared sweltering. "Thanks for dinner. I really enjoyed it." He leaned toward her. The breath caught in her throat. Before she could back away, he kissed her. As his lips moved over hers, she felt the heat all the way to her toes. A moment later, the soles of her feet started perspiring, he pulled back. "I'm really looking forward to roughing it." His rough thumb stroked her cheek.

Tremors ran through her. Her mind went blank. All that remained were waves of raw emotion, which she'd buried years before.

A scream rent the air.

Ariel remembered to breathe.

"What the heck?" Stone whirled toward the sound.

Tempest sniggered. "You made Mozart jealous Mr. Stone."

"Cute trick," he said.

"He's a very silly bird." Tempest grinned. "If you want to finish kissing Ariel, I'll take him into the other-"

When had her sister turned into such a little traitor? "That won't be necessary," Ariel said, as she backed away from him. "I'm sure Mr. O'Banyon is in a hurry to leave." She grabbed the doorknob and prayed her knees wouldn't fail her.

Link looked ready to burst with either laughter or anger as he pushed Stone outside.

Ariel closed the door, set the deadbolt, then knees still wobbly from the impact of Stone's kiss, she leaned against the wood.

Tempest's grin was mischievous. "Wow, was that a kiss or what?"

"Or what," Ariel snapped. "What were you thinking, begging to go into the middle of nowhere with them?" Tempest widened her eyes. Her innocent act steeled Ariel. "In case you haven't noticed, we don't know them."

"Sure we do. They're nice."

"All you know about Link is that he can catch and cook fish. That's nothing. You're a kid, he's a man, there's something really wrong about-"

"Oh!" Tempest fumed, "You're always such a fuddy-duddy! He's a nice person."

"Maybe, but he hasn't proved it to me."

"What, you think he's interested in me?"

"I think Link and Stone are the types that Peter hires and some of them were perverts."

Tempests eyes sparkled with anger. "Not Link."

With no proof to support her suspicions, Ariel changed the

subject. "You should get ready for bed."

"Insha' Allah," Mozart wailed.

"Sometimes I think he understands," Tempest said. "You really aren't upset about Link liking me, are you?" Ariel stared at her. "It's Stone, isn't it? That's whose got you all balled up inside, isn't it?" Her sister's perception was getting far too good. "Well, are you going to answer my question?"

Speechless, Ariel glared at her.

Tempest licked her lips. "That kiss looked hotter than anything I've ever seen on TV." Tempest hugged herself, her hands moving suggestively over her back. "What exactly was he doing with his tongue? What did-"

Ariel's circulation came back with a whoosh and she pushed away from the door. "Go to bed, now."

Tempest shrieked and vaulted up the stairs two at a time.

Ariel watched her go, then went to card-table and started collecting the black plastic plates and utensils. Compared to the dinning room she'd grown up with, everything looked pathetic, but neither Link nor Stone seemed to have minded. She closed her eyes, remembering the lead crystal candlesticks, platinum-edged china and etched glass goblets she'd always associated with fine home dining. Peter had smashed more than half in angry fits before her mother had understood that a monster lived under his 'too-nice-mask". Were she and Tempest making the same mistake about Link and Stone? Were they sociopaths, like Peter?

She opened her eyes and looked at the four for a dollar plates and sighed. Would her life ever be stable enough for anything but throwaways?

"What was it like to kiss him?"

Ariel whirled around. Tempest was halfway down the stairs, an impertinent grin on her face. "Why aren't you in bed?"

"Was that what they call a French kiss or was it just a deep one and how do you tell the difference?"

She didn't know, since she'd never experienced such a soul-touching kiss before, but Tempest was the last person she'd admit that truth to. "When Mom met Peter, she thought he was some sort of golden guy – perfect – like a knight of old, he virtually swept in, took care of all her problems and then swept her off her feet."

"And got her pregnant with me."

Ariel nodded. "It took a decade for her to figure out that everything that she thought was wonderful was a lie." Ariel took a step closer and lowered her voice. "About five percent of males have sociopath tendencies." Tempest gasped. "I'm not saying Link and Stone are in that bracket, but I'm trying to make you realize that sometimes people simply are not as wonderful as they seem." Tears swam in her sister's eyes. Ariel relented. "Go brush your teeth."

Tempest wiped her tears on the back of her hand, gave Ariel a mulish look, and then kissed the back of her hand. She wrinkled her nose. "I don't think I can find a way to make a real comparison."

"I'm warning you."

"Was that kind of kiss what a guy does when he wants sex?"

"Tempest! Didn't you hear a word I said about how people can pretend to be one person and actually be something worse?"

"You don't want me to trust Link and Stone. But I think

you're the one who needs to watch out, after all, I didn't kiss Link back, but you were kissing Stone like – Wowser!"

Ariel sprinted toward the stairs. Tempest shrieked and ran toward her room.

Ariel caught up with her a second before her bedroom door closed. Within seconds, they were rolling on the midnight-blue carpet, locked in a tickle fight. Tempest twisted out of her grasp, doubled over and yanked off her loafer. As Tempest tickled her arch, Ariel's entire leg went into a spasm. Shaking her off, Ariel pinned Tempest down and tickled her ribs. "Uncle!" Tempest gasped, tears streaming down her cheeks.

Exhausted, but exhilarated, Ariel flopped off her and lay on her back.

Tempest rolled onto her side and propped her cheek on her hand. "Want to talk about it now?"

"About what?"

"You really do like Mr. Stone, don't you? Isn't that why you're so worried about me 'n' Link?"

"He unsettles me."

"'Cause he reminds you of Father?"

"They have the same coloring and size."

"Stone doesn't give me the heebie-jeebies, like Father."

"Intuition is good, but it isn't infallible." Tempest stared wide-eyed. "That doesn't mean he's nice deep down." Ariel glanced at the ceiling's cottage cheese texture.

"I think that if some guy looked at me the way he looks at you, I'd just melt." Tempest sighed. Ariel rolled onto her side and studied Tempest's dreamy expression. "Maybe he's just as nice as he seems and you'll fall desperately in love with him. If you do, we can stay here and never have to hide again."

Tempest exhaled.

"Love certainly wouldn't cure our problem or make it possible to stay here," Ariel said. "If anything, a romantic relationship would only make everything harder." Tempest snickered. "You know what I mean." Her sister gave her an innocent look. "A romance would mean stronger emotions and stronger emotions mean a deeper hurt once it ends." Ariel knew that first hand. So did Tempest. Still, Stone O'Banyon could certainly kiss. Shoot, he could look into her eyes and make her forget the world existed. That scared her to death, because she couldn't forget about the world and the evil in it. Peter was out there, somewhere, looking for her and Tempest and once he found them, he would murder them in the most painful way possible.

"But for now, it might be nice to make everything harder." Tempest laughed like a hyena at her own joke.

Ariel refused to think about the possibility. "Did loving your father feel good?"

Tempest gasped, her amusement gone in an instant. "That's not the same thing."

"Isn't it?" Ariel challenged. "I know each relationship is different, but if you're going to have a close relationship love should be the basis of it." Ariel knew she was being harder than necessary, but she was still irritated at the way Tempest had forced her into agreeing to go camping in the middle of nowhere. Ariel gritted her teeth. "Just how is loving one man different from loving another?" Tempest started to make a flip answer, then snapped her mouth shut. Ariel held down a smile. "Don't know, do you?" Tempest reluctantly shook her head. Now that her sister was finally listening, Ariel softened her tone,

"That's because all men have the potential to become predators. Which means that they all can get angry and take it out on weaker ones."

"I don't believe you. And I don't believe those statistics you're always telling me about." Ariel raised a brow. "You know, like five percent of males being sociopaths."

"Why don't you believe the figures?"

"Uncle Link and Mr. Stone seem really nice, and you always ignore the fact that there is another ninety-five percent. Like you said, five percent of guys are whacko, not every male."

"True. Until we overheard Uncle Giovanni talking to Peter, we thought they were compassionate men, who would protect us." Ariel forced herself to keep her voice soft. "Is it better to know that you need to beware of the real person behind the smiles and bon-homme, or be wary to begin with, then happy to find out the person really is who you thought?"

"Neither." Tempest rubbed her eyes and sniffed.

Ariel hated to destroy her childish faith in people, but loving people was deadly. "How many years did it take us to figure out that they were criminals?"

Tempest wiped away tears. "Father will never give up looking for us will he?"

"I doubt it. Revenge is very important to him and I'll wager that every time we escape, he just wants us more. Despite the fact that no one is paying him to murder us, I'll bet we're at the top of his hit list." They both shivered.

"Don't get even, get ahead," Tempest quoted in a grave tone. She lay on her back, hands folded across her stomach. "Life stinks. I'll live in an igloo before I let him get revenge."

"I hope it never comes to that." How long would it take Peter to track them in the wilderness, where there weren't bureaucrats to pay off or computers to hack? Probably less time than it took him to learn compassion. Ariel swallowed, but the lump in her throat remained.

"Living in an igloo would be nifty," Tempest said.

"Why do you think that?"

"Just think of all the animals you'd get to see. It'd be better 'n a bird feeder."

"More dangerous, too." Tempest shook her head. "Hypothermia. Frostbite. Ravenous polar bears. And just what would we eat? Snow?"

Tempest sighed. "I suppose you're right, but I still think the wilderness is cool." She grinned. "At least you said yes to going camping. I thought for sure you were gonna say no."

"About the Arctic National Wildlife Refuge –"

"Don't you dare back out!" Tempest shot upright, like she'd been fired from a cannon. "You promised. You told Uncle Link and Mr. Stone we'd go."

"Isn't the refuge near the Alaskan oil field?"

"So?" Tempest glared at her. Ariel tried to hold her gaze, but failed. "Environmentalists wouldn't let anyone drill a well on a national refuge and if it's a refuge, that means there's no hunting, either. So, there's no way Father would ever go there."

That seemed reasonable. Peter wouldn't be there, but Stone would. Ariel contemplated the ceiling and wondered how she was going to endure a weekend in such close proximity to Stone O'Banyon. Worse, she would be at his mercy since he owned the airplane. The refuge loomed like a giant million-acre trap, and she was stepping into Stone's snare. Perhaps that was why a deep sense of dread overcame her when she thought about the trip. Ariel frowned. "I didn't say we weren't going, but I want you to know that I've got a bad feeling about this."

"That's cause you're the queen of paranoia."

"True, but when I get those feelings, something generally goes terribly wrong." Tempest grunted in agreement. Ariel added, "I wasn't going back on my word. I only wanted to let you know that you shouldn't wear your rose-colored glasses."

"Let me guess, I'm about to hear your life isn't like a fairytale speech."

"If you haven't learned by now, it's a waste of breath."

Tempest rolled onto her back and stared at the ceiling. "Life stinks." She sniffed.

"There are good parts," Ariel said.

"Not according to you. If I believed everything you said, I'd think every handsome dark haired guy was a murderer or some sort of monster." Tempest sniveled. "Well, I don't believe it. That's like saying every blond is stupid. We aren't dumb." Tempest touched Ariel's hair. "You may have dyed yourself some artificial intelligence, but I got myself a snazzy look."

Ariel laughed. "You think I look smarter as a brunette?"

"No."

"Me, either. Maybe I didn't have to dye my hair. Maybe I'm just paranoid, but I feel safer with dark hair."

"Do whatever you want with your hair, but I'm gonna keep my spikes. Maybe I'll go purple, though. This black looks sorta goth. Or maybe blue. Or how about orange?" Her face scrunched in concentration. "I know! I'll dye some of the spikes pink and leave the rest black! Perfect!"

Ariel sat up and crossed her legs Indian fashion. Unwilling

to get into the frivolities of a discussion on hair color, Ariel changed the subject back to a topic that worried her, "What you expect to see in the refuge?"

"Wide open spaces big enough for humongous herds of animals."

"I hope you do."

"What are you looking forward to seeing?"

Ariel shrugged. "I haven't thought about anything except my packing list. And that's more climate related."

"This is only Sunday. We don't leave until Friday. We've had a lot less notice a couple of times when we had to leave whole lives behind, so how come you're worried about a packing list?"

"For one thing, living in the Arctic in a tent worries me." Her sister appeared to accept that explanation. In less than a week, she'd be camping in the wilderness with the only man she'd ever met who turned her mind to mush and inflamed her body. Ariel groaned.

Tempest went to instant alert. "What's wrong?"

"I'm just tired. I didn't get much sleep last night."

Tempest flopped onto her belly and propped up her head. "I wish I could help more."

"You want to help me organize the curriculum?"

Tempest rolled her eyes, then stiffened. "Shoot!" She scrambled to her feet and dashed across the room. "I forgot to turn off my computer… Sherry, we've got a voice-mail." Her voice trembled. "I didn't think anyone had our magic jack number."

"Elizabeth has it."

Tempest's expression brightened. "She does?" She tapped some keys. "It's from area code 704, so it must be Grandma."

"Are you going to play the message?"

Tempest tapped the mouse.

"Hello. How was your trip? Is there any decent timber there? I miss you two... I know I never got to see you much even when you lived closer, but it was nice knowing I could have driven there, if I'd wanted to."

"If she hadn't figured she was being watched and her phone was tapped," Ariel said.

"Shhhh." Tempest hit the 'pause' button. "I want to hear what Grandma says. Maybe she'll send a crew up here to harvest lumber, then maybe we can see her."

Ariel laughed. "You really think she'd cross a nation to harvest these big bonsai for her paper mill?" Tempest's expression soured as she shook her head. "I don't think so, either, but it sure would be great to see her."

Tempest nodded, then pressed the 'resume' button. "Actually, Peter is the reason I'm calling. The investigator I hired lost him in O'Hare. I don't want you to panic, but we believe he took a flight to Anchorage."

Tempest smacked the mouse. "Sherry, is that anywhere nearby?"

Ariel's stomach felt like acid had been poured in it. "About four hundred miles south of here."

"Well, that's okay, right?"

No! He could still be in the same state. And she was being totally paranoid for thinking so. Unwilling to allow her terror to invade Tempest's happy mood, Ariel hedged, "We didn't drive within one-hundred miles of Anchorage. It's doubtful that he could pick our trail up from there." She wished she could believe as easily as her sister.

Tempest pressed resume. "Talking to this machine is almost as irritating as talking to your demented parrot." The sound of coins being deposited punctuated Elizabeth's words. "Mr. Bell and his money hungry machines... Now for the latest family news..." Ariel and Tempest sat in rapt silence, listening to the beloved voice. After more coins were added, Elizabeth's voice sounded tired. "Now for the bad news. Yesterday, Mitch stopped a speeder to issue a traffic citation." She sniffed. "The young man was high on drugs and shot him at point blank range. Mitch never had a chance." Elizabeth sniffed. "Sorry to end on such a sad note, I know how much you liked him. That's all the news. I love you. I miss you. Please stay safe." The recording abruptly ended

Tempest stared at her. "He can't be dead." She played it again, but the message was the same. Tempest rocked back and forth, clutching her stomach. "How could someone do something that awful to Uncle Mitch? He was so nice."

Ariel swallowed, but the lump in her throat remained. Had Peter figured out how much Mitch had assisted them? She'd hidden their friendship, to protect him, but now... Tears burned her eyes. "He was one of the few people brave enough to help us." If Elizabeth hadn't specifically said a doper murdered him, she'd be certain Peter had pulled the trigger.

"Poor Aunt Jade." Tears streamed down Tempest's cheeks.

Jade and Mitch had only been married a short time. Now this. Ariel wished life didn't keep reminding her how fragile it was.

"What will Aunt Jade do with the farm and horses?"

"I imagine she'll keep them."

"And Lucifer, too?" Tempest sniffed. "He's such a nice dog."

Lucifer was a powerful police-trained rottweiler-mix and the best guard dog Ariel had ever seen. "If I were Jade I'd keep him." When Jade and Mitch had decided to marry, she'd thought they had it all. Now, their hopes and dreams were destroyed.

"I always wished we were more like Aunt Jade."

Ariel wiped a tear from her eye. "How so?"

"She can stay there as long as she likes because no one is trying to kill her-"

"At least not that we know about."

Tempest's expression looked forlorn. "Aunt Jade has such a nice little house and pretty horses and she-"

"Now, she's even more alone than we are." So was Elizabeth, who had outlived both of her children.

"No she isn't. Aunt Jade can see grandma whenever she wants and call her or her mom or sisters, or just anyone whenever she wants. And she has Lucifer."

"Dogs aren't the same as a husband."

"That's right." Tempest straightened her shoulders. "They're better... I'm glad Aunt Jade didn't get hurt when she pretended to be you."

"So am I." Ariel couldn't get past the feeling that Peter had figured out how Jade and Mitch had helped them escape. What if Jade was next? Ariel shivered. "I should never have agreed to let them help us."

"They offered."

And look at the results. "I'll never endanger anyone like that again." It was too dangerous. Icy fear numbed her.

Tears rolled down Tempest's cheeks. "You don't think some psycho shot Uncle Mitch. You think Father had someone kill him because he found out they'd helped us."

"Maybe." It wouldn't be the first time Peter had paid someone to eliminate a problem for him. And they were certainly a problem. "If that's what happened, it's probably the Suburban." She swallowed. "There would have been a paper trail after that FBI auction."

"I didn't think Father was powerful enough to hack their files." Tempests forehead furrowed. "How would he even know to do that?"

"He probably didn't. The druggie was probably just a coincidence and I'm paranoid."

Tempest studied her. "Still, it'd be just like something Father would do." Ariel nodded in agreement. Anyone who helped them could pay with their life. And even if Peter never discovered it, if something horrendous happened to them, she'd never know if she was responsible for involving them or not. To keep family and friends safe, they needed to stay out of touch. Yet their need for Elizabeth's information made that impossible. Twice, they'd escaped Peter because of data provided by her private investigator. In addition to keeping track of Peter, the PI was building an incriminating file. One of these days, that file could free them by putting Peter behind bars. Ariel hoped she lived long enough to breathe without the shroud of paranoia. If the PI had lost Peter, it usually meant someone was about to die. And it would be just like him to fly to Anchorage, then switch flights. Ariel covered her lips with trembling fingers.

"Sherry, I love you." Tempest cuddled close.

"I love you, too, Sabrina." If they'd been discovered, there was no reason to hide. "Tell you what. Let's call Elizabeth."

"Could we?" Ariel nodded. Tempest scrambled to her feet. "Where's the closest pay phone?"

"Alaska bounces phone calls off satellites. I don't think there's any way to trace our number through both satellites and the Internet. Just make certain not to say anything which could give anyone a clue where we are."

"Because of the wire tap." It was a statement, not a question.

Ariel nodded. "Don't make it sound like we know about the PI losing Peter. And for heavens sake –"

"Don't call her grandma because she doesn't like being reminded how old she is. Aunt Jade has Lucifer, but Elizabeth has lost both her kids and for all intents a purposes, she's lost us, too. Understand?" Tempest interrupted.

"I was going to say don't give away that we know about Mitch's death because then they might figure out that she knows how to contact us. We've got to protect her." Ariel also didn't want to think of how Peter might have been behind the murder.

"If he knew, Father might have her tortured and killed to get the number." Tempest gulped. "Maybe we better not phone."

"By calling and playing our parts right, we protect her."

"'Cause Grandma knows how to get in touch with us and we want to make it sound like she doesn't?" Ariel nodded. "But don't-cha think Father could figure that out?"

Ariel nodded. "But he'd never be sure enough to interrogate her. And he will want her alive so he can keep tabs on the wiretap."

Tempest's hand hovered near the keypad. "So where do we pretend we're at? Obviously, we can't say we're here."

"How about Chicago?"

"Father was just there." Ariel grinned and nodded. Tempest stared at her, then snickered. "I get it. Make him go back."

Tempest snickered louder, as she pulled up the magic jack screen.

"Someone could get a phone number from that. Use the skype account."

Tempest nodded, switched programs and punched the well-known number. When Elizabeth answered, her face broke into a big smile. "Hi, Gr-Elizabeth! I miss you sooooo much."

"Sabrina, honey, I miss you, too. But you shouldn't call me here. You should never call me."

"Well it's not as if you know where we are or can call us." Tempest grinned through her tears. Ariel gave her a thumbs up.

"Is there something wrong?" Elizabeth asked. "Is that why you phoned?"

Forgetting that her grandmother could not see her Skype image, because she was using an actual phone. Tempest shook her head. "I just miss you." They talked for several minutes, then as Ariel took her turn, Tempest leaned close to the laptop, unwilling to break the tenuous contact to the real world.

"Sherry, you shouldn't let Sabrina phone me here."

"Why? Surely you don't think your phone is still tapped. Besides, Chicago is a big place. Peter will never find us here." To the best of her knowledge, calls from Skype to phones could not be traced, but they could be recorded.

There was a moment of silence. "Maybe there's no safe place from someone like him."

"Or maybe if we have to disappear again, we'll have to sever all ties."

Elizabeth's intake of breath was audible. "I would never –"

"I know," Ariel said.

After a moments silence, Elizabeth said, "Maybe you should

stop running." Tempest gasped.

"What are you suggesting?" Ariel asked. "Letting Peter find us?"

"No. Never that." Panic and tears suffused her voice. "Neither of you have the strength to stand up to him." Ariel raised her chin as she thought of how strong her kickboxing skills were becoming, but she couldn't tell their grandmother that. Because she was positive her phone was taped and she didn't need Peter to know what to expect. "I'm not necessarily talking about brute strength." Elizabeth paused. "It's Peter's immorality."

"The sociopath quality that allows him to do anything to get his way," Ariel said.

Tempest shivered. "Or because he's sort of the devil in living flesh."

"Precisely," her grandmother said. Her tone hardened, "I never liked him and I don't think you did, either. I think you were nice to him because you felt you had to."

Elizabeth's suspicions about her feelings were frighteningly close to reality. "How long have you known?"

"Known?" Elizabeth's laugh sounded sad. "About a second. Suspected? Since the first time I saw you with him." Elizabeth sighed. "I was wrong for encouraging you to testify against him."

"You thought justice would be served and he'd get convicted," Ariel said. None of them had foreseen Peter's ability to create `evidence' to support his lies or find everyone's weakness and blackmail them. Of course, having more money than some countries gave him the power to bribe guards, and if all else failed, he could tamper with a jury or find the perfect inducement for a judge.

"There has to be a way to make Father stop chasing us," Tempest murmured. "I hate him," she added, "I hate him. I hate him." Tempest's cheeks turned scarlet. "He's taken everything from us. Everything. But it'll never be enough to satisfy him until he tortures us to death."

Would that even be enough? The past five years seemed like several lifetimes, each with a new name and face, each discovered and ended. All Ariel could see of the future was more running and hiding. More dye, makeup and colored contacts. More new names. More mornings, when she looked in the mirror and wondered who the stranger was. Did Peter have any idea how devastating living on the run could be? Was he procrastinating on catching them because it amused him to watch their efforts? Or were they actually staying a step in front of him?

Ariel sighed. "He'll only quit if we die or he does."

"I vote for him," Tempest said.

Elizabeth sniffed. "You'd never forgive yourself if you stooped to his level." She had a point.

"I'm not sure we'd be rid of him even if he died," Tempest said. "Knowing him, he'd haunt us."

Elizabeth cleared her throat. "I don't want to think about Peter right now." She paused. "Kelsey is overdue by two days." They could hear the amusement in her voice. "Having a pregnant senator is creating all kinds of fervor." Elizabeth's voice warmed. "Bet the voters didn't see that coming, when they elected her."

"But she's okay, right?" Tempest asked.

"Certainly... Of course, Calhoun may never recover from this," Elizabeth said, alluding to her bigoted brother, Kelsey's grandfather, "But that's his problem. I'm confident that Kelsey will be able to manage both career and a baby."

Ariel's heart constricted with jealousy. If she could trade places with her cousin and raise a family with the man of her dreams, she'd do it in a heartbeat. Shoot, she'd even do it, if she had to do it alone, like her cousin, who'd decided to raise the son of her high school sweetheart, alone. Ariel blinked to rid her mind of the thought of having a love child, but she could nearly see her baby's big blue eyes and adorable dimples.

Chapter 4

"The pipeline looks like a snake going in and out of the ground," Tempest exclaimed, then immediately added, "Ooooo! Look! I see a bear." When Stone glanced at the ground, his lips tilted up. Ariel tried to see what they saw, but the body of the plane blocked her view.

Stone silently piloted Linkstone's plane toward the Beaufort Sea, while Link, who was sitting in the co-pilot's seat, kept glancing at his partner, but didn't say anything. Neither did Ariel. Not that any of them had had much chance of getting a word in over Tempest's endless string of observations. Had she even paused for breath since they'd taken off an hour ago?

"Ooooo! Look! There's a wrecked plane!" Excitedly, Tempest grabbed Link's upper arm and gestured to the ground. "Shouldn't we so something? Land and help them?   Radio someone?"

Stone's lips twitched. Link outright laughed.

Tempest punched Link's biceps. Ariel settled back in her seat, wondering what would come next.

"Stop that," Link said.

Instead, her sister smacked him, again, when he continued to look out the window and laugh harder. Tempest screeched, "Stop laughing. Someone could be down there, hurt or even dead. Someone has to-"

Link turned around and put a finger over Tempest's lips. "Relax. That wreck has been there for years. It may have been the first crash you noticed, but it won't be the last. It costs too much to salvage stuff like that, so the wrecks just sit out there until they rust away." Tempest made a sound of disagreement. "Trust me, you'll see a lot more before we get to Deadhorse. But perhaps you'll think you're seeing bears." Both men laughed.

"Uncle Link, I wish you wouldn't joke like that. It isn't nice."

"I'm not joking, am I, Stone?"

Stone glared at Link. Link raised a brow. Stone sighed and said, "He's right. That bear you thought you saw was a rusted snowmobile." Tempest twisted around in her seat, as she tried to look back at 'the bear'. "We'll be seeing a lot more crash sites before we get to Deadhorse. In fact, wrecks are some of the major reference points for the pilots who don't use the pipeline for VFR." He grinned. "We call it 'I follow wrecks'."

"I thought we were going to a wildlife refuge, Deadhorse doesn't sound like a good place for animals."

He rubbed the stubble covering his jaw. "I prefer landing on a runway."

"But Deadhorse?" Tempest's voice squeaked. "What kind of a place is that?"

"It's where people working for the oil companies live."

"Oil companies! Ick! Take me back!"

Stone glanced at Link, who shrugged and raised a brow. "Is there some reason you don't like oil companies?"

"I hate them," Tempest screeched. "They kill animals!"

Ariel put her hand on Tempest's forearm, in an attempt to quiet her. "Calm down, Temp."

But her sister's mouth flattened into a thin, hard line, as she leaned forward. "After that Exxon Valdez thing and all the poor creatures it hurt and killed, it's hard to see any good oil does."

She gave her sister a firm look. "None of us want to hear any more about those poor animals or your hatred of oil. Got it?"

Tempest grudgingly nodded, then turned to the window and silently stared at the wilderness passing beneath the Cessna's belly. With a sigh, Ariel settled back into her own seat and stared out the other window. Granted, the photos of affected animals had been heart wrenching, but she suspected Tempest had brought up the oil spill to cover her fear of the oil companies Peter worked for.

"We have business in Deadhorse," Stone said, "That first, then we'll fly over to the park." Ariel's bad feeling returned with a vengeance. She narrowed her gaze at him, willing him to tell them why he hadn't mentioned this detour previously.

"Is that where the VFR is?" Tempest asked.

Stone chuckled. "VFR stands for visual flying rules. The other term is IFR – instrument flying rules. VFR means a pilot needs good visibility because they use landmarks like rivers, roads, wrecks and the pipeline to navigate. Up here, visual rules are easier because magnetic north deviates."

Tempest scratched her ear. "You mean it moves?" He nodded. "How can north move?"

Trust her sister to latch onto something irrelevant, instead of demand to know why the stop hadn't been mentioned. Ariel bit her lip, with the knowledge that she couldn't bring herself to ask that question, either.

"North doesn't actually move; fact is that the magnetic north isn't exactly north, so the farther north you go, the more off you are from true north." Stone's forehead wrinkled, as if he knew how confusing his explanation sounded. "Luckily, VFR doesn't matter now days because GPS – that's the global positioning system – tells me where I am within a few feet."

"Is this GPS thing some sort of gizmo?"

Stone pointed to a small rectangular panel, which displayed ground speed, the distance to their destination and the time left before arrival. "See the needle? I just follow that line to stay on course. It's simple and safe."

"Uhhuh." Tempest pointed to another gauge. "How come that round one is pointing down?"

"It's broken." Tempest gasped. Stone calmly added, "If it mattered, I wouldn't have taken off. The altimeter only tells me how high I am above ground. I've flown thousands of hours in this plane and am pretty sure we're about five-thousand feet."

"The only time we need the altimeter is when we're flying IFR and we never do that unless it's an emergency," Link said, "if it makes you feel any better, we've got a new one on backorder."

"What kind of emergencies do you get?" Tempest asked. "The blood and guts kind?"

"Not generally, but we have had a few. Nothing fatal, though." Tempest pressed her nose against the window and gazed down at the terrain. Link pointed toward the horizon, where the flat expanse of tundra met a thin dark line. "Know what that is?"

Ariel leaned forward to see. "Prudhoe Bay?" She smelled Stone's rich masculine scent and quickly sat back.

"A lot of people call the whole body of water that, but that portion is actually the Beaufort Sea. We'll land in a few minutes, then Stone and I have to check on some things. You can come with us if you like, or just wander around."

Tempest perked up. "I wanna to see everything - except oil wells, that is."

Stone smiled. "We'll be checking on schedules and supplies. It'll probably take us a couple hours."

"So we can just walk around the town and the -," she squinted at the distant buildings, "uh, area? Nobody will care?"

"Stay away from the wells and pumping station." Stone glanced back, his expression amused.

Tempest's nose wrinkled. "I'd never go near something like that."

Stone laughed. Ariel had the feeling that her sister's response had told him something. But she had no idea if Tempest had simply confirmed her distaste for petroleum or given away more. As she studied his profile, wishing she could read his mind, he tightened his seat harness. Not good. Ariel tightened her seatbelt, too and wondered if he planned to crash the plane.

Stone wagged the Cessna's wings as they passed the pumping station. Ariel bit her lip and wondered what he'd just announced. Even Tempest got quiet. He lined the plane's nose up with a dirt strip that he apparently intended to land on. Or crash. When she could see individual blades of grass, she bent over, grasped her ankles and prayed for survival. To her left, Tempest did the same. Stone landed the 185 and casually taxied to the gas pumps. Before the prop stopped, Tempest bolted out of the plane. "I'm going to go see that river over there," she called over her shoulder, then she sprinted toward the desolate area, opposite from town.

"You should have told me you were afraid to fly," Stone

admonished.

"I'm not," Ariel snapped. Stone raised a brow. She glared at him. Since she was not about to explain, she turned her back on him and shouted at her sister. "Hold up, I'm coming with you." Ariel grabbed her dark green book bag then scrambled out of the Cessna, and headed away from Deadhorse, her step slightly unsteady on the springy ground.

She caught up with Tempest about a quarter mile from the plane. "This sure is a strange place," Tempest said. She kicked a clump of vegetation. "No trees. No roads, at least none I could see from the sky. I can see why they call it Dead Horse. A horse wouldn't be caught dead here."

"It isn't that bad," Ariel said." In fact, I wouldn't mind staying here."

"You just don't want to get back in the plane. Would you h've said okay to this trip if you'd known we'd hav'ta fly in something smaller than our car?" Ariel shook her head. "I didn't think so." Her impish look returned. "I'm glad they didn't tell you beforehand."

Ariel gazed into the distance. "I wonder if we can walk to the refuge from here."

"Probably not. Alaska is sorta like Russia, we can drive for days and not get anywhere." Ariel winced at the memory of a vacation Peter had forced them to join him on. Tempest grimaced. "Sorry for bringing that up." She cleared her throat. "Mr. Stone is a much better pilot than Father, don't you think?"

"Stone only seems better because he doesn't hot-dog and try to scare us."

"You mean Father flies like a lunatic because he *wants* to?"

Ariel nodded. "Everything is a power trip to Peter, but I think

Stone views flying as transportation."

"Well, I sorta guess it is."

"Look around. There aren't any real roads. I read somewhere that one out of every three Alaskans is a pilot. We can see why, can't we?" A chill washed over her and Ariel shivered.

"Are you cold? Do we need to go back and get you a sweater?"

"It's not that kind of chill." It was more of the premonition type and never a good thing to feel.

"You aren't having one of your prem-notions are you?" Ariel nodded, wishing she could figure out what had set her intuition off. Tempest shivered. "I'm glad I don't get those. It's bad enough when something nasty happens, I'd hate to have to know bad stuff was coming. So, what is it? Fear of getting back on that plane?"

"Possibly, but I never really know until disaster happens." She gestured toward the barren landscape. "This reminds me of Siberia." On that trip, Peter had piloted them to an obscure pump station in another small plane and executed so many roiling theatrics that once she'd finally got home, she had vowed she'd never get aboard one of those horrible things, again. And she hadn't, until she'd been tricked into agreeing to this trip. But Stone had proven himself an excellent pilot.

"The Russians use Siberia sorta like a barless prison. I wonder why Americans don't do that."

They stood shoulder to shoulder looking across the barren area. Another chill flickered over her. Was she reacting to the area, which looked so much like the place where she'd first suspected that Peter wasn't the upstanding white-collar businessman she'd thought? "It'd probably be too expensive to build an American type facility here."

Tempest snorted. "Maybe our country needs to get back to making prisons that are nasty places. I'm telling you, if the Turks had caught Father, he'd still be in their dungeon."

"We don't know that."

Tempest kicked a clump of grass, then stomped away from her. Ariel followed. For a while they walked along a narrow trail, the silence punctuated by the squishy sounds their feet made. "I wish we'd see some animals." Tempest exhaled noisily. "All we've seen since we got to this state are dogs, dogs and more dogs. I haven't even met Mrs. Cabot's cat. Not that I don't like dogs, I do. It's just that all the books tell about the wonderful wild animals and it sounds better'n a zoo, but what kind of zoo doesn't have anything but dogs?"

The wildlife probably could hear her five miles away and knew to hide. "There was that goat on the road and that wolf in the dumpster."

Tempest snorted. "It looked more like a mangy ole dog to me."

They walked along the path, sneakers squelching and socks becoming damp. "What about the ravens?"

"Mozart is cooler… Even his cussing sounds better."

Ariel looked skyward, wishing that Tempest didn't understand the Farsi curses their parrot spewed out at every opportunity. Distant birds cavorted beneath the filmy clouds, but nothing in the pale blue sky offered inspiration for a new, safer topic.

"Did'ya ever think land could be so cold and spongy?"

"Siberia was just like this."

After a few quiet paces, she said, "I suppose hell would be worse." Tempest kicked at a clod of muck. "Before we got here, I sorta wondered why Father never came hunting here." She squinted at the desolate landscape. "He'd have hated it here. No place to hide. No trophies to hang on the wall, no politicians to pay off. I don't get why Uncle Link seems to think this is such a great place."

"Not all men are like Peter. Link has different values."

"You mean he fishes."

"That's partly it." Much as Ariel disliked the conversation's turn to the subject that haunted her, the desolate path to nowhere was as good a place to talk as any. "I wish things were different." Tempest glanced up at her. "I wish there'd been a better way to survive than trying to hide."

"It's not your fault, Sherry."

"Isn't it? I was the one who was so certain that justice would prevail."

Tempest bit her lower lip, then exhaled hard. "Uncle Link and Mr. Stone are nice, yet somehow, I get the feeling that they're involved with oil. For the longest time, I thought everyone that worked with it got covered with slime and turned into an evil person. Kinda like those ole' Ninja Turtles getting changed in that toxic sewer."

Ariel chortle as she ruffled Tempest's spiky mop. "That's a clever comparison, and you're right, the problem isn't the oil itself, it's the power surrounding it and the way that power infects people."

"Yeah, I sort'a figured that out." They reached the river and began ambling northward, along its bank. "Do you think Uncle Link would turn out like Father if he was richer and had more power?"

"I don't know, but I think there's some sort of basic ratio of good and bad in any given person and the way they respond to situations can show us what motivates them." Tempest stared at her as if she was speaking Greek. "Okay, let me try to explain another way: some people are super good – Mother Teresa for instance – she would have done anything for anyone just for the satisfaction of helping or giving. That's the mark of a very good person. On the other hand, some people are willing to do most anything for power or some form of wealth and they never do anything nice for anyone unless they expect something ten times better to come to them because of it."

"Like Father."

Ariel nodded. "Peter will always be the standard I measure evil against."

"Until he found out that we knew about him, he sorta seemed okay." Tempest sighed. "Sometimes I wish we'd never found out who he really was." She glared at the river's calm waters.

"Me, too." If they hadn't found out and confronted him, their mother might still be alive. Ariel wondered if she'd be practicing pediatrics in some nice, safe, warm place, right now, if the truth had never been spoken aloud. The creepy feeling was getting worse with each step. "Let's sit down for a while."

"Here?" Tempest's voice squeaked with surprise. Ariel nodded. "But the ground is like a icky sponge."

"Then let's just slow down. We're not running a race, after all and so few people see this river, we should take our time and admire it." Tempest glanced at her as if she'd lost her mind. The ominous feeling was getting so bad that Ariel wondered if she was losing it. Even at a slower pace, her sense of impending doom worsened. Ariel clenched her teeth and tired to shove aside the unwanted feeling.

"What about preachers?" Tempest asked.

Ariel frowned, as she tried to understand the question. "What do you mean?"

"Well, you said Mother Teresa was good. Does that mean that you think everyone who is doing something with religion is good? I mean what about that evangelist guy who took all those donations and bought his dogs that great five-thousand-dollar doghouse? Was he doing good or not?"

"You can't judge goodness by a person's profession. The good or bad parts depend on the person's reason for doing what they're doing." Ariel chewed the inside of her cheek. "Maybe the guy who asked everyone for money to do good honestly thought those dogs needed a special kennel." Tempest snorted. "I think his choice was weird, too. A lot of time, people go into a profession like that because they feel it's something they need."

"Kinda like shrinks going into psychology because they're nutso?"

"Some have probably been motivated by that, but you shouldn't make such a big generalization." Ariel grinned. "For instance, would I be correct if I said all blonds were dumb?"

"No!"

She nodded. "You get the point - we can't judge religion by the charlatans, even if they make big headlines."

Tempest stooped down and picked a tiny blue flower. She twirled it between her fingers, staring at it as if it had all the answers in the universe. "I suppose you're right."

The uneasy sensation of approaching disaster tightened

around Ariel's chest, making it hard to breathe. She'd thought a walk would ease this awful feeling, but it was getting worse and worse.

Tempest leaned forward and touched the water. She jerked back, staring at her finger. "It's cold as ice."

So was the ground under Ariel's boots. "In the Arctic, things never really warm up."

"Who are they?" Tempest pointed down river.

Ariel looked downstream in surprise. They hadn't seen another living soul, since they left the airfield. But about a half mile downstream, two fishermen, dressed in the latest outdoors wear and carrying expensive looking poles, were organizing their equipment on the bank. "They look like fishermen to me," she managed to say, as a wave of nausea washed over her.

Tempest gave her an exasperated look. "Surely, fish can't live in that." She pointed an accusing finger at the water. "They shouldn't be able to move a fin."

"Plants and animals can exist in some amazing environments." Though Ariel wasn't watching them, she was as aware of the fishermen as if they'd been Peter and his brother. Something deep inside her urged her to flee as far away from them as possible. And another inner voice cautioned her that running would be a fatal mistake.

"I think I'm going to wet my pants," Tempest whispered.

Surely her sense of disaster hadn't transferred to Tempest. "This is a joke, right?"

"No." The word was barely discernible. "Don't turn around and look but I swear that's Father."

Unable to heed the warning, Ariel sneaked a peek. Sure enough, one fisherman was staring at them. Though he was too far away for her to be certain, he appeared to be the right build. Worse, he had dark hair and held his head the arrogant way Peter did. Had Stone and Link's friendship been a ploy to get them to walk into a trap? She wanted to look around for his companion but knew that if it was him, her interest would attract suspicion.

"Relax." Ariel tried to take her own advice. "Act natural. It's probably just some man starved for the sight of a woman." Her stomach knotted at the falsehood. Ariel picked up a few rock shards and tried to bounce them on the water. One by one, they landed with a plop in the frigid water and sank. "Link told me that the sun doesn't set for eighty-four days in summer."

"Sherry." Tempest's harsh whisper sounded near panic.

"I know he's still watching us. But we need to lighten up. Or at least appear to be relaxed." She swallowed. "The down side of so much sun in summer is that it stays below the horizon for an equal length of time in winter."

Tempest hopped from foot to foot "I want to leave."

"Please act calm."

"I can't."

"You have to try." Ariel casually took Tempest's hand. "Whatever you do, don't run unless someone starts shooting at us."

"It really is him, isn't it?"

"I hope not." Ariel hoped she appeared unconcerned.

"But how could he have found us in the middle of nowhere?" That was the stupidest question Ariel had ever heard. If Peter Baldwyn decided he wanted to find someone, the universe wasn't a big enough place to hide.

"I can think of two people who knew exactly when we'd be

here."

Tempest's eyes dilated. "No!" Tempest shook her head. "I will not believe Uncle Link works for him."

"Enough money would probably make the Pope Peter's lackey." Tempest appeared faint. Ariel put her arm around her sister's shoulders in what she hoped would look like a friendly fashion, and hauled her close to steady her, then brushed grass off her in an attempt to look like a fussy mother. "Get a grip," she whispered. "Breathe." Tempest managed to inhale. "That's it." She kept swiping at non-existent dirt until Tempest's color returned. "You okay, now?"

Her head bobbed. "I gotta pee." She grimaced. "Really, really bad."

Ariel did too. With what she hoped looked like a nonchalant gesture, she indicated a path that paralleled the one they'd come on. "There is no reason in the world for Peter Baldwyn to be in Deadhorse, Alaska today or any other day. We're probably just paranoid." Except that she knew in the marrow of her bones it was Peter.

"There's oil here," Tempest whispered.

"Which is why we are probably suspecting some poor innocent man of being him." She dusted off Tempest's back. While she was certain they didn't know every evil thing Peter had done, they had learned that normally his targets had 'accidents' after they challenged OPEC.

"Quit beating me or I really will pee." Tempest's sharp tone told Ariel that she was getting over her fright.

Ariel straightened and stretched. Despite her words, she'd know Peter anywhere. She prayed he couldn't recognize them. "Let's play a game."

"What da'ya mean?"

"Let's think of a song and try to walk to its beat."

"You're weird."

"Thank you." Ariel took a few steps. "I'm thinking of My Little Demon. Does it change my walking pattern?"

Comprehension suffused Tempest's expression. "I knew it really was him."

"Can't we do anything for the fun of it or practice for 'just in case'?" She hoped her tone was lighter than her sense of foreboding.

"I suppose." Tempest's walk resembled Elizabeth's favorite dance, the cha-cha.

Ariel mirrored her and she giggled. "Is he still watching us?"

"Yes," Ariel said. Odd that only Peter was watching them. The other fisherman sat slumped on the riverbank. "If I were him, I'd be watching the two silly females, too." Hopefully he'd turn his attention to the freezing water. She boogied a few feet down the thin path. When she spun around, Tempest was mimicking her and trying to put the scare behind her, but the lone fisherman was packing his gear. Ariel didn't see the second man or his gear. The realization that they might have been in the vicinity of a second murder, nearly brought her to her knees. Ariel fought the temptation to look for the second man. Some functioning part of her mind sorted through the likelihood of whether the other person was moving to block them, or if she'd just witnessed another assassination. Her gut told her that it was the latter and if they didn't get to safety, they'd be next because he never left any witnesses, if he didn't have to.

Peter picked up his gear; looked right and left, then took a deliberate step in their direction. Ariel's heart slammed against her ribs.

Tempest struggled for breath. "He's coming this way and he looks just like Father."

"Everyone has a doppelganger somewhere." Though she felt like screaming and running, she knew the only way to survive was act innocent and look oblivious. "Let's keep moving as if we don't have a care in the world."

"I've got to go to the bathroom."

"Me too." Ariel deliberately slowed her pace. "Remember the lesson Peter taught us?"

"Which one?"

"That man is an animal. Some are predators. Some are prey. Peter is a predator. If that's him and we move too fast, we'll trigger his need to chase us. As is, we're only certain where this path leads."

"So you lied," Tempest stopped as if turned to stone. "It really is Father."

"I didn't say that. I said we could use the practice, just in case we ever do see him." Tempest snorted. "Think about this, we're not blue-eyed blonds and I've lost a lot of weight. Some mornings, I don't recognize myself in the mirror … even if that is Peter, he can't possibly recognize us at this distance." And if there had just been another murder, any panic on their part would seal their fate, whether they'd actually seen anything or not.

The lone fisherman paused to look around the barren landscape.

Ariel swallowed, but the lump in her throat remained. "There are millions of dark men, probably hundreds of thousands of them have that build." A flock of birds swirled into the air, water dripping from the bellies and feet. Ariel and Tempest shaded their eyes and watched them escape.

"I wish I could fly away," Tempest said.

They could … on a claustrophobic Cessna … if Link and Stone weren't Peter's accomplices.

Were they walking into another part of Peter's trap or escaping?

Chapter 5

Tempest visibly shivered beneath the gooseflesh covering her arms. Ariel hoped that if the man behind them noticed, he chalked it to up the cool air. "If it is F-f-father, 'nd we'd stayed where w-we were, we could'a pushed him into the r-river." Tempest's teeth chattered from more than the permanently frigid soil beneath the soles of their hiking boots. "That w-water is s-s-so cold he'd of surely d-died and the current would'a carried him out to sea for the p-polar bears to eat."

Was that what had happened to the other fisherman? Ariel glanced at Tempest, who didn't appear to have carried her train of thought to the same conclusion she had. In an attempt to avoid emotional meltdown, she teased, "What do you have against polar bears?" A glare was her only answer. She sighed. "Much as I'd like to drown Peter, I'd never be able to live with myself if I killed him." To do so would be to behave like him and she wasn't at all sure she could. Worse, if anyone got thrown into the river, odds were good that it wouldn't be Peter.

"Even if it was an accident?"

"Well, maybe." And maybe every step they were taking approached the real ambush. Would she fight Link or Stone to the death if cornered? Definitely to defend Tempest. She hoped upon hope that no matter how suspicious the coincidence seemed, Link and Stone had not purposefully lured them into a trap. "I'd never plot to murder anyone or cause serious injury."

"That'd be too much like my father, huh?" Tears welled in her eyes.

"Exactly."

Tempest swallowed hard. "Gramma says meanness is in his genes." Her voice quivered. Ariel glanced at her. "And I feel it." She pressed her palm to her chest. "I want revenge and I think I really could kill him." Ariel shook her head. Tempest made a gasping sound as she inhaled. "I didn't give any vow to heal and protect, like you're stuck with and I would never want to." Tempest's tone sounded strangled. "What if Gramma is right and I'm turning out like him?" Tempest's chin trembled with the message she'd extrapolated from Elizabeth's casual comment.

"I don't think genetics define how a person will behave."

"But Gramma wouldn't lie about that."

"No, but you might have misunderstood what she meant. Genetics gave you mom's blond hair and blue eyes and Peter's long legs, but those are physical features, not reactions. Genetics can not determine what a person does."

"Well, why not?"

"Mainly, because it's a choice." Tempest frowned. "Okay, consider this – how did you decide to dye your hair?"

"Well, I wanted it totally different and I saw a picture in Rolling Stone with this haircut." She patted her spikes. "Then, when I realized all black was blah, I put a few hot pink ones in."

Ariel nodded. "You consciously made choices based on influences from external stimulus. That's how most behavioral choices are determined. So, when it comes to behavior, parenting is much more important than genetics." She tightened the arm around Tempest's shoulders. "Peter's father abused him and Giovanni, then they abused their sons and Peter probably would have abused you, if we hadn't found out about him and run."

"So Benji acts like Father because he was taught to, not because he was born to?"

Ariel nodded. "Peter's father was violent, so violence became his way of life."

"So you don't think there's any hope for Benji." It was a statement, not a question.

She shrugged. "I don't know if his behavior is an act or not, but he seems to like hunting and he certainly loves money."

"Spending it, you mean." Tempest sighed. "How come parents get away with teaching kids the wrong thing?"

"Lots of reasons, but most of them come down to our freedoms."

"I'm willing to kill Father to be free."

"Yeah right." She snorted. "You sobbed for half a day after mom accidentally ran over a squirrel." Ariel looked at Tempest. "Can you really picture yourself committing murder?" Tempest's tears spilled. She shook her head so sharply that a droplet flew in a glistening iridescent arc. "I didn't think so." If the man hadn't been following them, Ariel would have stopped and hugged her, but the necessity of trying to appear unconcerned about his presence made that impossible. "Thinking and doing are two different things."

"I know." Tempest wiped her eyes with the back of her hand, then blinked and squinted at the approaching airfield. "Oh, look, there's Uncle Link." She waved to the big blond. He waved back as if he was genuinely happy to see them.

To look at his body language, no one would think he'd been waiting to capture them. Tempest shook off her arm and broke into a run. Helpless, between a possible trap and certain death, Ariel knelt and pretended to tie her shoe. A huge smile broke over Link's face. Either he was innocent or he was an amazing actor.

Quickly, she offered a quick prayer that her suspicions about Link and Stone were simply paranoia. Ariel picked a wild flower and studied it and risked a quick glance at the fisherman. His pace had slowed. She stood up, then pretending a calm she hadn't felt in years, she followed her sister.

With a laugh, Link caught Tempest and lifted her high, then swung her around, as if she was light as a feather and young as a toddler. Laughing, he set her back on her feet. If he wasn't the enemy, then at least Tempest was safe. Link looked intently at Tempest, then bent over to see her face more clearly. When he touched her cheek. Or maybe she wasn't safe, if he was some sort of pedophile or something. Tempest pointed to the seed heads on a clump of grass and said clear enough for Ariel to hear, "Hay fever, except I don't think those are hay." Link hugged her, apparently buying the explanation for her tears, but the easy way he kept touching her sister didn't make her feel any better than finding Peter in the middle of nowhere.

Ariel hoped her loitering had convinced the fisherman that his presence didn't upset them. Her fist clenched around the tender stem with the intensity of her need, then she took a deep breath and moved toward Link and Tempest.

Stone approached Link and Tempest from the other side. She tried to casually check out the hangar behind him to see anyone lurking in the shadows. The mechanic who had greeted them had his head in the engine of another aircraft, but no one else was visible.

On one hand, Peter had always liked to have as few witnesses as possible; on the other, he liked to show others he could do what he wanted, when he wanted. So, everything boiled down to where Stone and Link's loyalty lay. Despite her fears, the scene looked innocent and peaceful.

"-and we saw some brown birds that had the biggest feet." Tempest aped their clumsy walk. "They weren't ducks. They were sorta chunky and looked real dumb." Link laughed.

Stone's dimples deepened. "You probably saw some ptarmigan."

Peter stalked past them close enough for her to see the scar near his left eyebrow. Oh, how furious he'd gotten when she'd thrown that lamp at him! Her heart thudded so loud, she was surprised no one looked at her. Though Peter gave the impression that he wasn't paying any attention to them, Ariel sensed the quick, intense scrutiny he gave each one of them.

"Pit-are-me-guns are pretty," Tempest said. She sidled next Link, as if his proximity offered protection. Deliberately, she turned her narrow back to her father and focused all her attention on the man she wanted to save her. "How come they didn't move until we almost stepped on them?"

"That's just the way they are." Link placed his hand on her shoulder in an unconsciously casual gesture that could be innocent or not.

Perhaps in another lifetime she'd been a ptarmigan. That would explain how she could willingly walk into what still might be a trap and stand there, surrounded by predators, trying to make them think she didn't know their game.

"Are you two finished admiring Deadhorse?" Link asked. "Or would you like more time to roam the bustling streets and gaze at the soaring skyscrapers?"

Tempest looked at him as if he'd grown two heads.

"Didn't you at least go shopping at the mall?" Stone's eyes twinkled. "I thought all females loved shopping best."

"We're done," Ariel teased back. "Poor Tempest had an allergy attack... It must have been from all the vehicle fumes. We should have spent our time shopping at the local mega-mall."

"Sh-Mama, we did not. You're lying." Tempest turned to Link. "We saw a dock that we couldn't walk on. Dogs that looked mean. Birds that were dumb and we threw pebbles into the river. Oh, and we saw a couple guys fishing, but I don't think the water is warm enough for there to really be fish in there." She put her hands on her hips, tilted her head up and glared at him. "Why didn't ya tell us there was a mall?"

Link laughed.

"I was joking," Stone said.

Tempest's expression hardened. "That's not nice."

"It was meant to be funny," Ariel said. She slanted her head toward Stone. "Adult humor."

Tempest's mouth flattened. "I do not like that kind of joke."

Stone gestured toward the blue and white Cessna, which was tied down near the terminal, within thirty feet of where Peter leaned against the wall casually smoking. "Shall we finish the last leg?"

Ariel looked from Stone's cheerful expression to the plane. Was the aircraft a vehicle of liberty or an instrument of incarceration?

She swallowed, then since she didn't see a third option, she took a hesitant step toward the plane. Peter turned, looked her square in the eye, and then smiled. Ariel shivered beneath her a thick gray sweatshirt. Stone edged closer to her. A tendril of smoke coiled upward from the cigarette dangling between Peter's fingers. Trap or not? Skittish as a wild colt, she moved toward to plane.

"What kind of an idiot smokes that close to fuel pumps?" Stone muttered with irritation.

She glanced back at him. His barely harnessed physical energy shrouded him with righteous indignation and it looked like he had every intention to confront Peter. If he knew Peter, he'd never tell him what to do. Or it could be a ploy to bring them into close contact. Ariel forced a smile to her stiff lips. "Obviously, he only cares about satisfying his nicotine craving."

Stone's mouth flattened. "Yeah." Tempest peeked around Link's elbow for a quick look, then ducked behind him. "The sooner I move my plane away from the fool, the better."

Tempest sped up and grabbed Link's left hand, then tugged on the sleeve of his black denim shirt with her free hand. "Could the plane explode just 'cause that man is smoking?"

Link leaned down. "Doubtful."

Tempest sighed with relief. "That's good." She wrinkled her nose. "Tobacco doesn't smell very good, does it?"

Peter blew a series of smoke rings. As if they were some unspoken signal, Link and Stone turned their backs on Peter and hustled them to the plane. Once out of Peter's direct line of sight, Ariel trembled with relief. They'd apparently passed some sort of test. Stone caught up to her, wrapped his arm around her shoulder and pulled her gently to his side. "You're cold as a glacier."

Unable to speak, for fear her teeth would chatter, she

nodded. He studied her face, his expression concerned. "You look sicker now than when you returned from your walk." Brow furrowed, he looked from her to his plane. "Does this have something to do with why you leaped out of the plane like you were fleeing incarceration?" She stared at him. Stone's expression softened. "Do you need some Dramamine?" he asked her. Ariel shook her head. "Aspirin?"

Again, she shook her head. "I'm fine."

Stone frowned. "For what it's worth, I don't make promises I don't think I can keep and I don't tell people I'm fine when I feel like tossing my cookies. So, what is wrong?" Stone placed his palm on her waist. Though she didn't return the quasi-hug, she didn't push his hand away, either.

"Allergies." She glanced back toward the terminal. "Now that I've move away from the smoke, I'll feel better, soon."

The mechanic's greasy hair emerged from his inspection of a nearby plane's engine. "I topped up the gas and added a half quart of oil."

"Thanks."

"You're gonna need an avionics tech to look at that altimeter."

Stone nodded in agreement. "Want me to bring you anything special on my next run?"

Chet chewed his lower lip and concentrated. Finally he shook his head. "If I think of something, I'll drop you an e-note."

"You have e-mail up here?" Ariel asked in surprise.

Everyone laughed.

"Mom, I think they had e-mail on the space shuttle." Tempest giggled. "So maybe they should rename the world-wide-web the galactic web or something."

Link surprised her by settled into the pilot's seat and starting the checklist. After they each secured their harnesses, Link taxied to the end of the runway and pointed the nose into the wind. As Stone settled into the co-pilot's seat to enjoy the ride, Peter casually walking toward Chet. Ariel slumped down in her seat and studied him. Was that his current plane or what?

The Cessna circled out over Prudhoe Bay, than Link put them on a heading for the Wildlife Sanctuary. A few minutes, after getting back over land, they were already descending. "Look." Link pointed toward a herd and of caribou.

Tempest, who had been uncharacteristically quiet since they left Deadhorse, squealed with delight. Link veered to fly over the caribou and began a running commentary about how the Eskimos relied on them, Tempest oooohhed and aaaahed with increasing enthusiasm.

Ariel pressed her forehead against the cold window, a tear quivering at the tip of her lashes and replayed their encounter with Peter, checking for any flaws.

"Uncle Link, where's the campground?"

"There isn't one."

"But I thought you said-"

"We'll set up camp on a dry spot."

After a somewhat bumpy landing, Ariel gripped the door handle, waiting for the plane to stop, so she could shove it open and gulp lungs full of cool air.

"My flying wasn't that bad," Link said.

"Only in your mind," Stone teased. "I don't think Ariel would look so green if she agreed." Heart slamming against her ribs, she glanced back at him. *Was he particularly pleased about something or did they joke around like this all the time?*

A slight gust chilled her exposed skin. She turned her attention from the occupants of the plane and studied the frozen, empty land surrounding the plane. Never, even in her worst nightmare, had she imagined anywhere so desolate. Was this part of one of Peter's plans: give them a sense of escape, when, in fact, he was tightening the noose and getting them to move to an even more isolated area – an area where a cannon could be fired and only those he controlled would hear it.

"You doing okay?" Stone asked.

"I feel fine."

"Sure you do." Stone didn't sound like he believed her, but Ariel didn't care if he did or not. What worried her was that in a desolate area, like this, a mass murder could be made to look like a plane crash and that was just the sort of thing that Peter Baldwyn would love to stage.

Wryly, she looked up at the pale blue sky, which should contain black clouds to match her mood. Stone opened the plane's door and scrambled out, a look of concern on his face. Black clouds emitting streaking lightening and booming thunder, would be appropriate if the weather wanted to mirror the tumultuous emotions she felt when she looked at him. Ariel gazed at Stone, remembering the safety she'd felt when he held her. How impossible it seemed that he would use his strength against her. Now, drained from fighting claustrophobia and fear, she waited to see what would happen next.

He held his hand out to her, palm up. When she placed her hand in his, his warmth invigorated her. The concern in his gentle smile restored enough of her hope to find the strength to step away from the plane. Did she really dare to believe that seeing Peter had been a coincidence? Stone held her fingers longer than necessary, while he studied her face. His expression seemed troubled. Regret? Guilt? Remorse? When he finally let go, his fingers caressed her palm. Concern? Worry? Caring? Those emotions seemed to fit his manner better.

Now, the pale blue, breezeless air seemed appropriate.

She followed Stone to the rear luggage hatch and reached for the bright red bag containing their dome tent. Stone grabbed it first. Their stares locked for a brief moment. She read heat in his look; thankfully it was not the heat of hatred. She also read concern in his eyes, too soft an emotion for one of Peter's men. He blinked. Released from his mesmerizing gaze, she took a step backward. She'd seen the heat of passion change to the heat of rage too many times before and every time Peter had screamed obscenities as he intimidated her mother. For years, she'd wondered why her mother stayed with him. By the time she was a sophomore in college, she realized her mother didn't believe she could escape from someone fanatical about keeping her subservient. In grad school, she began to understand that Peter controlled her mother in some form of sick power game and began to wonder if her father's 'accidental death' might have been planned. It had still come as a shock to discover that many of her worst suspicions about Peter were true instead of idle speculation.

Ariel took another step away from Stone. As if reading her distrust, he put her tent down a few feet from the Cessna.

Link grabbed several bits of grubby fabric and his folding shovel, then moved toward a shallow depression. Before she had a chance to ask what he needed rags for, he showed Tempest how to hold a filthy cloth bag open, while he filled it with dirt and sand. *Weird thing to do, especially first thing after landing.* Ariel could only hope that there was a good reason why anyone would prioritize filling bags with soil. Tempest looked trilled to find a way to help Link. Assuming Link and Stone really weren't Peter's minions or pedophiles, it was good that she had found a male-role model.

Doubtful if Peter would have waited to kill them if he'd been certain. Probable that he'd have wanted to scare them, first, then have them moved into assumed safety ... cats liked to play with prey, too. Of course, it could have been a twist of fate, but what were the odds of that? Ariel's jaw clenched. The most likely scenario was that Link and Stone had arranged for the supposedly chance encounter to verify their true identities. So the big question was if Peter had recognized them or not.

Ariel let out her breath. It made sense. Stone and Link's work had something to do with the Pipeline, it didn't take a big leap to see how they could have met Peter or suspected she and Tempest were the ones with the big bounty hanging over them. After all, they had an advantage, because not only had they seen them, they'd also seen Mozart and how many parrots matched his description?

Conceivably their lack of verifiable panic could have postponed the inevitable.

She had to stop thinking about the possibilities and analyze the here and now. Her life would have been different if her parents had never met Peter and he hadn't become obsessed with her mother. How different would Tempest's life have been if someone decent had fathered her? Or would her sister ever have existed? She frowned at that disconcerting thought.

If not for Peter, she wouldn't wonder about hidden agendas

and motives; she'd be able to relish the concern in Stone's eyes, the warmth of his embrace, the gentleness of his touch, and the sheer manly scent of him. She might even allow herself the luxury of fulfilling the fantasies she'd had ever since he'd kissed her.

But Peter had fathered Tempest and while that factor couldn't seem to kill the attraction she felt for Stone, it eradicated any possibility of her pursuing a relationship of any tall, dark and handsome man that made her tummy quiver when she looked into his eyes.

Desperate to refocus her thoughts, Ariel began assembling her tent poles.

"Mama, Mr. Stone." Tempest cleared her throat as if preparing for an important announcement. "Uncle Link is done with the bags and now he's taking me on a hike to see how many kinds of birds we can find." Tempest hunkered down next to her and leaned close to whisper in her ear. "Do you think he wants to shoot them? He's got the biggest gun… I don't think I want to go with him if he's going to see how many kinds he can kill."

Ariel squinted at the rifle, which appeared to have a bore large enough for an elephant gun. "If Link shoots a bird with that caliber, you'll be lucky to have feathers left." *It could really damage a human, too.* Ariel's hands shook as she began threading the rods into the tent's channels.

"So why the gun?" Tempest shivered.

She shuddered to think of the ways a corpse could be made unrecognizable with a well-placed shot. Of course, since they were in bear country, where nature would clean up most of the signs of murder, a corpse probably wouldn't get an autopsy.

Ariel whipped her sweaty palms on her denim-covered thighs, then cleared her throat. "From what I understand, there are bears around. It makes sense to carry a rifle." And a bullet that size might even stop one before it could exact retribution. Or, a bullet that size could mutilate a person.

"You mean he'd shoot cute little bears?"

It seemed more desirable than considering what Peter would do to them with that gun. But Tempest wasn't talking about Peter. This was her hero, Link. "The animals around here aren't the PBS type. They're wild and food is a survival issue for them." Though they'd seldom gone hungry since they'd been on the run, she could identify with basic survival issues. "What if a bear tried to eat you for lunch?"

Her lower lip thrust out. "I don't wanna see a poor little bear die." *And she believed she was a killer, like her father?*

"No one wants to see you die, either."

A large warm hand grasped Ariel's shoulder. She froze. "Link has never killed anything with that 308." Stone kept his hand in place as he squatted. His fingers didn't dig in, like Peter's had; the touch seemed much different. He spoke softly into her ear. She leaned toward him, drinking in his scent. "It's stupid not to take along for protection." Stone released her shoulder so abruptly, her body shifted toward him. He tickled Tempest under her chin. "Normally, we fire into the ground to scare them off."

"Into the *ground*?" Tempest demanded, "Aren't warning shots supposed to go into the air?"

"Only in the movies." Stone tweaked her spiked hair, then stood up. "In real life, we shot downward so we know where the bullet is going." Tempest gave him a doubting look. "Think about it. If a shot is fired into the air, it could come down most anywhere within a mile radius."

"That wouldn't be good." Tempest wrinkled her nose. "It could hit anyone." She looked around the empty land. "Or anything."

"Bingo," Stone said.

"So he's only taking it for in case." He nodded. Tempest scrambled up and gave Stone a quick hug. "Thanks, Mr. Stone."

"You really want to thank me?"

She nodded, black and fuchsia spikes quivering like the quills of a nervous porcupine.

"How about dumping the mister?" At her look of protest, he held up his hand. "If losing the title makes you uncomfortable, call me Uncle, like you do Link."

"Well-" Tempest's voice faded, as she looked for help. Ariel nodded. "Okay." She jumped to her feet, skipped to Link and grabbed his hand.

"Need some help with that?" Stone asked.

He was too close. Too helpful. Too male. Too kissable. Too sincere. Too desirable. "I can get it," Ariel said.

"Fine. Don't forget your bags." He pointed to the filthy pile of filled ones. Her confusion must have registered on her face. "Place them inside your tent for support." He gestured toward her tidy pile of tent stakes. Up here, those are no use." She looked from the tent stake in her hand to the grubby bags.

Heat crept up the back of her neck, as understanding dawned. "The ground is eternally frozen."

"Bingo." *Of course regular stakes won't work. How could she have been so obtuse?* "When you get a chance, I could use an extra hand." Ariel looked over her shoulder, to where his tent stood proud and green. "Getting the rain-cover on works better with two."

Ariel stood up and brushed the dirt off her hands. "A lot of things are easier that way." His smile became leering. A blush burned its way up from the soles of her feet into her cheeks.

~0~

Despite being a divorcee or widow or whatever Ariel was, she acted like a cloistered virgin. Other things were odd about her, too. Though she acted protective towards her daughter, there was something intrinsically different between their relationship and the way his mother treated his sisters. Perhaps it was simply because Windy and Brit were adults, but he sensed the difference went beyond age. He supposed whatever was nagging at him could be as simple as her parenting style. Single parent versus two parents; prosperity versus need ... any number of reasons could account for the disparity between their relationship and the mother/daughter interaction he was accustomed to.

Different strokes for different folks. Stone shrugged. Ariel Danner's body certainly looked caressable - particularly her full breasts. Were they really the perfect size to fit his hands? Her legs were lovely, too. It would feel great to caress her toes then move up to her arch, and he couldn't ignore her dainty ankles.

With a harsh curse aimed at his unexplainable obsession with one blushing brunette, Stone shook out the rain-guard. She cringed. His own neck heated. "Sorry. Guess I don't spend enough time with ladies. I'll try to remember not to cuss." He forced himself to focus on the project at hand and not wonder any more about her. Working together, they positioned the rain-guard and tied it into place. Ariel gave him a shy smile, dipping her head when her cheeks flamed scarlet.

They worked without speaking. He focused on tying secure knots. When his tent's rain guard was secure, they collaborated on hers. With a start, Stone realized that he liked her quiet shyness better than the sensual fantasies, which often kept him awake at night.

Stone said, "Care to take a walk?"

Caution suffused her expressive eyes as she took a quick look around the area. "Shouldn't we finish setting up the camp?" Her voice cracked. She winced. Tension? Worry? … Desire?

He glanced from the bedrolls, visible beyond her open tent flap, to her. "Fine, I'll show you the best way to arrange the gear."

She scrambled to her feet. "A walk sounds great. Just let me get my sketchbook." She yanked the duffel bag she'd just tossed into the tent back out, as if she was afraid to go into the tent for fear he'd trap her in it. What kind of a sex-crazed maniac did Ariel Danner think he was?

Stone stomped to the Cessna and grabbed his Winchester rifle. When he returned, he focused on the leather-bound sketchbook clutched in Ariel's white-knuckled hand. His sister, Brittany would have coveted its antiquated styling as well as the worn, well-used patina the leather had developed. Though Stone was tempted to ask Ariel where she'd found it, the way she held onto it gave the impression of long-term ownership, which made it unlikely he could acquire a similar one for Brittany's upcoming birthday. "Looks like you've been sketching for a long time." She nodded. He tried again, "Ever taught anything other than – what exactly is it that you teach?"

"Science… This is a hobby."

He gave her an encouraging look, but she didn't continue the conversation. "Did you bring your camera?"

She shook her head, then raised the sketchbook. "I haven't had one in years." Clutching the volume to her chest, she looked at the ground. "I promise not to waste too much time."

Anyone who preferred to sketch their memories instead of snap a quick picture intrigued him. He chuckled. "Relax. We don't have a deadline." She glanced up, her expression hopeful. What kind of a jerk had she been married to? One that took her so for granted? For his part, Stone was interested to see what the pages of the much-loved book contained. He tried to peek over her shoulder, but she turned away. He was as likely to see her etchings, as he was to see if her underwear equaled her sex appeal. His manhood quivered at the thought, then Ariel's tongue darted out and moistened her lips. He nearly groaned with the intensity of his body's reaction.

"I started sketching about twenty years ago." She clasped the worn leather to her chest in an embrace he envied. "I wish I found more time for it." Stone swallowed hard. "Drawing is so relaxing that I've done it ever since. The earliest sketches were pretty juvenile, but I've gotten better with time." Ariel clamped her lips together, as if irritated at having said too much. She looked tense enough to shatter. A kiss could calm her.

And another kiss could alienate her forever. Stone inhaled deeply and looked at the horizon. It had been close to a week since he'd tasted her lips, but the memory was still vivid; the temptation powerful. He had to keep it light or he'd kill any chance at gaining her trust enough to - to what? He wished he knew what he wanted from her. "I imagine being able to draw comes in handy."

"How so?" The charcoal pencils were clutched so tightly, her knuckles turned white.

Damn, she would have to pin him down on that comment, wouldn't she? "Biology was a core requirement." He grimaced at the memory. "We had to draw pear cells as seen under the microscope... I almost flunked the class." His tone hardened. Ariel shifted uncomfortably. Maybe he should have flunked it instead of asking Marishka, who had the best sketches in their class to help him. Failing biology would have been far less traumatic than having her set her claws into him and scar him for life.

She cleared her throat. "Are we going to leave and take that walk, soon?"

Stone resettled his Winchester on his shoulder and shook off his bitter memories. Ariel visibly cringed away from him. "What's wrong?" he snapped. He immediately regretted his angry outburst. How could he ever explain the way Marishka's manipulative methods still torn at his soul, when he wasn't even certain he understood?

Ariel focused on a distant spot. He turned, trying to see what held her interest. "I hate guns."

So did her kid and hadn't she agreed wholeheartedly with the points he'd made? Would she force him into the BS of going over the safety value of having a rifle, again? "You'd better get over it. Up here, everyone carries."

"That really reassures me." He stalked away.

Chapter 6

Ariel stared at his retreating back. Link had landed moments after spotting the herd. He and Stone had probably intended to hunt all along. The big question still was: did the prey they'd really come after have four legs or two? She would never have accepted their invitation, no matter how Tempest pleaded, if she'd known the trip was a hunting party. And she'd certainly never have accepted if she'd realized she'd come face to face with the devil incarnate.

The question remained: were Stone and Link Peter's associates?

Stone's wide shoulders thrust forward, as if matching pace with his long legs. Was he supposed to bring them to this remote location so Peter could torture them at his leisure? If so, why didn't he give any evidence of smug satisfaction in a job well done?

Did his behavior mean the meeting had simply been a coincidence?

Ariel's heart hammered at the hand pressed against her heart. What to do – what to do. She didn't want to walk into one of Peter's mind-games, if that was what this was. Ariel swallowed, but the lump remained. She didn't want to be left alone in the middle of nowhere with a chest of food and no protection from the predators, which might raid it, either. And she certainly didn't think her skill in kickboxing would protect her against something that would consider her lunch.

She didn't like how easily Link and Stone had separated her from Tempest. If this was just an innocent hunting trip, staying with Stone would be the least of the possible evils, but she didn't want to watch an innocent animal die, either. Ariel blinked away tears. Despite Stone's assurances that he carried the rifle for protection, she'd witnessed Peter's definition of self-protection one time too many. She looked from the plane she didn't know how to fly to the pair of forlorn tents to Stone's strong form. Being left alone in the desolate camp felt like the worst scenario – at least it would until she saw blood and death.

Ariel hurried after Stone.

Jogging behind a black-clad, silent hunter brought back bitter memories. For the hundredth time, she thought how it would be just like Peter to let them recognize him, allow them escape, only to have their get away, so they could land in the heart of his trap.

The real question was if he could possibly have identified them, when she could barely recognize her own reflection.

Doubtful.

Ariel stopped, looked around the frozen land and inhaled deeply, allowing the cool freshness deep inside as she gazed at almost desert-like landscape. If she hadn't testified against her stepfather, would she ever have come here? Had doing what was right actually given her a more interesting life than the cozy partnership in the pediatric practice she'd been offered?

Her life was definitely more exciting.

She grimaced at the truth.

In many ways, it was more interesting, too.

But while being on the run had brought her closer to her half-sister, it had also torn both of them away from family, friends, and security. Ariel studied Stone's wide shoulders and trim hips as he calmly kept walking, either unconcerned that she wasn't keeping up or not aware she'd accompanied him. If he worked for Peter, he would have noticed. She heaved a sigh. She really had to stop tormenting herself with what-ifs about Peter. And she needed to stop fretting about Tempest disappearing with Link and wondering if he was a pervert. She glared at the barren land. She had to stop thinking everything was some sort of trap. If their getaway was part of Peter's scenario, he'd be waiting for them, a smile on his lips, just over the next rise.

Stone's pace slowed. Her heart sank. She shook her head as if denial could fend off her worst fears. Don't let Stone and Link belong to Peter. Ariel looked back at their lonely little camp and wished she could silence the squirrel-cage of fear that kept playing and replaying in her thoughts. Would she die in this eternally frozen land, no matter what she did?

"Come on," Stone urged softly. "They should be visible any minute."

They who? Link and Tempest? Peter and whomever else he might have brought with him to witness the revenge he'd promised? Her legs felt frozen in place. Stone motioned for her to come, then when she didn't move, he disappeared over a rise, leaving her behind. If he was part of Peter's latest plot, running back could get her a bullet in the spine. Advancing could gain her time and perhaps even a chance to really escape.

Ariel took a deep breath and walked forward.

A cloud darkened the sun.

Not a good omen.

The last time she'd felt this cold and alone, she'd been three years old. Snow had coated the ground as her mother pushed her higher and higher with each sweeping arc of the swing. That time, she'd shrieked with delight. This time, she tripped on a something, fell flat on her face and hit her temple. Everything turned black.

Unseen rain bathed her face. Her body swayed, and she detected the faint taste of salt, but she couldn't hear any surf or the storm that had enraged the sea.

"Are you okay?"

Ariel's eyes jerked open. Stone's face, silhouetted against the pale sky, hovered close to her, his expression alarmed. She fingered her aching forehead, amazed that she didn't feel a bullet hole. Her body pitched forward, then from side to side and with every second she got closer and closer to the nausea she'd been fighting since seeing Peter in Deadhorse.

It took all her concentration to realize that Stone was sitting on the ground, cradling her in his arms while he rocked her like a baby. The concern in his eyes warmed her more than the heat from his body, because it was an emotion Peter didn't possess.

"Please stop. I'm getting seasick." Her world instantly stabilized. She wished her stomach would respond as quickly. "Thank you," Ariel said.

"For what?"

"Not treating me like I'm a moron."

"Why? Because you didn't take the Dramamine, when you

obviously should have? That is what's been wrong with you, isn't it?"

She moistened her lips and opted for a partial truth. "I'm terrified of guns and the violence they imply. The sight of blood-" She shivered, as she recalled a bloody memory. "I'm the last person on earth anyone would want to take hunting." Fortunately, she'd gotten past the revulsion before she started residency training, but she still thought the worst parts of her real profession were surgery and forensics.

He frowned as he fingered her forehead. "That rock you tripped on had some nasty consequences." Through the heavy fabric of his shirt, she heard the steady comforting beat of his heart. For the first time in years, Ariel relaxed in a man's arms. "Luckily it looks like you have as hard a head as I do." Dimples deepened next to his mouth. He nudged hair away from her temple and studied the sore spot, then his thumb tenderly traced the contour of her jaw. Stone O'Banyon had the most incredible bedside manner she'd ever experienced. He'd make an amazing doctor.

Sensual awareness surged through Ariel in a heated rush. The next wave of awareness carried terror of her reaction.

She couldn't keep forgetting that Stone might be the enemy. She had to stay focused or she'd end up dead. She scrambled to her feet, but a wave of dizziness hit her. She swayed, nearly falling, he grabbed her waist, without truly restraining her. She clutched the steel-like cords of his arm. Though it seemed unlikely, perhaps he really was the safe harbor she dreamed of.

"Steady."

What was wrong with her head? Had she somehow been drugged?

"You look ready to fall flat on your face, again."

She felt woozy.

"Here," Stone said, as he wrapped an arm around her, "let me help you back to camp."

Ariel blinked. If he wasn't forcing her forward, it might not be a trap. "I'll be fine if I just sit down for a bit."

His sapphire eyes studied her. "Are you sure?"

"No." She would be, if she knew what her problem was. Ariel took a step away from him, but immediately regretted the movement when she lost her footing and pitched forward.

A second later, the earth beneath her feet vanished, Stone swooped her into his arms, and he was carrying her up the gentle slope. "As long as you don't want to go back to camp and do want to sit, we might as well have a seat with a great view." He carried her over the ridge's low crest. Just beyond it, the sprawling herd of caribou grazed, each bite taking them a couple inches westward.

He hadn't lied; at least not about the herd. This was just another example of why she deserved to be crowned the queen of paranoia. "They're beautiful." Or at least they would be, until one or more lay bleeding on the ground.

Stone grunted in agreement, then settled onto the ground, all the while keeping a firm hold on her. A moment later, his face lowered, blocking the sun. A chaste kiss on her temple brought back bitter memories of times Peter had made a show of being the perfect, adoring stepfather. Her jaw clenched. Stone contentedly held her close, rested his chin on top of her head, and ignored her, as he watched the herd.

Peter would never have wasted a kind effort unless he had an audience or was pulling a con. She narrowed her eyes, as she looked up at him. He held her gaze, a smile playing at the corners of his mouth. He leaned a fraction closer, as if he intended to give her another get-better-kiss. If he worked for Peter and was simply stalling, then perhaps she could use her previous dizziness to her advantage or at least compromise his loyalty to Peter a little. Before she thought about the possible complications, or could talk herself out of it, Ariel twisted to face him, wrapped her arms around Stone's neck, pulled him close, and brushed her lips over his. Then, she trailed the tip of her tongue lightly across his lower lip. His massive body shuddered, but instead of following her lead, he pulled back. She tightened her grip, but he easily turned her so her so they were both looking in the same direction and tucked her head under his chin.

Ariel blinked, wondering what had just happened and why any red-blooded male would reject what she'd offered.

She tried to turn back to him, but only got far enough to press her ear against his chest. His ragged breathing hinted that he hadn't felt as totally indifferent to her as he had acted. She stretched upward and kissed his throat. His heartbeat escalated. Feelings she'd imprisoned years before somersaulted through her, leaving her as breathless as he sounded.

Touch by touch, taste by taste, the icy core within her thawed against Stone's warmth, while she consciously seduced him. All too soon, he pulled away, again. This time, he tucked her head under his chin, wrapped his arms around her and sat stiff as his name. Was he afraid of a woman being the aggressor or did this rejection mean he was more afraid of Peter? Or maybe he was just being true to his ladylove. She took a deep breath, wondering if she was more disappointed or relieved. She couldn't recall the last time she'd ignored logic and been driven by emotions, as she'd been when he'd initially responded to her clumsy attempt at seduction. Mentally, she chalked round one up to him, then sighed and faced forward. He hugged her close. She molded her spine against his chest.

After several minutes of silence, Stone softly asked, "What made you so afraid of guns and airplanes?" Though his words were soft, the question pinpointed the roots of much of the terror, which had permeated her youth.

Ariel tried to move away, but he held her against his heart. If he worked for Peter, he deserved to know the kind of demon her stepfather really was. "When I was small, my stepfather decided to take me hunting." Why had she started with that incident? Especially when she was trying to win over someone who was obviously a hunter. Ariel took a raged breath, then continued on the path her subconscious had chosen. "I had such high expectations. I mean, he'd asked me and not my stepbrother, his own son ..." Tears misted her eyes at the naïve kid she'd been. But she hadn't stayed immature. "It was the first time he'd actually noticed me and I was so proud." Somehow, telling Stone about the incident removed the sting from the memory and for the first time, she the full extent of what a trusting child she had been. Her stepfather had known exactly what he was doing and how she would react, yet it had taken her years to realize that he'd manipulated her, then, just as he had so many other times in her life.

When she remained silent, trapped in her thoughts, Stone's arms tightened around her. "But?" he asked, voice soft as the cool breeze.

"He told me we were going to see wild animals." She tried to laugh at her childish gullibility, but tears filled her eyes. She swallowed. "Silly me figured we were going to a zoo." Ariel leaned against Stone's arm. "Now that I'm an adult, I realize how stupid I was. My stepfather's den was filled with mounted heads and taxidermied animals he'd slaughtered. But it never occurred to me that those snarling, glassy-eyed creatures had once been alive and that he, personally, had killed them."

"What'd you think they were?" His voice sounded like a combination of amused interest. "Stuffed toys?"

"Hardly. I thought they were scary… They weren't anything like my teddy bears, even though some of those were pretty realistic." She frowned as she thought through childhood impressions. "Actually, in a lot of ways, I thought my toys were more real than those nasty things. Shortly after my mother and I moved into his place, I felt sorry for him for having such horrid toys, so I offered to share mine."

Stone laughed.

She sighed. "In my defense, I'll note that I was very young at the time."

"Too young to know."

She nodded. "I should have known there was a difference. My toy animals were cute and cuddly. The ones in the den seemed vicious, angry, and some even looked demonic." As memories threatened to overwhelm her, gooseflesh rippled over her. Stone's big warm hands rubbed her, as if he knew. Ariel swallowed the lump in her throat.

"How old were you?"

"When he asked me to go on the hunting trip?" He made a sound indicating agreement. "Seven."

"You were only a kid, operating on the values and facts that you had. Don't judge your beliefs or actions, now after you've had years to gain so much more information." Stone kissed her forehead. "I've seen museum exhibits like the one you described. I wouldn't I'd like one in my home."

She could hear the honesty in his voice. "I never went into his den unless I absolutely had to," she admitted. A compulsion to rid herself of this unpleasant childhood memory seized her. Ariel cleared her throat. "We rode in a jeep to a nearby forest, then sat in a hunting blind. He told me that it was a special place, better than any zoo I'd ever imagined - a place where we would see animals in the wild." She blinked as tears blurred her vision. "I could barely sit still for my excitement."

"I can imagine." His chin settled comfortably on top of her head. "I love coming out here to watch wildlife, too." She tensed. "But that wasn't what you stepfather had in mind, was it?"

She made a sound of agreement. He sighed, as if he shared her disappointment, understood that as she'd sat in the hunting blind, she'd let herself believe she'd become someone her stepfather valued and that Peter had come to care about her, as her father had. Oh, how she'd missed her daddy. Ariel blinked back tears. She and her father had always enjoyed spending time together, no matter if they were simply putting together a jigsaw puzzle or taking a grand trip somewhere exotic like a museum. The most fun had been their daddy-daughter days at an amusement park, but the best times had always been that half hour before bedtime, when she'd snuggled into her father's lap, they'd opened a bedtime story, and he'd rocked her while reading about magic carpets, frontier adventures, missions to mars or her very favorite character,

Minnie Mouse.

After the drunk driver had run over him, her mother had been too upset to read to her and she'd been forced to put herself to bed; try to learn to read to herself. Then she'd lie awake in her dark room listening to her mother quietly crying, while hot tears ran down her own cheeks and fear that life would never be more than just an existence, ever again nearly choked her.

Peter had started coming around more and more often, but he'd virtually ignored her, while playing the knight in shining armor for her mother. Gradually, her mother had stopped crying in the dark, but Ariel's eyes continued to shed tears long after her mother and Peter married.

Then, miraculously, Peter had wanted to spend time with her - her alone. The night after he'd issued the invitation, she'd understood he considered her a person of worth. That night, her pillow had stayed dry.

Sitting there, in the cold with Stone's warm arms wrapped around her, Ariel looked over the herd of caribou, recalling that 'special outing', which turned out to be the first time she glimpsed the sort of 'knight' her new stepfather truly was. "After what seemed like years, I noticed the most beautiful spotted cat. It's coat looked softer than velvet. I don't know if it sensed me or not, but it stopped and seemed to look right at me. Its eyes were beautiful and trusting, just like my toys." Her voice cracked. "I can remember thinking we were sitting in that awful blind so we could see animals that were so much nicer that any my stepfather had at home." She fought back tears.

"He shot it?"

Unable to speak, Ariel nodded. Stone's arms tightened

protectively around her and he growled something under his breath that sounded like 'scoundrel'. Perhaps Stone knew Peter really well.

Ariel remembered the incident so clearly, that she smelled the pungent scent of death and felt nausea over the realization that her stepfather had wantonly killed something so beautiful. She cleared her throat. "The explosions were so loud that I thought the world had ended." Her voice still conveyed too much, so she cleared her throat, again. "Blood gushed out of the big beautiful cat's forehead like a fountain. I couldn't look at the shock and hurt in its eyes, so I watched the blood splatter on leaves and soak into the dirt... When it fell down, I started screaming and crying." Tears trickled down her cheeks, just as they had the first time. But this time, instead of being ridiculed for being too soft, warm hands stroked her back.

"Sounds like a horrible memory." Stone's tone conveyed his disgust. "What a rotten thing to do to a kid."

She nodded. "At that moment, I knew that no matter how much he meant to my mother, I would never like my stepfather."

Stone kissed her temple. This time she didn't mind the way he treated her like a child. "The way I shoot animals is with my camera. I only use a weapon when I or someone else is being attacked."

She pulled away from him, turned, then looked at his big, horrible gun and narrowed her eyes. "What camera?"

His smile seemed boyishly embarrassed, but not guilty, as he dropped his gaze. "I don't have it this trip. If I did, I'd photograph her." He slowly raised his arm and pointed to a distant doe, which meticulously munched lichen, while twin fawns cavorted around her slender legs.

His sincerity assured her and prompted her to do something to atone for her suspicions. "Would you like me to draw her for you?"

"Sure."

She scrambled off his lap and headed toward the family. He lunged after her. The animals froze, muscles tense to flee. Stone's hand clamped onto her shoulder. "This way." He grasped her hand, and slowly led her back over the shallow summit. When she glanced back, a herd of suspicious eyes still watched her.

Chapter 7

Stone looked at Ariel's straight lips and the way her shoulders slumped. Angry or afraid? A blush edged up her neck, then she dropped her gaze to the ground. His arms felt empty without her and his chest felt cold. He took a step to close the distance between them. She stiffened. The caribous' muscles tightened in preparation to flee. He resisted the desire to touch her – to kiss her. His body protested, but one thing he'd learned from the two times he'd given into temptation, and touched Ariel Danner, she had reacted unlike any of the other sexy divorcee he knew and erected some sort of frosty barrier between them, which was the wrong direction on the thermal scale. Yet, just when he'd decided there was something about him she didn't want close, she had clung to him for comfort. Women. He let go of her thin shoulder.

She kicked at a rock.

"We need to be quiet," he murmured. Moving slowly, she looked over her shoulder at the herd, which continued to watch them with quivering attention. Ever so slightly, she inclined her head in agreement. He surveyed the barren landscape, and then added, "We'll come in down-wind, so we should be able to get close enough to see some details." Her eyes widened with excitement as her fingers cautiously gestured for him to proceed.

Holding her hand had been better than having her walk behind him, but pushing any physical stuff could lose the points he'd just won. Lord but she felt good in his arms. Too good. Stone's jaw clenched so tightly that a muscle jumped. He didn't understand this attraction any better than he'd understood what he'd felt for Marishka. Worse, kissing Ariel Danner had been just as good the second time as the first. Just as exciting. Just as dangerous. Just as confusing.

Why had he let male pride convince him that another kiss would help him forget first one? If anything, the second kiss rekindled feelings that had already monopolized too many unguarded moments.

He didn't want to become a stepfather, particularly after the one she'd experienced. Didn't want to give his heart to another person, only to have it ripped out.

It was dishonest of him to let himself or Ariel believe that they could ever share anything deeper. Not that he was certain Ariel wanted him any more permanently than he wanted her. Behind him, the air stirred with a sound that reminded him of Marishka, who had faked sighs of rapture over everything. Stone's jaw clenched at the memory of the way those sighs had sent him running in circles, like a dog chasing its tail. He should have seen through his ex's motives sooner. His stomach felt queasy. He consciously forced his muscles to relax so that the poisonous scars his wife had inflicted could continue healing. Immediately, the queasiness vanished.

Rounding a small rise, the grazing herd became visible below the hillock they were now on. The sight of their vast numbers were reminiscent of a dark brooding inlet. Ariel sank to the ground, and then slowly wrapped her legs into a classic yoga pose. Every unhurried motion, filled with grace and sensuality. Oblivious to the affect of her movements on him, she positioned her sketchbook on her lap, took a thick charcoal pencil in hand and soon, her deft, bold strokes began capturing the scene. Stone hunkered down, alternately watching the herd and Ariel as she drew the doe and two fawns, which had captured his attention. He looked from the caribou to the page and back again, amazed at how quickly she'd portrayed the animals' idiosyncrasies. She turned to a fresh page. Again, with minimal lines, she revealed the powerful strength of a superb buck, which Stone identified as the one staring at them, ready to sound the alarm.

Slow as a receding glacier, Stone settled into a lounging position beside Ariel. Casually, he shifted his gaze to her notebook. Sketch by sketch, she filled two pages with antlers, profiles, eyes that seemed to watch him, muscles seemingly ready to leap off the page and familiar expressions. A tiny illustration of moss appeared in a corner. Along one side, the horizon materialized. Bits and pieces of the life before him sprang into stark relief. Stone narrowed his eyes, trying to see what Ariel saw. Gradually, the buck accepted them and lowered its head to graze.

Ariel turned to a new page, her hand slowed as if she realized the threat of a stampede had passed. She turned her attention back to the doe and twin fawns, which has initially captured their interest.

Why did she teach science if she could draw like this? Shouldn't she teach art?

Suddenly, the herd raised their heads. Eyes centered on a spot to their right. Muscles quivering, nostrils flaring, they watched the unseen danger. Stone grasped his rifle and clicked off the safety. Abruptly, the herd wheeled and broke into a clumsy gallop, which swiftly changed into a steady ground-eating trot that quickly carried them over the tundra.

Ariel's pencil moved furiously across the paper, depicting the energy and motion with vigorous strokes.

Abruptly, a bear appeared, running with a gamboling gait. For several moments, it appeared to gain on the herd, but as Stone held his breath; the caribou began to put more distance between themselves and their cinnamon-colored predator.

Rippling fur, clouds of dust and flashing hooves were caught by Ariel's pencil.

The bear slowed, then stopped. After glaring at the dust cloud, it sat down, an expression of sheer disgust on its face.

Ariel chuckled.

He put his hand over her mouth, leaned close as whispered, "Shhhh. We don't want it to come after us." She stiffened, her pencil poised over a beady eye. He let go of her. Inch by inch, Stone brought the muzzle of his Winchester forward. Ariel's whiskey-colored eyes widened, the hand holding her pencil remained immobile and her breath caught in her throat. For what seemed like an eternity, they watched the bear sniff the air.

Stone prayed the beast would move away and he wouldn't have to harm it to save himself and Ariel. Icy tentacles reached up from the ground. Frozen glares came from Ariel. Mid-winter on a seventy below day would feel warmer.

~0~

Ariel tried not to shiver. Tired not to think about how secure she'd felt touching Stone O'Banyon. Yet, moment-by-moment, her body felt more paralyzed, but she wasn't sure if it was due to the frozen tundra beneath her bottom, his preoccupation with the bear or the sight of deadly steel in his hands.

Nose high, the bear searched for new prey. "Thank God we're downwind." Stone's soft words seemed more a thought than a statement. Ariel wrinkled her nose against the bruin's unwashed odor and marveled that the beast could smell anything other than it's own stench.

Which would come first, frostbite or freedom?

Stone's aim never wavered.

Frostbite, freedom or bloodshed?

Other than an occasional blink and the soft sound of breathing, Stone seemed petrified. Her muscles would be shrieking in agony if she had to hold a gun up that long.

Yet, as the chill wrapped her in its coils, she became aware of Stone's calm protectiveness and a strange peace permeated her.

After what seemed like an eternity, the bear rose and ambled away in the direction the caribou had taken. Freedom! With a soft groan of relief, Stone laid the rifle across his lap. He stretched the kinks out of his arms, back and neck, and then traced her jaw with the pad of his callused thumb. "Don't worry, I would only have shot him if it was absolutely necessary for our survival."

How endearing his dimples looked, how warm his gentle touch felt. Ariel shook her head to clear her traitorous thoughts. Tall, dark, handsome men were worse than Ebola. As if reading her thoughts, he gave her a sad smile. "You really think I'm that much like your stepfather, just because I own a gun?"

Ariel shook her head in denial then scrambled to her feet.

Had she unfairly categorized Stone O'Banyon based on his looks? Or on his choice of weapon? Perhaps. Ariel's right leg protested. She bent over began messaging the knotted muscles. "It's not every day someone is willing to save my life." She straightened in time to see him working his own kinks out. Without thinking, she moved behind him, reached up, grasped his solid, broad shoulders and began kneading the knotted muscles. Stone made a sound of protest. "This is the least I can do to say thank you." And it kept him quiet, so she could massage his muscles while she analyzed the past few moments. She'd always loved the beautiful harmony of nature and when she had the luxury of drawing, she tried to capture it on paper, but in one fleeting moment of pursuit, the bear had taught her that there was a harmony to all phases of life – even the dark side.

And Stone's behavior made her realize that she needed to reevaluate other beliefs and weigh their truth as well. Only one thing seemed certain: guns did not make a man evil, they only increased a malicious man's ruthlessness. The person's heart and true self were the important things. Ariel felt along Stone's tense muscles, then carefully applied acupressure at the critical spot and counted off fifteen seconds.

Stone tilted his head toward the pad she'd left open on the lichen. "You're better than my chiropractor."

"Thank you for protecting me."

"I was defending myself just as much as you."

"I know, and you really didn't want to kill that bear. Even if its head would have made a good trophy or its hide a rug."

"Don't make me out to be a saint. I killed a bear once."

"For the thrill of it?" She was gratified to hear how neutral her tone sounded.

He scowled. "There's no thrill to killing. Ever." He grasped her hands and turned to face her. She knew at least four people who could debate that statement with him, but if it looked like Stone might win the debate, any one of them would cheerfully shoot him between the eyes. "I've killed a lot of animals." He took a cleansing breath. "Back home, my parents butcher a couple head each year for their consumption. Usually bulls. I never liked helping them, but it was a chore we all had to do."

Ariel stared into his sincere eyes, and wondered what she could say that could possibly convey her gratitude to him for restoring a portion of her faith in humanity. When no words came, she cupped his face between her palms, and then brushed her lips against his. When his arms wrapped around her and his lips parted, she eagerly deepened the kiss.

~0~

Emersion therapy supposedly worked. Right? Stone frowned at the failure of its power to break his obsession with Ariel. Plunging into a situation, which forced him to see her practically 24/7 should have broken whatever attraction she held. It hadn't. His scowl deepened. Wilderness survival had effectively defeated other obsessions. It still rankled that he hadn't discovered the strategy until after Marishka scalded him. Emersion therapy had even effectively conquered his sister, Brittany's addiction to chocolate. Though she seemed just as tempting, Ariel wasn't chocolate. And he hoped she wasn't another Marishka.

She baffled him as much as she intrigued him.

Ariel Danner certainly danced to her own drummer. Instead

of trying to talk his ear off in the guise of friendly chatter, she lapsed into quiet companionship, which somehow made him even more aware of the way her curves met his angles. After he'd seen her distrust of guns, he'd forced her into a situation he calculated as being uncomfortable for her. A situation designed to drive her away. But she'd faced her fears. And she'd felt like she belonged in his arms. Stone glowered. The subject of weapons and the need for them had seemed like the ideal motivator to make her consider leaving the entire damned state, let alone her proximity to him, but then she'd explained how and why she'd come to feel the way she did and it had only made her seem more real, more fragile, more desirable and more damned kissable.

That thought slammed a riot of sensations through him.

She was making his plan impossible.

Stone chewed the inside of his cheek and recalled the way he'd responded to her probing tongue; the way he'd lost his senses to her intoxicating taste; the way he'd wrapped his arms around her; the way he'd never wanted to let Ariel go. She fit perfectly against him, as if she'd been made for him to hold. As the kiss had deepened, her body had molded more tightly to his. His body hardened at the memory.

The woman had gone from frigid one minute to hotter than sin the next. There was no explaining it. And Stone did not like unexplainable things.

He clenched his jaws. What the hell did Ariel want from him? Surely, it wasn't the citizenship, Marishka had craved. Of course, his ex had targeted him because he'd represented citizenship plus a seven-digit payoff. The muscles in the back of his neck knotted as he considered the myriad of motives women threw themselves at men. Usually their reasons came down to some form of power. Did Ariel know who his family was? Was she after prestige? Money?

Or did she simply want to fool with him?

At the divorce, he'd vowed never to fall prey to womanly wiles, again. If he didn't watch it, he could fail his pledge. A muscle in his jaw twitched with tension. Perhaps the best defense against her innocent act was a good offense. "You want to screw here or wait until we get back to camp?"

A blush rose from her neck to hairline. "Neither." She took several steps away from him and dropped her gaze, as if she was too shocked by his offer to know what to do. And thus, the ice queen returned. Was this another ploy? Whatever it was, he couldn't let her know that she'd gotten under his skin, like no one except his ex-wife. Until Ariel Danner, he'd been certain his marriage to Marishka had taught him how to deflect the most determined female aggressor.

So why was Ariel different? Was it the way she could swing between innocence and carnality? As if sensing the intensity of his thoughts, or perhaps thinking he'd jump her, Ariel took another backward step.

Stone shouldered his rifle. "If you don't want to get it on, it's time to start back."

Ariel clutched her notebook to her chest. Eyes low, as if feeling guilty for throwing herself at him, she began limping back toward camp.

Feeling like a heartless ass, Stone followed.

As they silently hiked back to the campsite, he nearly told her that in the future she should keep her hands to herself and not make him feel things like tenderness, but if he'd put his thoughts into words, it would have revealed too much to her. Instead, he clamped his teeth together and let his gaze sweep from her disheveled bun past her rigid shoulders, down to her gently swaying hips, then focused on the ankle, which she was favoring. Marishka would have demanded to be carried, perhaps insisted that she needed to be flown to civilization and a hospital. Marishka wouldn't have cried over an animal, either. She hadn't shed a tear when she'd had 'the inconvenience he'd deposited in her' cut away. What kind of woman considered a baby a nuisance? Not that kids didn't create problems, but they sure couldn't be considered to be one-hundred-percent irritant! Feeling cold as his thoughts, Stone looked away from Ariel. He bit the insides of his cheeks and studied the harsh scenery that he loved.

Had Ariel's fall been a play for sympathy? He glanced at her out of the corner of his eye. Her limp seemed consistent. So did the scratches on her arms and face. Marishka would never have spilled her own blood on purpose. Well, except to murder his child, that was. Stone scowled.

Did weapons really frighten her? If her kid was any clue, that part could be real. The hunting experience had sounded plausible, too. "Let's take a break," he said. Ariel stopped, her posture tense. Stone surveyed the scenery he loved. "Amazing isn't it?" Three furrows creased her brow, as she glanced from him to the surrounding view, as if trying to determine what he was looking at. Sunlight without warmth bathed the frozen soil, highlighting the soft curves of the stark land. Stone gestured in the direction of the vast plain, the shadow of his arm stretched far into the distance. "It's hard to believe this was once tropical."

Her frown deepened. "Tropical?" Her tone conveyed total

disbelief. "Here?"

Finally, he had her talking. He scowled. What kind of science did she teach? "Years ago, when the dinosaurs were king."

She blinked. "I thought this area had always been frozen." Ariel clumsily sat down and began massaging her ankle.

Stone glanced from Ariel to the plain. Paleontology should have been a safe topic with someone who taught science, yet she seemed genuinely amazed by his comment. "As far as human history goes."

"Do you think oil comes from some sort of rotting vegetation?"

He narrowed his gaze. "I've heard that some scientists believe it's the product of eons of continuing chemical changes made to sedimentary material by microscopic organisms."

"And they're probably right, but that seems so cut and dried."

"You don't follow research?"

"Not that type." Ariel turned her back on him, as if her answer should have satisfied him, when it only spawned more questions.

"What exactly do you teach?"

His sharp tone startled her. "Anatomy."

"Bones?"

She nodded. "Bones. Muscles, tendons, veins and glands, too." She gave him an apologetic smile.

Stone picked up a pebble, fingering it while he weighed her words. "I've always wondered if oil is partly responsible for the continental shift." What had possessed him to make that asinine comment?

Ariel's face registered interest. "Are all oil wells on or near coastlines?"

He shook his head.

She sighed. "Pardon me for not knowing much about the past history of this area or about oil."

"A significant percentage of fields are located near continental shelves, so I've often theorized that one function of oil is to lubricate the plates." He raised a brow and waited.

"My mother believed volcanoes and earthquakes were the reason Pangaea broke up in the Mesozoic Era." Ariel leaned back on her elbows, her eyes closed and her expression dreamy.

She knew more than she pretended. Stone studied her seemingly relaxed pose. Did she realize her breasts thrust against her shirt when she arched her back like that? He tore his gaze away from the tantalizing mounds and looked at the horizon.

"Did you ever wonder what sort of cataclysm it took to break the mother continent into seven?" she asked.

"Nope, never wondered about that." His attention remained riveted on her up-thrust breasts.

"I wonder what it would have been like to have one gigantic island continent without mountains or valleys in the middle of the prehistoric ocean."

"Think you'd have like to live then?"

Ariel's lids shot up and her gaze centered on him, as if she was surprised to discover he was there, and then she slowly raised one shoulder in a shrug that dried his mouth.

~0~

Would any of Peter's lackeys sit on frigid ground discussing theories about pre-history?

Doubtful.

Stone acted completely unlike anyone Peter had ever palled around with. Perhaps that accounted for her sense of security with him. Ariel's tension ebbed. "I like your idea about oiled continental shelves. It makes the world seem so mechanical and well lubricated." She grinned at him.

He gave her such a warm smile in return that the skin at the corners of his eyes crinkled with merriment. Wow he 'got' her sense of humor. Amazing to find a guy like him in this frozen wasteland. Still grinning, Stone held his hand out to her. Not sensing the Neanderthal that he'd seemed to turn into when he'd acted like he expected her to have sex, she grasped his hand without hesitation, then they headed companionably toward camp.

Not wanting to trip, she watched her step over the rough ground. After a half hour, the ground leveled out and smoothed flat as a road, but he continued to hold her hand. This was nice. Very nice. Unwilling to let him see her smile, she turned her face away, Their combined shadow moved across rugged land, looking ominously like fate was stabbing them in the back. A lump of apprehension formed in her throat. She swallowed and reminded herself to breath, as she looked at him to see what made the shadow. The gun he carried was casting the unsettling silhouette. Guns. They couldn't even look hopeful as shadows!

Unwilling to let horrible memories or paranoia ruin the day, Ariel focused straight ahead, determined to enjoy the day. As they walked back to camp, the air seemed fresher, the breeze sweeter, and the world less threatening. When their tents came into sight, a familiar screech rent the air.

"Ariel! Link and I had a grrrreat time!" Tempest hollered as she sprinted toward them, agile as a gazelle despite the rocky ground. "I saw a raven big as a eagle." Without missing a step, she threw her arms wide. "And it wasn't scared of us one bit. It just sat there eating and cawing as if it owned everything." Tempest skidded to a stop next to her.

"I'm glad you enjoyed yourself," Ariel said.

"Ohhhhh, I did!" Tempest bounced around with delight reminiscent of either a pagan dance or a puppet on a wire. "What'd you see? Any birds?"

"Some. Mainly, we watched the caribou until a bear chased it away."

"A bear!" Tempest stopped as if turned to stone. She clasped her palm to her heart. "You saw real live polar bear!"

Ariel glanced at Stone. He took the hint and said, "It was a black bear." Link gave him an incredulous look. Stone squared his wide shoulders and hitched up his chin, as if defending himself from an unspoken rebuke. Ariel glanced between Link and Stone, trying to decipher the undercurrents flowing between them. "They don't normally stray this far north, but it's not unheard of."

Tempest gave a dramatic sigh. "A real live bear! I wish I could have seen it."

Link shrugged. Stone raised an eyebrow, then focused his gaze on Ariel's notebook as he gave her a telling look. When she opened it and showed her sketches to Link, Stone crowded close behind her. She felt his heat from shoulder to thigh. It distracted her so much that she held up the journal without commentary.

"Ohhhhhh, what a wonderful animal! And so's that." Tempest's grubby finger jabbed the air above a sketch of the caribou. She bounced on the balls of her feet. "It's a boy. Right?" She looked up at Stone.

Ariel glanced over her shoulder, just in time to see Stone's dimples deepen as he nodded. "I thought so," Tempest said triumphantly, "but it's so hard to tell when they all have horns."

"Antlers," Link corrected, as he joined them in a tight cluster around her sketchbook.

Ariel held the notebook as Tempest paged through and cheerfully commented about their day as depicted by the charcoal lines, but she kept sneaking glances at the soft look in Stone's eyes as Tempest ooohed and ahhhed over the animals. Ariel was glad she hadn't sketched Stone or made any drawings, which could have revealed her secret thoughts since she'd found comforting refuge in his arms. She'd felt safer in his arms than she had in years, and that kiss! A wave of heat rushed from her cheeks to her toes. She managed to hold the book steady, instead of fan herself.

She sneaked another glance at Stone. His gaze locked with hers, bored into her, as if he knew she'd just been thinking about his taste. If she didn't have to keep her wits and protect her sister from Peter, she'd accept the sensual offer in his eyes, but the one time she had allowed herself to believe in romance, it had been a trap.

Ariel tore her gaze away from the promise in his eyes, trust the journal into Tempest's hands, and pleading exhaustion, hurried to their tent, where she climbed into her sleeping bag and wished she could turn back time to just before she'd agreed to this trip.

A moment later, Tempest entered their tent and hunkered next to her. "Sherry," Tempest whispered.

"What?"

"Do you think F-Father recognized us?" The barely concealed panic in Tempest's tone explained the thrashing. "I mean we were sooooo close. How could he not have recognized us?" The dim light filtering through the tent's red dome gave the interior a sinister cast.

Ariel shifted in her down cocoon. "We've changed a lot. Some mornings, when I look in a mirror I don't even recognize myself."

"But he was so close."

"I know." Ariel rolled to face Tempest. "We were wearing sunglasses, so he never saw our eyes. Our hair is dyed. I've lost a ton of weight –"

"But I know he knew."

"All he can be sure of is that he saw two females of approximately the right age. That's assuming it was –"

"Of course it was Father. You know that."

"Do I? For certain?"

"Of course you do! He followed us." The other sleeping bag rustled as Tempest climbed in. Her eyes looked large, the whites tinged pink by the dim light.

"Are we certain the man was following us or was he just headed for the airfield?"

"It was Father," she said with conviction. "He wasn't ready to deal with us. He was there to kill that guy he was fishing with. But he saw what plane we got on and he was plenty close enough to read the numbers. He'll get a plan and come after us. Maybe he's even at our place right now."

Gooseflesh erupted over her. She tried to laugh it off. "And I thought I was the queen of paranoia." Tempest gave her an evil look. "Be logical. Even if he could read the plane's number and bothered to research it, he still wouldn't know who Link and Stone's guests were." Ariel imagined Peter entering their townhouse, seeing Mozart and knowing he'd found them, but there was no way the plane's registration should turn up their apartment number. "If Peter recognized us, and that's a big if, he still doesn't know our names." She managed to keep her tone light, "do you really think he'd let us go for even a moment, if he'd recognized us?" Tempest frowned with uncertainty. Ariel tried to think of a concrete way to convince them both. "The man just leaned against that rough old wood and smoked a cigarette."

"Uncle Link and Stone are big."

"Has Peter ever gone anywhere without a gun?" Tempest made a negative sound. Elizabeth had often theorized that Peter needed to carry a weapon to make up for some form of male deficiency. Ariel cleared her throat. "There were five people at that airport, the four of us and that guy with the greasy rag. If that man really was Peter and he'd been certain of our identity, he'd shoot everyone and 'let the Devil sort us out'."

"You're right, there were only five of us … he'd have bullets left over."

Ariel nodded. The canvas overhead undulated; she hoped it wasn't some sort of malevolent omen.

"So you think we're safe."

Ariel looked up at the canvas ceiling and swallowed. "For the time being."

Tempest sighed as if a load had been taken off her

shoulders. "I'm glad. I like it here. I think I want to stay here forever."

"Do you think you'll get tired of sleeping bags and canvas ceiling before it reached a hundred degrees below zero?"

"You know what I meant." Tempest giggled. "I want us to find a safe, permanent home. Of course, if we really do stay right here, we might hav'ta build an igloo for the winter."

Dreams of a different life, a safer life never died, and since she'd found such peace in a man's touch other dreams had emerged, too.

"But I'd rather we settled down someplace a little warmer, like maybe where Mozart could live outdoors and I wouldn't have to clean under his perch." Tempest's tone became wistful. "We could get a place with a yard big enough so I could get a dog and maybe some bunnies," Tempest continued. "It'd be nice to get more birds and fish, too." Her tone sounded wistful. "I love Mozart, but he doesn't play like a kitten or puppy."

"If we ever find a safe place to settle down, you can have as many pets as you want."

"Anything?"

"No reptiles."

"Sherry," Tempest's eyes glistened with unshed tears, "I love you, even if you can't see beauty in fangs and scales."

"I love you, too ... even though you do have the oddest definition of beauty." Ariel reached across the narrow space and brushed Tempest's black spiked halo away from her face. "Do you think you'll be able to sleep now?"

She nodded. Gradually, Tempest's breathing slowed. The soft sound lulled Ariel. She closed her eyes allowing the calmness to soak in. Peace soothed her fears. Then the sound of stealthy footsteps retreating outside their tent brought her to full alert. She clamped her hand over her mouth to hold back her scream. Heart pounding, she listened to the guilty silence.

Had Peter found a way to follow them? He couldn't have, could he? Her sleeping bag became clammy with sweat. Surely it had been an animal in search of a morsel, and realizing there was nothing to eat in the tent, it had moved on.

Again, she sensed movement. She clamped her jaws together so her teeth wouldn't chatter and strained her ears.

Chapter 8

The aroma of coffee permeated the tent's canvas walls and perfumed the air inside with the promise of a new day. Ariel wriggled out of her cozy sleeping bag and grabbed her clothes. The cool, crisp denim of her jeans brought gooseflesh to her sleep-warmed skin, feeling like one of her scary premonitions. Remembering the footsteps, she might have heard, she held the chilled cloth of her red flannel shirt to her face and hoped the frosty fabric would sooth her, but nothing quieted fears, except facing them. She shivered more from nervousness than the cold as she tied the laces of her hiking boots. Then, she jammed her arms into her navy pea coat, took a deep breath and unzipped the tent flap.

Nothing happened.

Ariel ran her fingers through her hair then peeked outside. The only difference was that the scent of coffee permeating the crisp morning air was stronger. A blue-enamel pot perked on top of a small propane stove, which resembled a yellow briefcase. Link hunched over it, inhaling deeply. Had he been the one sneaking around the camp in the middle of the night? The one who had unburied so many of her fears?

She peered at the hard ground, but saw no sign of any footprints, so she crawled out of her tent and cleared her throat. "That smells wonderful. Will it be ready soon?"

Link jerked upright and twisted to face her. His blond mane appeared to have been finger-combed, too, but she didn't detect any guilt in his expression. Ariel hoped she looked equally tousled, instead of scary. "You're just in time." He moved the pot to the unlit burner and stood up.

Ariel perched on a red and white striped campstool. "You're up early." Link cocked a finger at her and pretended to fire it like a gun. She hid her shiver behind a chuckle. He winked, then chose two mugs, and looked at her expectantly. "I drink mine black," Ariel said.

"I inhale mine." Link sniffed loudly as he poured the brew, then carefully handed her a blue-enameled tin mug, which matched the pot. "Take the handle or you'll burn your hands."

Ariel breathed in the steam. The last time she'd smelled this blend was five years ago in London. "This reminds me of my mother."

"I take it that she made sludge." Ariel looked at him with confusion. "You look sad," he explained as he dropped his gaze and shifted uncomfortably. "When we get back, I'll change brands. Coffee is supposed to make you feel better – ready to face the day." His brows knit.

"You misunderstand. I miss my mother and this smells like her favorite brand. Remembering her is a very good thing." Ariel took a sip. "Mmmmm and it tastes good, too." When they got back to civilization, she would buy some.

"I understand." Link sat down on a folding chair, blew into the mug and stared at the horizon. "When I was living at home, I couldn't wait to move out. Be on my own. Do as I wanted, when I wanted." He shook his head. "The longer I'm away from them, the more I miss them."

"Big family?"

"Parents, two brothers and a sister. I miss Carmen the most, which is weird because I used to think she was the worst pest in Dallas."

"Is that why you adopted me?"

"Probably." He chuckled. "You have sisters and brothers?"

"One each sister and brother." Ariel gulped her coffee. As it burned down her esophagus, tears flooded her eyes. She deserved the pain for being such a blabbermouth.

"I'm the oldest. Carmen is two years younger. Nick and Nate are identical twins, but just about as different in personality and interests as two people can be." He smiled thinking of them. "They're in their last year of college."

"Miss 'em?"

"Sometimes, but not over coffee." Link tilted his head. Ariel took a sip, but he kept looking at her. When she realized she needed to tell him something, she admitted, "My brother is so much like my step-father that I hope I never see him again."

"Do you mean he's a big game hunter or a man's man?" Stone asked from behind her.

Ariel twisted around and looked up so quickly that scalding coffee sloshed on her hand. She wiped her hand on her jeans and hoped neither Stone nor Link had noticed how disconcerted his question had been.

Stone hunkered down, poured a cup for himself, then turned to Link and explained, "The guy sure isn't a woman's man or a kid's man."

"Your step-father is an avid hunter?" Link craned to see her over Stone's broad shoulder, his expression surprised.

Ariel nodded, and then studied the scuffed toes of her hiking boots. "He is the reason Tempest hates guns so much." She clenched her teeth together and willed herself to shut up.

Stone settled between her and Link. His expression serious as he asked Link, "What kind of man takes his seven year old daughter on a *special day*, makes her think where they're going is some sort of zoo, when it's really a hunting blind, then kills a leopard right in front of her?"

Link choked. "Was the cat hurt?" he asked, when he recovered his breath. She shook her head. He frowned. "Attacking people?"

Had it been? She'd never thought to ask. "Not that I know of. My step-father put its head on the wall in his study and had a chair upholstered with its hide." Gooseflesh rippled over her at the memory.

"Great guy," Stone said. "Don't you agree?"

"How come he didn't take your brother?" Link said.

"He was away at boarding school." When it looked like Link would continue with the subject, she said, "Do you mind if we talk about something else?" His mouth flattened, but he nodded. Several moments passed where the only sound was a distant bird cry or someone sipping their coffee.

"How come no one woke me up?" Tousled ebony and fuchsia hair proceeded Tempest's rumpled shirt as she crawled out of the tent. "Mmmmm, coffee." She stood up and ineffectively tried to smooth the creases out of her faded jeans. "Is there milk and sugar?"

Link rose. "I'll get some."

Tempest poured herself a half-cup of coffee then snuggled next to Ariel. The campstool teetered threateningly, but didn't collapse as she took a sip. "Ohhh, this tastes just like-"

"Your grandmother's favorite," Ariel interrupted. "I already told Link."

She nodded like a dashboard puppy. "Grandma's coffee was always the best." Tempest tapped her hand. "You've got goose bumps."

Stone sat up straighter then sandwiched her free hand between his warm ones. "Your skin is freezing." His thumb lazily circled her palm. Heat radiated through her. The thumb continued in its slow sensual path. Warmth spread through her, centering on her core. He smiled as if he knew the effect he had on her. The short hairs on the back of her neck quivered.

Ariel yanked her hand free. "I'm fine."

He arched a brow at her and grinned. How dare he play with her emotions, like she was some sort of toy!

"It just hurts to remember Grandma," Tempest announced. "She died in a terrible accident." As if realizing she'd said too much and now they might need to embellish a lie, Tempest bounced to her feet and handed her mug to Link, who was placing creamer, sugar and eggs on top of the cooler.

Ariel took a quick swallow of coffee. The heat tingled on her tongue, but she swallowed reflexively. The liquid burned all the way to her stomach, where it expanded into a burning ball. Ariel breathed through her mouth and hoped Stone didn't suspect the depth of his effect on her.

"You sure you're okay?" Stone studied her, as if he knew exactly how unsettling his attention was.

"Of course I am," she said stiffly. Stone chuckled, while his thumb caressed the mug's smooth enamel. Ariel turned to Tempest. "Why don't you go find our sandwich maker and the bread and pie filling?"

With a whoop of excitement, Tempest dashed toward the plane.

"It must be rough being a single parent," Stone said. "Even rougher when you don't have family to help."

Ariel shrugged, took another sip of burning coffee and willed herself not to notice his tantalizing maleness or remember the tenderness of his touch.

"I can't find the can opener," Tempest wailed as she jogged back.

Stone retrieved a tiny object from his pocket. He flipped it like a coin, then caught it in his palm. "We can use this."

Dubiously, Tempest handed him the can of cherry pie filling. Stone rocked the odd bit of metal around the top of the can. "Haven't seen a P-38 before, have you?" Tempest shook her head. Stone handed her the half-open can. "You put the cutting blade over the rim and rock it up and down like so." His big hand covered Tempest's smaller one for a moment, while she started, then he let her finish.

"It's working! This is neat," Tempest said. She handed Ariel the open can, then studied the simple object.

Link picked up Tempest's cup, filling it the rest of the way with milk, then stirred in a big spoonful of sugar. He handed it to Tempest. "This is the way I liked my coffee when I was your age."

She took a tentative sip, quickly followed by a big gulp. "This is so good! Thank you."

Ariel prepared the picnic pies while Link made scrambled eggs. Every time she looked up, she caught Stone watching her. What did he want? Was he playing some sick part in one of Peter's mind games? It took every ounce of self-discipline to pretend she didn't notice his attention.

After breakfast, Link said, "Who wants to go exploring?"

"Me!" Tempest jumped up, waving both hands. "I do."

Stone raised his hand.

"You three go on," Ariel said. "I'll clean up then do some sketching."

Link and Tempest didn't need a second invitation, but Stone was slower to follow through. "I really should take a look at the altimeter and see if there's a bad ground or something," Stone said.

Check the altimeter or keep an eye on her? Ariel turned her back to him and picked up the frying pan. Her hand tightened on the handle as she tested its weight. Link shouldered his rifle. She pretended a calm she didn't feel and started cleaning her makeshift weapon. When she finished everything, she got her sketchpad, then avoiding the plane, where Stone had torn out the instrument panel, she headed toward an interesting clump of vegetation. She hunkered next to a six-inch tall pussy willow, and began a charcoal sketch of the perfect little bush. As she was finishing, a shadow touched a catkin, she looked up and found Stone gazing at her. She inhaled sharply. "Do you always sneak up on people?" she demanded before she thought better of taunting him.

He grinned. "I like watching you draw. You're really good."

She wet her lips and forced a smile. "Thank you."

His grin widened. Dear Lord, either he thought she was the stupidest woman alive or he suspected that she suspected he worked for Peter.

She cleared her throat. "How was the plane? Everything all right?"

"I found a loose screw under the console. When I tightened it, it popped back out." He shrugged. "It's probably stripped, but that's no biggie. I think I've got it fixed, at least for now."

Probably fixed so only he or Link could use the radio. It's what Peter would have done. "How," she asked, "if the screw is bad?" Hopefully he would believe she accepted his story.

"I twisted a bit of aluminum foil around the screw's shank."

Somehow that didn't sound either believable or safe. But it did sound like one of the lame excuses Peter came up with when he played dumb.

"Last night," Stone said, "I thought I heard something, so I went out to check." He cleared his throat. "Tempest was whispering something to you and she sounded terrified… Who was the man you were talking about? Your ex?"

Ariel tried to breathe, but air wouldn't come. "You were eavesdropping?"

Chapter 9

Stone straightened his spine. "Not intentionally." Damn, but the woman was testy. He shrugged and told her the truth. "Like I said, I thought I heard something."

"And?" When she started walking toward their campsite, he fell into step beside her.

What did she want? "While I was trying to find out what woke me, I overheard Tempest." Ariel's expression snapped with anger as she motioned for him to continue. "Yes, I stopped to listen, I think anyone would have. She sounded terrified and I thought perhaps whatever had passed through the camp had gotten into your tent."

Ariel folded her arms across the sketchbook and pressed it into her stomach while she stared at the toes of her shoes. "She had a bad dream."

Why wouldn't she look at him? Did she feel guilty for some reason? Stone kneaded the taunt muscles at the back of his neck. "I found a bear's tracks near the Cessna." Ariel blanched and her head jerked up to look at him fast enough to give herself whiplash. "I'm glad it just passed through." He smiled reassuringly, but it didn't seem like anything he said or did penetrated Ariel's distrust for any length of time. "What was Tempest's nightmare about?"

"Her father." Ariel's expression equated the man with week-old-roadkill.

Strange how two people could initially believe they were so in love, then so quickly fall into hatred. Remembering Marishka made him feel similar things to the unspoken message Ariel's muscles were sending. Too bad he had never known the real Marishka until it was almost too late. He suspected Ariel felt the same way, but would clam up if he asked a question that personal. "Does she often have nightmares?"

"Not as often as she once did." Ariel closed her eyes, then when she opened them, she looked directly at him. "While we were wandering around Deadhorse, we saw a fisherman that looked and moved like him." The tip of her tongue traced her lips in an unconsciously sexy way.

Stone focused on her eyes. "When's the last time you saw him?"

"Years … unless that really was him, yesterday."

The abhorrence in her tone made him want to smile. Stone didn't stop to analyze why Ariel's obvious hatred for her ex husband pleased him, but it did. He said, "So he doesn't have visitation rights?"

"No!" Her eyes widened and she took a deep breath. "Sorry. It's just that I hope I never have to have anything to do with that man again."

"Except for the alimony and child support checks." Sarcasm burned in his tone, as he relived the judge's unfair ruling.

"Excuse me?" She glared at him. "You think I'd accept his money?" Her mouth thinned and fire snapped in her eyes. "I'd rather starve than accept a penny from him. That'd just make him think he had the right to run my life."

Damn, he should have bit his tongue, instead of take his

hostility toward Marishka's five blood-sucking-years of alimony out on Ariel. He made an apologetic gesture. "Forget I said that. You have a kid, so you deserve it."

"For your information," her voice rose and anger snapped in her gaze. "Tempest and I literally walked out with only the clothes on our backs and I'd do it, again." She glared at him at enunciating each word, "Anything we have is what I earned. Me. By myself. And if you think I ever intend to trust another man for anything, you're wrong."

Stone held up his hands for a truce. "I believe you. It's just that when the subject of divorce comes up, I always think of Marishka and the lies she concocted-" He gritted his teeth against the bitter memories.

"You're divorced?"

He gave a sharp nod.

"I'm sorry it didn't work out."

Stone opened his mouth to answer, but didn't know what to say, so he snapped it closed, again. One thing was certain, he didn't want to continue talking about Marishka's deceit. Narrowing his eyes, he focused on the woman who'd pried too much. Perhaps she needed a bit of probing in return. "Didn't your divorce decree stipulate child support?" Ariel shook her head. He frowned with confusion. "A father should be responsible for his children."

"Shoulda, woulda, oughta-" Ariel clamped her lips together, as if she'd said too much, then studied the ground around the plane. Was she looking for the bear tracks or avoiding answering his statement?

"Sometimes there's just no justice," he murmured, as he pointed toward the bear's prints. "Guess you found that out the hard way, too."

With a shudder, she stared at the impressions, then she looked past him. Before she turned her back to him, he glimpsed an odd mixture of confusion in her expression before she moved toward the tents. "What I make is enough for myself and Tempest. Don't worry, you'll get your rent checks on time."

"I didn't mean-" She turned to look at him over her shoulder, her expression vulnerable. "You're right," he hastily said, "your finances aren't my business." He heaved an inaudible sigh, when her facial muscles relaxed, but she continued to look at him as if he was the enemy. With a stepfather and husband like she'd had, it was no wonder she distrusted men. Of course, it also explained why she had married a bastard and why it was doubtful that she would ever be attracted to him. Yet, after the way she'd kissed him, perhaps the theory that women fell for guys like their father wasn't completely true. He frowned. Marishka certainly was nothing like his mother. "I hate to think you aren't getting a fair shake." She trembled. With three strides, he caught up with her, close enough to see the tears brimming in her eyes. One oozed over, hung on her lower lashes a moment, then it slid down her cheek. "Oh, hell!" He hugged her tight. Her entire body shuddered against his. Despite her obvious misery, it felt erotic as hell.

Stone forced himself to think about the bastards in Ariel's life – the one who had taken her on a trophy hunt and the other one who didn't pay for his own kid. "I'm not worried about the rent." Muffled sobs proceeded a damp spot's spread across his chest. What kind of a jerk had she married?

Soothingly, Stone ran his hands over her back. Ariel melted

against his body, molding her curves to his hard planes. He tried to focus on her bastard ex. His hand slid under her heavy flannel shirt and grazed the heat of her back. She became rigid. Startled by her obvious fear, he paused. The men in her life had been psychological abusers, had they been physical, too? "I'm sorry for-" He released her then gestured helpless to express his suspicions without further alienating her. It looked like more tears were poised to follow the first. Before the water-works could start in earnest, he hurried toward camp. Once there, he sat down on a stool and wondered how he'd ever gotten sucked into her emotional problems.

Moments later, she settled onto the edge of the stool next to him. When the silence lengthened, he admitted, "I had a rotten divorce, too. The one thing I learned is that it got better when I started talking about it."

She chewed on her upper lip, then her expression relaxed and she gave him a quivering smile. "How bad was yours?"

"Total humiliation." Though Ariel's gaze rolled upward, he sensed that she understood, as only a person who has experience that sort of hell can. "I fell in love with Marishka the first time I saw her." He looked away from her and admitted, "At least I thought it was love, though I now know it was just lust. I thought she looked like an angel."

"She had wings?" she joke

"Wings?" He laughed. "Believe it or not, yes, but no harp." One corner of her lips tilted upward, beneath her confused expression. "Marishka had platinum blond hair, long legs and big blue eyes and the first time I laid eyes on her she was dressed up like Tinker Bell – wings, wand and all." His first impression had been that she looked like either a high priced model or a wet dream. Probably both. He should have known she was trouble and steered clear. But he hadn't been thinking with the right head. Ariel looked like what she was – the girl next door, which was the antithesis of Marishka. Logic told him to shut up, but for some reason, having Ariel understand the reasons for his failed marriage seemed important. Stone shook his head at his youthful stupidity. "I didn't think I had a chance with someone like her, so I told her I'd take the trick." He wished he'd just given her a fist full of candy. Ariel looked startled. He laughed, "It was Halloween." Stone shook his head. "We got married after knowing each other a week."

"You're kidding."

He wished he was. "I didn't get to know the woman behind all the cosmetics and goop until after she had that damned slave-band on my hand."

"You married her just because of her looks?" Her tone spiked high with disbelief.

The sex hadn't been half bad, either. "Stupidest thing I've ever done."

Ariel blinked.

He kneaded the knotted muscles at the base of his skull. "It took a while to figure out why she'd picked me, and even when I figured it out, it took a lot longer to believe it."

She frowned.

He stared at the horizon.

"Well?" She asked, "Why did your wife marry you, if it wasn't for love, or the fact she was as shallow as you and thought you looked gorgeous together?"

How would she know if they'd looked good together? And why did she think he was shallow? He was tempted to tell her that it was because he was so good in bed, but that wasn't a smart thing to tell the 'girl next door', so he opted for the truth. "Marishka wanted U. S. citizenship."

"She what?"

"She was an exchange student from Novosibirsk." He grimaced. "I was too young and too naïve to realize how superior the U.S. was to other areas – Siberia, for example."

She shoved a stray curl behind her ear. "It's difficult to imagine you being immature or easily manipulated."

He gave a short bark of laughter. "I learned a lot during the summer between my junior and senior years of college... I call it my two months in hell."

"That was when you were married?"

"Actually before Thanksgiving in my sophomore year. It took a while for me to figure out her motives, because she acted so devoted that she even took some classes with me, but it was all for her green card." His nod felt harsh.

"You think of your marriage as hell?"

Oh, yeah. "At least being used by Marishka made me into a better businessman. Before it mattered, I knew enough to read the fine print, knew never to take anything at face value, knew that if something seemed too good to be true, it probably was and to never trust anyone."

She leaned forward, surprise filling her expression. "That's totally paranoid."

He focused completely on her. "Are you trying to tell me your marriage didn't teach you to toss away the rose-colored glasses?" She stared at him open mouthed, than sat back on her stool and snapped her jaws shut. He slanted his body forward and rested his forearms on his knees, lest he shake her secrets out of her and thus prove to her that all men were the same. "I just bared my soul and showed you the scars. What went on with your ex? How come you cringe every time I touch you? ... Did he beat you?"

She shivered, as if chilled by a miserable memory. "My past isn't any of your business."

Bingo, she'd been beaten. What else had the bastard done? "What other kinds of abuse did he put you through?" Though Stone used a gentle tone, she stood up, and took a step away from him as she her lips clamped into a thin line. "If it wasn't because of abuse, how come you're supporting your kid all by yourself?"

She swallowed twice. "That's none of your business."

"True," Stone said. His honesty seemed to surprise her. "Don't blame yourself. And don't blame me."

"Who should I blame? Satan? God?"

"How about your father?"

She looked like she'd been slapped. "W-w-what about my f-father?"

"I meant your step-father. He was the first man who disillusioned you, right?" Stone remembered the way she'd looked when she told him about the leopard. "Up until the moment he shot that cat, I suspect you thought he was one step below God."

Ariel's eyes watered. Not again! He turned to mush when females cried. "My real father probably deserved being God's right hand, but never my mother's second husband. I never liked him." She paused, deep in thought. "You have one thing wrong – he didn't think he was one step below God, he thought he *was* God." She shook her head. "I always knew he wasn't, even though everyone else seemed to." She clutched her sketchbook so tightly against her stomach that it bent. "I have a terrible headache, I think I'll go find an aspirin." With that, she fled into her tent.

Stone watched the canvass flutter until it, again, hung motionless. He mulled over the bits and pieces of the conversation he'd overheard. "Do you think he recognized us?" Tempest's tone had sounded fearful. If he hadn't heard the anxiety in her voice, he would never have paused to listen, then weighed the wisdom of bursting into their tent and decided not to. Though Ariel's voice had contained a trace of nervousness, it had immediately become apparent that the threat wasn't eminent, and it had something to do with why they'd seemed so disturbed after their walk in Deadhorse. By the time he figured that out, he'd been too intrigued to leave.

"But he was so close." When she'd made the statement, he'd heard the fear. Why wouldn't Ariel openly admit her ex had abused her? Obviously the jerk had mistreated Tempest, too. Stone's teeth ground at the thought of a man using his size and strength against others – particularly kids. Did she realize that hiding the truth made everything ten times worse? He'd doubted that fact until he'd experienced the liberty of sharing the biggest mistake of his past.

Stone rubbed his temple and told himself there was no reason why he should feel strongly about someone who he was unlikely to meet. But he did.

~0~

The tent's undulating canvas made the shadowed interior seem like she was inside a peacefully sleeping creature. But peaceful was a far cry for how she felt. Without the bag to kick,

Ariel couldn't work out her aggressions, so she did the next best thing and picked up her sketchpad. As she added texture, to the tiny twig, she heard nearby snuffling. Ariel shook her head to shiver ran down her spine, as she recalled the enormous tracks she'd seen. She dropped her charcoal pencil and grabbed her small knife. When the rhythmic sound didn't move, she crept to the flap. With every inch forward, the odd vibration sounded louder; more like the purring of a large, contented cat then the hunger pangs of a bear. Or so she hoped. Hair tingling at her nape, Ariel peered around the campsite. She held her breath and listened. The source of the sound seemed to be coming from the men's tent. Had something huge and furry crept in there? Eyes unblinking, she watched the structure. When nothing happened, she looked around camp for Stone. Slowly, she realized she was alone in camp with a – something – a 'something' that sounded like it had huge lungs – a something that probably ate people – a something that was probably impervious to kick boxing and tiny knives. She hunkered back from the tent flap and told herself she should have gotten over her fear of guns years ago. The thin canvas rippled in response. It might be good to keep out rain, but it wouldn't offer any protection against something with slashing claws. Of course, since she didn't have slashing claws, it would certainly hold her for whatever wanted to eat her. She crept out of her tent and edged closer to the cooking area, which might offer some form of threat. Unfortunately, she had to move close to Stone and Link's tent to get to there. Inch by inch the purring sound intensified. The when the other tent flap fluttered. She froze, expecting an attack. Instead, she saw Stone sprawled face down on top of his navy sleeping bag; appearing dead. A scream welled in her throat. Ariel clamped her hand over her mouth. She stared at the tent, wondering how he'd been murdered there. The flap moved aside, again. There were no maul marks on him. In fact, he appeared peaceful. Her gaze narrowed on his face. His lips moved in concert with the odd noise. She stood up, shamelessly staring at him, innocent as a babe, Stone snored on mere feet from her. Her cheeks burned with proof of her paranoia.

Since the first time since she'd met Stone O'Banyon, Ariel had wanted to study him and understand what it was about him that made her feel so different from other men. Now that she had the opportunity, she tiptoed back for her sketchbook. Clutching it, she stared at the man who simultaneously seemed hard as diamonds and gentle as a kitten.

Kneeling in the shadow of his tent, she flipped open to a new page and began portraying the man who haunted her dreams. Hard muscles contrasted with his gentle smile while light and shadows conspired to give him an air of mystery.

A distant shriek startled her as much as the shadow of an eagle passing over the sketch of Stone's face.

Fearful that he would awaken and catch her, Ariel scrambled to the campstools and flipped to a new page, then made sweeping lines that captured the bird's flight as it rode the unseen air currents.

One day she and Tempest would be free as that bird.

One day, they would be able to scream into the wind and not mind who heard or saw them.

One day...

Chapter 10

Stone purposefully grabbed his fishing gear, slung his rifle over his shoulder and walked away from their camp. Halfway out of camp, he stopped, turned and said, "Come on."

"What?"

"You heard me. Come fishing with me." Her mouth flattened and she shook her head. Stone took a deep breath, then used a gentler tone, "Look, it isn't safe to be alone, unless you have a weapon... Do you?"

"No, and I never have." But she might have to rethink that personal rule if she intended to live in bear country.

"Then come on."

"What is it with you?" Ariel looked him up and down, as if she was wondering if he liked caveman tactics. "Since when do you have the power to tell me what to do and when to do it?"

Stone exhaled and looked to heaven. "Fine. Stay here with just pencil and paper to beat off predators." He looked ready to spit with frustration. "At least let me leave my spare rifle with you." She shook her head. "It's that or I stay."

Teeth gritted in distaste, Ariel held out her hand.

Stone studied her. "Do you know how to use a rifle?"

"You point the barrel and pull the trigger." She looked like a rancid taste permeated her mouth. "Stone, I appreciate your concern, but I am not going to kill another living thing."

"I didn't ask you to." He took a calming breath. "Can you at least fire three shots into the ground?" She nodded. "Good. If there's a problem, that'll alert me and Link about it, but you won't have to compromise your sensibilities." She looked skeptical but determined. "In truth, most predators flee at the first shot, but a series of three is the international distress signal, so fire all three. Okay?"

"Fine."

He swung the Marlin off his shoulder and offered it to her. Ariel grasped the barrel in one hand and the stock in the other, her nose wrinkled in distaste. He set down the fishing gear and with a step, moved behind her. "Here, put this hand here." He placed her left hand under the stock. "See how it balances?"

"It does, doesn't it?" Her tone sounded surprised.

"Right. Now you place the butt here on your shoulder. This is a little long for you, but that doesn't matter, since you'd only need to use it as a signaling device, not win a marksmanship trophy." He positioned her other hand near the trigger. She reacted as if it had scorched her fingers. Stone pointed to a black button. "See this?" He pushed it, so a red shaft emerged. Some of the tension in Ariel's spine eased, as she focused on the small part instead of the whole weapon. "This is the safety. Red is hot, black is not. Red has to show for this to fire." He quickly put the safety back on before her shivering created a disaster.

"I think I can manage." Her words sounded more confident than her tone. "First red for ready, then 3 shots into the dirt.

"Yep it's dead simple." She became rigid. Stone massaged her shoulders, but with every rub, her back remained as unyielding as marble. What had her ex done to her that she usually couldn't stand any sort of physical contact with a man? He dropped his hands and said, "If you see a bear, what do you do?"

"Push this, point there and pull that."

"Three times," Stone said.

She nodded.

With nothing else to say, Stone got his other rifle then left. But with every step away, he wondered what it was about Ariel Danner that put his body on red alert. God must have a cruel sense of humor to first have him fall for mercenary Marishka and now have him dreaming of Ariel, who switched between steamy and glacial for no reason.

No sooner had Stone cast his line, than Link joined him. "Catch anything?"

"Not yet." Stone offered Link his rod.

"Nah, you keep it. If I start fishing, I'll forget everything else.

Stone wished fishing was as enthralling for him.

"The kid is fun, but-" Link turned his hands palm up. Stone grunted in agreement. "This is a strange camping trip. Think we'll ever take a couple females camping again?" Stone shrugged. Link frowned. "You still pissed at me for inviting the Danners?" Stone shook his head. "Will you cut with the silent treatment and tell me why you're angry?"

"I'm not mad."

Link snorted. "You haven't been yourself for days."

"I've had a lot on my mind."

"Such as?" Stone shrugged. Link scratched a mosquito bite on his neck. "Mavis would have told me if something special was going on with the company. And there's nothing unusual at home. That leaves Dolly."

Stone started reeling in the fishing line.

"That's it, isn't it?" Link scrutinized him. "There's a problem with Dolly. That's why you've been acting strange." Link warmed to his theory. "You're having a problem with the love of your life and it's infuriating you."

Stone shook his head and clipped the hook securely in an eyelet.

"One way or another, it has to be Dolly," Link said. "What's wrong?"

"Nothing."

"When you saw her and had to have her, I warned you that she was totally incapable of returning the love you wanted to lavish on her. It's finally sunk in, hasn't it?"

Stone thrust the fishing rod into Link's hand. "Link, you fish. I'm going for a walk." He pivoted and marched upstream.

"A couple weeks ago, your mom told me she'd seen Marishka," Link called after him. Stone squared his shoulders against the onslaught of emotion her memory always brought. "She's remarried and is expecting."

Memory of the way Marishka had lied to his family and friends came back cold as the arctic day. Stone turned and glared at Link. "Good for her, now catch something for dinner."

Link fingered the pole. "Is that what's eating at you? Marishka, not Dolly?"

"No. But I pity any kid she has."

"Until this minute, I never believed the rumors."

"What rumors?"

"That she wanted children and you didn't."

"Bull. I wanted them. All she wanted was US citizenship. When she got that, she moved out." *Period, end of his stupidity.*

Link scratched his neck. "Then why was she moaning and groaning about losing you and her future during the divorce?"

"Theatrics."

"Marishka was emotional. Is that Dolly's attraction?"

Stone thrust his hands into the back pockets of his jeans. "I don't know. You seem to be the shrink of the day, why don't you tell me?"

~0~

Tempest threw her arms wide as if she wanted to encompass the barren tundra. "You gotta love a place with no trees to hide behind." Ariel glanced up from her sketchbook. "For the first time since Ireland, we don't have to keep looking over our shoulders or wondering how close he is to finding us."

Ariel replaced the cover on her charcoal pencil. "So you feel safe here?"

"Look around." Tempest pirouetted in a circle. "You can see someone coming for miles and miles and miles. This isn't like being in a city, where someone can spy on you from all sorts of spots or sneak up on you at any corner." Tempest lowered her arms and hugged herself. "Besides, even if someone did come here, Uncle Link would protect us."

"You really like him, don't you?"

"Oh, yes." Tempest rubbed her upper arms in an oddly sensual manner; reminiscent of the way Stone's hands had felt on her neck. "I think he might be the one."

"The one what?"

Tempest gave her an exasperated look. "The one and only love of my life, of course."

Ariel nearly laughed at the absurd thought. "He's old."

"Not much older than you."

Was Tempest looking for a father figure or what? And what about Link, who seemed only too happy for her sister's company? What was he looking for? Why did Tempest view Link as a boyfriend? Could he be a pedophile? An icy chill whispered across Ariel's skin.

"I like Uncle Stone, too," Tempest said. "But he isn't fun like Uncle Link. I think something is bothering him." Her brow furrowed. "Sometimes the way he looks reminds me of you."

"You've got to be kidding."

She shook her head so hard, her two of her stiff spikes flapped. "He's so serious and responsible and all that stuff that makes you boring." *Her sister thought she was dull*? She'd given up her education, her career and her future, to keep them together. To keep them alive. And Tempest thought she was boring? "Uncle Stone never plays, and he always works." She wrinkled her nose in a cute way that normally would have made Ariel forget she'd just been called boring. "He's sorta like you've been since – uh, never mind."

"Since London." Tempest nodded. Five years, one month, two weeks and four days ago, they'd started running for their lives. Ariel sighed as she acknowledged the truth: she'd become someone she never wanted to be. "Things have been too tense for too long. I wish I could tell you we could stay here forever, and with time, we'd feel like we had real lives, but I can't."

"I know." Tempest sniffed. "Unless he dies, we'll be on the run forever."

"Maybe this is-"

"Don't. Every time you start hoping that our new identities will be the one, he finds us and we're on the run again. I mean, I know that even if Link is the right guy for me, it'll never work out because we already saw Father and he's checking out that tail number." Ariel shook her head in denial. Tempest gestured toward the plane. "Don't be stupid. Of course he is, so we're only safe out here in the middle of nowhere. Once we take off, it's only a matter of time."

"*If* he recognized us - and I don't think he did, at least not for certain." Tempest gave her a skeptical look. "If he'd been certain, do you think we'd have left Deadhorse alive?"

A glimmer of hope shone in Tempest's expression, as she shook her head, then she bit her upper lip and her eyes got huge as saucers. "Right now he could be setting traps for tomorrow. Oh, God, tomorrow! I hope it never comes."

Ariel hugged Tempest. "Shh. Enjoy today. Don't worry about tomorrow." She repeated the advice to herself, and hoped she could at least appear to be worry-free.

Tempest trembled. "I can't help it." Her thin arms wrapped around Ariel's waist in a vise-like grip. "Every time I think about seeing him, I get so scared I'm afraid I'll pee."

"You did great."

"He has such a terrible temper."

"It'll work out, somehow." Ariel stared over Tempest's shuddering shoulder.

"He said he'd kill us and you know he will."

"Only if he finds us." Ariel realized she was staring at the rifle Stone had forced her to accept. She licked her lips. "If he tries to kill us, I'll stop him." Somehow.

Chapter 11

The following day, as her seatbelt clicked into place, Tempest's fears haunted Ariel's thoughts. If Peter had recognized them, he might be waiting at the apartment and they really could be walking into a trap. By the time the plane had taken off and they began flying into the mountains, a chill seized her so hard that she shook.

"I didn't realize how badly flying terrified you," Stone said, as he settled into the pilot seat. "I'll try to keep it smooth."

She stared at her clenched hands, unable to speak.

Out of the corner of her eye, she noticed that Tempest was squinting at the gray clouds above the Cessna, which were obviously pouring rain, and then she glanced at the dry windscreen. Frowning in confusion, she peered down at the rocky peaks of the Brooks Range. She tapped Link's arm. "How come the rain isn't hitting the plane?"

"Virga."

"Viagra?" Ariel asked, startled.

Laughing, Link twisted around in the co-pilot's seat, until he faced her. "V-I-R-G-A," he spelled, "Virga." He focused on Tempest, then launched into a discourse on Alaskan climate and weather phenomena. Ariel's cheeks flamed with heat. She glanced at Stone, grateful that he had to keep his attention on the plane and whatever else pilots needed to focus on. After that humiliating comment, she pressed her lips together and vowed to be quiet.

Stone tapped a round gauge on the instrument panel, frowned, then tapped it again. Ariel held her breath, wondering what was wrong. He tapped it a third time. She peaked around him to see what the thing was for. She squinted at the innocent white numbers on the black face, which claimed they were ten-thousand-feet high. Ariel looked down at the ground and doubted it they were more than a mile high. A pit of dread opened in her stomach, as she wondered if Peter had sabotaged the plane and intended to kill them all.

"Uncle Link? How come you keep saying how dry it is here? A lot of this," she gestured to the ground below, "is boggy."

"Tundra is formed by old peat quagmires. That's the black, mucky little mounds you see all over, and yeah, they're usually in water, but that's because about three feet below ground level, everything is always frozen, so what rain or runoff we do get just stagnates."

Tempest made a face. "They're no fun to walk on. I tried hopping on the ones near home and landed in freezing water up to my armpits."

"I've heard of shocks like that killing people with bad hearts," Stone said. "It's best to stay out of the bogs."

"We can certainly see a lot of detail," Ariel said. "How high are we?"

"My best guess is about two-thousand-feet, but I can't be sure." He tapped the gage a forth time.

"You mean the plane is broken?" Tempest asked, panic in her tone.

"Just an old problem we thought we'd fixed," Link assured

her. "Don't worry, an altimeter is only necessary when we're flying blind." He gestured ahead to the clear blue sky. "Trust me, today, we don't need it."

Ariel stared at the ground as if watching it would help Stone keep the plane airborne. Tempest and Link spoke in soft tones, which barely permeated the peripheral area of her awareness, while her mind grappled with the events of the weekend.

When she and Tempest had first gone into hiding, they'd fled to her mother's country, the United States, and stayed in urban areas. Years of worrying when she saw the same vehicle too often, and avoiding looking into stranger's face for fear they were Peter's lackeys had taken their toll on her nerves. The only thing worse was when Peter did find them, and they had to run, again. The past five years had been filled with close calls, changing their appearances and so many new names that some mornings, she couldn't remember who she was.

Fleeing to the wilds of Alaska was supposed to have broken the pattern and given them security.

Instead, it had provided one of the closest face-to-face encounters she'd had with Peter since he'd sworn revenge.

Stone chuckled at something Tempest said. Ariel's heartbeat quickened. Why had fate stuck her next door to a man whose every word and move stirred her soul? Maybe if she'd met him at some other point in her life, they could have made a life together, but there was no chance of that, now.

Fact: Stone had a woman and she was neither willing to break up a relationship nor become the other woman.

Fact: Ariel had never wanted a relationship with a man, after seeing what Peter did to her mother.

Fact: Alaska was not a sanctuary. And if the locals thought

this chilly weather was nice, winter had to be horrible.

Fact: She was tired of living on the edge and wanted permanence and security. So did Tempest.

Fact: Now that she'd actually been to Fairbanks, she realized the city was a trap with few means of escape.

Fact: If Peter had recognized them, today was probably her last day on earth.

Assuming they survived reentering their apartment, today, they needed to begin choosing new identities, a new location and profiles. Perhaps, if they took their time, planning their next step, instead of run, in a panic, this time they'd really succeed in losing Peter. Forever.

Hope bloomed within her at the thought.

Another continent might do the trick. But that would create another set of problems. When Mozart had gone through customs and quarantine, Peter had easily followed them to North America.

Fact: Transporting Mozart made them conspicuous. So, no matter how hard Tempest cried and how badly she felt, they needed to find him a new home. Ariel swallowed hard, but the lump in her throat didn't budge. The thought of leaving Mozart behind felt devastating. Her father had given him to her for her birthday and he's been her one true friend through all the years and fears.

A sickening lurch brought her back to reality.

"Sorry about that," Stone said. "Geese were on the runway."

A moment later, the plane settled onto the runway with a thump. *Dear Lord, they were already in Fairbanks and Peter might be waiting for them, a smug smile on his evil face! Please, God, help us survive and find a safe future.*

As the plane moved down the runway, each runway light took longer to pass. With every drop in speed, the place seemed smaller and more vulnerable, as did Ariel. She looked sideways at Tempest, whose profile centered in the small window. How easily a sniper could pick off her sister. Ariel Grasped Tempest's arm, pulling her away from possible death.

"What?" Tempest demanded.

Ariel pulled her arm downward, until she was below the window. "Help me find my lip balm." Ariel gestured under their seat. Soon, they both had their heads between their legs and were looking at dusty blue carpet.

There was a firm thud, then the sound tires made on an asphalt highway, which signified that the Cessna had landed. Still, Ariel held Tempest down.

"All I see is a Cheerio," Tempest said.

"Keep looking, it's my favorite pina colada one."

Tempest sniffed her lips then sat up and gave her an accusatory look. But they were nearly inside a hangar and probably safe. Still, Ariel's heart hammered against her ribs. Her nails dug into her palms, and the cabin walls seemed to inch inward. Her lungs burned for fresh air and the dark maw of the hanger looked like a gaping mouth waiting to consume them.

She yanked on the seat belt release, but her fingers slipped off because the sheen of perspiration made it impossible to grip anything.

Tempest grabbed her hands and whispered, "Ariel, what's wrong with you?" Tempest squeezed her fingers, then said in a louder voice, "You know the rule: never take off your seat belt until we're parked and the engine has stopped ... or doesn't that apply to little planes?"

The urgency of Tempests tone and the panic in her expression got through. Ariel tried to smile. "I forgot where I was for a moment. Sorry."

Tempest gave her an odd look, then let go of her hands.

Link glanced back at them, as he took off the headphones he'd used to speak with the tower. "Welcome back to Fairbanks."

The plane entered the dim hanger and a man dressed in dark coveralls materialized from the gloom. He raised his grease-stained hand and Ariel ducked.

"How long has Drew been working on that Chieftain?" Stone said.

"Why?" Link said, as the plane came to a halt.

"I'd like someone to look at the altimeter before I need to go back to Valdez." Link made a sound of agreement as the engine shutdown and he opened the door.

Ariel realized they were talking about the man in the jumpsuit and told herself that meant he was safe. Except she still wasn't positive Link and Stone were safe.

Despite her fears, no assassins materialized as they were unloading their things, no sniper took a shot as Link drove them home, no one even peaked at them from around a corner. Now, all that she had to do was survive entering her front door and finding out if Peter was waiting for them inside. If they weren't killed on the spot, she vowed to develop a new set of identities – ones that would keep them safe until they were one-hundred-and-three, assuming anyone really lived that long.

As Link parked the truck, Stone muttered an angry curse then got out of the truck and let out a piercing whistle.

Tempest's eyes rounded. "Ariel would wash my mouth out

with soap if I ever said that."

He looked at Ariel and gave her a lopsided smile. "Apologies." He gestured toward his backyard. "The gate is open and the dogs are gone."

Peter would have slaughtered animals that made that much racket so he could sneak around. Or perhaps he'd kill them just because he liked killing. If he'd murdered Stone's dogs so they couldn't sound the alarm, it was her fault. Ariel swallowed the threatening bile. She placed her hand on Stone's biceps. "I'm so sorry." Tears distorted her vision. "I'll help you look for them."

Stone gave her an odd look. "It's nothing to cry about. And it's hardly the first time."

Tempest bounced on the balls of her feet as if looking for the dogs was an adventure. What would she do when – if – they found mangled carcasses? "Oh! Look!" Tempest pointed across the road.

Two huskies were trotting toward them.

Ariel's skin tingled with hope.

"Come here, you two," Stone said, as he hunkered down. When the dogs stopped in front of him, he scratched their ears. "Where were you?" Both dogs gave him smug-looking doggy grins. Stone continued stroking them. "Not talking, huh? Okay, where are Agamemnon and Hercules?" The dogs only gave him more canine smiles and lolled their tongues as they panted.

Stone sighed and stood up. "Okay, girls, back into the yard." The chubbier dog started toward the gate, but the other looked undecided. "Go on, Athena, you don't want to have your puppies away from home." The chubby dog appeared to agree. "Go on Aphrodite, get in there." The dog sat and looked up at him, her big blue eyes pleading. Stone stood and put his hands on his hips. "If I have to chase you, I'll put you on a chain." Reluctantly the second dog moved toward the gate. He shut it with a sharp click, then looked around the area.

"Would it help if I walked down the street and looked for them?" Ariel asked.

"Would you know them if you saw them?" Stone's expression was skeptical.

"I would if I read their tags."

He appeared to be stifling laughter. "You intend to read every collar of every husky you find?"

"Can you think of a better way?"

"Yeah, go home. Take a long hot bath and –"Stone shrugged. "I'll look for them."

Anything was better than going into that townhouse and confronting Peter – assuming he was in there. Ariel hitched up her chin, then stalked up the street.

Halfway down the block, she heard feet running behind her. Fighting the urge to run, Ariel glanced back. Tempest sprinted up to her, eyes aglow with happiness. In the distance, Stone was marching the opposite direction.

"Uncle Stone laughed."

"Why?"

Tempest snickered. "Uncle Link was afraid that some strange dog would bite you if you tried to read its collar." Ariel rolled her eyes heavenward. "Don't worry, I told them that only one dog had ever dared bite you."

"You told them about that?"

Tempest nodded. "I told them you bit it right back and were spitting fur for a week." Tempest beamed. "Uncle Stone can actually laugh."

Would he still laugh if he knew she hoped to find one of his dogs so she could avoid her townhouse for a bit longer, then force his pet inside before she went in to see if Peter was really there?

"Let's go find those huskies," Ariel said.

Chapter 12

"Where are we going?" Tempest gasped, after they'd speed-walked several blocks.

Ariel gestured toward the stand of pines ahead. "The park by the Chena seems like a good place to look." She'd seen Stone take the dogs there, previously. The first time, his behavior had been so unexpected – why walk a dog, when it had a yard to 'do its thing in' – she'd followed him and watched as he and the largest dog played Frisbee until they were both so worn out they collapsed in a laughing pile. She'd stayed behind the pine's thin trunk, afraid to leave for fear they'd see her. She had been equally unwilling to leave the scene of a man who cared for his pet that much. "It stands to reason that given an opportunity, the animals would go there to play on their own."

"Right," Tempest scoffed. "Play." She snorted. "Remember how Father always said that a dog was merely a walking stomach? If they're here, they're here for the food."

"Maybe." She glanced at the open area where Stone and his dog had played, marveling how different he was from Peter, at least where his pets were concerned. Of course, it was probably unfair to call Peter's half-starved guard dogs, pets.

"What were you thinking about on the flight back?" Tempest asked.

"Nothing." They stepped off the sidewalk and followed a

vague trail through the sparse grass.

Tempest snorted. "You didn't even take lip balm, so what was that dust inspection about?"

Ariel sighed. "I'm tired and I want a bath."

"Then why are you looking for dogs instead of soaking?"

"If we were missing Mozart, wouldn't it be nice if Stone helped us look for him?"

"Well, yeah, but he's too smart to get lost."

Something white moved beyond the park's picnic tables. Ariel shaded her eyes with one hand and pointed with the other. "Is that one of them?"

Tempest squinted then grinned. "Hey, Agamemnon!" When the dog didn't respond, she gave a faltering imitation of Stone's piercing whistle. "Come here, boy." She knelt and threw her arms wide.

After four thudding heartbeats, the dog took a step toward them. Tempest whistled and called, again. The same dog she'd seen knock Stone to the ground, broke into a canter, then a full gallop. As sixty pounds of black and white fur covered muscle focused on Tempest, the hair on the back of Ariel's neck stood up, but fangs and claws were on Tempest before she could move.

Tempest shrieked as the dog pounced on her, then somersaulted backward onto the grass, the dog landing on top of her. Ariel screamed and tried to grab the dog's collar. The dog sprang upward, twisted in mid-air, turned, then landed next to Tempest and dashed around her. Ariel tried to catch the beast a second time.

She failed, again.

Tempest sat up. The dog rushed at her. Tempest screeched

and caught it, as it plowed into her. Soon, the two bodies were rolling in the dirt.

It took a moment to realize that the dog's tail was wagging and Tempest's screams were delighted.

Ariel sank to her knees and waited for her blood pressure to lower. As the two tussled and played, she bit her lip over their sheer happiness. The same joy she'd witnessed between the dog and Stone. Perhaps she should consider getting a dog. Tempest had certainly begged for one often enough. She studied the muscular furry body and wondered if the dog could check their apartment for intruders without eating Mozart. She sighed as she realized she wasn't even certain how she could convince the animal to come home.

Tempest sat up as she brushed dirt off her shirt. "Get off me, Agamemnon. It's time to go home."

The dog sat down, tongue lolling out of the side of its mouth and watched Tempest with woeful eyes, as if he understood that he'd soon lose his freedom. Strange how simple some sorts of freedom were and how anyone could see a fence. It must be so nice, not to imagine watchers behind every tree and a trap in your house, just waiting for you to come home.

Or maybe she was simply being paranoid. Again. "I think he likes running free," Ariel said.

"Do you?" Tempest ticked his ears, then stood up and patted her thigh. "Come on, boy."

The dog remained seated.

"Pull-ease."

Ariel studied the mulish creature. "Do you think he'd cooperate if I used my belt for a leash?" And an even more crucial question was, if she used it for the dog, would her pants fall off, because of the twenty pounds she'd lost?

Tempest blinked in surprise. "What if he ran off with it?"

Ariel laughed. "I hadn't thought of that possibility." She studied the dog. "It's not like it's my money belt." Something she kept their most necessary documents and emergency funds in, and only took off when in the shower or was working out with the boxing bag, and knew her torso would become slick with sweat Moisture was not good for documents, which made the difference between life and death. "Do you think he's likely to try to run?"

Tempest blew a limp lock out of her face. "He's stubborn." She wagged a dusty finger at the black muzzle. "You will not be naughty."

Ariel took off her brown, braided belt, then untucked her shirt and flared it over her pants. Losing all that weight in the past year had given her confidence, an entirely differed profile, and made her feel better than she had in years – until now, when she was faced with the possibility of becoming a public spectacle.

Tempest grabbed the belt and easily slipped it under Agamemnon's collar. The dog appeared to accept that playtime was over. "Come on, boy." With apparent submissiveness, Agamemnon got up and began walking beside Tempest. Ariel clutched her waistband and followed them. Tempest glanced back at her. "He's a lot like us, isn't he?"

"How?"

"He's gotta stay locked up to be safe." Tempest's forehead crinkled into three small ridges. "He's never really free to do whatever he wants, like maybe chase a squirrel or whatever dogs dream of doing. And we aren't any freer … not really."

So her sister had noticed the similarities, too. "We're able to make more choices than he is," Ariel said.

Tempest snorted. "If you were free, you'd finish your residency and become a pediatrician, like you planned. But if you used your degree, you'd have to admit you're Sherry D-" Ariel put a finger to her lips. Tempest's eyes widened and she shut her mouth, but after a quick look around and seeing that the dog was the only one listening, she added, "It'd be a way for Father to find us and you wouldn't want to leave any patients behind when we had to hide." Tempest gave her a superior look. "And if you were free, like you think you are, you'd have your own house and never move again."

"Know me pretty well, don't you?" Ariel tried to smile, but the stark truth of her sister's observation made that impossible.

"Of course."

"What would you have that you don't have now?"

"I'd have a bunch of animals. Maybe raise dogs, like Uncle Stone."

Ariel nodded. Convincing her they needed to leave Mozart behind was going to be hell, but maybe if she shared her half-made plan in the right way, she could persuade Tempest it was better for the bird and them. Of course, she could promise her a puppy... Ariel studied the dog, wondering if dog's personalities varied as much as people's.

When they got back to the townhouses, Tempest put Agamemnon inside the gate, slipped off the belt, then tossed it to her before Ariel could suggest they take the dog home with them. As she caught the belt, she felt her pants droop. Hastily, she looped the belt in place and cinched it tight.

She looked up, just as Tempest entered their apartment.

Ariel froze an unuttered scream cutting off her breath.

Mosquitoes buzzed and ravens cawed, but Tempest didn't scream. Neither did she hear the sound of a struggle nor gunfire. Dare she hope that hiding their anxiety behind the mask of weight loss, brown contacts and hair dye had tricked him? Please, God, let it be so.

Step by step, Ariel approached the townhouse door. Her hand slipped on the knob. She rubbed the perspiration on her pants and opened the door an inch.

"Mamnoon am, Agha," Mozart said.

"You got that right, feather-brain, I'm your Excellency," Tempest said. Ariel opened the door far enough to see behind it, then stepped inside. "But you gotta learn to speak English and say hello like a real American parrot would. She poured sunflower seeds into his bowl, while he squawked and fanned his wings.

Ariel leaned her forehead against the door and started to laugh.

"What's so funny?"

"Nothing."

Tempest snorted and slammed the cupboard door closed. "You were laughing at me, weren't you?"

Ariel shook her head and wiped her eyes. "I'm laughing to let off steam." She took a deep breath and confessed, "All the way back, I kept imagining coming in here and finding Peter waiting for us." She ran her hand over her face. "Coming in and finding everything normal-" She sighed and wiped her eyes, again. "I needed to let of steam and I just started laughing."

"You really thought he'd be here?"

Ariel shrugged.

"And you let me walk in?" Her voice hit a high C. "Into a possible ambush!"

"Not intentionally. You move pretty fast."

Tempest studied her. "So you did think he recognized us, but you didn't want to admit it."

"If he'd been certain, we'd be dead and he'd be gloating."

"But you knew he suspected."

"Freaked out because he followed us."

"We have to move again, don't we?" Ariel nodded. Tempest fingered an ebony spike. "Just when I was starting to get into this punk look, too."

"It is cute." Ariel sat down on the stairs and looked at Tempest. "Know what I want?"

"Real freedom."

Ariel concurred. "Since he obviously isn't here, now, I think we've got a bit of time to plan our next move. If we do it right, we'll never have to relocate again, and we'll even be able to throw away these contact lenses."

"And never dye our hair again?"

"Only if we wanted to."

"I don't know if I'd recognize myself if I saw blond hair or blue eyes looking back at me."

"Half the time I think of my reflection as the roll I'm playing, sort of like the image is a separate identity." Ariel ran her hand over her dark wavy hair.

"So what do you figure? That since we've always dyed our hair when we changed our names that if we went back natural, Father wouldn't recognize us?"

"Something like that." She glanced toward the door to the basement. The need to kick their body-bag and take out the frustrations she'd masked over the weekend nearly overpowered her.

Tempest plopped down on the step next to her. "I'm not a baby, any more."

"Okay, here's the idea." Ariel took a deep breath. "First we call Elizabeth and see what her detective knows. Then, if Peter hasn't altered his pattern, we know we have time to plan our next move."

"But I thought he lost father in Chicago."

"That doesn't mean he hasn't picked his trail up since then."

"I'll skype her right now." Tempest scrambled to her feet. "And I won't say my name. I know the drill." Tempest exhaled. "If she's not there, waiting for her to call back is the absolute worst."

Ariel motioned for Tempest to go, then she made a beeline toward the basement with the intention of kicking and punching the bag until she was too tired to stand upright.

Chapter 13

Elizabeth cleared her throat. "When he was questioned, Peter was properly shocked by the 'accident' and claimed he had no idea what had happened until the next day, when the sheik's body was pulled out of the Bay." Elizabeth's sarcasm crackled with malice. "

Tempest plumped her bed pillow, centered it on her bed then sprawled face down on it.

"So they're ruling the man's death as an accidental drowning," Ariel said.

"A real surprise, isn't it?" Elizabeth said. Ariel shook her head. Either Peter was one of the best assassins in the world, or he was one of the luckiest at avoiding police investigations.

"We might'a been there when he did it," Tempest whispered, her face flushed, as she fought to hold back a flood of tears.

"What did you say, Dear?"

Tempest cleared her throat and inched closer to the microphone. "There were two people fishing when we got to that river, but Father was alone when we got ready to leave and he followed us back to the airplane. I thought I was gonna pee myself."

"You could have walked in on him while he was committing another murder," Elizabeth said, her tone grave. Ariel tasted bile. She stood up and took two paces toward the door, then realized she wasn't going to throw up - yet.

"We thought he could have recognized us, when he followed us, but if he thought we'd seen him kill that man..." Tears gushed down Tempest's cheeks, so Ariel left the thought hanging in the air.

"Get out of there," Elizabeth said. "Now he's got two reasons to need you dead."

"This is just like last time..." Tempest wailed, "Even if we did say anything and he got arrested, he'd be out on bail in minutes." She snapped her fingers. "And if it went to trial, he'd tell the jury more lies about me being a vindictive little bitch and say I'm trying to punish him for something." Sobs wracked her thin body. Ariel crossed her arms over her stomach and fought down a panic attack as, she too, relieved the bitter memories.

"It's only a matter of time," Ariel said, "but I don't think we have to leave today. I think we have time to make a decent plan."

"Don't wait," Elizabeth said, her tone tense.

"Grandma, I'm scared."

"We need time to make a good plan," Ariel said, even though the only thing she wanted to do was to leap into the Suburban and drive out of town just as fast as possible. "First off, he doesn't know what we saw and if we stay quiet, maybe he will realize that a second 'accident' so soon could attract more unwanted attention than he likes. Secondly, we were in Deadhorse and flying on a private plane. We acted cool and calm, and didn't give away that we recognized him or had seen anything suspicious."

"And thirdly, Father is Father and he just plain likes an

excuse to kill things," Tempest concluded. Ariel winced at the truth.

"I don't like you staying in such an awful place," Elizabeth said.

"I like it here, I especially like Uncle Link - he's soooo nice. I just love him to death. Uncle Stone raises huskies and I think he's sweet on Ariel, but he's too shy to say so."

"Tempest!" Ariel said.

"Well, it's true!"

Elizabeth cleared her throat, then asked, "Are these men really worth dying for?" Tempest's face blanched and silently stared at the speaker as if it was a rabid grizzly.

Loud knocking came from downstairs. Ariel jumped. "Elizabeth, someone is at the door." She went out, closing Tempest's bedroom door behind her before she ran down the stairs.

Halfway down, the person hammered on the door again. "Coming."

She opened the door to find Stone leaning against the frame. "Hi. Can I assume you and Amber were the ones who returned Agamemnon?"

She nodded.

"Thanks. I found Electra at school. She was playing Frisbee with a bunch of kids. I hated to break it up." He gave her a lopsided grin that warmed her core. "Where'd you find the King? Cramer's kennels?"

"Beg pardon?"

"Agamemnon was the King of Mycenae." He looked away from her, then softly admitted, "I've always liked Greek Mythology."

"He was chasing rabbits near the river." Why was she making him stand on her stoop, where any spy could photograph them at his leisure? "Want a soda?"

He grinned and stepped inside.

Ariel fled to the kitchen. He followed her. She grabbed two Pepsi's from the refrigerator and handed him one. His hand caressed her fingers as he took it.

"Thanks." His eyes sparkled with warmth. Ariel backed into a corner and tried to look calm. Stone raised his can in a silent toast. "How come you teach science? Talented as you are, I'd think you could make a living off your art."

"You know what they say about starving artists." She shrugged. If it hadn't been for lab sketches, she'd never have discovered the soothing hobby. "I like to eat and teaching pays enough to do it."

He gave her a contemplative look, as he took a sip.

She edged around him. "Would you like to sit in the living room?" She escaped before he answered. Scooting across the living room, she sat on the inflated chair next to Mozart's perch.

Mozart screeched and flapped his wings when Stone entered the room. An emerald feather fluttered free. Stone caught it in mid air, twirled it between his fingers, then tucked it into his shirt pocket, as he sat down opposite her. The cheap inflated plastic squeaked in protest.

"I forgot to thank you and Link for inviting Tempest and me. We had a wonderful time."

"You're welcome." He took another sip, but never took his gaze off her.

Ariel swallowed. "I know this sounds crazy, especially after what happened up at the Refuge." He raised a quizzical brow.

She grimaced. "My fear of guns must have been pretty obvious." He grinned and inclined his head. "Well," she stammered, "since you showed me how to use the thing, I've been thinking that it might be good for me to have one of my own – for when Tempest I and go on walks alone." Ariel bit her tongue and told herself to slow down. She wet her lips. "Would you be willing to help me pick out a gun and recommend someone to teach me to use it?"

He stared at her as if she'd turned into a stranger. "You want to buy gun."

Did he need to act like the axis of the Earth had tilted? Before he could ask any questions, which she didn't want to answer, Ariel said, "I've had time to think about it and I've concluded my attitude was wrong. You taught me that they're not just instruments of death and destruction, but that they can scare away trouble and call for help at the same time." She tried to smile with confidence, but her stomach kept flip-flopping.

He leaned forward and studied her. She felt the flush of unsaid truths burn its way up her neck. "Have you gotten over your aversion to guns?"

"Do I have to do that to buy one?"

"If you buy it, you live with it."

"Oh." She swallowed. Would she become what she hated and feared if she bought the weapon? Lord, what a mess her life was becoming.

"What sort of weapon were you thinking of purchasing?"

"One with a loud enough bang to scare a bear and call help."

The corners of his lips twitched. "Then you definitely don't want a handgun. A rifle would have the stopping power you'd need if the bear didn't scare-"

"If it didn't run, I don't think I could shoot it, so that wouldn't matter."

"Understood."

"Then you'll help me choose one?"

"What time frame were you looking at?"

"Next weekend?"

He shook his head. "Next Friday I'm heading down to Valdez and Dolly." His lady friend. A lump formed in Ariel's throat. Stone furrowed his brow. "How about tomorrow after four?"

"That works for me."

"Excellent."

"Sherry! You'll never guess!" Tempest hurtled down the stairs and lunged into the living room. "Aunt Kelsey and Uncle Devlin had a baby boy! They named him Matthew and call him Mick. He's almost two feet tall and weighs seven pounds nine ounces! Isn't that exciting?" Ariel nodded. "I mean he's just been born! Uncle Devlin called grandma on her cell phone while we were talking. He was still at the hospital."

Stone straightened up. Tempest jumped, then shifted from foot to foot and looked guilty of seven kinds of sin. "Oh! Hi. Did you find Electra?" He nodded. Tempest gave him a Cheshire cat smile. "I was gonna go back out and look for her after I got done talking to Elizabeth."

Stone cocked his head. "You call your grandmother Elizabeth?"

"It makes her think she's younger."

He chuckled and looked at Ariel. Before he could ask any more questions, Ariel said, "How's Jade doing?"

"Fine. Ariel, can we get the baby a present?"

"We'll figure out something later. We don't want to bore Stone with girl talk."

"Goody!" Tempest skipped out of the room and she was left alone with Stone's interested expression and a life to hide.

Chapter 14

Stone poured a jigger of Scotch, then sat down on the sofa. Cradling the glass in his hands, he studied the News Miner's front page story, where a banner-headline compared Alaska's murder and suicide rates. For some reason, the topic made him think of Ariel and her about-face on guns. Had the article spurred her change of heart? Was Ariel being honest about why she wanted a rifle? She had seemed genuinely terrified of weapons, a situation, which he had initially attributed to her stepfather's coarseness, but had later modified to include abuse from her ex-husband.

Tempest had sounded terrified of her father, and from what she'd said and her tone of voice, he'd deduced that she'd recently seen the man. What if Ariel wanted to learn to shoot so she could murder her ex?

Stone's stomach clenched.

If that was her plan and he taught her how to use a rifle, could he be considered an accessory? Stone downed the contents of his glass in one gulp. It burned its way halfway to his stomach before he started coughing. Liquor surged back up burning his throat and nasal passages. He hurried to the kitchen, turned the water on full force and drank straight from the tap.

By the time his eyes stopped watering, he'd determined that

since Ariel's ex was an abuser, he probably had a criminal history. Therefore, the law enforcement files should have a record of him.

Stone propped his hip against the kitchen counter, picked up the phone and punched in his sister's number.

"Hello." Windy's sunny voice sounded like Texas heat.

"Hey."

"Stone! This is a surprise…. What's wrong?"

He should try to keep in better touch and not wait until he wanted a favor. "Is there some law that says shit has to hit the fan before I phone my favorite sister?"

She chuckled. "So, what's wrong?"

And some people wondered why the FBI had been so eager to hire her. "Link and I have a new tenant and certain – things – about her don't jive with my gut feeling." Windy made an interested sound. "Would you do a background check on her and her ex?"

"What's it worth to you?" The childhood love of negotiating tinged her tone.

Stone rolled his eyes to the ceiling. "What do you want?"

"Brit and I are planning a big party for the folk's anniversary. We want you to be there."

"When?"

"Third weekend in August."

"Done." He'd planned to be there, anyway, all he needed to do was tweak the date he arrived. "How much do I need to send for my share?"

"I'll tell you later." Windy sounded disappointed at achieving such an easy victory. "Give me the particulars. Let's start with the name."

"Ariel Danner." He frowned. "But her kid often calls her Sherry."

"Cheri? Are they French or something?"

"Maybe … they do have a faint accent." He shrugged. "I never thought about it."

"Perhaps you should."

"Yeah." By the time Stone hung up, he realized how few facts he knew about Ariel and how much emotional frustration he felt. Why did he have such a strong feeling that he needed to protect her?

~0~

As soon as the door closed behind Stone, Ariel headed toward the basement door, but paused when Tempest asked, "When are we gonna go shopping for the baby?"

The only thing Ariel wanted to do was kick-box until she was black and blue, but she paused and turned to her sister. "Do you realize that you called me Sherry in front of Stone?"

"I did?" Ariel nodded. "When you were coming down the stairs." Tempest scrunched up her face. "Then how come you didn't say anything?"

"Calling you on it would only have brought his attention to it. You really must listen to yourself and -"

"Think before I open my mouth." Tempest finished with a sigh. "I know, but knowing is easy and doing is really, really hard."

Some of the tension ebbed out of her muscles. "How would you like to live in mountains?"

Tempest stared at her as if she'd lost her mind. "You think we hav'ta run just because I goofed up and-" Ariel shook her head. "I'm not talking about moving soon – we aren't even finished unpacking." She hadn't even hung the painting of the two white calla lilies, which was her favorite and always made her feel as if she was finally home. "But I thought that now would be the time to preplan our next move." Tempest plopped down on a stair step and looked dejected. "I really like it here."

"Me, too."

"Mountains are okay, so's the beach. I didn't like the plains, though, they were flat and boring."

"I want the next move to be our last."

"We've wanted that for how many moves?" Tempest's laugh sounded suspiciously like a sob. "It's no wonder I can't remember your name. Some days I can't even remember my own."

Ariel nodded in agreement. "But it takes him ten times longer to track us when we get our names changed."

Tempest's eyes held unshed tears. "How soon will we have'ta move?"

"I'm not certain, but until now, all of our relocations have been panicked escapes after he found us. What I have in mind is pre-planning the next move so we can do it right and not leave a trail."

"How'll doing it slow make things any different? One way or the other, he'll just find us, again."

"Every time we run, we follow a pattern. We hang onto things we love and keep in touch with –"

"That's why you asked Grandma how she'd like a parrot!" Mozart squawked and flapped his wings. "You want to get rid of him! And what about Grandma? Are we gonna lose her, too?"

"Not if we do this right."

Tempest eyed her suspiciously.

Ariel wet her lips and tried to organize her thoughts. "Okay, we're pretty sure that he found us in Kansas because he taped phone calls Elizabeth received and our Topeka number was the only new one." Tempest nodded. "So, what if we weren't so quick to call? What if we wrote her letters instead?"

"You mean actual paper ones with stamps and everything?"

"Yes. It's so old fashioned he might not think we'd use them."

"You don't think he bribes her mailman?"

"If he didn't, I'd be shocked … What I'm getting at is we find ways to break the old patterns that didn't work."

"Not keep Mozart." Tempest ticked the items off on her fingers. "Not make phone calls or use skype. Not keep the same name and hair. Not use charge cards."

"Not stay on this continent and don't use our current identities or real passports to leave it." Leave absolutely everything behind... particularly Peter.

"But how?"

"If we pose as illegal immigrants trying to enter this country, Customs officers might just escort us out."

"Sherry! That's brilliant! But Canada is still North America."

"So we get to the Lower 48, as Stone calls them, and go into Texas, Arizona, California or maybe New Mexico. Once there, I figure we can pose as illegal Mexicans and Customs will take us back. Then, we head south to maybe Brazil or somewhere."

"How're we gonna convince anyone we're Mexican? Our Spanish is terrible. Last time we were in Madrid, you thought you ordered Red Snapper and ended up with tripe."

Ariel grimaced at the memory. "Guess we'd better start

learning Spanish and Portuguese."

"Huh?"

"They speak Portuguese in Brazil."

"Can't we just go to a country that speaks Spanish? I don't want to learn two languages."

"Fine. How about Costa Rica?" Ariel asked.

Tempest frowned. "How come Costa Rica?"

"They speak Spanish. I've heard the cost of living is lower and if we settle in a rural area, where there isn't much technology and that minimizes his chances of finding us."

"I like Jennifer Lopez. Could our last name be Lopez?"

"Sure, but you'd better pick out a different first name. Ariel studied Tempest, as she gazed at Mozart. If Peter had been the oilman he'd portrayed himself as instead of an assassin, she'd have finished her doctorate and Tempest would have a normal life with a yard full of pets.

"Grandma is gonna worry herself sick when we disappear and don't tell her."

"If we enclose a detailed letter to her with the baby's gift, she'd know what we were doing and not worry."

"Ooooh … then we can get them something! Is that what you and Uncle Stone are gonna go shopping for tomorrow?"

Ariel winced. "No. He's going to help me find a good rifle then teach me to shoot it."

"You're kidding!" Ariel shook her head. Tempest stared at her, eyes wide. "Are you gonna kill Father?"

"Dear Lord, I hope not. I hope I never see him and if I do, I'd never want to be like him."

Tempest got up and stuffed her hands in the back pockets of her jeans. "I want to learn to shoot, too. And I'm not going to lie about why."

"I'm not lying. We don't know what kind of dangers we'll find in Costa Rica and we have to cross all of Mexico to get there. I've heard there are all kinds of criminals in Mexico."

"So you're willing to shoot them, but not Father?"

"Actually, I'm hoping not to shoot anyone. Stone taught me how to fire three shots into the ground to summon help and he said it usually scared off bears and stuff, too."

"Sherry, don't lie to yourself or me. You know we hate Father. You know we'd be better off with him dead."

"Not if we went to jail for killing him."

"He's killed bunches of people, but no one ever caught him."

Ariel sighed and sat down on the stair step. "You really want to live with murder on your conscious?"

She started to nod, then got an odd expression on her face and sighed. "No, I guess not."

"Me, either."

Tempest perched next to her. Ariel put her arm around her sister's thin shoulders. Tempest nestled close to her and said, "Know what I wish? I wish Mama had never met Father. If she hadn't ever met him, he'd never have fallen for her or killed your dad."

"We don't know for a fact he did that." Tempest looked at her as if she was a moron. "We can't change the past. And if they had never gotten together, I'd probably never have a sister."

"I hadn't thought about that ... I'd have liked to have your dad for mine."

"I wish you could have, too."

"Did you like Father when you first met him?"

"I was too young to remember and he was just 'some adult', who had something to do with my dad's work." Ariel sighed. "Over the years, he started coming around more and more." She frowned as she remembered the way he'd always seemed to swagger into their home, acting like he owned it. She gritted her teeth, even as a toddler, she'd never liked Peter. "I don't remember if Mama paid much attention to him. I do remember that after dad died, she cried a lot and we had some really bad money problems. That's when Peter started taking care of everything and worming himself deep into our life." Ariel had wanted to help. She'd given her mother every penny she'd saved from her allowance, but there was only so much a kid could do. What her mother had needed was the life insurance, but the insurance company had claimed that the policy was invalid because there was suspicion that her dad's accident had been a suicide.

Tempest snorted. "Mama should have known what Father was really like."

"Should'a, could'a, would'a … we can't change the past or the fact that Mama liked having a man in charge." Ariel patted Tempest's shoulder. "That's one reason why I've never wanted to be dependent on anyone else."

Tempest nodded in agreement.

Chapter 15

The glassy eyes of the buffalo seemed to sparkle with malicious intent as Stone ushered Ariel into the gun shop. He escorted her down the corridor of glass cases filled with knives and brass knuckles on her left; ninja stars and weird metal playing cards on her right. Behind the corridor of glass counters, one wall supported archery equipment and targets, while another was plastered with posters of bleeding animals and taxidermy specimens. She gave an involuntary shudder. The Marquis de Sade would have loved this shop.

Every step took her one pace closer to the huge buffalo head. Though its horns were a scant foot short of the twelve-foot ceiling, its nose hovered over the clerk's curly red hair.

Stone gestured to the left of the buffalo. "We'd like to see one of those."

The red head nodded. For the first time, since she'd entered the store, Ariel noticed that racks of rifles flanked the buffalo. She leaned heavily against the end case and looked down. This part of the U-shaped case displayed handguns.

She straightened. Her breath came too fast and sweat dampened her back, causing her shirt to cling. This place was bad as the snake house at the zoo... Worse than Peter's hunting blind... Almost as bad as facing Peter, himself.

The clerk spread a thick white towel on top of the glass

display case then, with a lingering caress, laid the double-barrel shotgun on top of it. Ariel's skin crawled.

"Well, what do you think?" Stone said.

That it looks like two snakes lounging on a polished bit of wood. She shrugged, afraid to voice her true thoughts.

Stone picked it up and held it to her. "Try it out for weight and balance."

Her stomach churned. Ariel forced a smile. "If you think this one will be okay, I'll take it."

The clerk blinked. "An excellent choice." He nodded toward the back wall. "Will you be needing ammunition?"

Ariel eyed the weapon. "I suppose it wouldn't be any better than a baseball bat without some."

"What type would you like?" The clerk grinned at her, his syrupy sweet demeanor making her certain he worked on commission.

Helplessly, she looked up at Stone. He said, "A brick of buck-shot and one of magnums."

If the salesman smiled any wider, his jaw might break. He handed her a sheaf of papers and a pen. "Fill these out." He then opened a lower cupboard and chose two boxes.

Ariel turned her back so she blocked out the awful glass eyes, then focused on filling out the forms. Still, it was impossible to block out Stone, who'd folded his arms and was leaning a hip against the display case next to her. He was so close that she could feel his heat from shins to shoulders. She glanced his way. Though he appeared to be studying the knives in a nearby case, she had the distinct feeling he was more interested in what she was writing. She hunched farther over the questionnaire. Stone moved away. When everything was complete, she handed the paperwork back to the redhead.

"Cash or charge?"

"Cash."

Though Stone appeared to be oblivious of everything except the display of hunting knives, he was writing something down on a ragged piece of paper.

While the salesman wrapped her purchases in plastic, she edged over to see what he'd written down, but he pocketed it. "What are you looking at?" she asked.

He pointed at an evil looking blade, with a stunning scrimshaw handle. "It's beautiful. Are you thinking of buying it?"

"Possibly. My father would like it, but it doesn't seem quite right for an anniversary gift." Stone shrugged. "Too bad Christmas is so far away."

"My step-father would appreciate something like that, too." She glanced around the store. Glassy eyes stared back at her. "He'd adore this place."

"But you hate it."

"It could be worse." She grimaced at an old memory. "At least there isn't a stuffed panther in here."

Stone laughed and caressed her under the chin. The clerk handed her the wrapped package. When she made no move to take it, Stone did. "Thanks, Buddy." Holding the cumbersome parcel in once hand, he put his other hand on the small of her back and directed her toward the door.

Ariel didn't need any encouragement to leave. Once outside, she drank in the clean, fresh air while the cool air dehydrated the thin sheen of perspiration. She shivered.

"Want to head over to a rifle range and try this out?"

"I need to check on the roast." Stone raised a brow. "You

wouldn't want me to burn your dinner, would you?" His expression suggested perplexity. "Perhaps we can go after dinner." Stone's skeptical look intensified. "Or maybe tomorrow or the day after."

"Whatever works for you, but I'm gone on Friday."

Ariel's muscles loosened. "Thanks for helping me pick the stuff out." She gestured to the package. She forced a smile. "Somehow, yours didn't seem so sinister."

"Why do you really want this?"

Ariel stopped halfway between the store and her Suburban. How much did Stone suspect? She shook her head and told herself that she had to stop being paranoid. "What do you mean?"

"I find it hard to believe that someone who can cry over a cat that's been dead for – years – and hates guns so much that when she touches one, she nearly cracks her teeth gritting them together would want to be a member of the NRA, much less own a gun. So, I figure there has to be a damn good reason. And I don't think it's to scare bears. You can get a pocket full of firecrackers a whole lot less expensively and they're lighter to carry around, too. So what's the real story?"

"What's the NRA?"

"National Rifle Association." His tone was tinged with exasperation. "Quit changing the subject."

"I filled out an application for that?"

He held up the package. "Is this to scare bears or kill your ex?"

"What!" Her knees felt weak. If Stone hadn't grabbed her elbow, she'd have collapsed onto the uneven sidewalk. "How could you think such a thing?"

He scrutinized her as if reading her soul. "Never mind." He used her elbow to propel her toward her suburban.

She stumbled against him. "Sorry."

"I'm glad you didn't tell me. I'd hate to become an accessory."

"You really think I'm planning murder!" He stopped next to the driver's door and dropped her arm. When her knees buckled, she leaned against the door. "For your information, I have never willingly killed anything except a bugs and I didn't like doing that. I value life." She enunciated each word precisely. "At one point in time, I'd hoped to become a doctor because I thought that I couldn't aspire for anything better than living up to the Hippocratic Code. I still think it's something to strive for."

Stone's expression softened and he caressed her cheek. "What happened?"

"You do not want to know." Dear Lord, how could she have told him so much? With shaking fingers, she pulled her keys out of her pocket. "I don't feel very well. Would you mind driving?"

He paused a moment, then took the ring, unlocked the doors and helped her into the passenger seat. It felt nice to have a handsome man act so solicitous. She'd miss Stone when they disappeared. It was good that she and Tempest were leaving because too often, she started daydreaming about a future with him that did not include his girlfriend, Dolly.

Stone backed the suburban out of the parking spot. "You must be stronger than you look."

"Why?"

"This thing handles like a ton of bricks."

"The bulletproof panels make it heavy. Mitch called it an urban tank." She stiffened as she realized how much more she'd revealed.

"Is Mitch your ex?"

She shook her head. "He was my cousin's husband." It felt scary, yet good to tell him the truth.

"You used the past tense. Is he alive?"

"He passed, recently … What? Did you think he was a mobster or something?" Stone shrugged. "For your information, Mitch was a police officer with SLED." Dear Lord, if she kept talking, Stone would have her entire life story. "I have a headache."

"Worried about firing the gun?"

"Wouldn't you be?" He looked at her with surprise. "No, I guess you wouldn't." She leaned back in the seat and closed her eyes while he drove.

~0~

When Stone stopped at the first red light, he studied Ariel's tense profile and the white lines around her lips. Maybe she'd told him the truth.

Maybe not.

Regardless, if someone had told him that he'd fall in love with a liar, he'd have told them they were crazy, but then he'd never imagined meeting someone like Ariel Danner. From the moment he'd first seen her with Mozart tangled in her hair, he'd started falling down the rabbit hole. He hoped that a Jabberwocky wasn't waiting to ambush either or them. What had his emotions gotten him into and why didn't he want out?

Stone didn't like admitting the truth, but the fact that he loved Ariel Danner was as undeniable as the fact he could become an accessory to murder.

Could his conclusions about her be wrong?

Was there a valid reason for Ariel to avoid meeting his eyes? He could understand why Tempest dyed her hair the funky black and pink, but could it be part of the disguise he'd overheard them talking about? And why did Tempest keep calling her Sherry instead of Mama?

Could Sherry be a nickname? Heaven knew that after growing up with a mother who was obsessed with ancient cultures, particularly druids and defending the name Stonehenge on the kindergarten playground, he understood the need for pet names. His sister, Gaelic, otherwise known as Windy, might be correct about Cheri simply being a French endearment, which would be equal to Sugar or Honey.

Stone rubbed his aching temple. The light turned green. He accelerated and thought of the Suburban's original owner. If Mitch had existed, had he been a good or bad cop?

While embroiled in thought, Stone parked the Suburban. Ariel opened her eyes, then straightened. "Did you like driving the Burb so much that you decided to keep it?"

Huh?

She gestured out the front windscreen. "Is there another reason why you parked in behind your own place?"

If he got the vehicle's serial number, Windy could research it along with the other information he'd collected. "I was going to change the oil on Link's truck and my Harley. I thought I'd change yours too. One mess to clean up and all that."

She blinked. "You can't be serious."

"Why not? You volunteered to cook dinner for my help and-" He made a dismissive gesture. "You hardly spent any time choosing your shotgun. I figure I owe you."

"But –" She paused then smiled. "Thank you. I'd appreciate

that." She went into the house.

Stone got a pencil stub and scrap of blue paper out of his pocket, and then popped the hood and started looking for the engine number. Funny how people forgot to change them when they scratched out the vehicle's number.

Chapter 16

Ariel looked out the window as she peeled potatoes and watched Stone drain the oil from his bike and Link's truck with assembly line precision, until he reached her Suburban, then he spent an inordinate amount of time under the hood before she spotted the trickle of black liquid going into the pan. She shrugged off paranoid thoughts and told herself that he'd worked on the other vehicles, before, and it stood to reason that it would take anyone more time to find the spigot, or wherever oil drained from on an unfamiliar vehicle.

Ariel sliced cucumbers and tomatoes into the salad bowl while she wondered if she was being overly paranoid about Peter. She'd contemplated ways she and Tempest could assure vanishing without a trace a dozen times in the past five years, but she always seemed to overlook some dumb little detail. Having Peter after them was like getting away from Sherlock Holmes.

Stone's muscles rippled beneath his cotton shirt as he reached deep into the Suburban's engine.

Had Peter recognized them? Even if he hadn't, did he realize they must have witnessed him murdering the other fisherman?

The world would be so much better without Peter. If only they hadn't seen him in Deadhorse; then they would be safe here, for the foreseeable future.

Stone began adding new oil to the engines. No one had ever done anything so thoughtful for her.

Ariel folded a bed sheet in half, the draped it over the card table. She then placed the pot roast and other items on the kitchen counter and as she began setting the card table, she asked Tempest to tell Stone and Link that dinner would be served in ten minutes. Before the door closed behind her, Link arrived with a bottle of burgundy.

A few minutes later, Stone arrived, held up a hand, which had grease under the fingernails and headed for the half-bath. Tempest came in last, all smiles and bright eyes, and wearing telltale dog fur. She eagerly grabbed Link's hand and pulled him into the living room. "We got Aunt Kelsey and Uncle Devlin a blanket for their baby. It's so cool! See?" She shook it open. Mozart squawked. Tempest draped the hand-woven coverlet over a chair.

"That's nice," Link said.

Ariel sighed and reminded herself to tell Tempest that men weren't interested in baby things.

Stone returned. Without even looking at the blanket, he leaned over to pick up a CD cover. "You're learning Spanish?" Stone asked.

Tempest rolled her eyes heavenward and nodded. "This has to be the worst thing I've ever had to learn. My computer has this microphone thingy and I have'ta say the words into it. Well, that's the sassiest program I've ever had to learn anything from. Nothing I say is right, even though I'm certain I've said it right."

Stone and Link chuckled.

"Dinner is ready," Ariel said as she handed each of them a plate and motioned them to serve themselves.

As they sat at the table, Link said, "Maybe Stone and I can help you."

"You speak Spanish?" Tempest said.

Link fluttered his hand in a 'sort of gesture'.

"Where I grew up," Stone said, "it was almost the primary language." Tempest's brow furrowed. "I lived in Texas until the last few years."

"You did? So you know where all the Mexicans cross the river and where they always get caught?"

Link chuckled. "It's a really big state - there are lots of places like that.

Ariel's stomach clenched. She frowned at her sister, but adopted a teasing tone. "You must be desperate for something to talk about." Tempest's eyes widened. Before Tempest could say anything more, Ariel turned to Stone. "I always forget how late it stays light. Would you like to give me that lesson while Tempest tidies up after dinner?"

He raised a brow. "I didn't know you were that anxious."

She wrinkled her nose. "I'm not, but I figure the quicker I get it over with, the less time I have to dread it."

Link grimaced. "You sound like you're talking about going to the dentist."

Wasn't it interesting how people shrank from simple things? She could only hope that learning to touch a deadly weapon and learning to use it would turn out to be simple and eventually her phobia would seem laughable. All things considered, she needed to get past her fear of guns and learn to use them. The quicker, the better.

Stone drove the Suburban down a narrow dirt track, then parked next to a half-dead pine. Wild roses blooming under scraggly pine trees gave the area an oddly romantic feeling. The previous night, Ariel had dreamed of him holding her on his lap, as he had when they went camping, but now, as she prepared to grapple with the phobia she'd had since childhood, her spine stiffened at the thought of a tender interlude coming between her and independence from fear.

Out of the corner of her eye, she saw him raise his arm and turn in her direction. No! Her heart slammed against her ribs, as she dove for the floor. "Drop something?" She glanced behind her. Without pause, Stone reached into the back seat and yanked a small duffel bag into sight. He paused and gave her an odd look. She'd never felt so foolish. "When you find whatever your after, get your gun and the ammo."

He got out of the car.

Heart still slamming against her chest, she raised her head until her eyes were over the dashboard. Without a backward glance, he strolled down the path toward the clearing. When he got to the sunlit area, he put his bag on a rickety picnic table, then finally looked back. Ariel felt like ducking back down, again. *I will not give into fear.* Instead, she slowly got out of the Suburban and opened the back door to get out her gun. She watched Stone open his bag, but instead of a blanket, he pulled out a thick magazine and a small translucent case. How stupid could she be? The man had a steady girlfriend, he didn't need to make moves on her. Ariel took a deep breath, grabbed the gun and headed over to deal with her fear.

Something crunched beneath her foot. A glance down revealed brass casings of assorted sizes mingling with the gravel. She hopped on one foot, but then realized the entire area was sprinkled with bits of metal and in some spots were thicker than the rough gray pebbles. *They are empty and cannot harm you.* Ariel squared her shoulders, lifted her chin and didn't allow herself another downward glance.

Treading lightly, she approached Stone, who was sitting on a weatherworn picnic table and flipping through a magazine featuring various types of yachts. She perched on the opposite end of the bench seat and looked around the clearing, which was a somewhat barren area within the ring of pines and wild roses. In fact the only oddity was the amount of metal bits on the ground.

"This is the rifle range?"

"Not what you expected?"

"It looks like a picnic area." Or it had until she stepped on millions of bullets, now it looked more like a place where the monster would lure its victim. "I expected targets."

He held up the magazine. "We brought our own." She blinked. He grinned. "Photos work fine, and I didn't think you'd like shooting at real targets that reminded you of – the past."

"Thank you." She put down the shotgun. "What should I do first?"

Stone tore an ad for Absolute Vodka out of the magazine, then handed it and a box of tacks to her. "Pin this up." He gestured to a jagged stump on the other side of the clearing.

Finding spots firm enough to hold the pin was a challenge. When she finished, Stone had the shotgun and two boxes unwrapped. "Now, load your gun."

She hesitated. "Which box are the blanks in?"

His incredulous look made her feel like her IQ was somewhat lower than a rock's. "I'm here to teach you how to hit what you aim for. How can you know what you're hitting with blanks?"

The flush burned her face. "That was a stupid question, wasn't it?" He nodded, but it looked like he was trying to keep a straight face. "I should have asked which box the target rounds were in. Rounds is the correct term, isn't it?"

He started to laugh. Ariel's jaw clenched. She turned on her heel and stalked toward a large patch of roses.

Something crunched behind her. She jumped. Stone touched her arm. "Sorry," he said, then he broke into a full belly-laugh.

"What's so hilarious?"

"You're angry." The man was Einstein. "I expected that you'd know more about weapons than you obviously do."

"Why?"

He made a brusque gesture. "When you told me about your stepfather's den and the hunting expeditions, I assumed you'd grown up knowing about guns. Forgive me?"

Since he looked contrite, she nodded.

He got serious. "Manufacturers make bullets and cartridges for specific purposes, but I don't think any are exclusively for targets." He steered her back to the shotgun. "You have a shotgun and proper term for its ammunition is cartridge."

"Boy, I'm dumb."

He shook his head. "Just uneducated about weapons." He hunkered down and picked a reddish tube out of a box and handed it to her. "This is double-aught buckshot. It's accurate up to twenty yards and is used to kill something the size of a wolf."

Her stomach roiled at the thought of hurting such a beautiful animal. She dropped the horrid cylinder of death. Stone caught it in mid-air, and held it between his thumb and forefinger. "By itself, cartridges are no more lethal than pyrotechnics. It's the human intent that makes the difference."

"Like when we sing about bombs bursting in air and it sounds more like fireworks than a war."

Stone nodded.

Ariel took a calming breath, and then grasped the cartridge. It didn't feel lethal.

Stone caressed her under the chin. "Do you have any ideas about killing anyone?"

"No! Never! I only want to protect Tempest and myself."

He studied her for a long moment. Until he relaxed, a moment later, she didn't realize he'd been as tense as she was. Somehow, Ariel found that reassuring. Stone pointed to a red tube. "Inside the casing, there are nine thirty-two-caliber-balls. If any one of them hits your target, it'll do some damage." He handed it to her

She gulped, as she held it up between her forefinger and thumb.

The corner of Stone's mouth twitched. He held up a second cylinder of death. "This is a magnum slug. Use this for bear."

Ridiculous. "You mean to tell me that I have to get a different type of ammunition for every type of animal I want to scare?"

He blinked several times then pretended to cough. Damn, she'd obviously put her foot in her mouth – again.

"That's not far from the truth," he said. "Actually, there are different types for what you plan to kill." Ariel felt the blood drain from her face and her head begin to spin. "There's also bird-shot, but we didn't buy any."

"I'm sure Mozart will be grateful for that." Her voice squeaked. Stone had another coughing fit. Why didn't the man laugh in her face? Then she could demand to know what was so funny. This ammo business was the stupidest thing she'd ever heard of. "So what you're tell me is that I need to know what creatures will be in the woods before I take Tempest hiking. Is that about it?" He blinked. "Should I load my gun with bear-scarers and pray I don't need to frighten away a rampaging caribou? Or do I have to take a selection of noise-makers and load an assortment when I don't know what I might need to scare away?"

Stone rubbed the back of his neck. "My rule is to load for the most lethal thing you're likely to encounter, and possibly need to bring down." Peter, but only if he tried to hurt them. "Around here, that's normally either a bear or moose," Stone said. "You can use the magnums for either one."

"Moose? You're kidding, aren't you?" He shook his head. "Bullwinkle seems-"

"Like a cartoon version of the real animal."

"Oh." She stared at him a moment, then forced herself to focus on learning as much as she could, so looked at the papery cylinder in her hand. "So the green ones are louder."

"Not necessarily."

"Why would I want to scare away Bullwinkle?" Ariel put her hands on her hips and tapped her foot.

"Because real moose are damned lethal. Bulls routinely take on the pipeline and cars – they even fight trains. Locomotives are the only ones that are up to the cont-"

"This is a joke, right?"

Stone solemnly shook his head. "I'd rather face down a grizzly than a bull moose." He appeared dead serious.

Ariel clamped her jaws shut and adjusted the straps of her ever-present book bag, then spent the next ten minutes listening to Stone explain the differences between ammunition, when and how to fire her shotgun. He concluded, "If you have a deranged bear and the first shot doesn't scare it, fire to kill. Not to wound. Bears don't die easy and if you wound it, it'll shred you before it keels over.

She shuddered. "I get the point. What else do I need to know?"

He put one foot on a long, low rock, placed her gun on his thigh and pointed. "This is a Remington 870 pump-action shotgun. It's the hunting model and holds either five magnum slugs or ..." He cracked open the gun. By the time Stone finished his detailed definition and demonstration of every nuance of every part of loading, firing and cleaning the weapon, her head was pounding. Suddenly, he plucked the gun from his makeshift lap and thrust it at her. "Here, you load it."

Ariel knelt and used the rock as a table. She held her breath as she repeated the sequence. When she finished, she looked up at him. For once he look pleased instead of amused or distrustful.

"Excellent, you learn fast."

"Thank you."

His dimples deepened. "Now shoot the target." He tilted his head toward the vodka ad. She swallowed hard, then stood up. Gingerly, she raised the butt to her shoulder, as he'd showed her. "It's too heavy to hold like a dead mouse," he said from behind her. "Use your hands, so you have better control and less chance of dropping it and shooting something painful." She put the gun on the picnic table, wiped her palms on her jeans, then, before she lost her nerve, she grabbed it in a firm grip and assumed the position. He smiled. Hoping he didn't notice her shaking knees, she sighted down the barrel. The wretched thing looked ten times longer from this perspective and the magazine page looked a thousand miles away.

When the photo centered, she gripped the barrel as hard as her hands would allow and slipped her forefinger over the trigger. Gently, she pulled. Nothing happened. She tried harder.

With a resounding boom, the barrel whipped upward and knocked her off her feet. She was thrown backward against a solid wall. Her breath rushed out and everything dimmed as she slid downward.

For a long moment, she lay with her eyes closed and listened to a bird shriek. Pain radiated from her right temple and shoulder. She suspected she knew what concussions and pulverized joints felt like.

A warm minty breeze fanned her face. "Are you alright?" Stone sounded terrified.

She raised her left hand and touched her forehead. Her fingertip felt sticky. "Let me guess, if the bear doesn't run away, after the first warning, shotguns are designed to knock us out so we don't feel it when the beasts rip us limb from limb."

"Thank God, you're okay!" Stone's sounded nervous. "Damn, you scared me."

She opened her left eye and tried to sit upright. "I think I'll buy some firecrackers and forget guns."

He helped her up. "It was my fault. You were holding it wrong and not standing right."

"I thought I'd copied what you showed me."

"Close. I would have corrected your stance, but you pulled the trigger before I −" He shrugged and looked away from her. "You hit the target."

She squinted at the tattered paper. "Wow, I did!"

Stone placed a supportive arm around her shoulders. "The

stock is too long for you. I'll cut it down an inch or so – that should make it easier to handle. Tomorrow, we'll try again."

"No, not tomorrow." Ariel carefully shook her aching head.

"It'll be okay. I won't let you get knocked out again. Next time, I'll help you hold the gun. I'll only make you do it alone when you feel you're ready." He was nearly begging.

Ariel sighed. "Fine. Tomorrow." That would be soon enough to finish dealing with her phobia.

Chapter 17

Mozart sidestepped back and forth across his perch while Tempest, a thin sheen of perspiration over her forehead, jabbed her way through a tae-kwon-do routine. Across the living room, Ariel pushed the Spanish tutorial into her Walkman then secured the headphones over her ears and gingerly curled up in her favorite inflated chair. Closing her eyes, she found a comfortable position and focused on rolling R's.

Suddenly, the headphones were yanked off. Ariel lunged off the chair, landing in a fighting stance. "What the?"

Her sister laughed. "Aren't you gonna work out with me?" Tempest danced out of reach.

"Not tonight." Before Tempest could argue, Ariel sat back down, then added, "When I fired that dratted gun, I bruised myself from head to toe and came close to giving myself a concussion. I need to rest."

"Lazy, lazy, lazy. That arc over your eyebrow looks cool. When do I get to shoot the thing?" She kicked at the imaginary nose of an attacker, who was at least a head taller than her. Mozart squawked and beat his wings, as he always did when Tempest did high kicks.

Ariel gently fingered her tender brow. "Believe me, you don't want to."

Tempest did two swift jabs followed by a kick about three

feet off the floor. "Stone isn't here to see, so quit acting like a wilting violet."

"Are you trying to insinuate that I'm faking being hurt?" Ariel would have shaken some sense into Tempest if it hadn't seemed like too much of an effort.

"You need to exercise or you'll really be stiff tomorrow."

"I can't lift my right arm."

Tempest turned to face her, hands on hips. "Since when do minor problems stop you?"

Ariel unbuttoned her shirt and eased it off her right shoulder. Even though she babied the joint, waves of pain shot through her bones.

"Ooo-ugh! That really looks bad. I'll get you a cold compress." Tempest hurried into the kitchen and the freezer door whined open. In a moment, she was back with a bag of frozen corn. "This should do." Tempest gently laid it over the angry flesh.

"This does feel better. Thanks."

"It's what Mama would have done."

True. It was nice not having to play the nurse roll. "I miss her."

Tempest bit her lower lip as she sank to the floor in a classic, cross-legged, yoga pose. "Sometimes I feel like the only things I can count on are you and Mozart."

"What about yourself? You have yourself all the time, you only have me part of that time."

"Mozart's around as much as I want."

"For now."

"Are you back to sending him to Gramma?"

Ariel wanted this conversation like she wanted another

lesson about shotguns. She wet her lips. "We've been lucky so far, but what if at some point in the future –"

"Is this another of your lectures about patterns and running away? Because if it is, I'm tired of running every time you get paranoid. I like it here. I like having Uncle Link, Uncle Stone and the Greeks next door. I like knowing I can play with them. I like knowing there will soon be puppies there. I like –"

"I like it here, too," Ariel said. "I don't mind teaching a couple classes and I feel like I'm being useful, which is something I haven't felt very often in the last few years. It makes me feel good to see you so happy, too."

"But?"

Across the room, Mozart tilted his head to the side, as if he was interested in the answer, too. Ariel opened her mouth, but all she could think of was her confusion over Stone O'Banyon, a man who obviously had a live-in girlfriend at his home in Valdez, but traveled enough to think he could get away with two relationships. Ariel shut her mouth and shrugged.

Tempest's eyes sparked. "Can't lie about why you like it here, can you? I've seen the way you watch Stone. He watches you the very same way when you aren't looking. Know what I think? I think that you're afraid of getting lovey-dovey close to him because of Father. And I think you're just using the glimpse of Father as an excuse to run away."

Perhaps Tempest was correct. Even the thought of leaving Stone O'Banyon gave a dull ache to her core. There was no way they could have a future, much less a fairytale ending. He was a womanizer, who didn't even bother to hide it. How many times had he mentioned Dolly with tenderness in his voice and a gleam in his eye? Too many. She had to end any possibility of a relationship before things got even more complicated between them.

Ariel cleared her throat. "I don't know when we'll have to move, or if we will need to. I was just having a conversation. Mozart is over 20 and parrots aren't immortal, all this moving and changing climates can't be good for him." Her skin felt dry to the touch. "I'm really concerned how the low humidity up here affects him."

"He's got a bunch more good years left. He'll probably outlive me and I intend to live for ages."

"I hope you're right." Ariel readjusted the thawing corn. "I hope Peter won't come looking for us, either, but we can't hide our heads in the sand, like ostriches."

Tempest relaxed her cross-legged pose. "So we still have to learn Spanish, don't we?"

Ariel nodded. "While we hope we never have to use this plan, if worst comes to worst, at least we'll have a strategy, so we won't blindly run. And we'll learn something new, too. You never know when something will come in handy." Mozart tucked his head under his emerald wing. "When we came to Fairbanks, I thought it was going to be so great. A wilderness place, yet progressive enough to have a university."

"It's that."

"True, but have you noticed how isolated it is?" There's basically one main road plus a railroad south to Anchorage, and plenty of wild country for ambushes. Then there's another road heading southeast to the Yukon Territory. Once other roads get out of town, they come to nothing. It wouldn't take much to catch us."

"Maybe instead of learning Spanish, we should get a cute

little plane and learn to fly it."

"There's only one airport –"

"Two. Fort Wainwright has one, and there might be little ones."

"How would we get onto the military base?"

Tempest flushed. "What about the river. We could paddle away."

"The Chena flows into the Tanana. It'll be winter soon and even now, the water is barely above freezing. You couldn't pay me to paddle my way to freedom for hundreds of miles. For one thing, we'd be stuck on the river and, like every other form of transportation, Peter would only need one simple ambush." She blinked away the threatening tears. She'd thought Fairbanks sounded so wonderful, but it had turned into a restraint. Probably, ten years from now, they'd only be missing persons in some dusty case file.

"Fairbanks is a freaking trap," Tempest concluded. Ariel nodded. She hoped they had the luxury of time to lay the framework for one more escape. Hoped that it would be the last time they ever needed to run for their lives. It was the same hope she had held close for over five years.

Chapter 18

Stone trimmed the Cessna's tabs and followed the pipeline south to Valdez. He settled back and waited for the tensions of the past week to evaporate. Instead, the thrumming of the engine reminded him of Ariel's low-pitched chuckle.

Out the windscreen, the sun glinted off the pools of water, which meandered through the river's mud flats. From two thousand feet above ground level, the mud looked like the same shade of innocuous brown as Ariel's hair and eyes. He ran a hand over his eyes and blinked. Until meeting Ariel Danner, he'd never been particularly fond of brown, now the shade haunted his dreams.

Damned but he needed to get to Dolly and spend the weekend working off the confusion and sexual frustration that had built up. Agreeing to teach the woman to use a shotgun had been one of the stupidest things he'd ever done.

He vowed that this trip, he wouldn't get distracted by the camaraderie of his pals or the dubious anesthesia of liquor; he'd spend every moment polishing Dolly's brass and anything else he could think of doing to work off the memory of lemony perfume mixed with wild roses or how good it felt when Ariel's buttocks were hurled against him.

Strange that he'd never appreciated how damned romantic and isolated the rifle range was. Too bad she'd turned stiff as a board when fate had literally thrown her into him.

And to think he'd been stupid enough to take her back there a second time, even after he'd realized how alone they were. At least she'd learned to stand properly and handle the shotgun. The one good thing about the exasperating time they'd spent together was that he was certain she had no intention of killing anyone.

He hoped Windy had found enough information to terminate the last of his suspicions. Perhaps she'd even dig up something, which would stop the obsession. The way Ariel occupied his mind was enough to make him believe that witches, possession and the supernatural existed. By the time he slammed through Linkstone, Inc.'s door like a rampaging bull moose, Stone was focused on demolishing the week's paperwork so he could get to Dolly and run his hands over her calming contours.

As the door connected with the coat rack, Mavis jerked in surprise. "Good afternoon, Mr. O'Banyon." Her tone held reproach and her back – always straight as an arrow – straightened even more as her narrow shoulders squared.

"Anything urgent?"

Piercing pale eyes, which were closer to white, then the blue, regarded him from behind bifocals and even her perfectly coifed snow-white chignon seemed to bristle at his abruptness. Guilt surged through him. He gently closed the door and forced his tense muscles to relax. "Apologies, Mavis, I was preoccupied. Athena will whelp soon." He gave her a broad smile. "Can I interest you in a puppy?"

She loosened up, though her militaristic bearing made it difficult for anyone, who didn't know her well, to differentiate between her moods. Link didn't work in their main office enough to gauge her moods, so one of Stone's amusements over the past decade was watching his partner grovel to Mavis in an effort to win the affection that he'd had for years. "No thank you, Stone." Something close to a smile touched her lips. "If I wanted something with fur, I'd get a cat. They don't require constant care or eat furniture."

"Dogs make better companions."

She steepled her fingers. "I thought you always had people standing in line to pay top dollar for your puppies. Has that changed?"

Puppies were easier to talk about than the real reason for his temper. "Just thought you might like one as a sort of bonus." For the first time since Mavis Cardew started working for them over a decade before, she looked flustered. Perhaps he should find her a kitten or gift her with tickets to something a sixtyish widow would enjoy.

Mavis lowered her gaze, then plucked a stack of pink phone messages from under the crystal-encased gold nugget, which she used as a paperweight. She rifled through them, and selected one. Putting it on top, she handed them to him. "A Peter Baldwyn has been here three times asking for either you or Link." Her nose delicately wrinkled, as if detecting a foul odor. "He has also phoned no less than eleven times and all but accused me of lying when I told him neither of you were in the office."

Stone grabbed slips and stared at the unfamiliar name and number on top. The thing Mavis detested most was phone calls. It was no surprise she was bristling like an enraged porcupine, if the stranger had phoned eleven times. His fingers itched to crumple the message and toss it. "What's he selling?"

Her mouth flattened into a thin line. "The man refused to speak with someone as lowly as a mere office manager." She picked up her letter opener, which was a replica of a very sharp medieval sword.

Stone suspected Mavis would love an opportunity to pin Baldwyn's hat to the wall, as she had the last Neanderthal, who had antagonized her. One flick of the wrist was all it had taken. He prayed Mavis never got angry with him.

Mavis tested the letter opener's balance. "Whatever he's selling, he is the most obnoxious man I've ever met."

"Perhaps he's an insurance agent."

She snorted. "Baldwyn made that Franklin fellow seem pleasant." Stone winced at the memory of the pompous politician who had had the temerity to solicit a donation after admitting to a pedophile relationship. The wanna-be-major had been lucky to get out of the office with his jewels intact.

"If he's that obnoxious, I'm surprised I don't have to help you bury the body." They both laughed. "Seriously, I hope you told him to peddle his wares elsewhere." Stone crumbled the paper and tossed it into the wastebasket.

A smug look of satisfaction softened her expression. "I most certainly did."

"Good."

Mavis selected a pile of papers. "The letters you need to sign are on top. The rest are contracts that should to be looked over."

He nodded as he took the stack into the adjoining office he and Link shared, though they rarely were in Valdez at the same time. Stone placed the stack on his half of the L-shaped desk, then opened the Venetian blinds, which had come with the building, then he settled into his worn burgundy leather chair, opened the top drawer of his desk and put on his gold-rimmed reading glasses. Eventually, the dull legal language of the documents consumed his attention and all thoughts of Ariel Danner dispersed. Periodically, the phone rang and Mavis ran interference. Occasionally, he heard the fax run and someone enter the outer office, but, as always, Mavis kept all the distractions at bay and allowed him to focus on the paperwork.

As he signed the last contract, his stomach rumbled. He thumped the stack into a tidy pile, and then glanced at his wristwatch. It confirmed that he'd missed both lunch and dinner. He got up and stretched, then took the finished work into the outer office. Mavis was already gone. Whistling tunelessly, he placed the pile on the center of her immaculate desk.

His stomach growled. Fish and chips would be good. He'd pick some up on the way to Dolly. With that in mind, Stone locked up and went out into the humid evening. Lord, but the sea smelled good. One of these years, perhaps he and Link would divide their business interests so that he could focus on the Valdez assets and let Link take care of their Fairbanks property. Then, he could live near the ocean.

He started his Jeep and headed down Hazlet Avenue. Horns honked. He glanced in his rearview mirror and saw a dark mid-sized car execute a U-turn. Dumb tourists didn't think they needed to obey common sense traffic laws.

After eating, he stopped for groceries. By the time he turned off South Harbor Drive, the sun was dipping below the horizon, the gulls were roosting for the night, and squadrons of mosquitoes buzzed out in search of unsuspecting prey.

Stone hefted the full bag of food and locked his Cherokee.

As he got out, a black Taurus cruised slowly past. He turned his attention to the marina and his first glimpse of Dolly. As always, her beauty struck him to the core of his being. Ariel affected him in much the same way. No, he must focus on Dolly. He squinted at her. Even though she was fifty-two, she was perfect in every way. It looked like she'd gained some water weight over the last week though. He frowned. He'd have to check that out.

He started toward her. This weekend, he'd give her a good oiling and polish her brass. If he got time, he'd take her out, but first he needed to pump her bilges. She needed to do what she'd been built for – cruising. Her twin V-8's needed to be run so they wouldn't rust and he needed to taste the salt and the freedom of the sea.

Stone began whistling row-row-row your boat and his stride lengthened. When he was beside Dolly, he grasped her brass railing and vaulted onto her weathered teak sun deck. As always, a sense of well being surged through him the moment his sneakers touched her.

With a sigh, he unlocked Dolly's hatch, stowed the groceries and then popped open a can of hard lemonade. The citrus flavor was perfect after a hard day of reading. He stretched his back until his vertebrae popped, and then took a second swallow.

Umm, it tasted just like Ariel.

Stone stiffened.

Why couldn't he get Ariel Danner off his mind? Memories of Marishka had never invaded Dolly's hallowed galley. Why did his infatuation follow him to his sanctuary?

Love.

Damn.

Stone poured the rest of the drink down the drain, then stomped off to check Dolly's bilges.

Chapter 19

Ariel locked the front door then double-checked the latches on the windows. Entering the living room, she stepped over Tempest, who was sprawled on the carpet reading a magazine. Mozart rolled one eye toward her before he resumed preening his feathers.

The scene seemed peaceful and normal, yet it was an illusion. For the past five years nothing had ever truly been serene, though many days had held the appearance of tranquility. It seemed like by the time she felt comfortable with an alias and new life, circumstances forced them to run.

Ariel drew the thick curtains to block out the seemingly perpetual sunshine, then leaned her forehead against the room-darkening brocade and thought about might-have-beens. If only the authorities had proved Peter was a murderer. Ariel closed her eyes and inhaled deeply, she knew in her heart that he had assassinated her father because he wanted her mother. She wondered when she'd ever accept the fact that justice had a price and that Peter Baldwyn had enough money to bribe the Pope, or at least enough to get away with executing her mother after she realized what a monster her second husband was and asked for a divorce.

She and Tempest should have run for their lives and never agreed to testify… if they'd disappeared when Peter was playing the grieving husband, he would never have known what they'd seen and they might have been able to live their lives in peace instead of on the run.

But they'd wanted justice and had believed truth and justice would win. How naïve they'd been.

She perched on the chair and looked around the room. Despite the cheap thrift shop look, it felt like home. That was something she hadn't experienced since her father had died. Perhaps it was time to hang up the calla lily painting.

Or not.

They couldn't stay in a place with so few escape routes.

Ariel shook her head. Actually, it was good they had to leave. Stone O'Banyon made her feel things in ways she'd never felt before, but there was no future there. Stone loved Dolly. She was an idiot to dream of a man who was involved with someone else. The bitter taste reminded her that if she tried to break Stone's bond with Dolly, she would be no better than Peter. The man had never led her to believe that his intentions were anything but neighborly. The only time he'd acted differently was the one kiss, which had been filled with burning ardor... the one he'd given her shortly after he'd returned from Valdez and Dolly. If nothing else illustrated his passion for his girlfriend, that kiss had.

Ariel traced her lips with the tip of her tongue.

"Sherry, you don't look so good. Are you still hurting from the rifle range?"

She gently touched her bruised shoulder and gave a slight nod. "What are you reading?"

"A quiz on how you know if your guy is the right one. I think Link is my right guy."

Ariel wanted to laugh at her innocent sincerity, but knew that at that age, she'd had an immense crush on the hunk who lived down the street and if anyone had told her he'd never be interested in a chubby, brainy girl, she wouldn't have believed them any more than her sister would believe that a grown man would be interested in a kid. At least a grown man wouldn't be, unless he was a pervert and since the trip to the refuge, she was certain neither Stone or Link were pedophiles. "Want to study Spanish?"

Tempest wrinkled her nose, but dutifully put aside her magazine. "Do you think we'll be able to get rid of our accents with enough practice?"

"I hope so. You'd think we'd sound Southern or something, but when I listen to the tapes I make of my pronunciation, I think I sound French." She shrugged. "It must be because of all the summers we spent there."

"Or maybe just because we speak French and it's sorta close to Spanish." Tempest brightened and added, "What if we got a fake Pyrenees address on our passports? That'd explain why we speak Spanish with a French accent." She frowned. "Wouldn't it?"

Ariel smiled. "That could actually work."

Tempest's head bobbed up and down so fast that a pink lock bounced in her eyes. "Don't forget that I've got dual citizenship. Instead of continuing to follow Mama's nationality, maybe we should try using that."

"We'll think about it."

Tempest studied her. "Even if we did, it'd still mean another move." Her nose wrinkled. "Link really is the right guy for me, but he's old. What'll happen if he dies of old age or marries some other chick because he gets tired of waiting for me to come back?"

Ariel blinked. "What makes you think there's only one Mr. Right for you?" Tempest held up her magazine. "Maybe they're wrong."

"Can't you admit that you don't want to move, either?"

When had she ever said she wanted to leave? "It doesn't matter what I want or don't want, I think we'll have to."

"You sure?"

Ariel nodded.

Tempest studied her for several moments. "That's what you tell yourself and me, but is it really true or are you just afraid to feel comfortable?" She leaned closer. "I think you know that Stone is the guy for you and you're scared 'cause he's big and dark, like Father. I think we're safe here and that you're just running because you're used to it and you're afraid Uncle Stone will turn out like Father. Well, he's nothing like him and never will be."

Whoa! "What do you want us to do? Stay here? Wait until Peter tracks us down? Then what? Do you expect me to negotiate a truce with him?"

"Shoot him."

Ariel shook her head. "Deadly confrontation is against my principles."

"You're just chicken." She was a healer, not a murderer, something as different from Peter as night and day. Tempest kicked the carpet. "I'd hoped you'd fall in love with Uncle Stone, so we could live here happily ever after."

"Life isn't a fairytale. Furthermore, if I cared about Stone, it would make leaving harder, because we'd need to leave him behind." Though she refused to admit it to anyone else, it was going to hurt to leave him behind worse than the cousins she'd already had to separate from. "Loving someone makes more problems than it solves."

"Like Mama and your dad and how he never showed her how to pay bills and stuff?"

"That's one example." Though hardly the one she would have chosen.

"How come Mama never figured out about Father?"

Ariel shrugged. "Peter is a good con-man. He seduced her when she was vulnerable. If I'd fallen for a felon, married him and had a child with him, I think I'd have a hard time believing what he was really like, too."

Tempest pushed her pink mop out of her eyes. "Can anyone ever really, truly know someone else?"

"I wish I knew."

Tempest appeared deep in thought. "Do you think Benji is okay?"

Ariel licked her lips and wished Tempest hadn't brought up their stepbrother. "I hope so. I wish he'd come with us, but-" She shrugged. "He's as stubborn as Peter." And had refused to believe them, when they'd told him what they'd seen. Benji had been angry at them for testifying against his father. Possibly even angrier, than Peter, if that was possible.

"He always thought Father was perfect. I bet'cha he turns out just like him."

"I hope you're wrong."

"Benji always acts unsympathetic. Is that cause of Father or because he's a boy?"

Who knew? "Years ago, I thought I was immortal." Ariel

sighed. "Things change when you grow up and realize you aren't the center of the universe and people aren't perfect."

"So you don't think I'm weird." Ariel smiled and shook her head. Tempest stared at her. "Father really screwed a lot of kids out of a really good pediatrician when he forced you to hide."

Ariel tousled Tempest's wild pink and black spikes. Loving people hurt, particularly when it was necessary to do something for their own safety, which they didn't want – like sending Mozart to Elizabeth or turning one's back on their feelings for someone like Stone, who obviously loved his longtime girlfriend.

What would her life have been like if Peter had not obsessed over her mother? Ariel shivered. She would not consider the possibility of a future with Stone O'Banyon. Doing so would only lead to temptation and she would be no better than Peter Baldwyn.

Chapter 20

Stone sat back on his heels and stretched the kinks out of his aching back. The sun blazing down on Dolly's newly oiled deck made the shine look a mile deep. Satisfaction simmered warm and satisfying.

"Hello Dolly O," said an accented tenor with a demanding tone.

Stone looked over the gunwale. A stranger's dark gaze appraised him. Unlike the Marina's regulars or the clients, who tracked him down here, this stranger was immaculately dressed in a black three-piece-suit and wingtips. His scarlet power-tie sparkled against his immaculate white shirt. There wasn't even a glossy black hair out of place.

He could only imagine what his own hair was doing. He glanced at his ratty T-shirt that had been white a zillion washings ago to his scruffy jeans and bare feet, the traditional outfit he wore when in residence. Stone wiped his palms on his Levi's. "Are you lost?"

White teeth flashed across the tanned face, and mirrored sunglasses reflected back Stone's laid-back image. "I pass by and see you take break." Stone eyed the stranger with a wariness, which he had previously felt as a child confronting a coiled rattlesnake. The dapper man studied him with the avid interest of a predator surveying his prey. Who was the guy? Satan come to bargain for his soul? "I see boat last week and admire."

Stone's nerves went on full alert. "Thanks." The guy gazed at him as if memorizing his face. "The Dolly O isn't for sale." And neither was he. The man chuckled, but it sounded so false that Stone stood up straighter. Despite the fact that he felt he'd met the man before, he sensed this stranger could have the best deal in the world for him, but if it meant having to work with the man, he doubted any amount of money would make a contract worthwhile.

With fluid movements, the stranger leaped aboard Dolly and advanced across the newly oiled deck.

Stone held up his hand. "Stop right there." The man smiled at him as if he'd said 'welcome aboard' Stone gritted his teeth and pointed to the deck. "You're ruining the finish."

The congenial smile didn't falter as he thrust out his hand. "Peter Baldwin."

The name sounded familiar, but he still couldn't place him with any of their clients. Worse, up close, Stone was certain he'd seen the man before. But until he could verify when and where, he wasn't going to be any more civil than necessary, so he put his hands in the back pockets of his Levi's. "You're ruining your shoes and my deck. Please disembark."

The man didn't spare a glance at his footwear. Instead, he put his hand inside his perfectly tailored jacket and removed something. "I look runaways." He thrust a photo toward him. "You see?"

If looking at the stupid paper would get rid of the obnoxious man, he'd look at it. Still seething over the footprints in his perfect finish, Stone pretended to seriously study the photo of a skinny girl, who was giving the camera a big gape-toothed, squint-eyed smile. The kid's pale blond hair was pulled back into pigtails, which were dominated by huge blue bows. He handed the photo back. "I don't see many kids in my business. Not too many around this part of the Marina, either. Sorry. Now, how about getting-"

The man thrust a different 5 x7 at him. This portrait had been done in a studio and the kid was at least ten years older. Her hair lay in soft curls around her plump shoulders. Her eyes were blue as Marishka's and there was something oddly familiar about her smile. Was his conniving ex up to another scam? "Still haven't seen her." He thrust the portrait at Baldwyn

A perfectly manicured hand pushed the photo back at him. "Not one. Two. Miss for five year. You look again." He pointed to the portrait. "That Sherrill. She child doctor." He held up the original photo. "This Sabrina, my daughter." The Arabic accent was as phony as the story.

"Your kid's doctor kidnapped her?" Against his better judgment, Stone found himself getting interested in the man's situation.

"They runaway."

Stone nodded. "Why?"

"I need to find."

Suddenly he recalled how disgusted Mavis had been with the man who'd been pestering her. "You came by Linkstone earlier this week." Finally being able to recall where he'd heard the name seemed to disconcert the man. "Look, I don't know why you're trying to make me feel sorry for you, but all you've managed to do is piss me off by coming abroad uninvited and ruining my deck." Stone glared at his reflection in Baldwyn's sunglasses. He wanted to toss the man into the harbor and be done with it, but to do so would necessitate touching the man. "Disembark now and either send me a proposal for whatever business deal you're really after or if you're selling something, talk to my office manager."

"No business. No leave."

Stone's hands clenched at his sides.

"You at Deadhorse with woman and girl-child."

"So?" Stone went on red alert. Overhead, a gull cried. He shrugged and smiled. "I was with my partner, Link, too."

"Maybe same." Baldwyn fluttered the photos.

"I doubt it." Dolly rocked back and forth, as if contemplating throwing their unwanted guest overboard. Baldwyn sidestepped to keep his balance and grabbed for a line. He dropped a photo.

Stone grabbed the one Baldwyn had called Sherrill before it hit the deck. The woman had Ariel's smile. If Ariel were a doctor, it would explain several things, including why Tempest occasionally called her Sherry. And if this jerk was her ex, it explained why she would rather live with rubber furniture than accept child support. Stone thrust the picture back to Baldwyn.

"Is possible same?" Despite the rolling deck, the man didn't show any intention of giving up.

Stone studied his reflection in the mirrored lenses, then laughed. "If you want a kid that bad, you need to talk to my partner. Much as Link loves his niece, I'm sure you could find a day where she frustrated him enough that he'd give Tempest to you."

Baldwyn shoved the photos back in his pocket, turned and tracked more footprints across the once-perfect teak. The bastard was lucky he didn't have his rifle.

As Stone repaired the damage, he alternately wondered if the jerk was actually Ariel's ex and why he was tracking them. How had Ariel gotten involved with such a slimeball? Worse, why was he looking for them?

After he finished the deck the second time, he went below, picked up the phone and dialed.

"Hello." His sister sounded cross.

"Hey, Windy."

"Three calls in one week! What gives?"

"Did you find out anything?"

"The vehicle was a snap, but I can't trace anything on the names other than what you already told me."

"Is it possible that they changed their names?"

"Absolutely. People do it all the time."

Criminals did, but after having met the ex, doing so just to evade him would be a valid reason. "Could you check out Baldwyn? Sherrill and Sabrina?"

"You sound tense."

"I think I just met Ariel's ex. God, what a creep."

"Do I detect jealousy?"

Stone took a deep breath. "Let's just say that I finally understand what you mean about meeting certain criminals and feeling like the hair on the nape of your neck is going to jump ship."

"One of those charmers." Windy's tone was laced with sarcasm and sudden interest. "Does he have a first name?"

After giving her all the information he recalled, they discussed plans for their parent's upcoming anniversary.

"You will be there." The order implicit in Windy's voice

amused him.

"Wouldn't miss it." Stone grinned. "If you think there's any chance I'll try to worm out of it, you can fly up here, handcuff me and haul me home while telling everyone you see that you're taking a notorious felon back to Dallas."

Windy laughed. "Deal."

Stone spent the next thirty hours impatiently waiting for Windy to come up with more information than the odd bits, like a South Carolina State Trooper had purchased the Suburban at an FBI auction and resold it to a Blythe Danvers within twenty-four hours. Had Ariel used that name? Did the cop's assistance with the Suburban have anything to do with his subsequent murder? If so, and his imagination wasn't simply going overboard, after meeting Bladwin, what kind of man had she married? And were they in mortal danger, as the conversation he'd overheard, had suggested?

No matter how hard Stone polished Dolly's brass, Windy never called. By the time Stone flew back to Fairbanks, he was torn between believing Ariel had been unable to work within the legal system to save Tempest from her pedophile-father, and believing she was a runaway wife from an abuser, who considered females inferior. He also started thinking he needed a reality check for himself.

As Stone secured the Cessna in the hangar, Wade sauntered over. "Good trip?" Stone nodded. "Your bird need any work?"

"Gas, of course, and do you have time to take another look at the altimeter? It's still giving me indication problems." Like telling him he was flying at forty-thousand feet, when he knew the mountain he was next to was only ten-thousand.

"I don't do avionics."

He knew that. "But you could schedule someone who is licensed to look at it and maybe do something temporary until that backorder finally get in."

Wade gave him a thumbs-up, then tapped his curly blond head. "You know why the blond dyed her hair black?"

Stone shook his head.

"Artificial intelligence." Wade cackled at his own joke. "Tell Link."

Stone nodded then headed home.

As he entered the kitchen, Link was placing a bottle of Chardonnay in a familiar basket. "Let me guess. You're on your way next door for dinner."

Link cocked a finger at him and pretended to fire it like a gun. "Coming?"

Stone raised a brow. "You expect me to cook when I can eat and have great scenery?" Link shrugged. "Remind me to tell you the joke Wade told me."

"The one about holding a flashlight up to a blonde's ear and being able to see it from the other side?"

"No, but it's on that line..." Stone chuckled. "Perhaps we should consider hiring a different mechanic. One with avionics expertise."

"The altimeter is still off?"

Stone nodded. "Don't take her out IFR."

Link fired a second imaginary shot at him.

Stone grinned. "Ever considered dying your hair black?"

Link laughed. "I think Wade is the one who needs dye." He glanced at his wristwatch. "Hurry up or you'll make us late." Link gave him a meaningful look. "Megara's close to whelping. May have already."

Having checked her kennel before he came inside Stone, shook his head. "I'll check her, again, after dinner," he said, then he hurried upstairs to change into a fresh shirt.

As they ate desert, Stone and Tempest talked about raising dogs and the kid bounced with excitement about Megara's imminent puppies. Stone studied her and thought about how good she seemed to be with the parrot, how much she loved playing with the dogs and how well she followed the rules, then he thought about what a chatty little thing she was, compared to her mom, and how it might be easier to get the answers that eluded him from her. "I travel about half the time," he told Tempest. She nodded, as if she'd figured that one out long ago. He held her gaze. "Perhaps we can work out a deal." Her eyes narrowed, in distrust. He hurried to finish his offer, "If you take care of the dogs and the puppies, once they get here, when they're old enough, I'll let you have your pick."

Tempest looked like he'd offered her a million dollars. "To keep?" She leaped off her folding chair and threw her arms around his neck. "Oh, thank you, Uncle Stone!" She planted a juicy kiss on his cheek and hugged him tight. "That's the nicest thing anyone has ever offered me."

"You're welcome."

Ariel cleared her throat. Tempest glanced over his shoulder and quickly stepped away from him. "But I can't have a puppy. I'll help take care of them as long as I can, though." With that, she slumped into her chair. Eyes downcast, she blinked several times, then repeatedly stabbed her half-eaten slice of apple pie with her fork.

He turned to Ariel, but she pretended nothing had

happened. A look at Link generated a shrug. Mozart ruffled his feathers and muttered something unintelligible. He focused on Ariel, "If you break it in young enough, it won't bark at Mozart."

"It's not that," Tempest muttered, her voice choked with tears. "Uncle Links says your dogs sell for thousands." She peeked at him, her eyes swimming with unshed tears.

"I was offering it as a wage."

Tempest blinked hard, then looked down. "I still can't." Her shoulders shuddered.

"Why not?" Because your mom doesn't want it? Would the kid admit the truth?

"Because it'd break my heart when we have to leave and I won't be able to take it with me." Her comments were cut off with a sob.

Stone placed his hand over the one clutching the fork. "You don't have to leave any time soo-"

Tempest leaped up, knocking her chair backward and dashed for the stairs.

A cold sensation swept through him. He turned toward Ariel for answers, but her attention was focused on her plate. He thought about Baldwyn's veiled accusations. Did they know Tempest's father had tracked them here? Were they planning to run, again or did they expect Tempest to be forced home?

He didn't ask Ariel, because he knew she would only change the subject, so he wasn't surprised when he was still wondering the same thing when he and Link returned home.

Sunlight glared off the windshield of an unfamiliar Ford Bronco parked a half block down the street. Worse, he thought he saw the dapper, dark haired man walking toward it. Had he led the jerk to them? He hoped Windy called with something solid, soon, because he wanted to help Ariel, but he couldn't rely on gut instinct, he needed verifiable facts. Facts she obviously didn't intend to share with him.

Chapter 21

Ariel daubed ochre on the caribou she was painting for Stone. Senseless as it was, she wanted him to have something to remember her by. She cleaned her brush, then picked up her detail brush and added a tiny touch of white to the eye. She didn't know why she wanted Stone to think about her after she reneged on her rental agreement; after all, he was serious about Dolly, but no matter how illogical it seemed, she wanted to leave a piece of herself with him. The black plastic, which she'd placed over the blue carpet rustled under her feet, as she stepped back to survey the canvas. It stood proudly on its makeshift easel and dominated the corner of her bedroom.

"How ya coming?" Tempest leaned against the doorway, her hair standing on end as if she'd been electrified. Ah, the wonders of gel.

"You tell me."

Tempest eagerly came into the room and stood next to her. She cocked her head to one side, as Mozart often did. "The baby looks good, but its Mama looks a lot like a really weird Siamese cat."

Ariel grinned. "It does, doesn't it?" She chuckled. "Until you pointed it out, I hadn't noticed that caribou and Siamese are about the same color."

"She'll look okay once you get her antlers on. The bull looks really lifelike. How'd you get his eyes to make it seem like he's looking at me?" Ariel shrugged. Tempest plopped down into a cross-legged pose. "I'm going to miss Uncle Link and the dogs like crazy." She pouted. "Father ruins everything. I hate him."

Ariel nodded. Ever since the Sunday evening, when Stone had returned from Valdez, the hair on the back of her neck had quivered and gooseflesh broke out over her arms whenever she went outside. Though she'd long since learned to listen to this subtle warning, this time she couldn't decide if her reaction had something to do with Stone's presence or if she was being watched. Was Stone the cause of her escalating paranoia? If so, why? She knew him well enough to know he was nothing like Peter Baldwyn, nor did she still believe he was one of Peter's hirelings.

"Sherry?"

Ariel looked at Tempest.

"Are you going to miss them, too?"

"Definitely." More than anyone would ever know. Almost as much as she missed her mother. "This is the first time in years that I've actually felt close enough to anyone, other than family, to consider them a friend." Ariel sat down next to Tempest and took her hand. "I didn't realize how much I'd missed that."

Tempest squeezed her hand. "At least we've got each other." She blinked away tears. "Sunday night, when Uncle Stone offered me a puppy, it was the hardest thing in the world to turn it down."

"I know."

"You don't think he suspects, do you?"

"About what?"

"Well, I nearly told him that we'd have to run away."

"I doubt if he understood it that way. Adults don't listen to kids as closely as they do adults. Some of them don't even listen to other adults and try to claim their own words were in the other person's mouth." Tempest gave her a strange look. "Sorry, just venting."

Tempest's expression became glum. "Maybe most adults don't listen, but you and Uncle Link aren't like that." She frowned. "It almost seems like Uncle Stone sorta understood, though. He's been real quiet and watchful this week. And have you noticed how he didn't go to Val-wherever, like he usually does? Do you think that means something?"

"Aside from his dog being close to having her puppies?" Ariel asked. Tempest smacked her forehead. Perhaps his change of routine was why she'd felt eyes on her, but it didn't explain why she'd had the sensation everywhere – home, university, even the grocery store. Worse when she glanced over her shoulder, she often saw someone turning away or ducking.

Tempest sighed. "Have you told them about the painting?"

Ariel shook her head. "It's a surprise. Kinda like an apology for breaking our rental agreement."

"It's really good, you know. You're good enough to go professional."

Ariel laughed. "Do you want to live in a garret and starve?"

Tempest snickered and nodded. "I'm not sure where that is, but I know that I'd rather just stay here."

"We've already stayed too long."

"I know … Think Uncle Link and the dogs will miss me?"

"Of course they will." Ariel assured her.

After a moment Tempest got up. At the door, she paused

and looked back. "I know Uncle Stone will miss me, 'cause he said so and he said it like he really, really meant it."

When had they had this conversation? With a sigh, she got up and cleaned her brushes, and then she headed to the grocery store to get a special desert to go with the salmon dinner Link had invited them to. Link was always the one who issued the invitations. Would Stone miss her? Would he have invited her for dinner, if Link hadn't beat him to it?

As she backed the Suburban onto the street, a dark Ford Bronco pulled out of a parking slot a block away and followed her. She checked her rearview mirror for it several times, but two turns later, there was only a dump truck behind her. Ariel shook her head and muttered, "Peter doesn't need to kill me – I'll kill myself with stress."

Hours later, she juggled an overflowing bag of groceries and pressed Link and Stone's doorbell with her elbow.

"Come on in. It's open," Stone called from somewhere within. She made a sound of exasperation, but managed to get the door open. As she kicked it shut, she heard The Moody Blues, Elizabeth's favorite band, playing in the kitchen. Stone was singing along and he sounded great. Worse, she could imagine him being her knight in white satin.

How could one man have such a peculiar effect on her?

No matter how much she dreamed about calling what she felt love or pretending that he was the one, she knew it must be simple lust. She felt heat rise up her neck and onto her cheeks.

As she entered the kitchen, Stone poured batter into a steaming cast-iron pan. She plunked her bag on the counter. "Smells good. What are you making?"

"Johnny cake."

Ariel raised a brow.

"I thought either you or Tempest said that you'd lived in the South. Don't tell me you've never had it."

What all had Tempest told him while she petted dogs? "I've never seen it made."

He placed the hot pan in the oven. "Mom always made it this way."

She chuckled. "I like the fact that you still call your mother Mom."

He turned toward her. "Family tradition. Just like the way you call each other by your first names." Ariel blinked. Stone gave her an easy smile. "Tempest calls you by your given name and you call your mother by hers."

He must mean Elizabeth. Ariel smiled and nodded. "Do you have a large family?"

"We're pretty average. Mother, father and two younger sisters." He set the oven timer. "How about you?"

"Just a step-brother and sister." The truth popped out before she could dodge it. "What can I do to help with dinner?"

"Nothing. I've got it under control."

"I expected Link to cook."

"He got tied up, so I volunteered." His chuckle did funny things to her heart. "It's fun to cook for a change. I never get to at home and when I'm at Dolly." He shrugged. "Take out is easier."

A discussion about his girlfriend was the last thing she wanted to hear. "Tell me about your family."

"What do you want to know?" Less than two feet separated them. She couldn't think, let alone breathe. Ariel shrugged. His lips twitched into a crooked smile. "My father raises beef and horses. It keeps him tied down most of the time, but he loves working the land … we never got many vacations when I was young. I guess that's why I wanted to see somewhere new."

"Living in one place sounds like heaven to me."

He cocked his head to one side. "The grass is always greener, isn't it?"

Ariel nodded.

"Where all have you lived?"

She should have kept her big mouth shut. "My father was a geologist and moved all over world. My mother and I went with him." She gave Stone a lopsided smile. "Was your mother a homemaker?"

"Hardly. Mom was – is – a scholar. Her passion is ancient civilizations. She teaches Medieval Studies at the University of Texas, Dallas campus."

"She sounds interesting. It must have been great to grow up with her."

"It had its moments, but most of the time, I halfway resented her eccentricity."

"Why?"

"My name for one thing." He grimaced. "Windy and Brit feel the same way." Ariel waited for him to explain. He frowned. "Don't you think Stone is an unusual name?"

"Not especially. I like it and figured it was a family name or something." She shrugged. "Perhaps a Stonewall Jackson sort of name."

Stone chuckled. "His parents really socked it to him, didn't they?" Ariel didn't know what to say. "My actual name is Stonehenge. Windy is Gaelic and Brit is simply Brittany."

Chapter 22

As she and Tempest drove past a black Ford Bronco, which was parked down the street her skin crawled. Ariel noticed how black and sinister its windows were. Perhaps that was what had made her shudder.

Or maybe it was whoever hid behind the dark panes.

Ariel shook her head at her continued paranoia and drove to the University to deliver her lecture. As she pulled into the drop-off circle to let Tempest off at the library, the black Bronco passed her. She caught her breath.

"Sherry, what's wrong?"

She gestured to the Ford.

"Oh. I didn't know the new tenants were profs, too."

"You know them?"

"Not really. Uncle Link said a couple guys rented the last available townhouse."

Somehow Tempest's explanation didn't sooth her. "I'll be back to pick you up in two and a half hours. Whatever you do, do not - repeat, do not - talk to strangers, even if you think-"

"Sherry, you're repeating yourself. I know not to talk to anyone. I know to sit with my back to the wall and nowhere near a corner. I'm not stupid." She hopped out of the Suburban and headed for the imposing doors, her step jaunty.

Ariel swallowed hard as she fought the temptation to call her sister back. The driver behind her tapped the horn. She squared her shoulders and accelerated. As she parked on the other side of campus, she chewed her lip and tried to convince herself that it was better if they were split up.

Twenty minutes later, she stepped behind the lectern, put her doubts aside and launched into a lecture on kinesiology as it related to the anatomy of the human hand. As she spoke, students stared at the palms of their hands. "While this technique does not replace conventional forms of testing, it can corroborate results." She smiled at her silent audience. Only one pair of familiar dark eyes looked back. Her throat went dry and the man sitting in the back of the room gave her a slight smile. Ariel's knees loosened. She grasped the lectern for support and looked down at her notes, but they blurred.

She took a deep breath. *I can do this.*

"In summary, many physicians believe applied kinesiology can be used to diagnose and treat problems in their early stages. Now, I have an assignment for you. Write a thousand word report on the comparison between the non-invasive diagnostic techniques of kinesiology and acupuncture." The students groaned. "Calm down. I'd like it one week from today."

While the undergraduates gathered their belongings and trekked out of the hall, Peter leaned back and studied her. Ariel forced herself to appear calm as she collected her notes. Once she escaped out the side door, it was all she could do to keep a sedate pace as she went to the parking lot.

She spotted Tempest waiting near the Suburban. When she realized her sister was talking to a tall, thin man, wearing a leather jacket and mirrored sunglasses, a chill ran over her arms. *Uncle Link said a couple guys rented the last available townhouse*. More chills ran up and down Ariel's body. Was she just being paranoid or was Peter gathering information and verifying their identity in tandem with an accomplice? As Tempest looked up, Ariel waved at her and pointed to the Suburban.

Tempest shook her head, then simpered up at the man.

The idiot.

Ariel jabbed her finger at the car.

Tempest glared at her, then looked back at the man and smiled. Ariel quickened her pace and prickles crossed her back. Her heart pounded against her ribs and she fought the temptation to look over her shoulder to see if she was being followed. With a fluff of her hair, Tempest opened the car door, then leaned against it and continued what appeared to be a flirtation with the stranger. Ariel glared at the little fool across the tops of two cars. "Get in the car, now. We're running late." Tempest's thunderous expression suggested that the only thing on her mind was having lost the chance to pretend she was a coed.

The tingling sensation at the back of her neck intensified until all she could think about was turning around and finding out how close Peter was. The ten feet separating her from the Suburban felt like miles. Was that thudding behind her footfalls? She hastened for the last three steps. Her hand shook as she slid the key into the lock.

A man chuckled behind her. Ariel tensed, remembering how Peter loved torturing people. "And then what did you do?" a strange voice asked. A woman giggled, but blood was pounding so loud in her ears that Ariel didn't hear the response.

She slid into the driver's seat and slammed the door.

Tempest hopped in. Ariel locked the doors and started the engine. "Sheesh, what's wrong with you?"

"You were talking to a stranger." She rammed the transmission into gear and accelerated out of the parking slot. The next row over, a dark Bronco moved.

"Josh? He's at the library all the-" With a squeal from the wheels, Ariel accelerated. Tempest was thrown backward. She grabbed the edge of the seat. Face white, she asked, "Practicing your defensive driving or are you that mad at me?"

"Duck," she snapped.

Tempest flattened herself. Ariel spun the wheel and sped onto College Road. "You are mad at me." Tempest's muffled voice sounded angry.

"We're being followed. Probably by your wonderful new friend from the library, who probably works for your father. And by the way, Peter sat in on my lecture, today." Tempest moaned. "Possibly he's driving the vehicle that is following us or its the jerk you were drooling over." Ariel spun the wheel and took the corner onto Steese on two wheels.

The Bronco's driver matched her skill as she floored the accelerator and headed for Chena Hot Springs, the Bronco kept an even distance. City quickly gave way to country. Within a mile, the traffic dropped to half what it had been.

This was not working.

She slowed to a sedate pace. So did the Ford.

"Is it safe now?"

"We're still being followed, but I don't think they want to shoot us." Probably whoever was in the vehicle was being paid extra to allow Peter that privilege. Ariel looked for a turnaround. "You can sit up."

Tempest straightened and looked out the back window. "That car belongs to our new neighbors." Ariel made a noncommittal sound. "You think they work for Father."

Ariel spotted a turnaround and whipped onto it. Tempest yelped and grabbed the seat. The Bronco followed them. "What do you think?"

"He recognized us."

"If he didn't, I was stupid enough to confirm our identities when I ran." Tempest's eyes looked enormous in her ashen face. "There's only one way out. We're going to the police station." She floored the accelerator.

"No!"

"Can you think of a better plan?"

"He'll kill us."

"Either way, he knows where we are. It's only a matter of time."

"We've got to run. Leave Mozart, just run."

"Where to? We've only got a quarter tank of gas. For a state that makes the stuff, you'd think there'd be more stations." She turned right. "One thing I didn't notice when I accepted this job is that unless I want to hit a dead end in the middle of nowhere, there are about two roads heading out of town." She whipped the Suburban into the police station's parking lot.

Tempest wailed.

Ariel winced.

The Bronco slowed, then parked three spaces away from her.

Ariel unsnapped her seatbelt.

"What – where are you going? Sherry, don't go out there," Tempest hissed.

"Do you remember our current bio?" Tempest's nod was shaky. "I'm Ariel. I'm your mother." Tears pooled in Tempest's eyes. "As soon as I get out, lock the damned doors and stay low." Tempest nodded. "And for God's sake, quit thinking people aren't strangers just because they tell you a name!" A tear trickled down her cheek.

Before she lost her resolve, Ariel slammed the door. Squaring her shoulders, she stalked to the Bronco's driver-side window and knocked.

She looked at her reflection and tried to look angry instead of afraid. Seconds seemed like hours. Finally, the black glass rolled down and she faced the man from the parking lot. Thank God, her plan just might work. "Do you mind telling me why you've been stalking me and my daughter?" she demanded, her tone loud enough to attract the attention of a passing woman.

The man's thin lips tilted up. "I wasn't following you, lady." Red crept up his neck at the lie. Whoever he was, she'd bet Peter wouldn't hire him, again.

Ariel's knees stopped knocking. She snorted with disdain. "Then perhaps you can explain why you're here."

"What's wrong with parking here?" He couldn't meet her gaze.

Ariel put her fists on her hips and glared at him. As an officer came out of the police station, she took a breath. "I don't believe you." She raised her pitch. "You followed me from the University, first North, than back into town. Now you're here. Why are you stalking me?"

Hand on his holster, the officer turned to study them.

"I saw you follow me from home earlier, too. What kind of a pervert are you?"

The officer unsnapped his holster and headed her way, hand on the butt of his gun.

"Look lady, I don't kno-"

"Is there a problem here?" the officer asked.

"Yes," Ariel said.

"No," the man said.

Ariel glared at the man than turned to the officer. "This man followed me from my home to the University this morning. He was standing in the parking lot chatting up my fifteen-year-old daughter, when I finished giving my lecture. And he's spent the last twenty minutes following me from the University. I'd say that qualifies as a problem." She swiveled back to the man. "What kind of pervert are you?"

Perspiration beaded his face.

"Is that true?" the officer asked.

"Yes it is," Tempest called from the cracked window of the Suburban. "He's scaring my mama and me."

"I'm not a stalker."

"You sure act like one," Ariel snapped.

"I've been hired to find —" He rummaged in some papers on the front seat. The officer half-drew his gun. The man held up her college graduation photo. He held up a second photo of Tempest at six. They quivered in his hands.

Ariel arched an eyebrow at the long-gone chubby cheeks and blond hair. "Surely you don't think either my daughter or I are these people."

The officer looked from the photo to her and seemed torn between amusement and suspicion.

"He said you like to disguise yourself."

"Who said?" Ariel demanded.

The man's face flushed. "My employer. I'm an investigator-"

"Is he?" Ariel asked the officer. "Don't they need licenses or something? I mean surely, people can't just say they're investigators than stalk people at their will."

"Sir, would you please get out of the car?"

"This has all been a misunderstanding."

"Please, get out."

"Are you arresting me?"

When the officer hesitated, Ariel said, "I'll be happy to file charges, if that's what you need." Before the officer could respond, the man started the Bronco and accelerated out of the parking lot.

Relief left Ariel weak. "Thank you so much. I don't know what I'd have done if you hadn't come along."

"Would you still like to file a formal complaint?" Ariel nodded, then motioned to Tempest.

She scrambled out of the Suburban, ran to her and threw her arms around her waist. "I can't believe you did that." The muffled words still conveyed fright.

"I can't believe I found the guts to confront him, either."

"Ladies." The officer motioned toward the step of the Police Department as he ushered them inside.

Chapter 23

Stone put his feet up on the coffee table, leaned back in his favorite chair and dialed the phone. As Windy's phone in Austin, Texas rang, he watched the headlines move across the bottom of CNN's muted broadcast. Since it was after seven her time and no new airline crashes were a top story, she should be at home. But after the forth ring there was a musical tone. "You have reached 555-2951." He groaned. Was she avoiding him and using her answering machine to run interference? "If this is the number you wanted, please stay on the line and leave a message. I will return you ca-"

He slammed down the receiver. "Promises, promises." He'd already left three messages, which she hadn't returned.

Stone clicked off the mute button. "OPEC's security team is partnering in the investigation with —" Stone turned off the television, effectly cutting off the anchorman's confident tones. He'd had quite enough of the big brouhaha the media was making over a stupid fisherman, who just happened to be part of OPEC and how the media was turning the guy's ignorance into some sort of murder cover-up.

He picked up the newspaper and flipped through the pages, but The Miner's reporters were just as bad. Why couldn't there be an article on why women acted devious? Perhaps he should write and ask the editors if all women resorted to deception or if he attracted the ones that did. Did women feel a need to hide personal faults? Did he need to harden his heart before it was shredded? What if he ignored the Danners and later discovered their sudden interest in weapons and self-defense had its roots in a real threat?

Knowing the truth about them would make it much easier, especially after Marishka's pathological lies. He jaw tightened. If it hadn't been for his beautiful ex, he'd bet his last dollar that Ariel had intentionally mislead him because of past pain and a distrust of men. Her ex must be a real piece of work. Worse, he knew how people chose mates that consciously or sub-consciously reminded them of their fathers and thus perpetuated a cycle of pain and humiliation, so Ariel had probably been abused as a kid. He frowned, remembering her account of the cat's murder, which defiantly sounded like emotional abused. And that was normally worse than physical abuse, because too often it went unnoticed.

What had Ariel's mother been thinking when she agreed to let her husband take the kid on a jungle hunt?

There was a jangle of keys then the back door squeaked open. He needed to oil that hinge, instead of think about it. Of course, there were myriad of things he should do instead of think about doing, like getting the Cessna's altimeter repaired.

Link's distinctive tread moved across the linoleum.

"Need any help?" he called.

"You can set the table," Link said. Stone winced because Link had asked him to do that before he'd run to the bakery. "Or if you're busy, I'll just have Tempest do it when she gets here."

Stone threw the paper down and surged out of his chair. Because Windy was ignoring him, he would be forced to face another evening of playing brotherly neighbor, when what he really wanted to do was kiss Ariel senseless. He went to the kitchen door and looked at Link, who was putting away some groceries, while leaving items he intended to use on the island-counter, around a huge chocolate cake.

"You planning something special or should I just set a basic table?"

Link rolled his eyes and laughed. "You expect me to put on a feed like your mother or something?"

Stone shook his head. A big Chinook sprawled over a large portion of the sink-counter. "Near miss?" he asked, as he reached for the plates.

"Only fifty-six pounds."

King salmon needed to be at least sixty pounds to qualify for a trophy. "Too bad."

"Good for us," Link said. He began honing his filleting knife.

Stone put napkins and silverware on top of the plates. "Want me to make a batch of Johnny cake?"

"Sounds good to me." Link deftly slit the fish.

Stone put his favorite skillet in the oven then turned it on. While it heated, he set the table. Upon returning to the kitchen, he spotted Tempest's elfin face peering through one of the backdoor's panes. He motioned for her to come in. Her eyes rounded and she looked pointedly at the pile of fish entrails next to Link and shook her head so hard that her hair looked like a black and fuchsia blur. He laughed.

"You think this is funny, you get over here and stick you hand into-"

"I wasn't laughing at you," Stone cut in. "You should have seen Tempest's face when she saw the salmon." Link glanced over his shoulder, at the now empty pane "She either went back home or is with the dogs," Stone explained. Link grunted.

Stone cleared a section of counter, which was closer to the cake than the fish and began mixing batter. After he poured the mixture into the hot pan, he went to the window and watched Tempest engage Agamemnon in a rollicking game of Frisbee. She was a great kid. It'd be fun being her dad. He shook his head, at the thought, turned his back to the door and sniffed. Lemon overpowered the scent of fish and mingled tantalizingly with the aroma of jalapenos and corn. "Smells good."

"Thanks."

There was a commotion at the front door. "You want the desert in the kitchen or on the table?" Ariel called.

"No space in here," Link said.

Stone headed for the dinning room. She looked beautiful. He felt his muscles relax and a smile form. "Need any help?"

She shook her head and placed a pineapple upside-down cake at the center of the table. "What's Tempest doing? Helping Link?"

"Playing Frisbee. I don't think she wanted to deal with fish guts. And I gotta admit that I don't blame her."

Ariel wrinkled her nose. "I can appreciate that."

She adjusted the placement of a cherry, so it stood at the precise center of the pineapple ring, then she brushed past him and went into the kitchen. "Oh, you already had desert." Parts of him sang with glee at the brief contact. Other parts shouted for more. He clenched his hands so he wouldn't reach out and grab her.

Link laughed. "Cake is always good and the more the better."

"Surely you don't expect the four of us to eat all that," Ariel said, pointing to the filleted salmon.

"I have hundreds of recipes for left over salmon," Link assured her.

Ariel shook her head. "What you need are hundreds of people that are really hungry. Have you considered the local Food Bank?"

"I hadn't, but it's a good idea. I was going to freeze most of this, but it's not like we need more salmon."

As Ariel brushed her hair back over her shoulder, her hand came tantalizingly close to his chest. Stone bit back a groan of frustration. She tensed and looked backward. He smiled. Her look turned frosty. Damn, but her ex must have been a piece of work for her to distrust him so much.

During desert, when Link started talking about their upcoming business trip to Valdez, Stone couldn't resist teasing him. "Aren't you afraid Mavis will eat you alive?" Link choked on a cherry.

Ariel gave him a sharp glance, but when she realized Link was dramatizing a non-existent illness, partially in jest, her attitude thawed.

"No." Link finally said.

Stone forced himself to ignore Ariel and focused on Link. "Could have fooled me. You've avoided the Southern run for the past couple months. I figured you'd taken her threats to heart."

"What threats? Who's Mavis?" Tempest asked. Her expression became belligerent. "His girlfriend?"

"Our Office Manager," Stone said. He tried not to look at Ariel, because she was staring at them as if she'd never seen two grown men banter.

Link stabbed a huge fork full of pineapple cake.

"What'd you do to Mavis to make her angry at you?" Tempest asked.

Stone pantomimed talking on the phone. Link grimaced. Stone laughed. Tempest frowned and said, "I don't get it."

Link sighed. "Mavis hates phones with a passion. About six weeks ago, I got myself on her roster when I called one too many times."

"He does this all the time. I think he figures I like the Valdez run because I keep Dolly down there."

Link snorted.

Tempest laid down her fork. "Well if she works for you, you should make her be polite or fire her."

The thought of anyone making Mavis do something she didn't want to do made him laugh harder. Ariel's eyes widened. Tempest's mouth flattened.

Tempest threw her napkin on the table. "I don't get what's wrong with you people." She glared at them. "You are her bosses, aren't you?"

"If we fired her, we wouldn't know what to do or when to do it," Stone admitted, then he smiled across the table at Tempest. "Mavis has been with us since the beginning and in a lot of ways she knows more about our business than we do."

"Why are your offices so far away?"

"Because Mavis lives there and we have contracts all over the state, so it doesn't matter where we live," Link said.

"And we like it here," Stone added. "Fairbanks is in the middle of the state, which makes it more or less convenient for most any job." His voice faltered, when he realized all of Ariel's attention was focused on him.

"I still think you should fire her." Tempest pouted.

"She's really good at her job," Stone admitted. "We'd have to hire at least three people to replace her."

"How come you have to go down there at all?"

"Mainly to look over the new contracts and sign them." He grinned at the kid. "Mavis always has everything organized so it goes quick, then I get to spend my time on Dolly."

Ariel nudged the cherry from her pineapple cake into the chocolate frosting. As she toyed with it, red tinged her cheeks in such an attractive way that he forgot what he was going to add.

Link cleared his throat. "Either Stone or I could run the business, if we had to, but neither of us really likes typing contracts or making sure the accounts are collected. Mavis revels in that and she's worth every penny we pay her."

"She knows it, too." Stone added a chuckle to soften the statement. He squinted at Link. "Exactly how many times did you phone her the last time?"

"One too many times while she was nit-picking the Haverguild contract."

Stone winced. "That one was a pup."

Link nodded in agreement, then added, "Actually, technology did me in." He looked simultaneously disgruntled and embarrassed by the statement and Stone sensed Link was telling the truth. Nevertheless, Tempest laughed out loud. Link flushed crimson. She put her hand over her mouth and appeared mortified.

"Technology, huh?" Stone said. Link nodded. "The redial button get you again?" Link nodded, looking as forlorn as a lost lover, but the Danners appeared to be suppressing laughter. If either of them had ever witnessed Mavis in full fury, they wouldn't think it was so funny. Thankfully, her anger was directed at Link. "You have to understand Mavis," Stone explained. "To her, Lucifer and Alexander Graham Bell are one in the same."

Link took a gulp of wine, then started coughing. Stone couldn't tell if he was acting or not, but Ariel and Tempest let our shrieks of laughter, as if they thought it was a big joke. For the first time since she'd touched him while flicking her hair, she looked at him as a person instead of a potential rapist.

What kind of pervert had her ex been?

"She can't be that bad," Tempest said around a mouth full of chocolate cake.

"Worse," Link and Stone said in unison. Tempest clasped her hands over her mouth and laughed until brown oozed between her fingers.

As the merriment died, Stone studied Link and asked, "You sure you're ready to face her? It's only been a few weeks."

"I have to go sooner or later. Might as well make it sooner so she doesn't get the idea I'm scared of her."

"Where's Valdez?" Ariel asked.

"Just off the Prince William Sound," Stone said. She looked mystified by his point of reference.

"It's the south terminus of the pipeline, where they pump the crude onto tankers," Link said. Ariel got a 'now I understand look' on her face. "If you're not busy fussing over Dolly, I thought we could take her out fishing."

"Great idea!" Stone grinned. "I knew there had to be an ulterior motive for getting your apology over with. Is there a competition?" Link looked at the ceiling as he shook his head. "But you are after a prize," he said. Link nodded. "Okay, we'll all go fishing. An ocean run would do Dolly good."

"All?" Tempest said. "Do you mean we get to go, too?"

"If it's okay with Ariel" Stone said. Maybe the freedom of the high seas was what she needed to feel she could be frank with him about her past. Face flushed, and lips slightly parted, Ariel stared at him. Tempest bounced in her seat, as excitement gushed forth. If he was lucky, Windy would get in touch with him before the trip and he'd know whether to comfort or confrontation was his best bet. He focused on Ariel. "How about a weekend in Valdez? Dolly has plenty of space."

Her blush deepened.

"Oh, can we, sh-Mom? Please? Pretty please?"

Ariel swallowed twice, then nodded. Tempest shrieked with glee and leaped out of her chair to do a victory dance. Stone hoped Windy returned his call soon.

The sooner, the better.

Chapter 24

As they walked home, Tempest bubbled with excited anticipation over her first deep sea fishing trip. "It's going to be so much fun!" she concluded the thought with a twirl. Ariel stared at her, marveling at her ability to compartmentalize her emotions. "What's wrong with you? Aren't you excited?"

Ariel didn't want to tell her sister that the only reason she'd jumped at the chance to meet Stone's lover was because Valdez represented their best possibility of escape, so she said nothing.

Tempest barred the door with her body and glared at her. "Trust you to be the wet blanket."

"Trust you to forget that we're being followed," Ariel hissed. Tempest stared at her. "Did you ever think about the fact that Broncos can't follow planes or boats?" Tempest swallowed and shook her head. "Well, I did." But mostly, she'd thought about the fact that she didn't want to see Stone with his girlfriend. Still, this was an opportunity to escape the trap Fairbanks had become.

Tempest's eyes watered. "Are we suggesting, that we pack everything possible, because we won't be coming back?"

"Would you mind leaving Mozart?" Ariel's throat felt blocked and her own vision began to blur. Tempest stepped aside and allowed her to unlock the door. It took several tries to get the key into the lock.

A tear dribbled down her cheek. "I don't wanna think about it, but if that's what it takes t-" Her voice broke.

Both of them managed to keep the real deluge in check until they got inside, but as soon as the lock clicked, there was no stopping them. They held each other tight in the dark and cried. "I hate myself," Tempest wailed.

"No you don't. You just hate the lifestyle we've been forced into. We should have sent him to Elizabeth, long ago."

"Poor Mozart won't understand."

From the living room, Mozart squawked.

"He just said that he loved us and wants us safe." Ariel's throat constricted. "Want to go downstairs and kick the stuffing out of the bag?" Tempest nodded. After working out to the point when she could barely climb back up the stairs, Ariel went to her bedroom. Keeping the lights off, she tugged a folding chair close to the window, so she could sit down while she studied the street below. Then, she cracked the curtain. The midnight light illuminated the to-do list lying on the vinyl drop cloth, but it also allowed her to watch for the Bronco.

If Peter hadn't taught her anything else, he'd taught her not to become complacent. And regardless of his faults, Peter always investigated everything thoroughly before an attack. His preparedness to win despite any fluctuation in circumstance made him a worthy opponent because he did not get caught committing crimes and generally his felonies were labeled accidents. Anyone likely to implicate him either disappeared or was involved in another 'accident'.

To evade Peter, she had to plan their escape as thoroughly as he would an assassination.

Since he was still having his lackey follow them, and had personally attended her lecture, he obviously wasn't certain of their true identity – yet. But she knew their time was limited and prayed they could afford to wait for the weekend. She hoped that when she'd finished her lecture, then confronted the Bronco's driver and filed an official report, instead of running, she'd confused him.

Before he totally gave up, he would search their possessions and find Mozart. And no matter how well they'd built their new identity, they were caught. It was how Peter had caught them the first time. Since then, they'd kept the drapes drawn, which had probably become one of the things Peter looked for. She frowned at the parked cars and wondered it the Bronco's driver had already peeped in their windows and noticed that the thick curtains were always closed. He'd had three days between the time she'd first noticed the new vehicle until she'd confronted the man, and whatever he'd reported to Peter had been enough to get him to try a personal confrontation.

Gooseflesh swept over her.

The hand holding the curtain turned clammy, but she couldn't stop staring at the street. Couldn't stop imagining Peter was watching their townhouse, while she peaked out from her hiding place, like the trapped prey she was.

The only things she could really do between now and when they took off for Valdez were write explanatory notes to Stone, Link and Elizabeth about Mozart, then pray for the best. She picked up her sketchpad and a fine-tipped charcoal pencil. Hand unsteady, she poured her hopes, fears and dreams unto the paper, but she stopped herself from revealing her deepest feelings. As her hand hovered above the white space, she began sketching Stone's profile. She inhaled deeply, thrust her pad away and told herself to get a grip.

Make a plan.

Perhaps create a diversion, to get a head start. She frowned, trying to think of something that would trick Peter, but she couldn't even figure out how to get Mozart to the airport, so she could send him to Elizabeth.

Shoot, she wasn't even certain she and Tempest would make it to the airport alive.

Too upset to do anything else, she peeked out the curtain. And stared at the road. Time seemed to simultaneously zoom by and last forever, as she tried to think of a way out of the trap she'd planned them into. All other thoughts were thrust aside when the black Bronco slowly cruised past. Its mirrored windows hid the watcher, but such a numbing chill gripped her that she knew in her heart of hearts Peter was in the vehicle.

They needed run now, not wait.

Her heart slammed against her ribs like a trapped animal. Was this how rabbits hiding in a briar patch from fox felt? If so, she needed to control her panic and stay quiet. Her dry tough flicked over her lips and she wondered if every hour she procrastinated was a step closer to triumph over Peter or disaster.

After the Bronco disappeared, she glanced at her alarm clock. The ominous red numbers glowed 2:30. She groaned and knew it would be a long night.

And it might be her last one.

She shut the curtains and lay, fully clothed, on her bed and prayed she'd made the right choice.

Chapter 25

Stone dreamed of gulls flying through ocean spray as he taught Ariel to steer Dolly. He smiled at the way she leaned against him. Suddenly his dream was shattered by the phone. Blindly, he grabbed the receiver, heart slamming with the knowledge that it had to be an emergency for anyone to call in the middle of the night. "Hello!"

"Are you all right?"

"Windy! What in the hell are you calling for?"

There was a pause. "Sorry. I forgot to reset my watch. I'm still on Central time. I'll call b-"

"No!" The fierceness of his response surprised him. "I'm awake." His heart rate returned to normal. "Have you found anything?"

"I wish I could tell you what you want to know, but I haven't had much time to check out the Danner info."

Or she hadn't wanted to bother. "Strange. I haven't seen any airline disasters making headlines."

Windy chuckled. "That's the problem. My division finished their analysis of that Boeing crash and I got put on temporary assignment in Anchorage. Isn't that great?" His grunt must have sounded like agreement. "I'm taking the weekend off. I don't care who dies or what falls out of the sky."

"And?"

"Well, do I have to invite myself or are you going to ask?"

He chuckled. "What do you think?"

"I called to find out what you were doing this weekend. After all, I'm three quarters of the way to a visit with my favorite brother."

"I'm your only brother."

"Same difference."

"A few of us have a deep-sea trip planned this weekend. Want to meet me in Valdez?"

"You sure I won't put a cramp in your style?"

"My style is so wrinkled no one would ever notice." He smiled at his own attempt at humor. "How about it? Can you get there by Friday?" He glanced at his clock. "Er, later today?"

"Count on it."

"And can you find the time to check out the Danners by then?" She mumbled something. "They're the ones we're taking fishing and I'd really like to know what they're hiding." This was turning into a nice convenient way to nudge Windy or it could turn into a major fiasco.

There was a soft rustle of papers being shuffled. "Stone?" He grunted. "There's only one entry for Ariel and Tempest Danner and I had to backtrack to find it."

"Well?"

"Do you know of any reason why they might have had their names changed twenty-two months ago?"

"She's divorced. Maybe she took back her maiden name."

There was an ominous silence then Windy cleared her throat. "Their previous names were Joan and Nancy Harmon." Her tone spoke volumes.

"You think they're criminals."

"Between your frantic need to get this info and the fact people don't change their identities on a whim-" Her voice trailed off.

He swallowed and tried to think of a new topic. Anything so she wouldn't figure out how desperate he was to know Ariel's background. "At least their name didn't used to be Baldwyn."

"Why do you say that?" There was a frown in her voice.

"That obnoxious ass who tramped all over Dolly's deck before the oil dried."

"Ah, yes, Peter Baldwyn." Stone grunted. Her tone became guarded, "Why did he focus on you, again?"

"His kids were runaways and he was looking for them." There was an odd silence punctuated by the rustling of more papers on her end of the line. "What?"

"Was that one of the names you already gave me? It seems familiar." The frown in her voice was stronger. "The most interesting one you asked about was Mitchell Keen, who was a North Carolina State Trooper."

"Who?"

"Keen was the officer who initially bought the suburban at an FBI auction. He immediately sold it." Paper rustled. "Odd that I don't have the name of the new owner." She paused. "He recently died while performing his duty."

A chill shook him. "Are you saying the car was stolen?"

"Nothing like that." She cut off his worst fear. And he remembered Tempest making some fly-by comment about her Uncle Mitch who had died. "From what I can gather, Keen was a good cop and if he hadn't been shot, he would have died of cancer. According to the coroner's report, he was quite ill."

"Perhaps he's Tempest's uncle."

"She the kid?" He grunted in agreement. "Doubtful. He had one younger sister, Danielle, who was married to Franklin Pendleton, both deceased."

"Murdered, like Keen?"

"Franklin died in a car accident eighteen years ago. Five years ago, Danielle stepped in front of a busin London, England. Hmm, it says 'suspicion of foul play' in both files." She paused and he assumed she was reading. "Franklin was a hit and run. They never found the driver." Papers rustled in the moody silence. "I don't understand why Danielle's death was listed as possible foul play when she probably forgot which side traffic ran on ... let me log onto the system and see if there is anything more about this."

"So you think Danielle killed her husband, then years later faked her death, changed her name to Joan and now Ariel?"

Windy chuckled. "Ariel couldn't be Danielle. I mean cosmetics are good, but you couldn't hide twenty-some years with them. Particularly if you'd been hit by a bus. And even if she could, five years isn't enough time to give birth to teenager."

He's figured Windy's information would sort the facts from theory, but she was only making him more confused. "Bummer to die on vacation."

"That's an assumption."

"And that's something you never make?" He hoped his teasing tone masked the confusion he felt.

Windy snorted. There was the chime of a computer logging on then the sound of typing. "Okay. Here's the file. Hmm. That's interesting." He was going to strangle her if she didn't start reading out loud. He made an impatient sound. "Oh-ho-ho! Guess who Danielle was married to when she died and who was accused of her wrongful death, but wasn't convicted."

"Little Bo Peep."

"Nope. Peter Baldwyn."

His intestines suddenly felt watery. "You're kidding."

"Nope."

The man hadn't cared enough about others to even apologize for ruing Dolly's deck. He hadn't been concerned about anything except the oil on his own hand.

"And," Windy added, "he was arrested for pushing Danielle in front of the bus."

Windy made a sound of agreement. "He testified that he'd been trying to grab her out of harms way, but lost his grip. Darn, I wish there was a transcript of that trial here. I'll get one by the time I see you."

"I'd bet anything that jerk Baldwyn pushed her."

"Had a rough time cleaning up the deck, huh?"

Stone growled. "More like the look in the guy's eyes. Dark, darting and sinister."

Windy snickered while she typed. Abruptly, there was an odd stillness on her end of the line. "Scotland Yard has some interesting comments in Baldwyn's file."

"What is he some sort of international criminal?" He was willing to believe it.

"Let's just say that his movements coincide with certain events and that makes him appear suspicious."

"Such as?"

"I'll print it out and bring it with me. When are you heading to Valdez?"

He glanced at the clock. "We'll be at Dolly for dinner. What about you? Want me to fly over and pick you up?"

"I'll wing it, but for certain I'll be there for the fishing, tomorrow. Uh, and Stone?" He grunted. "This isn't going to be like the last time you took me out, is it?"

"What do you mean?"

"The brass. I'm giving you fair warning that I will not polish my fingernails off on that stuff, again."

"Trust me, I did it last month." By the time he put down the receiver, he was too keyed up to go back to sleep and too tired to stay alert. He got up, tugged on some sweats and went downstairs to brew a pot of coffee.

Chapter 26

"The Bronco just passed, again. That's the third time he's been by in," Tempest looked at the clock, "fourteen minutes."

"He's trying to flush us out, just like a fox does a rabbit, who is safe in the briar patch." Ariel swallowed. "There's no way we can get Mozart out of here without him seeing."

"But we can't leave him!" Tempest stared at her.

"We'll ask Link to send him to Elizabeth on Monday. We'll just have to leave out enough seed and water for the weekend." She gestured helplessly. Tempest's lower lip trembled as she got the bag of sunflower seed. Mozart rolled his eye and cocked his head as more seeds clattered into his bowl, then she went back to keep her vigil behind the curtain.

Ariel tried to swallow the thick lump in her throat. Perhaps this was best in the long run. They'd always snuck Mozart out, so Peter wouldn't realize they weren't planning to come back until their trail was cool. Cold would be better, but that seemed impossible to achieve. Still, she hated putting Link in the middle of her problems. Knowing Peter would probably pick the lock as soon as they left, was even worse. Knowing how much Peter loved to kill things, and that he might take his fury out on Mozart made it impossible to think. But she had to survive and to do that, she had to make everyone else believe things were okay.

Oblivious to his impending abandonment, Mozart preened

his feathers, preening was the first thing he had done when her real father had given him to her. She took a deep, shuddering breath, then began writing out instructions for Link. When she was done, she folded the sheet along with airfare and tucked everything in an envelope.

"There he is, again," Tempest called from the living room. "Sherry, I'm scared. What if he shoots us on the way to the airport?"

"You think he'll get close after yesterday?" Tempest's irises looked like islands in a white sea. Ariel forced her tension into hiding and smiled. "If he ran away from me, he'll run away from Link and Stone. They're pretty big and intimidating looking."

"Father always said, 'guns win over knives'. What if that guy is pissed about yesterday and just decides to shoot us? What if he shoots poor Uncle Link?"

"We'll make it." They had to.

"You can't know that."

"People who shoot others get sent to jail. Do you think one of Peter's hired thugs is willing to go to jail for shooting a stranger?"

"I hope not." Tempest didn't look convinced, and Ariel couldn't allow herself to think of the hundreds of awful things that could happen before they got to Valdez. "Sherry, are you okay?"

"Just a few cramps. I'll be fine." She gestured toward the window. "What's really sad is that the Bronco's driver doesn't even know the truth about who he's spying on or why."

"Why d'ya say that? 'Cause Father always lies?"

Ariel made a sorta gesture. "Do you think Peter is going to admit that he was arrested and put on trial for suspicion of killing his estranged wife so she couldn't testify against him?"

Tempest shook her head so hard that her hair flew in her eyes. She wiped it and tears away on the back of her hand.

Ariel started climbing the stairs two at a time. "Let's get our luggage piled by the door, then as soon as he's past, we'll run out and throw a bag or two in the back of Link's truck. That way, even if he sees us leave, he'll think we're empty handed." With luck, the lackey would focus on the Suburban and townhouse and not even see them in the back of Link's truck.

And if he thought they were inside, Mozart might be safer. At least for the weekend, which would have to be enough time for them to get far away.

Tempest ran up the stairs. "I'm gonna copy all my computer files on a CD then reformat my hard drive so all my notes are gone."

"Why? There's nothing on it, is there?"

"Father doesn't know that I only use it for homework and skype." Tempest tried to laugh. "He'll think there was information on it that I deleted and spend lots of time trying to get it back."

"Now you're thinking!"

Later, as she climbed into the backseat of Link's truck. Tempest looked out the side window, then half dropped, half threw down her teddy bear. As she ducked to retrieve it, Ariel plunged down, too and her forehead collided with Tempest's jaw with an audible thunk.

"Ouch!" Tempest yelped. She grasped her ankles and remained doubled.

"You okay?" asked Stone.

Ariel made an affirmative sound. "Just being a tad clumsy."

She silently counted off the seconds it took the Bronco to pass, then added another twenty for good measure before she inched up with the bear. She was just in time to see the Bronco make a left hand turn into a driveway.

Stone's expression was concerned. Ariel gave him what she hoped was a disarming smile, but most of her attention was on the Bronco, which was executing a three point turnaround. She switched her attention to Link. "So, how do you think your chances are of winning your contest?"

Link rolled his gaze heavenward, then shrugged and started the truck.

As the Bronco returned, Ariel sneezed and bent forward, her arm across Tempest's shoulders to keep her down. She faked four more sneezes and stayed down. By the time she found the nerve to take a second peek, they were cruising down Airport Road and the only Ford in sight was a battered green pickup truck. She heaved a sigh of relief.

Tempest straightened, her bear clasped tight against her chest as if it was a lifeline. Link glanced at them in the rearview mirror. "You two sure you want to make the trip today?" You don't look so good, he left unsaid. Stone turned to look back at them, his gaze suspicious.

"I want to go," Tempest said. She sneezed. "You clean in here with pepper or somethin'?"

The mirror reflected the fact that Link's attention was now totally centered on her. So was Stone's.

Ariel forced a smile. "Sorry if I'm not the life of the party."

"She's got cramps," Tempest said. Neither Stone nor Link wanted to know that tidbit. It amused Ariel that neither of them realized a female could get cramps from stress and she was grateful that the remainder of the ride to the airport was conducted in silence and without the sight of a black Bronco.

Once the Cessna was airborne, she leaned back, closed her eyes and dared to believe they might actually have made the first step toward safety. Though the ache in her stomach eased, she couldn't completely believe that this was more than a short reprieve. The more she relaxed, the more she was reminded of the middle of the night call Stone had gotten. While she hadn't been able to hear much through the wall, his tender tone had suggested that he was talking to his girlfriend. Ariel opened her eyes and saw Denali's peak glistening to the right side looked just as cold as the dose of reality she'd gotten when Stone said the hated name, Dolly.

Even though she knew there had never been a chance for them to have a relationship, the memory of that call still hurt. Would she feel any better after she'd left Stone O'Banyon far behind? Or would she torture herself about might-have-beens? Ariel leaned against the cold window, which felt wonderful against her feverish skin. Eventually the calming throb through the hull brought the escape of slumber.

"Look!" Tempest's excited yelp woke her. "Is that a real, honest to goodness glacier?"

Ariel blinked sleep out of her eyes and peered out the window.

"Yes," Link said. "If we have time, do you want to go see it up close? Perhaps hike on it a bit?" Tempest nodded. He turned his attention to Ariel. "There are safe sections."

Tempest grabbed her biceps. "Can I? Please? Purty pull-ease?"

"Valdez's airport is at the base of Chugach," Stone said, as if her silence was an evaluation of proximity.

"Pull-ease? I may never, ever get this opportunity, again. Just think how educational it would be."

There wouldn't be any glaciers where they were heading. Ariel wet her lips as she looked at the ancient packed ice and snow. What the heck, they deserved one last bit of pleasure; something that she could think about instead of Stone in Dolly's arms. She gave a short nod.

Tempest tried to throw her arms around her, but was held back by the seatbelt. "Oh, thank you, thank you, thank you!"

"But I get to come, too."

Tempest nodded so hard, it was a wonder she didn't sprain her neck.

Ariel leaned back in her seat and looked at Stone's hair. How had she allowed herself to fall for a man who loved another woman? After witnessing the way Peter had pursued her mother and been willing to murder to have her, she'd vowed never, ever to even look at an unavailable man. She's kept that oath, too. It had been easy since she'd had limited time. And until Fairbanks, no man had really caught and held her attention.

A tapping sound brought her attention to the present. She peeked around Stone's broad shoulder and saw him rap the face of an instrument. Both he and Link were frowning at it.

"Is some'thin wrong?" Tempest's eyes looked frightened.

"The altimeter still isn't reading right," Stone said.

"Instruments," Tempest said, with a superior grin.

Link nodded. He looked from the panel to the mountains below. "Looks like we're reading about twenty-two-thousand-feet higher than we really are." He turned to Stone. "When did you last confirm the setting?"

"Prior to take off." Stone gave him an annoyed look. "I always check."

Tempest tugged on Link's sleeve. "Will we need any instruments before we land?"

"No," Stone said.

Link patted her hand, then pointed out the window. "There's the airport, now. See it at the base of the glacier?"

"Oh, wow!" Tempest flattened her nose against the window.

Stone chuckled. "How about we all plan a picnic-hike?"

Tempest squealed with delight. Ariel hoped he didn't bring along his ladylove. She'd like one more great memory of him to hold in her heart.

Chapter 27

"Just toss your stuff in the back of my truck." Stone gestured to a Dodge Ram, which was identical to Link's truck. Tempest tossed her Mickey Mouse duffel bag in.

Ariel towed her big, wheeled suitcase to the truck, then with a groan, Link put it in the back of the truck. "Think you packed enough?"

Ariel made an 'I don't know' gesture. "I've never been fishing before."

After Stone finished securing the Cessna, he announced, "If you aren't too tired, I'd like to go to the office and let Link get his confrontation over." Link grimaced. That office manager of theirs must be a cross between Genghis Khan and the Marquis de Sade.

"Of course," Link said, "if you're tired, we can go over to Doll-"

"No," Ariel said. "I'm fine." She looked at Tempest. "We're both fine. I'd like to see your office." Anything was better than meeting Stone's girlfriend.

Link straightened his broad shoulders and got into the truck. On the trip from the airport to the old clapboard two-story building on the main street of the small town, silent tension emanated from Link and bubbling babble from Tempest. Stone's profile seemed set, as he drove through traffic while Ariel's stomach churned with acid as she looked for something that would inspire a spur of the moment escape plan.

After Stone parked the truck, Link marched to a heavily varnished wood door and opened it to reveal stairs to the second floor. He took a deep breath and stepped into the dim passage. Tempest's elbow jabbed between her ribs. "Will Uncle Link be okay?"

"He wouldn't face her otherwise," Ariel whispered back.

Stone gave them a lopsided smile as he held the door open. "Don't worry. Mavis isn't half as formidable as either she or Link think she is."

Tempest glared at him. "Uncle Link is the bravest man I've ever known. Mavis must be Mrs. Godzilla." He tried to hold back laughter, but failed. Tempest looked ready to kick him in the shins.

Ariel shoved Tempest toward the stairs. "Don't take it out on Stone. If Link needs defending, use your karate." Tempest took the stairs two at a time.

Stone doubled over laughing.

Ariel gave Stone a final disgusted look, then ran upward. As she got to the upper floor, she saw Tempest standing in an open doorway, mouth agape. Dear lord, the woman must be Amazonian to scare Tempest that much. It was silent, except for Stone's laughter. Ariel tiptoed forward and peaked around the doorframe.

Link was standing in front of a highly polished mahogany desk, his posture as petulant as if he was a child being reprimanded. A tiny white haired woman was on the opposite side of the desk, her blue eyes sparkling with triumph as she twirled something silver between her fingers.

Stone edged past her. "Afternoon, Mavis." He gave her a warm smile. Ariel's heart picked up a beat. "How've you been?"

Oblivious to Link's discomfort or perhaps pretending to ignore it, the perfect little granny seemed to focus all her attention and warmth on Stone. "Never better." A corner of her mouth twitched, as if she was holding back a smile. "That fool insurance salesman finally quit pestering me."

The news seemed to startle Stone. "Did you have to shoot him?"

Tempest's jaw dropped. Mavis' eyes twinkled. "Unfortunately, I was deprived of that pleasure." A bead of perspiration broke out on the back of Link's neck.

Revelation struck. The nefarious pair were using Link's illogical fears against him and finding entertainment in his discomfort! Ariel stepped around Stone, her hand extended. "Hello, ma'am." I believe I had the pleasure to speak with you on the phone a few weeks ago." Mavis' piercing gaze focused on her, but she didn't try to shake her hand. Ariel ignored the attitude. "I'm Ariel Danner and this is my daughter, Tempest. We live next door to Link and Stone and they were kind enough to let us tag along on this trip." Ariel smiled at the little lady as if she were the Madonna. Mavis' mask of superiority cracked a trifle and she smiled. Some of Link's tension seeped away and Mavis put down the silver thing and took her hand.

"I've heard of you." Mavis looked past her and Stone chuckled.

"Mavis," Link said, "I need to apologize to you. I was exhausted that day, and-" She waved away his words with an indifferent motion. "I should have paid better attention," he quickly concluded.

Mavis gave Link a sharp look. "I suggest you glue that redial button in place before it gets you in real trouble."

Stone laughed outright. Link looked as if a death sentence had been removed and Mavis had the expression of a cat that had dined on an entire cage full of canaries.

"Good idea," Link said. "I'll do it."

Mavis smiled as she thrust a pile of papers at him. Link's relief was palatable as he took them.

Stone put his hand on the small of her back. Ariel's vertebrae seemed to melt against his touch. "Come on into our office. We won't be long." She allowed herself to be urged forward into a large airy room dominated by two desks that matched Mavis'. He caressed her spine. Have a seat. Knees weak, she settled onto a comfortable burgundy leather wing chair. He went behind the unoccupied desk, opened the top drawer, pulled out a pair of wire-rimmed reading glasses and put them on.

Every joint melted as she noticed his lack of concern for his ego, and the need to have help reading.

"You aren't what I expected," Tempest said. Ariel looked around. Her sister still stood in front of Mavis' desk. Link sat up straight, as if torn between saving Tempest from Mavis or fleeing from what might come. Stone hid behind a sheaf of papers. Ariel tried to hide in the chair. Tempest leaned her elbows on Mavis' desk and studied her. "I thought you'd be taller."

Link scrambled to his feet. "Why don't you three go over to Dolly. I'll take care of the paperwork."

"Bu-"

"Go!" Link cut Stone off.

Obviously amused, but trying to hide it, Stone rose and offered her his hand. She took it. Though he didn't appear to hurry, Stone had Tempest in hand within a minute. Though the drive only took a few minutes, Ariel felt as if she aged a decade, as she tried to figure out how to greet Dolly. She wondered if she was getting a reprieve from being presented to his ladylove when Stone turned into the marina, which seemed odd, until she noticed that several of the boats had laundry hanging outside.

He'd had that Yachting magazine and used an advertisement as a target. Apparently he and his girlfriend shared a love for water. Landlubber that she was, Ariel had never had a chance with him. It was good that she was leaving. Good that nothing ever came of her thoughts and hidden feelings.

Stone parked between a turquoise sports car and a dark utility van. As he shut off the engine, a shriek of glee echoed over the parking lot. Ariel looked out the windshield and saw a gorgeous, long-legged woman leap over the railing of a majestic-looking sailboat and sprint toward them.

Stone tore off his seatbelt, leaped out of the truck and raced toward her.

"Who the hell is that?" Tempest asked, from the back seat.

"Probably Dolly." To look at them, a person would think they hadn't seen each other in ages. Stone picked up the dark haired woman and swung her around in a circle.

Tempest snorted. "That can't be Dolly."

If the woman wasn't the love of Stone's life, who was? With leaden legs, Ariel got out of the pickup and took a step toward the happy reunion. Though Stone put his girlfriend down, he didn't remove his hands from her. "I didn't expect you until later,"

Stone was saying as Ariel got within earshot.

"Meeting you gained importance." The woman was as dark as Stone and nearly as tall. Of course he would go for a woman as gorgeous as he was and not some nothing little wren of a woman.

With every step, Ariel felt uglier, fatter, shorter and dumber.

The brunette noticed her over Stone's shoulder. "That them?" He looked back, then grinned and nodded. Though he removed one hand from her, he kept an arm firmly around her shoulders. She gave them a big smile and held out her hand. "So, you're Stone's neighbors. I'm so glad to finally meet you." Ariel took her hand and looked at her in confusion. "How do you like Alaska so far?"

"Fine," Ariel managed to say.

"I love coming here." Did the woman have to have beautiful dimples, too? Ariel's smile felt brittle enough to break her face. The woman poked Stone in the ribs. "Well? Aren't you going to officially introduce us?"

He jerked. "Sorry. Windy, Ariel and Tempest Danner. Ariel and Tempest, my favorite sister."

Ariel blinked in confusion.

"Oh, you're the one with the FBI," Tempest said. "That's so super cool."

"Where's Link?" Windy craned her neck. "I thought you said he was coming with us.

"He'll be along."

Windy grinned and winked at Ariel. "Of course he will, if there's a fish involved." She gestured toward Stone. "He's been trying to marry the two of us off for the past ten years and-"

"I have not," Stone said. Windy laughed as she mouthed not

to believe him. "Besides, it's only been five years."

"You think I want to hook up with someone who is like a second brother?"

Stone blinked with confusion. Windy laughed, shook free of his grasp and tugged Ariel forward. "Come on, you're going to love Dolly." If it hadn't been for Windy's firm grasp, she would have thrown herself into the quay.

"Is Brit here, too?" Tempest asked. Stone and Windy shook their heads. "Oh, I kinda wondered." Her forehead furrowed. "How come you're here?"

"Weekend get away and deep sea fishing," Windy said as she pulled Ariel onto a beautiful wooden deck. "Well?" Windy asked expectantly. "How do you like her?"

Who?

"She's old," Tempest said. "And she has a whole lot more wood than any boat I've ever been on."

"She may be old, but she's very stable," Stone said.

Ariel still couldn't see what they were discussing and wondered it Dolly was keeping out of her sight out of sheer dislike. She wished she'd never allowed herself to be brought here. Wished some other memory of Stone O'Banyon would be the one she took with her.

"When I got here, I noticed she was sitting a little low in the water, so I turned her bilge pumps on. Hope that's okay."

Stone nodded. "She puts on water weight every week." He touched Ariel's elbow, with a warm caress. Even knowing his girl was somewhere watching, she felt the touch all the way to her toes. "Well? Do you like her?"

Ariel mutely nodded.

Windy cocked her head to one side and looked from her

face to her brother's and a slow smile began to form. "Well, I think I've figured out the details you didn't tell me."

Stone gave her an odd, warning look. "Later."

Windy nodded, then turned her full attention on her. Ariel felt herself shrink. "He really wants you to like Dolly. That's very telling." *Dear Lord, strike me dead.* Windy patted the boat's gleaming brass railing. "For years after that witch, Marishka, screwed up his mind, Brit and I had a bet that he'd never care about a flesh and blood woman, again. Mom will be thrilled to find out she won't have to consider that dingy a grandchild."

"Windy." Stone's tone held a warning. She laughed at him.

Ariel blinked in confusion.

Tempest looked at her as if she were from another planet, then tugged on Stone's sleeve. "Uncle Stone, isn't Dolly kinda a weird name for a boat?" He shrugged.

Comprehension nearly floored her. Dear Lord, how dense could she be?

Stone grasped her biceps, "Let me give you a tour."

Chapter 28

Later, Stone pretended to sort fishing lures, while he watched Windy try to draw Ariel and Tempest out. But the Danners were very skilled at changing the topic and avoiding Windy's innocent appearing questions. His sister had never been this interested in Marishka and he suspected she was fascinated by the deflection and what wasn't being said.

What information had she unearthed that inspired her to catch a flight to Valdez ASAP? It had to be something earth shaking for Windy to arrive hours early.

He glanced at the small brass clock bolted to the cabin wall as Link stepped into the salon. 3:12. How much longer would it be until he'd get a chance to speak to Windy and find out what she'd discovered?

Abruptly, a heavy hand clapped his shoulder, and a stabbing pain ripped through his finger. He winced. "Uncle Link!" Tempest scrambled to her feet and launched herself to Stone's port side, then she paused to ask "Are you okay?" Despite the wound only shedding a drop of blood, her expression looked panicky.

"I'm fine, it was only a nick," Stone said, as he put down the lure and applied pressure. Windy's spine straightened and for the first time since he'd noticed her smug expression while being introduced to Ariel and Tempest, she seemed uncertain about something. Stone put aside the lure box, stood up and stretched. "I'm going to the store for provisions and bait. Windy, would you like to tag along?"

"Uh-oh." Windy laughed and leaned toward Ariel. "He's got this policy that if you buy it, you cook it and if you cook it, you clean the galley."

"Are you telling me you don't want to come?" he demanded.

Windy nodded.

Tempest wrinkled her nose. "Me neither."

Link held up his hands in a 'don't look at me' pose.

Ariel shook her head.

"Fine," he said, "Just remember that you had the chance to avoid my cooking."

Windy sighed. "Fine, I'll come, but this is under protest." She looked him in the eye. "Understand?" He nodded.

Stone ushered her to his truck. As soon as both truck doors closed, he demanded, "What'd you find out?"

"What I've got so far are bits and pieces of what looks like it might be a very ugly, confusing puzzle." Her expression became tense, as she pulled an iPad out of her shoulder bag. "Where do you want me to start?"

"With Ariel and Tempest." What if that Peter person was some sort of bounty hunter? "They're not felons or anything, are they?"

"They're hard to track and that makes me very suspicious," she hedged. He made an inquiring sound. She added, "I can't think of any good reason, other than marriage, for someone to make one name change, much less four within five years."

"You've got to be kidding." But the acid in his gut and the

way the Danners avoided answering innocent questions told him she wasn't, just as surely as the sad expression on Windy's face as she shook her head.

She stared at him. "You're hung up on Ariel. That's why you're so interested in her background check. You're serious about her and afraid of getting burned, again."

"Reading a lot into this, aren't you?" He asked, hoping he sounded flippant. She held his gaze. He turned his attention back to the road. "They're my tenants and I don't want felons living next door." He gave her a hard look. "If I was interested in her, would I end up with another Marishka?"

"No, Marishka was only a manipulative bitch." Cold coils wound around his heart and he swallowed. "I'm still not certain what your new girlfriend is." Windy's brow furrowed. "I can't find a direct connection between Baldwin and the Danners, but-"

"Baldwyn? You think he's involved?"

"Perhaps."

"How?" Why did the way she kept giving him bits of information make it feel like she was skirting something?

"I've got bad vibes about Peter Baldwyn." She shivered, and she hadn't even met the guy. "You should read the file Scotland Yard has on him. Interpol's is even longer." She made a growling sound. "Our own file is more than ninety-five-thousand words long, and it's the smallest. He's been brought in for questioning on several occasions, but always has an ironclad alibi-"

"For what?"

"Murder, mostly."

Murder! Stone cleared his throat. "And you think there's a connection between him and the Danners."

"I'd bet my badge on it." Dear Lord, could things get any worse? Windy's chin hiked up a notch. "If there's a relationship there, I'll find it." Her tone indicated that she'd bet the farm there was a link. He prayed she wasn't the guy's accomplice, but he sensed there was a deep connection and it wasn't the distraught parental one Baldwyn had claimed.

At this rate, he'd have a perforated ulcer within the week. "Who has Baldwyn killed or been suspected of killing?"

She tilted her head. "Now that's the interesting part." He turned the truck left into the grocery store's parking lot. "The only one that he was indicted for was his wife."

He slammed on the brakes. Tires squealed and people gawked. "His wife!" She nodded. "Well, did he?"

She shrugged. "The charges were dropped due to lack of evidence."

After Marishka, he could certainly understand the temptation to strangle certain people. Of course, Marishka would have been more likely to disappear and make it look like she'd been murdered. Stone pulled into a parking lot and turned off the engine. If there was lack of evidence, could it mean that there wasn't a body? Would Ariel have set up her husband for a murder wrap then changed her name and taken their child? He didn't want to believe it, but their fear of discovery and evasion of simple questions made it seem like a suspiciously possible scenario.

Windy was giving him an oddly appraising look, then closed the file she had been skimming and tucked her pad in her purse. "What are you thinking about?"

"That people often marry someone who is just like their parent." She raised her eyebrow. "Like if a girl has a scumbag of a father, she'll choose a guy who is just like him."

"Are you talking about yourself? Because if you are..."

He shook his head. "Marishka was an exception.

"But in many ways, Ariel seems a lot like mom."

He shrugged and got out of the truck before he fell victim to the temptation to ask in what ways. Windy caught up as he grabbed a grocery cart. They silently headed for the produce section. As Windy chose tomatoes, she glanced at him. "Scotland Yard's file on Baldwyn nearly goes back to his diaper days." She grinned as if she could see the chill that had washed over him. "The most accepted theory is that he's either an enforcer for OPEC or that he works for another organization that wants to control OPEC's decisions."

"That seems unlikely."

"Not when you take everything into account and dismiss his iron-clad alibis." Her soft tones sounded more menacing than if she'd shouted fire at the top of her lungs.

He remembered the tracks on Dolly's deck and could see the man as a killer. Could see why a wife would fake her death and hope the law convicted her husband. If the man really did have ties with OPEC, Stone could see how his connections might have gotten him off. He grabbed a head of lettuce.

"Don't get any ideas about taking Baldwyn on and mauling him, like that poor produce, Windy hissed. "Even if no one can make anything stick to him, my instincts tell me the guy is bad news. I mean it's just too much of a coincidence how often Baldwyn is near a place when there's a suspicious accident. Take that drowning in Deadhorse-"

"Deadhorse!" Stone interrupted, as a memory fell into place. "That's where I saw him. He was following Ariel and Tempest."

Windy's frame tensed. "What day was that?"

He told her. They stared at each other in confused horror as both put bits and pieces together and realized the presumed drowning could have been an arranged murder. Stone's gut constricted as he recalled how upset Ariel and Tempest had been when they returned to the plane.

And they'd come from the river. Christ, had they killed the guy? Unlikely, since they hadn't even known they'd be landing there. Helped kill him? Equally unlikely. Seen it happen? Possibly. If they were able to identify Baldwyn because of something they'd seen, maybe he'd concocted the phony story to track them down and arrange another 'accident'.

Windy was the first to find her voice. "No wonder they act evasive and have changed their names so often." Yeah, but why was Baldwyn after them? "Though the kid seems kinda young for a murderess."

"What are you talking about?"

"Well it makes sense to me, but I'll try to explain. Baldwyn is a licensed PI and several times when he's been questioned concerning a suspicious accident, he's stated that he was tailing this or that person – usually unfaithful wives or husbands." Windy clutched his wrist. "What if the supposition is partially true and Baldwyn works for OPEC, not as their hit-man, but as someone who is trying to track the real killer?" He didn't buy that theory, but Windy barreled ahead with the idea, "What if a woman is the killer? It would have been easy for a female to get close."

"You should know," he said. "But I'd bet on Baldwyn. There's something sinister about him." He gripped her arm. "You said that there wasn't a link between him and the Danners.

What if the connection is new? What if he thinks they could have seen him push that sultan into the water and knows they have the power to testify against him?"

Windy looked at him. "They'd be in danger."

He nodded. "The question is, do they realize how much danger they could be in." She winced. Silently, they loaded up the cart with fruits and vegetables, then headed toward the bakery section.

Stone chose a loaf of pumpernickel while Windy picked crusty French rolls, then she tapped her pad and scrolled through several pages. "The names MacLennan, Keen, and Smyth-Reynolds pop up alot." He looked at her, wondering what she was talking about. "In the South, the MacLennan name equals big money and lots of power – political power. The MacLennan comes with the highest pedigree and a load of political power. There is a load of money behind the Keen name. The Smyth-Reynolds family seems to have several powerful connections."

"You mean crime-wise?|

She nodded. "The question is still why anyone would want an alias if they rightfully were a family member."

"Are you trying to say that's who they really are?"

"I'm still trying to backtrack to be certain, but it looks possible. The most direct link is to Mitchell Keen, but only due to selling the vehicle." She bit her lower lip as she studied her notes. "Do you know if Ariel has more aliases and if one of them might have been Daniels?"

Stone stared at her and wondered why his sister. "You seem determined to find the worst in Ariel."

"Someone has to protect your heart." She frowned. "Don't

tell me you think it's normal for someone to chose to drive a bullet-proof car. That's one reason why I suspect them of something sinister and am willing to give Baldwyn the benefit of doubt."

"I wish you weren't so persuasive." He wished even more that part of him didn't agree with her assessment.

"The safest thing for you to do would be distance yourself from them, both physically and emotionally."

Despite the impossibility, he nodded. "But what if she's a victim?"

"If she is, I don't think you'll be able to protect her from someone like Baldwyn."

"What aren't you telling me about him?"

"For one thing, his talents could rival one of Stephen Segal's characters."

"You mean he has the capability of being an assassin?" Windy nodded. "Then why do you seem to think it's more likely that Ariel is the killer?"

"None of the victims have died of a sniper shot between the eyes or a well-placed karate blow. The string of suspected murders all seem to be accidents and Ariel seems a lot smarter than she's letting on."

"You think she's a potential killer just because she's smart?"

"I also think she could be a lot older than you think. I had Duke fax a yearbook photo of Phyllis MacLennan-Smyth-Reynolds. Except for coloring, they're practically identical. It's a miracle what plastic surgeons and hair dye can do. And before you say another word, Ariel dyes her hair and is wearing colored contacts. So is Tempest."

"Any idiot would know Tempest dyed her hair." Windy's

expression was a mixture of sorrow and worry. "What are you going to do? Arrest them for needing glasses and liking dye?"

"On what charge?" she shot back, "Dying without a license?" She sighed and began pushing the cart toward the checkout lane. "I'm going to watch them and talk to them. See what makes them tick." She turned to him and poked him in the chest. "And I'm going to do my level best to make certain no woman hurts you, ever again."

It would be nice if another person could actually protect his feelings like that.

If Windy was correct, Ariel may have been married to Baldwyn and perhaps still was. She was at least ten years older, than he'd guessed, too. He scowled, then shrugged. The cashier, who was ringing up their order paused and looked at the produce waiting to be bagged, her expression confused. "Thinking about a business problem," he assured her.

Windy groaned. "More like monkey business."

He arched a brow. "This landlord-tenant situation has nothing to do with apes."

The cashier snickered.

"It could," Windy warned.

Stone had to think her cryptic comment through for a moment until he understood the thinly veiled warning. Had there been thugs nearby when Baldwyn tracked up his deck?

Windy silently watched him. Finally the groceries were bagged and stowed in the rear of the king cab.

As he backed out of the parking slot, a horn honked. He braked, and then realized that the warning had been for a black bronco with dark mirrored windows. "That's strange."

"What is?"

He gestured toward the Ford. "Recently, I've frequently seen a vehicle identical near our townhouses."

"Identical to it or the same one?"

A chill gripped him. "Surely you aren't suggesting that—"

Her solemn nod stopped him cold. She leaned close and whispered into his ear. "Believe me, if Scotland Yard and Interpol each have a massive file on someone, they're probably guilty of something. It's just a matter of time before the right bit of damning evidence is found. Didn't you get my meaning in the store? I think Baldwyn is dangerous and so is everyone who works for him."

"Or else he's just a PI doing his job and downright unlucky," he said, even though he didn't believe a word of it. He glanced at his sister. "Do you really think Ariel helped kill that sheik?"

"No, but if Ariel saw something, she might be in danger. There have never, and I do mean never, been any witnesses. A string of odd accidents to people, who were suspected witnesses, but no one ever was found this side of the dirt."

He cleared his throat. "What a charming thought."

She straightened and gave him a penetrating look. "If they saw something, let me take them into protective custody. If Baldwyn is half the bastard I think he is, and they're witnesses, I need them to put him where he belongs."

"From what you've told me, it's more likely they'd end up six feet under."

"I could get them in the Witness Protection Program."

"One of the things the Witness Protection Program does is change a person's name. Could that be why they've done it in the past?"

Her eyes widened. "I'll check it out."

As Stone turned onto the street, he tried to understand his feelings for Ariel.

Chapter 29

Windy leaned slightly forward in her seat as she concentrated on the reflection in the passenger-side rearview mirror. "It's been a long time since I've been to Valdez and I'd like to see what's new. Can you take the scenic route back to the boat?"

"Why? You afraid that once we get there all you'll see is the inside of Dolly's galley?" Or did she think they were being followed? He turned down a side street.

"Not exactly." She paused, as she studied the mirror, then leaned back and gave him an equally intent look. "How come you brought Link and everyone along? That's not very romantic."

"He can fish while I check out the pipes." Windy snickered. He suddenly realized how she'd taken the remark about his job. A burning sensation rose on the back of his neck. Stone hadn't felt this embarrassed since Junior High School. The hotter his neck, the harder Windy laughed. As he debated if it would be worthwhile to remind his sister what he did for a living, the Bronco slid around the corner. His hands tightened on the wheel. When traffic cleared, he turned left. Windy stopped laughing and intently watched the mirror. He forced himself to keep the pace slow so it didn't look like he was trying to lose the

Bronco, which kept veering in and out of sight in his rearview mirror, then turned right.

"Stop there." Windy pointed to a drug store. "I forgot to get something at the grocery store." She leaned close in what probably looked like an ear-nibbling moment to anyone watching. "Drop me at the door, then slowly drive to a slot at the end of the lot. I want to check the guy's license plate number."

He winked. "Get a couple boxes of Trojans, while you're getting whatever you need," he said. Windy's face flamed red, as she got out. He smiled with satisfaction, as he leisurely cruised toward the far side of the lot. After the Bronco passed her at a snail's pace, she hurried into the store.

He parked his truck, then looked around the cabin for something to do while he waited. A USA Today lying on the rear floorboards offered a way to peak at the Ford without being obvious. As he opened the paper, he recalled that he'd seen the article in a previous News-Miner about the man who had drowned the week before Baldwyn had trampled Dolly's decks. Worse, the more he thought about it, the more certain he became that the fisherman who had followed Ariel and Tempest back from their walk was Baldwyn.

What if the creep had murdered that sheik? He knew the man must have had opportunity because he'd seen him walk up from the river path behind Ariel and Tempest. What if he'd followed them back to the airfield and then taken down the Cessna's tail number? What if Baldwyn was some sort of international killer who had never been convicted because he didn't leave witnesses?

Or, what if Ariel and Tempest had done the deed and PI, Baldwyn was trying to gather enough evidence to convict?

His skin went cold. He turned the page, making note of where the Bronco parked. Baldwyn had hounded Mavis and he hadn't stopped at any of the other boats to show his photos to anyone else who was out working. Why had he been singled out unless the guy wanted to test him to see if he'd recognized him? He wet his lips, wondering if he'd passed the test, or if his hostility had made the jerk feel like he needed to be watched.

Stone hurried into the drug store. After a few minutes, he found Windy crouched behind a display of contraceptive products, tucking her cell phone into her pocket.

He hunkered down and leaned close. "Did we talk about Baldwyn at the boat or in the truck before we spotted the Bronco?"

"I think so. Why?"

"I've been gone a few days, so if he's into high tech stuff, like some PI's, he's had time to bug everything."

"But no way of knowing when you'd be back or that you'd bring the Danners." She patted his face. "I did a basic search when I got here. Dolly was clean. For all I know they're just watching, but it's always better to be safe than sorry." She held up two boxes. Then loudly asked, "What do you prefer? Ribbed or nubby?" He tipped so far backwards on his heels, he nearly fell over. Windy surged to her feet, while tossing back her mane of long dark curls and collided with a brown haired man coming around the end cap. "Men!" She looked at the stranger and said, "And you call us the indecisive sex." She marched up to the register with both boxes. Face burning, for the second time in minutes, Stone stepped around the bemused-looking man and hurried after her.

After she paid for her purchase and they left the store, he

hauled her to a desolate corner of the parking lot and pointed to the horizon as if it were interesting. "I can't believe you actually bought them." How would his prude of a little sister surprise him, next?

Windy touched his face. "The guy I bumped into is the Ford's driver and I wanted a good close look at him."

He wrapped his arm around her shoulder. "You certainly got it."

"Yeah, too bad he isn't anyone I remember from Baldwyn's file."

"That would have made it easier to figure this out." He frowned, as tried to figure out what Ariel and Tempest might have seen in Deadhorse, which would have motivated Baldwyn to track them over a thousand miles. "You mentioned that the murders always appeared like accidents on the surface. What type of accidents?"

She looked up at him and in a voice that barely carried to his own ears said, "Faulty brakes on cars that were going too fast for mountain roads. Gas leaks in ovens that resulted in exploding houses. A civilian shot between the eyes when the home owner supposedly mistook them for a burglar."

"You're kidding."

"I wish. And that was just the past eighteen months. The latest was that drowning."

"The one in Deadhorse?" She nodded. "We were there for two or three hours that day."

She stiffened. "Are you positive it was the day he died?"

He nodded. "I figured out the timeframe a few minutes ago."

"Too bad you can't place Baldwyn at the river or have a photo of him pushing Kowiss in."

"Link and I were in a meeting. Ariel and Tempest seemed upset when they returned from a walk near the river." The moment the words were out of his mouth, her expression became suspicious and he regretted telling her the facts without admitting that he and Link had chosen the itinerary. Windy didn't say anything. "Listen, it's not what you think."

She arched a brow. "What am I thinking?"

"They had nothing to do with the accident. They couldn't have because they didn't know we were stopping there to sign a contract until an hour after we were airborne, so they wouldn't have had time to find out where that sheik was, but they were both visibly upset when they met us back at the plane. Tempest looked like she'd been crying, but they explained it as allergies. I'm positive Baldwyn was the guy who followed them."

"Why were they with you to begin with?"

"Link invited them camping." Stone frowned, as he recalled what a pivotal day that had been. How Tempest had latched onto Link as if he was life personified, after the walk. How Tempest's nightmare had woken her. How Ariel had chosen to get a shotgun shortly after that fateful trip.

Did she know something? Suspect it?

He'd been confronted here in Valdez, which made sense since their office was here and corporate address was where their vehicles were titled. What if Ariel and Tempest had seen something suspicious, but not been certain of what they'd seen? What if Baldwyn was the assassin? He certainly wouldn't want to leave any witnesses but by the same token, he wouldn't want more dead bodies, which would make the authorities suspicious.

Dear Lord, what if his innocent invitation to go deep-sea

fishing was bringing them straight to the killer?

"Stone?"

"What?"

"You okay?" He gave a sharp nod. "You're shaking." He tried to breath deeply. "For what it's worth, I don't think your girlfriend is the actual killer, but I think that somehow or other she's in this thing with Baldwyn up to her ears." Windy took a deep breath, then added, "And I'm not one-hundred-percent certain she didn't put the idea in Link's ear to invite her."

"I was there."

"You spend a lot of time here." She gestured in the direction of the harbor. "Ariel is smart. She had plenty of time to work on Link and make both him and you think it was his idea to invite them along."

"To the nature preserve, yes, but how'd she know we'd need to stop in Deadhorse? I didn't even know, myself, until Mavis called."

"When?"

"Just before we left." He'd barely had time to print out the faxed contract before they left.

"You're probably right about them being innocent, but you're the only brother I have and I kinda want to keep you around." She gave him a mischievous smile. "How would you protect you, if you were me?"

"Have my sister check her files."

Windy laughed. "And after I checked them, I'd tell you to ask her about Deadhorse." She moistened her lips. "If a relationship is worth having, she'll tell you the truth. If she doesn't-" Windy made a tossing away motion. "Get her in the right mood. When you have her between the sheets and after you have her so hot she's on fire, then ask."

He stared, not believing what he was hearing. "You expect me to seduce her for information?"

"You mean you haven't."

"Not since Marishka."

"But-" Now, it was her turn to blush.

"My reputation is mostly unfounded gossip," he admitted. A breeze gusted. "Females aren't the only ones that get emotionally attached to their sexual partners."

Windy looked at him, hard, then her face softened and she hugged him. "I never realized how much she'd hurt you." She whispered, "You love Ariel, don't you? And after that witch-" She searched for the word.

He winced. Yeah, he probably loved her and after Marishka, the thought of being that vulnerable to another person, again scared him shitless.

A soft chime emanated from Windy's pocket. She plucked it out and huddled against him, so that he shielded her from view of the Bronco. "Yeah?" The short conversation became one-sided with mostly murmurs on his sister's part. He suspected the call was about Ariel and Tempest, but Windy's phone didn't broadcast the conversation. Finally, she concluded, "Keep me posted, and send a backup team here." She slipped the phone out of sight.

"According to the files, Baldwyn left Deadhorse the day before the accident." Stone shook his head. "Exactly. For the first time, we can place him in the vicinity on the exact day. It's still only circumstantial evidence, but at least it's something."

"Thanks."

"For what?"

He shrugged, then took her arm and started walking back toward his truck. "Know what?" She made an inquisitive sound. "I'm tempted to do what you suggested and if Ariel tells me she's in danger, weigh anchor and simply sail away."

Windy studied his face, as she mentally weighed the ramifications of what he'd just told her. "You're serious." He nodded. There was something about Ariel Danner that spoke to his very soul. Windy stared at him as if he'd spoken his thoughts aloud. "Will you at least come to the folk's anniversary?"

"Count on it."

Chapter 30

Ariel glanced up as Stone's truck turned into the marina's parking lot. Two seconds later, the familiar black Bronco turned in. She ducked out of sight into the cabin pressing her spine against the bulkhead. *How in Hades had it gotten here so quickly?*

Her rubbery knees knocked and she began hyperventilating.

A car door slammed, then a second one. A woman laughed. The high-pitched sound seemed as if it were a mask for tension. And it sounded like Stone's sister. What was she hiding from her brother? That fact that they were being followed? It seemed plausible the if Windy was half the FBI agent that Stone seemed to think, she should know when she was being followed.

And that would freak anyone out.

Wouldn't it?

She risked a peek. Stone and Windy appeared casual as they hauled groceries out of the truck, while the Bronco tried to appear inconspicuous as whoever was inside watched.

She took a deep breath, then another and forced herself to think logically. The Bronco had followed Linkstone's truck here, not her or Tempest. What looked like the same vehicle had cruised by her townhouse, but Link and Stone lived next door, so it could simply be her paranoia going overboard when she thought the occupants were watching her.

How much did she know about Linkstone's business?

Next to nothing.

There was every reason to believe the surveillance was aimed at them. Legs weak with relief, she slid down the wall and sat on the floor. Were Stone and Link into something they didn't want made public? Had the brown haired man been researching them instead of her? Had he only followed her and Tempest because he'd seen Link and Stone frequent their house and vice-versa?

Dolly gently rocked to one side. "Careful." Stone sounded close.

Ariel scrambled into the head and latched the door with trembling hands, then she sat down, until she felt strong enough to stand without fear of falling.

Paper rattled.

Something shut.

"He still watching?" Windy asked.

Stone made an affirmative sound. "May he bake in that black oven." Ariel gulped in a lung full of air. So, they knew. Had Stone asked Windy to be here this weekend or had she asked to join them? If it was the former, Stone must know why he was being followed. Was he using her and Tempest as some sort of cover? Would he put them in harm's way?

She shivered.

"I don't see how he could be the same person that's been casing your townhouse," Windy said. Ariel knelt next to the door and pressed her ear against the solid wood surface. "What is it by road? About 500 miles?"

"Closer to 375." There was a significant silence. Ariel blinked and focused on breathing like a rational person. "It's unlikely to be the same car, just one that looks like it."

"Which seems like a bizarre coincidence."

He grunted in agreement. "Why is it following me?"

"Some companies have been known to use intimidation to cut out the competition."

"So?"

"Have you outbid a sore looser on any contracts recently?" Windy asked.

"We subcontract with a limited number of clients. Our newest account is Haverguild. We negotiated it about two months ago." Ariel could hear a frown in his voice. "Think their previous supplier could have just gotten their notice?" Could it truly be? Had she been paranoid for nothing? Ariel didn't know whether she should weep with relief or kick herself.

"If the previous supplier is a large company, they might have black Broncos for everyone," Windy said, "Have you noticed any prior to the last week or two?"

"If they were around, they weren't obvious," he said. Ariel looked at the wooden ceiling and shook her head at how oblivious the dear man was. "I get it." Stone sounded ready to smack himself for stupidity. "You think they're trying to be obvious as an intimidation tactic." He snorted. "That's juvenile."

"But often highly effective," his sister said. Ariel nodded in agreement.

Ariel got up, washed her face, then stepped into the cabin. "Hi," she said. Stone jerked in surprise. "Link and Tempest went for a walk around the harbor." She pretended she hadn't been eavesdropping.

He frowned. "Are you feeling okay?"

"Yeah." Looking as if he didn't believe her, he brushed her

hair back then touched her forehead. She stood silently. He studied her as if she was an amoeba under a microscope. "I had an upset stomach, but I'm feeling better, now." He caressed the side of her face as he took his hand away. Tingles went from head to toe.

"Probably a mild case of seasickness. I'll get you some Dramamine, and then we'll go for a nice slow walk around the harbor. You'll feel like a new woman by the time we get back."

Windy gave him a sharp look.

Ariel took the hint and protested, "But your sister came all this way to see you."

"Go," Windy said. "Once you feel better, we'll all be happier."

Ariel sighed. If the Bronco was actually following Stone, the only immediate jeopardy was her heart breaking when she left Stone behind. Perhaps she could break their plans to him gently, as they walked. Windy offered her a glass of water with one hand, a tiny white pill with the other.

As soon as she swallowed it, Stone placed the half-full tumbler on Dolly's tiny counter, took her hand and tugged her toward the hatch. The moment her feet touched the dock, his arm went around her waist and he pulled her close, as if afraid she'd run away. What had gotten into him? Whatever it was, she liked it. And hated that whatever was developing between them would end before it actually began.

She put her arm around his waist. It felt right, except for the handgun, which was stuck in the back of his jeans. She jerked. He looked down at her. "Don't worry. I'll guard you."

Her spine stiffened. "Why do you think I need protection?"

He arched a brow. "Don't we all?" He matched his pace to

her, his eyes continually roving the area and seeming to peer into every shadow.

And she'd thought she was the fearful one. What kind of contract had he signed? One with the devil?

His hand seductively caressed her side. "Down in the Lone Star," he said, "riggers have a saying 'don't bring a knife to a gunfight'."

"And you've brought that philosophy to the new frontier." He chuckled and hugged her closer. "I like your sister."

"Me, too." He suddenly stopped walking and turned to her. "How'd you like to go to my parent's anniversary with me? It's in August?"

"You're kidding." He shook his head. "But-"

"At least think about it."

"Fine." She'd disappear from his life in the very near future, but she'd wonder what might have been for the rest of her life. How long would he remember it?

As if by unspoken agreement, they continued their walk in silence. Would he be angry when they disappeared? Worried? Ariel tore her thoughts away from him, focused on the soaring gulls and fought a consuming sense of desolation. She took a deep breath, but the scent of kelp mixed with salt and Stone O'Banyon. Her steps faltered. He pulled her close as he slowed his pace.

"Stone, I can't go to Texas with you or anywhere else." The confession burst from her, leaving relief in its wake. Yet, he looked like she'd slapped him. Ariel put her fingers over his lips, silently beseeching him to understand. "The decision has nothing to do with you and everything to do with me."

He clasped her hand, moving it from his lips. "Are you

married?"

"What? No!" Out of the corner of her eye, she could see the black Bronco. If he had problems like hers, surely he could understand part of the truth of her life. "By August, Ariel and Tempest Danner won't exist."

"Are you planning to die?" She shook her head. "Then don't make your decision now. Think about it." His tone was husky.

"Why? What's so important about it? I don't know your parents and it's not like I'm your girlfriend or something."

"That can be changed." The look he gave her made her bones melt. "I should have told you how I felt about you sooner. Instead, I kept fighting it."

Dear Lord, this had to be a dream. She shook her head. "Don't say things like that." He couldn't tell her that, now. They didn't have a future or even a real past. They each only had what might have been.

Stone gently wrapped his arms around her and hugged her close. Through a veil of tears, she saw his head edge closer. She put her hand up to fend off his kiss.

Gently, his teeth raked her finger, and then sucked it into his mouth. Fireworks of feeling rocketed through her. She yanked her hand away before the moment overpowered all reason.

He smiled as he lowered his head to claim a kiss.

Whirlwinds of passions swirled through her. Ignoring the warning from her mind, she felt her defenses slip away and her willful body mold itself to him. The reality of Stone O'Banyon wanting her as much as she wanted him was more amazing than any girlish daydream and ten times more devastating because it could never be.

He groaned and broke the kiss, then gathered her against

him and tucked her head under his chin. Her ear pressed against his pounding heart.

"Now you know how I feel," he said. Tears choked her. One broke free and slipped down her cheek. "Don't cry." He caressed her back. "I want you. I want our futures twined like the plaits of a rope."

Her tears fell like rain. "It can't be. We don't have a future. We don't even have another week."

"Why not?"

"I can't tell you." Confusion and pain converged in his expression. He let go of her and tried to step away. She clung to him. "Listen to me. This has absolutely nothing to do with you or how much I care about you. It has to do with problems in my past that just won't go away."

He went very still. Silently, he watched her. "Tell me what's wrong."

"I can't."

"Can't or won't?"

"There's too much in my past that is terrible." Unable to look him in the eye, she spoke to the front of his denim shirt.

"I'm listening."

Her tears can hotter and faster. "I'm not the person you think I am."

"Ariel, I love you." She shook her head. He nodded. "I want us to have a future. Let's both forget our pasts." The salty smell of dead fish wafted on the breeze. "I want you to meet my parents."

"I wish I could." She wiped away her tears with the back of her hand. "But -" His kiss swept all objections from her mind.

Chapter 31

Knees weak, Stone raised his head. A brown haired man walking by gave him two thumbs up. He ignored the jerk and hugged Ariel close enough to feel her thundering heart.

"I love you," he whispered.

She trembled, but didn't utter the words he longed to hear.

"Ariel, who are you?" he whispered.

She stiffened. "What do you mean?"

So she could speak, but chose not to. He closed his eyes and took a steadying breath. "Obviously you aren't Tempest's mother."

"Why do you say that?"

"Partly the age thing and partly the fact she calls you Sherry."

"What gave away my age? I though I'd easily added on ten years with the makeup and bun."

Added what? He opened his eyes and stared at her. "So who are you, other than someone she obviously cares for?"

She sighed. "Her sister." It sounded like the simple truth, but was the last thing he'd expected.

"Will you please tell me why you're playing this role game?"

For a second, he though an invisible wall had gone up, then she looked at the empty sidewalk and her expression cleared. "It's a long, horrible story." He guided her to a bench. When they sat down. she leaned against him and stared at the harbor. "Five years ago, when I was home from university for the summer, I made a promise to our mother."

He hugged her close. "What was the promise?"

"To protect Sabrina, Benji and myself from our step-father."

"The leopard hunter?" She nodded. "Sabrina is Tempest and Benji is -?"

"My older step-brother. Unfortunately, he acts like he's Peter's clone." Her mouth flattened and she struggled to swallow. "Benji worships the ground my step-father walks on. I wish-" She swallowed, again, then cleared her throat. "I can't prove it – I can't seem to prove anything. But I know that if Dad hadn't done any work for OPEC, he'd never have run across Peter and, and, and, I think that drink in Amman was the beginning of the end."

"You mean your brother is dead?"

"No, my father. I think Peter killed him because he was obsessed with my mother and wanted her for himself." She looked up at him, her face a mask of misery and running mascara.

"Obviously he succeeded, since you refer to him as your step-father."

"Mother had never handled money. It started out with Peter helping her 'deal with things'. Eventually, she got pregnant and married him. She lost that baby three days after the ceremony." Ariel rubbed her arms, which were covered with gooseflesh, as she wondered how different her present life would be, if only her mother hadn't been in such a hurry to legitimize the baby. Stone hugged her tighter. "Look, I know you're curious, but I really don't want to think about any of this. It's very painful."

"What do you want to talk about?"

"Nothing you want to hear."

She couldn't have been more wrong. "If Tempest's real name is Sabrina, what's your real name?"

"Our real names are Ariel and Tempest Danner. We had them legally changed. However, I was born Sherrill Francine Pendleton, after my father's mother and Tempest was born Sabrina Petera Baldwyn." She grimaced. "Peter named her after Ann's daughter. He's always been obsessed with her."

"Who is Ann?"

"Princess Ann is part of the royal family." She gave a slight shrug. "I shouldn't be surprised that you've never heard of her. Even dead, Diane makes the tabloids, and no one hears about Ann."

"Were you raised in England?"

"Partly. My father traveled a lot and my mother took us with him on long assignments. More of a nomad life than anything else." She looked out at a ship leaving the harbor. "Stone, I don't want to talk about my family." She shivered. "You've told me that you love me and that's very nice."

"Nice!" He let go of her. She wet her lips, but didn't look at him as she stared at the water. "That's all you have to say? Being told someone loves you is nice?"

"I wish-" She bit her lip and tears flowed down her cheeks. "I wish I didn't have to go."

"You don't."

She shook her head. "I have to keep my promise."

"The one to your mother?"

Her head made a jerky nod. "I can help you."

"You have no idea." Her voice broke. She cleared her

throat. "I think Peter killed my father. I know he pushed my mother in front of a bus, but he's worth millions and the case was thrown out for lack of evidence, even though at least a dozen people saw him do it."

"Why would he kill her if he'd wanted her so badly that he'd murder to get her? That doesn't make any sense." She wiped her face and turned to him. Zebra like streaks of mascara marred her cheeks, but the oddest thing was that one eye looked blue and there was a brown area over the white. He frowned and peered closer.

"My mother found evidence that Peter was an international assassin." She took a deep breath. "Instead of going to the authorities, she confronted him. He acted all contrite and gave her a big sob story about how he was being forced to kill these men and if he didn't kill them, the person controlling him would murder all of us."

"And your mother believed him?"

Ariel shrugged. "I'm sure she wanted to. But I knew that if he was murdering people, he was doing it because he liked killing."

"When did your mother tell you all this?"

"When I went home for summer vacation. Then, she made me give her that promise. After I did, she asked me to take Tempest to the park." Tears muffled her voice. "At the time, I figured she was being melodramatic or something." She blinked away tears. "Tempest fell into the fountain, so we went home early. They were screaming at each other when we got back, so we snuck in and I got her cleaned up." She took a shuddering breath.

"Go on. Tell me about it. You've held it inside too long."

"After Tempest was dry, they were quiet, so we decided to go back to the park." He smoothed her hair out of her face. "Instead of going straight there, we stopped for frozen yogurt. That's when Tempest spotted Mom and Peter walking hand in hand, weaving in and out of the crowds. I stood up and put my hand up to wave at them, but just then, he shoved her right in front of a bus. I watched him kill her and couldn't do a thing to stop it."

He hugged her. "You should never have had to see anything that awful."

"Peter didn't think if was awful. The only thing he thought was awful was that we told the authorities what we'd seen. Then, we testified against him, but his lawyer twisted our testimony into some sick form of dealing with our grief." Her laugh sounded bitter. "The judge dismissed the case. As I walked past him, he acted like he wanted to reconcile with us. Smiled and hugged me and while he was doing that, he told me I was next." She looked up at him. "Until I met you, every time a man touched me, I remembered that threat and flinched."

His arms tightened around her. "I'll never let anything happen to you or Tempest."

"He can pull a trigger and kill people from a kilometer away. You'd never be able to protect yourself, let alone me."

"And you think you have a chance?"

She nodded. "It's personal and he wants to see the fear in my eyes when he murders me. He once told me I might even be worth jail time."

"He told you all that in the courtroom?"

"Some then. Some more when he tracked us down the first time. If it hadn't been for Uncle Mitch..." She started sobbing.

'*Keen was a good cop and if he hadn't been shot, he would have died of cancer.*' He could almost hear Windy's voice. Dear Lord, had she watched her uncle die, too? Did she know he was in the last stages of cancer and the bullet might have saved him months of suffering? Should he tell her?

"Ariel-" The brown haired man appeared between two nearby parked cars, then sauntered toward the black Bronco. "Sail away with me."

"What?"

"The earth is mostly ocean and Dolly is available. The three of us can stay at least a mile off shore so he can't shoot any of us."

"You're serious."

He nodded.

"Why would you give up everything to help me?"

"You know why." Because I love you.

"When would we go?"

"Tomorrow morning, just like we planned. We'll start out deep sea fishing, then take Windy and Link to a harbor and let them make their way back." He ran his thumb over her chin. "What do you say?"

"Yes." It looked like the agreement scared her almost as much as the thought of facing her creep of a stepfather.

Chapter 32

Tempest stared at her wide-eyed. "You're kidding." Ariel shook her head. "Oh, wow! Just think of spending the next few years cruising the South Pacific in this great ole boat. That's just too cool."

"It'll be a lot of work and you won't get a break from home schooling."

"I don't care." Tempest ran her fingers over the polished wood. "Not even about the prom." She clutched her heart. "I'll know Father can't sneak up on us or be behind the next tree. Because there won't be any trees! How cool is that? I'll have my own room and no matter where we go, it'll be there, too." Tempest hugged herself.

Ariel wished she could hug herself, too, but nothing could match one of Stone's embraces. Never in her most optimistic moments had she believed that she could be this happy or hopeful. Warmth spread through her.

"I just wish Mozart could come Tempest looked out the porthole and sighed. "And I wish I could touch that glacier, just once. Can you believe that people can just walk up and feel something that incredibly old?"

Ariel gazed out the porthole and shook her head. "I can't imagine anything surviving as long as it has."

"Could we go see it after dinner?"

"I don't know." The thought of leaving the sanctuary of the Dolly O sent shivers over her.

Tempest fluffed her hair. "I'll ask. For certain Uncle Link'll take me." She breezed out of the cabin.

Though Ariel felt like the side trip was a terrible idea, the only solid reason she could think of was the black Bronco's continued surveillance. If Peter had been behind the wheel, he'd have acted by now. And if the watcher had a shred of evidence that they were his quarry, Peter wouldn't have given them time to plan an escape. No, those dark mirrored windows obviously hid someone who was interested in Linkstone or its owners. Perhaps that was why Stone really wanted to sail away and give observers in far away ports the impression of a family trip versus a single man on the run.

Was that all she was to him? Camouflage?

Tears stung her eyes. Even if he wanted to use them as a cover to escape something, wasn't she doing the same thing?

Ariel groped in her duffel bag. Her fingers found her sketchbook. After pulling it out, she sat on the bunk and paged through the charcoal chronicle of their life. So much black in her past. Perhaps she should try to capture the glorious white of the glacier and its enduring promise of a brighter future.

Later, while Windy and Link cleaned up the galley, Stone ushered them into his king-cab Dodge pickup. Somehow this didn't seem like the beginning of a new life, but more like a continuation of the one they started building when they moved to Alaska. Ariel hugged her ever-present backpack against her stomach, then tossed it into the rear and slid next to Stone. He smiled. Tempest, in the rear seat of the king cab, wiggled with excitement. Stone looked around the marina as if he was silently saying goodbye to a favorite place. "Looks like a fog is rolling in. That could be good and it could be bad."

"How come?" Tempest asked.

As he backed out of the parking slot, a thin wisp of mist seemed to give the truck a gentle lingering caress. "When it comes in at this time of night, it stays. That'll make it trickier to get out of the harbor in the morning, but it'll also make it easier to get out without anyone noticing."

Tempest squinted at Stone, then turned her attention to her in silent question of how much he knew. When Ariel shook her head. Tempest's mouth flattened.

Stone glanced at the rearview mirror and his jaw tensed. Ariel looked back. The Bronco was being blatantly obvious about following them. Stone turned north. Tempest giggled and pointed at the sign stating Meals Avenue. "Who named the streets in this town?"

He shrugged and made a left, heading toward the airport. After he passed the place where the Cessna was tied down, the road narrowed and the terrain became isolated. Stone kept his attention more on his rearview mirror than conversation. "Idiot drives like he thinks he's on a race course."

Only one person drove like that. A chill paralyzed her from head to toe. The black broncos were not following Stone; they were the target. The idea that they were following Stone had just been wishful thinking and it was about to get them killed.

"Go back!" Tempest yelped. She hunkered down in the back seat, but kept sneaking peeks at the Bronco. "I don't wanna see the glacier." Stone gave Tempest's reflection in the rearview mirror an odd look. "Can we go back to town? Pull-ease?"

"Why?" he asked.

"Because we've got to get away from that car." Ariel enunciated every word, knowing each syllable could be her last.

Tempest grabbed her hand in a white knuckled grip a moment before they were catapulted forward against their shoulder harnesses. The sound of crashing metal resonated in the cab.

"What the!" Stone looked back into his mirror. She didn't need to turn around to know the Bronco had crashed into them and would do it again.

"How'd Father find us?" Tempest flattened herself against he seat and shook like a leaf in a blizzard.

The Ford hit the Dodge a second time. Stone's muttered curse was an apt description their situation. He slammed on the brakes.

"Don't stop," Tempest screamed.

"He'll kill us all," Ariel said. "Just stop long enough to let me out, then escape with Tempest."

"No," Stone and Tempest shouted in unison.

The third impact sent the Dodge hurtling into the ditch. For a moment, the front end hung like a drunken seesaw with engine racing, then it slowly tipped forward. Stone rammed the transmission into park and turned off the engine.

In the quiet, her heart thudded like a jackhammer.

Tempest sobbed. "It's all my f-f-f-fault."

"Hush," Ariel hissed at her sister, while she tried to get Stone, who obviously still didn't understand their deadly situation enough to flatten himself. It was like trying to move a mountain. "Get down," she shrieked. When he still didn't immediately comply, she threw all her weight against his arm and yanked him down. "I warned you about his love of long shots."

"You told him?" Tempest said.

"We're sitting ducks here," Stone said. "On the count of three, I'll open the back door, then we'll slip out the front and use the ditch as cover." His handgun was in his hand, but he looked like an under-armed match for Peter. "Ready?"

Tempest's face was white, as she nodded.

"One."

Behind them, the Bronco's motor revved, as it pushed the Dodge forward, into the ditch. Stone's side scraped against rock with a mind-numbing yowl. The cab's sickening angle increased.

"Two."

Tempest put her hand on the door handle.

"Three!"

Stone dove into the back seat then hurled the rear passenger door open. A thunderclap of bullets ripped the metal. The window burst into a shower of glass shards and the smell of cordite increased.

Tempest slammed open the front door and dove headfirst into the ditch. Ariel landed across her legs, her face hitting frigid water. She gasped, inhaled water and gagged and Tempest wriggled out from under her.

More shots, but spaced, as if Peter was aiming instead of reacting.

Something heavy landed on top of her, forcing her deeper into the mire.

Large hands gripped her waist and yanked her upright. "You okay?" Stone whispered into her ear.

Afraid to open her mouth and taste the fetid water, she nodded.

"Keep your head down and move down this trench toward the airport," Stone hissed. "If we get separated, meet me at the hangar near the plane. Got it?" Tempest stared at him, white eyed. "Move." The gun boomed, sending a spray of muck flying mere inches from Stone's head. Tempest tore down the ditch as if the hounds of hell were after her.

Stone peered under the Dodge.

"Come with us. Please," Ariel begged.

"In a minute." He pointed the handgun, which appeared in his hand in the narrow opening between the asphalt and truck frame then squeezed off a shot. With a loud hiss, the Bronco's tire blew. Metal howled, as its grill slid off the Dodge's bumper. "Hurry. Leave." He lined up aimed at the other rear tire and fired. The tire popped. "I'll be right behind you."

She grabbed her backpack, then slid back into the freezing, murky water. Though the prickles of frigid pain, only came as high as her ankles, she bit the inside of her mouth against a welling scream of panic.

Something big splashed into the water behind her. Praying it was Stone, not Peter, she sprinted downhill, glacial runoff splashing waist high.

Four more shots boomed, but she didn't sense any slugs landing close.

She tried to peer ahead to see Tempest, but the fog was too thick to see any farther than the next step. Dear Lord, please guide her to the rendezvous.

The report of Stone's gun ripped through the fog. It sounded close. Almost immediately, Peter's gun boomed. There was a grunt of pain and something heavy hit the water, sending a shower if freezing daggers over her back.

Ariel turned on her heel, tripped and fell to her knees, then frantically felt for Stone. He was lying face down in the icy trench. She rolled him onto his back and felt for a pulse with numb, shaking fingers. The gun dropped from his grasp. She jammed it into the waistband of her soggy jeans and, again, tried to find his heartbeat.

Something grabbed her hair and yanked her upright. With a triumphant laugh, Peter shook the fist clutching her hair. It felt like she was being scalped alive. His face twisted into an evil smile as he leaned toward her. "Thought you'd beat me again, did you, you fucking bitch?"

She stared at a long black something, which trailed from his mouth.

He yanked her up the bank to the road. Her sneakers squished with each step, her sodden book bag lay like an empty hope against her spine. He grunted with satisfaction and hauled her back toward the car. "I got her," Peter said, triumph suffusing his tone. "Where are you, Ben?" The fog swirled thick around them, making it seem like they were the only two inhabitants of a nightmare.

"You didn't have to kill Stone."

His laugh had a maniacal sound. "Don't worry, I'll take my time with you and 'Brina." He yanked her hair so hard she yelped. "Before you die, you'll beg for death and regret every time you've gloated over getting away."

Tempest stumbled out of the haze in front of them and fell to her knees gagging. A second later, Benji appeared behind her. Ariel lunged to help her, but was hauled up so quickly, her neck felt like it snapped. Pain swept from her head to her toes. A belt wrapped tight around Tempest's throat, the other end was gripped in Benji's hand, as if he was dealing with a rabid dog. The expression on his face was a perfect match for Peter's.

Ariel gave Benji a pleading look. "Why are you helping him?" But she knew. Had known for years. Benji adored Peter and had always wanted to be like him.

She saw Peter's fist a second before it hit her ear. Then she was falling. Pain radiated through her as her face impacted the road. The next moment, everything went black.

Every cell ached when her hearing returned. It took a careful breath to realize that the hot ooze in her eyes was blood and that she was lying on the road. Tentatively, she moved her fingers. Pinpricks for pain radiated up her arms, but she was free of Peter. Somewhere in the cold, clinging shroud, Tempest was softly sobbing. Peter's laugh sounded close.

She opened her eyes and blinked into the darkness. There was a dull thud to her right. Tempest screamed. A 'now or never calm determination' bolstered her to move past her dizziness and pain. Ariel rose an inch and turned toward the sound. Something hard pressed against her belly.

She froze.

Stone's gun. Did it have any more bullets? Painfully, she pulled the weapon from her sodden jeans and gripped it as Stone had done. She awkwardly planted her palms on the still-warm road and heaved her body upward. It felt as if every muscle in her body had been kicked and battered while she was unconscious. Knowing Peter, they probably had.

Fearing she would fall over if she stood, she crawled up the steep fog-shrouded road, feeling along the uneven edge, so she stayed straight. A light flared, then a flame appeared to move magically through the gloom. Like a ghoul, Peter's face appeared as he leaned down, but he wasn't looking at her, his attention was on Tempest. He grabbed a fist full of her hair and pulled her up as if she was a doll. The more she screamed, the more he smiled.

"You cold?" Peter asked, his voice filled with false concern. Tempest whimpered. While holding her head up, Peter moved the lighter under her chin. "Here, let me warm you."

"No!" Ariel surged the rest of the way to her feet, raised the gun and pulled the trigger. Peter stumbled backward and Tempest dropped. She fired again and again and again toward the last spot where she'd seen Peter.

She kept pulling the trigger long after the only sound was a click.

"Sherry, it's empty," Tempest said.

"Are you crazy?" Benji shouted from the murk.

"No. You are." Ariel hurled the gun at the source of the voice and heard the gratifying thud of metal on flesh. Pain forgotten, she moved into defense stance, prepared to die in hand-to-hand combat, if that's what it took.

Something cold and trembling grabbed her leg. She aimed a killing blow, only to have it deflected. "It's me," Tempest gasped.

"Dad," Benji said. A groan answered him. "Can you stand up?" There was shuffling in the gloom.

Ariel managed to stand, then she grabbed Tempest's hand and pulled her up. As quietly as possible, they half-carried each other to the other side of the road, once there, they melted into the blackest shadow they could find.

"Damn, Dad, how many times did she shoot you?"

"Hell if I know, but she didn't hit anything serious." Tears filled her eyes and emotions warred within her, as she tried to decide if she was glad she hadn't killed him. Or not.

"Lean on me. I'll get you to the hospital."

"I've had worse. Where are your bitch sisters? I need to finish what they started."

"But-"

"I will not go to the hospital and leave a paper trail. Those kill you. Little 22 poppers don't."

"But-"

"Shut up and bring them to me."

There was a lot of shuffling in the murk. "You can hardly stand." Ben said.

"Hell, I know that. The fucking bitch got lucky and lodged a fucking slug in my damned thigh."

May the bastard limp for the rest of his miserable life.

"I'm taking you to the car."

"No! Find the bitches!"

"I can't in this soup. I'm taking you back to the motel, patching you up, then, once this mess burns off, I'll come back."

Peter made a sound of protest.

"Where they gonna go? They're trapped. And the longer they wait, the more scared they'll be."

Peter grunted in agreement. Shortly afterward, Ariel heard the sound of feet shuffling through the cloying cloak that protected them.

Tempest's quivering hand found hers. Silently, they listened to Peter's angry progress. When the car door opened, the fog glowed luminous. As soon as Benji managed to turn the car around, the headlights would find them.

Ariel tugged Tempest back into the cold, wet ditch, felt

around, then crawled up the other side. Thorns tore at her face and dug into the palms of her hand. A motor revved, but the sound seemed different. Shriller. Had he broken something when he rammed the truck? She hoped so.

Tiny sounds of crying came from Tempest. "Hurry," Ariel whispered. Half standing, she barreled into a barely seen thicket, each step a sodden squish of misery. Each movement brought daggers of pain.

A squeal of tires preceded the cry of tearing metal. Ariel stopped moving and dropped. The only thing she could see was Tempest's wild hair. She pulled her sister to her, covering her body with her own, expecting to be fanned by headlights.

They never came.

Something large moved down the road. Tempest silently trembled.

They crouched in the briars long after the car was past. Finally, Tempest stopped shaking, by then, Ariel was too numb to feel anything. Ariel bent forward until her lips grazed Tempest's ear. "It could be a trick."

There was a tiny gasp, then silence as if she were biting her lip. Ariel counted to one thousand, then started to count to two thousand. At 1,793, headlights began moving slowly through the fog, the car making short, choppy zigzags as if someone was looking for them on the sides of the road. When Stone's pickup was illuminated, the vehicle stopped, it's engine's high-pitched whine making Ariel grit her teeth against a scream, which would doom them both. After what felt like an eternity, the car continued downhill in the same slow crisscross pattern.

Tempest quivered with relief, when the lights disappeared around a curve and Ariel rolled off her. "It's all my fault."

"No, it's not," Ariel whispered back.

"Yes, it is." She sat up, her face streaked with dirt and what smelled coppery like blood. She pulled a leaf from her hair, then crumpled it in her fist. "I was the one who wanted to touch old ice."

"Shhhh," Ariel breathed. "One of them could still be out here, just waiting for us to make another mistake." They sat silent and still as the heavy mist. Waiting. Listening.

Finally, another car moved slowly up hill. Or was it the same car, coming back for whoever had stayed behind? It was impossible to tell in the cloying murk. Hazard lights went on, making the fog pulse with recrimination. Car doors slammed. "There's a trail of blood," a woman's excited, high-pitched voice shrieked.

Tempest moved toward the light. Ariel grabbed her shoulder. "It could be a trick." She stiffened, then nodded and became still as the breathless air. When they heard people splashing in the thin water, Ariel touched Tempest's arm, then silently as possible, they worked their way through to the far side of the thicket and into a mat of cold, soggy grass. The frosty blades felt like a blessed relief. Exhausted, Ariel lay on the frigid ground. Tempest sat next to her and quietly cried.

Ariel wished she dared release her choking tears, too, but she knew if she started, she'd never stop.

In the distance, something big boomed. Unless they'd gotten turned around in the fog, the sound had come from the ocean. The marina! Her mouth went dry and she knew that in a fit of anger, Peter and Benji must have blown up the Dolly O with all aboard in his fury over losing them, at least temporarily, again.

She should have left as soon as they landed. It would have been better for everyone. And Stone would still be alive.

Ariel knew she'd relive this nightmare over and over and over for the rest of her life.

Chapter 33

Agony hammered at every joint and mosquitoes buzzed around her like a hoard of buzzards. One side on her face felt hot; the other was numb. Something shook her aching shoulder, grinding thorns and rocks into her back. She tried to open her eyes, but the lids seemed glued shut.

"Sherry." Tempest's whisper sounded frantic. "Wake up." The dizzying shaking got worse.

"Stop it," Ariel groaned. The agitation ceased but the throbbing pain stayed. It felt as if she'd been run over by a steamroller.

Or been kicked all over by Peter. She considered herself lucky to be alive.

"I can sneak into town and get you a doctor."

Ariel moved her head from to the side, but it hurt too much to do more. Stone was dead. A sob wracked her body.

"You need a doctor!" Tempest sounded near to panic.

Experimentally, she ran the tip of her tongue over her lips; the taste of blood mingled with tar and mud. "Peter and Benji are looking for us. You'll get caught if you go for help." She shivered.

"Oh, Sherry, I'm so, so, so sorry. I should never have asked to touch that glacier."

"It's my fault."

Tempest burst into sobs. "No it isn't."

"I told myself the Bronco wasn't a problem."

"You need a doctor. You're all sorts of colors."

"They could give me meds, but not do anything else. These injuries need time to heal."

"You sure?"

"Yes," she lied.

Tempest chewed her lower lip. "They took Stone away in an ambulance. I think I saw a sheet over him. Is real life like movies?" Hysteria filled her whispered words.

"Not always." But too much so in their case. She forced as eye open. The deserted road was barely visible through the thicket of wild roses and lingering wisps of fog. As the sun burned the mist away, Benji would be back, determined to finish what he'd begun – take them to Peter.

"A wrecker took the truck. At least I think it was a wrecker. They pulled it onto a truck that bent down in the back and when they pulled it up, sparks flew all over." Tempest began crying. "I'm scared and I still think you need a hospital."

Every nerve protested as Ariel raised her arms and hugged Tempest tight. Her sister threw herself against her chest and quietly bawled. Ariel closed her eyes against the briar patch of her existence, but then there was only darkness.

When Tempest's sobs reduced themselves to dry heaves, she patted her back. "We can't stay here."

They should have left as soon as they could see. Not that she could see that well through bloodshot eyes and swollen lids.

Face bloated with misery, and hair crusted against her head with mud, Tempest inched back and looked down at the barely visible road. "He'll start looking for us here. Won't he?"

Ariel was surprised that bloodhounds weren't already howling all over the area. They needed to get far away from this area without leaving a trail. "Help me stand up."

Horror crossed Tempest's face. "I'm afraid to touch you. Father kicked you and kicked you and punched you and-"

"I get the idea, but death is worse." She grimaced as Tempest pulled her upright.

"You got it!" Relief lit Tempest's face. "I thought it was still in the truck. So we do have a chance!"

Ariel forced her fingers upward and felt to familiar security of her backpack's strap. Her other hand gingerly touched her waste. Despite torn flesh on her fingertips, she recognized the stitching of her money belt. So, they did have the basic minimum to survive and build another new identity.

If she could survive long enough to get somewhere safe.

Tempest shivered. "This reminds me of when Uncle Mitch helped us." Ariel nodded. "I still have nightmares about the way those dogs chased us."

"Lucky for us they raise sled dogs around here, not blood hounds."

Tears welled in Tempest's eyes. "I'm going to miss the Greeks so much and poor Mozart! You've had him since he was practically an egg!"

Heat burned her tortured eyes and the scenes blurred but she forced herself to put one foot forward, then another. "At least there aren't any bloodhounds." Step by painful step she inched away from the road.

"Where are we gonna go?"

She swallowed the suffocating lump in her throat. "For now, we try to circle the glacier and get to a road." Tempest groaned.

"Then we somehow get a ride to Texas and go back to our original plan." Ariel pointed a shaky finger toward a gap in the ice mass. "We'll see if we can work around to the other side of it there."

"Letting him kill us would be easier."

True. Living with the guilt of suspecting she had caused Uncle Mitch's death and now, knowing for certain she was responsible for Stone's death's seemed worse than the beating she'd taken. When they came upon a downed tree, she sat down. Through the underbrush, she could still see the raw wounds in the bank where Stone's truck had been. They were still too close. Way too close.

Painfully, she opened her backpack and got out two power bars. They chewed in silence, then Ariel squared her acing shoulders. "Nostros vivirmos, Senorita Lopez." With that, she took her first step toward the low part of the glacier. Over the next seventeen days, *'we will live'* became her mantra and her dirge.

~0~

Tempest's face was smeared with purple juice when she returned to the riverbank. She held out a stained hand, piled high with the fat fruit that they'd practically existed on since they'd found the hovel of a shack and taken refuge inside. "Here."

Ariel's stomach flinched at the sight of the blueberries. She shook her head. "I'm not hungry."

"But you gotta eat!" Her hand shook. "Sherry, what am I gonna do if you get sick? I need you."

Stomach revolting, Ariel took a berry and swallowed it whole. Tempest gave her a lopsided smile. Thankfully, the berry stayed down and the turmoil in her stomach subsided a bit. She took another.

Tempest sat down next to her and stared at the glacial melt that formed an icy river. "We've gotta get somewhere to get real food."

Ariel nodded. They'd eaten their last power bar three days before and had been on starvation rations for two weeks before that. Her money belt was cinched tighter than she'd thought her waist could get and if they didn't eat soon, Peter wouldn't have the satisfaction of killing them. "Any ideas?"

Tempest gave her a quizzical look. "Maybe."

"Well, go on. Anything has to be better than the choices I've made, which only seem to be benefiting the mosquitoes."

"I found a wrecked plane and I think we could make the wings into a raft. Float down the river and we'd have to end up somewhere that's better than this."

"VFR - I follow wrecks," Ariel whispered. Tempest blinked hard. Ariel cleared her throat and got up. "Show me the plane."

"You look better greenish yellow than you did purple."

She stared at Tempest, who looked like something too filthy for a vulture to claim and wondered how bad she must have looked.

Two days later, their makeshift raft floated under the pipeline and for the first time since Stone died, she realized they might survive the ordeal, which had begun as the simple pursuit of justice.

Tempest cocked her head to one side. "Do you hear that?" She pointed downstream. "It sounds like a big truck motor. She shaded her eyes, then excitedly pointed. "It is! I see a semi!"

They dug the struts into the water, using them as clumsy

paddles to beach the rusty wing into the muddy bank.

A half hour later, they peered through the undergrowth at the Tonsina Lodge. Tempest chewed her lower lip as she studied the half full parking lot. "I don't see a black Bronco."

"I doubt if he'd still be driving it after using it as a battering ram." More likely that Peter had made it into a mobile bomb and used it to blow up the Dolly O. Tears choked her.

"So what's our story going to be?" Tempest asked.

Good question. Spiked black hair with blond roots showed through the mud. If their descriptions had gone out, it would certainly have been mentioned. The brown contacts were long gone; that could be good or bad. Ariel scratched at a mosquito bite. "How about if I go in and register. Claim I had a falling out with my old man and we literally had a mud fight. That I need a room for the night. You sneak in so we won't be seen together."

Tempest stared at her, then slowly nodded. "But I got dibs on the first shower." Ariel nodded in agreement.

Later, as she wiped steam from the mirror, she stared into eyes that reminded her of one of Peter's stuffed animals. Hurriedly, she looked away from her reflection. She tore off the filthy clothes she'd spent nearly three weeks in. As she wadded up her shirt to throw it away, she saw the rust-brown stains across her heart. Blood. She hadn't been cut there. It had to be Stone's. Her eyes closed as she remembered hugging him that one last and, oh so final, time.

It felt like her heart was being ripped from her chest. Why did her last memory of those she loved seem to end in death? Worse, she knew her lack of caution had been what cost him his life. Quickly, she wadded up all her clothes, stuffed them into the trashcan and got into the shower. Though the puny spray managed to wash away the grime, nothing could sluice off the guilt.

She dressed in the clothes she'd found in the dumpster, then went out to purchase the basic things they would need and more clothes for Tempest.

Chapter 34

"Get with it Lopez," the cook hissed, as he thrust a steaming order of shit-on-a-shingle at her. "Your stations are backing up." Ariel flinched and grabbed the gravy-covered toast. "Don't just stand around looking dazed, serve your damned customers," he hissed.

She pasted on a smile to hide her nausea and served the vile looking stuff with a flourish. Then, she grabbed the coffeepot and began refilling cups. After the customers seated at the counter were served, she moved to the tables, which seemed to attract a more intellectual caliber of patron, at least their snippets of conversation were of a higher caliber, though their tips tended toward stingy and most of the men paid more attention to their newspapers than trying to flirt with her.

At least the morning breakfast rush wasn't as bad as lunch, when the blue-collar types dominated the café and seemed to try to outdo each other embarrassing her. She wished she knew if all the unwanted attention was due to the simple fact that she was female or if they figured they could cop feels and pinch because of her Mexican disguise.

One more month of preparation and language emersion and they'd be ready to cross the border. One more month of upset stomachs and nightmares and she'd have a full-fledged ulcer.

She bent over the table occupied by three well-dresses

middle-aged women. The trio looked like they were trying to look like triplets, with their battered briefcases, subdued professional suits and spinsterish buns. The chubbiest one smiled a thank you at her as she added three packets of sugar to her coffee, then she turned back to the woman across the table from her. "Are you going to Jennie and Mick's this weekend?"

The woman indicated that she didn't want any more coffee. "Are they still planning the party?" The plump one nodded. "Oh! Well, I guess I am." Ariel poured coffee into the third woman's cup. "I'm surprised," she said. "After everything she went through with her poor son, I thought they'd cancel."

The overweight one shook her head.

"Poor, poor Jen."

Ariel smiled at them. "Can I get you ladies anything else?"

"Just the bill," the second one said.

"Poor Jen?" The third scoffed. "More like poor Stonehenge. He was the one that got shot!"

Ariel dropped the pot. Coffee and glass exploded across the floor in a searing arch.

"Oh!" the plump one yelped.

"I-I-I'm so s-s-sorry." Ariel hunkered down and began picking up shards of glass with trembling fingers.

"Lopez!" A mop slatted into the mess. She grabbed it, grateful for something to hold onto. "Sorry, ladies," her boss said. "Good help is hard to find. Breakfast is on the house and bring me your dry-cleaning bills."

As she struggled to her feet, she saw coffee splattered across her white apron. It looked just like Stone's blood. The tears that she'd managed to hold off for weeks broke free.

"There, there, dear." A motherly hand patted her arm. "It was only coffee."

"Dammit, Lopez, clean up your mess." The cook's face looked bloated and red through her tears. Ariel thrust the mop at him, ripped off her apron and threw it into the mess, then sprinted out the door. "Damn you, you freaking 'can, get back here!" She ran the entire seven blocks to the seedy motel that asked no questions and turned a blind eye to the activities and legal status of its patrons. Her hand shook as she inserted the key in the lock. When she finally got it right, the chain lock stopped her. "Sabrina, let me in."

"Sherry, what's wrong?"

Ariel threw herself across her bed and bawled. After her pillow was saturated and she felt like a hollow shell, she realized Tempest was sitting next to her, patiently stroking her back.

"What's so terrible?"

Every bit of common sense told her that since Tempest was finally getting over her nightmares, she shouldn't burden her with her own. But she needed to talk to someone and her sister was the only person available. She swallowed. "I got fired today."

Tempest's expression was incredulous. "We watch Peter murder Mama and you don't even blink, but you cry your guts out over being fired from that crappy job?" She folded her arms across her stomach and shook her head. "Tell me what really happened."

Ariel rolled onto her side and took Tempest's hand. "I- This- They-" Words failed her. Tempest stared at her as if she'd sprouted a second head. Ariel closed her eyes against the ridicule and the shabby motel room with its cheap vibrating bed.

"Did you know that Stone was raised near here?"

Tempest's eyes widened. "He was?"

"Today, in the café, I overhead some women talking about his parent's anniversary."

"How do you know it was his parents?"

Ariel looked at Tempest. "How many women name their sons Stonehenge?"

Tempest frowned. "It could be common around here."

Ariel shook her head. "It's his parents. I know it. He asked me to go to their anniversary party with him."

Her sister silently studied her. "And what'd you tell him?" Ariel bit her lip and raised her brow. "You said yes! Oh, Sherry, that means you really loved him! Oh, I'm so sorry, so very sorry. I should have realized how upset you were. The way you've been losing weight and looking so sick. This is so much worse than when Uncle Mitch died." Tempest's words tumbled out in a torrent. "I mean, I loved him and all, but he was a cop, and he was trained for dealing with someone like Father. Poor Uncle Stone never had a chance." She burst into tears. "It's all my fault. Everything is always my fault."

"No." Ariel hugged her.

Tempest sobbed against her shoulder. "But it is. If I'd listened to you, I wouldn't have gotten wet and if I hadn't been so upset, we wouldn't have stopped for a snack and seen Mama get killed and Father wouldn't need to kill us, so Stone and Uncle Mitch would still be alive and-"

"I would have never met Stone O'Banyon…" A lump of tears made it impossible to finish the statement. Tempest bawled harder. Ariel clasped her sister tighter. After several attempts, she managed to say, "It's better to have loved and lost than never to have loved at all." She wished she could believe the platitude. Wished the loss didn't hurt so badly. Wished she'd trusted her instinct. "I'm as much at fault as you are. More-so, because I saw the danger and didn't react. Didn't want to, because I wanted the hope I saw with Stone." More tears washed down her cheeks. "Neither of us is the real guilty one. It's Peter. If he wasn't so vindictive, most of the terrible things in our life would never have happened." She gave a decisive nod. "He's the one to blame."

Her sister stared at her. "Who will he kill next?"

Ariel didn't know what to say. "Maybe he won't find us this time." Tempest snorted. Ariel sighed.

"I think he's killed Grandma."

"Why do you say that?"

Tempest wouldn't look her in the eye. "I tried to phone her. Just for a minute to find out if she'd got Mozart."

"Oh, no," Ariel wailed. "You promised."

"I know," Tempest yowled, "but I had to know."

"And?"

"The secretary said she was gone."

Ariel blinked rapidly. "That doesn't mean she's dead." Tempest hopelessly shook her head. "Well, it doesn't!"

"Must you always try to be so optimistic? Nothing is ever going to turn out right for us."

"Don't say that."

"Can't take the truth, can you?" Tempest hopped off the bed and pushed her brown fingers through her wavy black hair. "Face it, Sis, we're never going to get away from Father no matter what we do. How many hours did I spend learning self-defense? Hundreds? Thousands? Yet what good did it do me when Benji grabbed me?" Her bare toes kicked a brownish stain on the drab gray carpet. "Nothing. No matter how many moves I made, I couldn't do a darned thing to save myself, or you or Stone."

Ariel's eyes were too dry to cry. Instead she stared at the sickly yellow light coming from the closed drapes.

Tempest threw herself onto the mustard-colored chair. The fake leather squawked in protest. "Instead of running and running and running, and everyone around us getting killed, maybe we need to just go back and give ourselves up." She brought her feet up, wrapped her arms around her knees and buried her face in her lap. Her sobs wrenched at Ariel's heart.

Slowly, she got up and moved to her sister. As she stroked Tempest's back, she realized facing her worst fear would be better than living the paranoid life, which they now had. "You're right."

Tempest shuddered and looked up at her.

Ariel nodded. "Death might be better." She looked around the cheap room. "If you're serious about this, instead of Mexico, we'll go home."

Tempest indicated agreement. "Can we do one thing before we leave here?"

"What?"

"Go visit Uncle Stone's parents. I'd like to apologize."

"Oh, Sabrina —"

"I need to do this. If it wasn't for me—" Her eyes welled with tears and she bit back a sob. She didn't have to list all the people who she thought had died in her place.

Ariel hugged her close, the chair's arm dug into her stomach. She closed her eyes and prayed for guidance, but the only thing that came to her was Tempest's plea to visit Stone's parents. "If that's what you need to do, we'll do it." Decision made and fate accepted, it was easier to breathe.

Chapter 35

Tempest stared out the taxi window at what seemed like miles of parallel white planks that bordered the wide paved drive beyond the O'Banyon sign. She leaned close. "Uncle Stone said he grew up on a farm. This isn't a farm." She shivered. "His dad must be as rich and powerful as Father."

"Want to forget this and go back?"

Tempest nodded. "But I have to do it. If I don't, it'll be worse."

Ariel studied Tempest. "You're awfully smart for someone your age."

She gave her a tremulous smile. "Walk me to the door?"

"Count on it."

The cab stopped in front of a huge white-columned home that looked more like a stage set for a rich land baron movie or a swank bed and breakfast, than a home. A chill swept through Ariel at the thought of having yet another wealthy man seeking revenge.

Stone's father would just have to stand in line.

The driver turned around, hand out for his fee. "We'll only be staying a few minutes," Ariel said. She plucked a one-hundred-dollar bill from her pocket and tore it in two. As she gave him half, she added, "Wait for us, then take us to the airport and you get the other half."

He scrutinized the bill. "Fifteen minutes."

A lifetime when faced with a wronged parent. They'd probably be sprinting back to the cab two minutes after Tempest started the speech she'd rehearsed until she complained her throat was sore. She looked, again, at the massive house. Or it could take his parents an hour just to get to the door. "Half hour." Before he could barter for more money, she hopped out of the cab.

Fingers twined with Tempest's, she climbed the steps onto the shadowed front porch and approached the door, which looked at least ten feet tall. Hand trembling, she grasped the heavy brass ring on the bull's head knocker and let it fall. The clang reminded her of the sound movies used signifying the closing of a jail cell. Tempest's sweaty hand tightened.

After what felt like forever, but was probably a moment, she heard faint footfalls approaching. Tempest squared her shoulders. The door swung open and a tall blue-eyed woman looked at them. "May I help you?"

"Mrs. O'Banyon?" Tempest's voice cracked. She stared at her, jaw working, but no sound coming out. Tempest inclined her head toward the elegant woman.

Ariel smiled at her. "You don't know us, but we knew your son and daughter—"

She brightened. "Friends from school?"

Ariel shook her head.

"We were in F-Fairbanks," Tempest said. "Mrs. O'Banyon, I – we came here because we needed to apologize to you. If it wasn't for us … actually, for my father –" Tears welled in her eyes. She looked helplessly at Ariel, who made an empty gesture, unable to articulate her stepfather's villainy. Tears poured down Tempest's cheeks. "I'm so, so sorry," she gasped out the words she'd worked to hard to get right, losing much of her message in the torrent of tears. "It seems like everyone who cares about us gets killed, but-"

The woman's posture straightened and she stared at them. "You have to be Ariel and Tempest!" She grasped their wrists in a viselike hold, turned her head and screamed, "Stonehenge!" The name echoed over the porch and through the massive foyer as Mrs. O'Banyon yanked them inside and slammed the door shut.

Tempest automatically moved into a defensive position. Ariel put her free hand up in surrender. Dear Lord, this was worse than she'd ever imagined. She should have remembered the mother bear was the dangerous one. Whatever was in store for them, it was time to stop running. Ariel focused on Tempest. "Relax."

Mrs. O'Banyon leaned against the door making escape and relaxation impossible. "Stonehenge!" She screamed, again. "Gaelic!" Dear Lord, she hadn't realized Windy had been murdered, too. But of course, she must have been on the Dolly O when it exploded. This was worse than she'd imagined. Mrs. O'Banyon barred the door with her body, as if she intended to fight to the death to prevent the escape of those responsible for her children's' deaths. Fortunately, to do so, she let go of their arms.

"If we'd known Peter had found us," Ariel said, as she fought the desire to rub her bruised arm, "we would never have stayed and endangered their lives."

Tempest dropped her defensive pose and sobbed, "I'm so s-s-sorry." Tempest rubbed her eyes. "It's all my f-fault. If I hadn't wanted to touch a real live glacier..." She fell to her knees and prostrated herself at Stone's mother's feet.

His mother stared at them, her shocked expression looked as if she was unable to comprehend their regret. Didn't the woman realize that they were suffering, too?

As Tempest sobbed, Ariel tried to think of words that would express her guilt, her lose, her misery, but all she could think of was the simple truth. "I loved him." The woman nodded and shouted Stone's name for the third time. From the distant recesses of the house, running footfalls of at least two or three people could be heard. If they all got here, Tempest would never get closure. "Please forgive us," Ariel said. She grabbed Tempest around the waist, hauled her close as she looked for an escape route.

Mrs. O'Banyon threw her arms around them in a half hug, half grab. "You have to stay."

"What the heck is going on here?" a man asked from behind them. I had to be Mr. O'Banyon because he sounded amazingly like Stone. Mrs. O'Banyon gestured helplessly. It was enough for them to get free and halfway to the door. Afraid to face a second parent, Ariel yanked open the door, she looked back and shouted, "We're sorry for-" Her eyes locked with the man's stunned blue gaze. She dropped Tempest's hand as she fainted.

Chapter 36

He stared from the crumpled Mexican on the foyer's rug, then looked at his mother's frazzled expression, as she tried to hold a second scruffy female. When the she lost her hold, his mother knelt next to the women who smelled of grease and cheap soap. His mother rocked back and forth, as if in pain. This was the woman who had been tranquil even when a tornado touched down within fifty feet of the house. The woman who had been calm when her son came home more dead than alive. Her stressed expression stunned him.

"Mom, what the heck's going on?" Windy shouted from the back hall. "We could hear you all the way out at the duck pond." She sprinted forward, skidding to a stop inches from him then stared open-mouthed at their mother, who wordlessly pointed at the scrawny Mexican, who'd collapsed at her feet.

The standing one was blubbering incoherently, yet seemed familiar, but he couldn't recall where he might have met them. Couldn't identify her from her back. Couldn't see much of the other one because of his hovering mother. Windy knelt next to her, fingertips searching for a pulse beneath the dirty dark hair, of the one that had landed face down.

"They're alive," his mother said.

After assuring herself, Windy turned her attention to the other one, gently touching the kneeling one's hand. "Breathe in."

The ragged shoulders quivered. "That's it." She turned, her expression as anxious as their mother's, as she looked her gaze with his. "Do something." When he stood there, she snapped, "Now!"

"Like what?"

Her look snapped with fury, but instead of screaming at him, she focused on the kneeling one. "Slowly breathe out. Good." Windy glared at him, again, tilting her head in an obvious command to kneel on the other side.

Muscles protesting, he hunkered down and rolled over the comatose one. A long black wig flopped off to reveal clean, short, dark hair. What the heck? He squinted at her familiar profile. Ariel? No, it couldn't be. She and Tempest had been kidnapped by her stepfather and died in a fiery hell, when Peter Baldwyn crashed his stolen Cessna. He leaned closer. The woman's tan seemed uneven, almost as if it was makeup.

The smaller one continued to wail. She sounded like Tempest.

Hoping against hope, he turned the girl around. Black eyes stared at him from an unfamiliar, bloated face. As her gaze focused, white surrounded her irises and she froze in mid-scream.

"Tempest?"

"Am I dead?" she whispered.

He shook his head. What a strange dream. He turned to the other woman, half expecting to shove the wig aside and see something totally incongruous. Something, which would assure him that, he was still dreaming in the hammock. What he saw was a dark, emaciated version of Ariel. A lump was swelling on her forehead.

Stone grabbed her to him and carried her into the parlor. He laid her on his grandmother's antique chaise, then knelt next to her. A moment later, Tempest snuggled against him. He wrapped his arm around her thin shoulders and hugged her close.

"Are you really alive?" she whispered.

He nodded. "Obviously, you are, too." If he'd known there was the slightest chance they hadn't been in the Cessna, he would have moved heaven and earth to find them. "The authorities said that there were at least two bodies in the plane. I thought-" He couldn't go on.

"What plane?" Tempest frowned. "Sherry said that Father shot you and you died in that ditch. She said she tried to save you, but you didn't have a pulse." She looked at him as if he was Lazarus.

Windy placed an ice bag over the bump on Ariel's head.

"They're the ones, aren't they?" his mother asked.

Throat too tight to speak, he nodded.

"I'll call the crew and tell them that they can stop looking for DNA of a third person," Windy said. She offered Tempest her hand, "Will you come with me and get some chocolate or something?" Tempest snuggled tighter against him. "Please? I really need to ask you some questions, then Link will want to see –"

"Is Uncle Link here? He isn't dead, either?"

"He's out riding wi-"

Tempest let out a war whoop of sheer joy and vaulted straight up. She danced Windy around in a wildly ecstatic circle that had the fringe on the thick brocade curtains swaying.

Ariel moaned. Stone adjusted the ice pack. Her eyelashes

fluttered.

His mother's fingernails dug into his uninjured shoulder. She leaned close, kissed his temple, the whispered, "Don't let her get away. She came here to apologize for everything that weasel did."

He put his hand over his mother's hand then squeezed her fingers. "She won't get away, again." If the bullet hadn't ripped through his shoulder, smashing bone and rendering him unconscious, they would never have been separated. For a moment, he'd held onto awareness, but there had been more shots fired at close range and someone had fallen on top of him. The doctors said that if he hadn't been in the cold water, he would have bled to death.

The doorbell chimed. With a final squeeze, his mother left. "I dropped a couple 'Cans off here and they didn't pay me," said a whining voice.

"Did they have any luggage?" his mother asked.

Ariel's eyelids opened. For a long moment, she stared at him, then, she closed her eyes and raised her hand to feel the icepack.

"Ariel." He wished he knew what to say. Her lashes moved as if she'd taken a peak, but didn't want to look at him. "How did you get away from that lunatic?" he asked.

She looked at him, face white under the ugly yellowish glaze of artificial tan. "I'd think I was dead, except my head is freezing and my back is all prickly."

"I'm alive." He caressed her face. "I only needed three pints of blood."

"Only −" She swallowed, then lifted a trembling hand and touched his heart, then tentatively felt for the bullet wound. She found the scar an inch above his heart. "If I'd known." Tears welled and her dark contacts drifted free. "I would never have left. I would have stayed with you until death."

He smiled. "Careful, or I'll hold you to that for the next fifty years or so."

She shook her head. "No. I will not endanger you a second time. If I'd known you were alive-"

He put his finger over her lips. She kissed it. "Peter Baldwyn and whoever else was with him when they stole our 185 – they crashed it – they're dead." She stared at him. "It's over. You're safe." She frowned, as if trying to adjust to the concept. "Ariel, since I'm down on both knees, will you agree be my wife?"

She inhaled. "You don't even know me. Not the real me. You don't even know what I look like. I've really got blond hair and blue eyes. And-" He placed his finger across her lips.

"None of that matters. I love you, whatever your name is. I love you whatever you look like."

Her expression looked as if storm clouds had vanished and the sun appeared. "I love you, too. I have for so long." Tears welled in her eyes. "You got hurt because of me. Because of Peter's hatred, and … you nearly died. How can you possibly forgive that?"

"That's all in the past. It's time to make a new future. Take the name O'Banyon and whatever first name makes you happy."

"You make me happy." The ice bag fell aside as she sat up and threw her arms around him. Her kiss was the only answer he needed and more than he'd ever hoped for. "And I think I like the sound of Ariel O'Banyon – it sounds so much better than Sherry Ann O'Banyon and besides, I don't think it's worth going through all the paperwork to go back to my original name."

He wrapped her in a bear hug and for the first time in weeks looked forward to the future.